I0614432

Dan Sugralinov

The Destroying

Plague

May every new day in your life become a Level Up day!

Dan Sugralinov

DISGARDIUM Book Three

Magic Dome Books

All books by Dan Sugralinov:

Level Up LitRPG Series:
Re-Start
Hero
The Final Trial
The Knockout (with Max Lagno)
The Knockout: Update (with Max Lagno)

Disgardium LitRPG series:
Class-A Threat
Apostle of the Sleeping Gods
The Destroying Plague

World 99 LitRPG Series:
Blood of Fate

Table of Contents:

Book 1 and 2 Recap.. 1
Chapter 1. Breaking Out of the Sandbox.................... 5
Chapter 2. Plan B.. 23
Chapter 3. Saving Private Crag................................ 41
Interlude 1: Wesley... 59
Chapter 4. Home Sweet Home................................ 72
Chapter 5. Fort Kharinza.. 99
Chapter 6. The Treasury of the First Mage............... 126
Chapter 7. Path of Courage.................................... 142
Chapter 8. Patrick Again.. 163
Interlude 2: Melissa.. 188
Chapter 9. A Still Unconquered Herald..................... 206
Chapter 10. The Worms Will Eat You From Within...... 222
Chapter 11. Walking Dead...................................... 239
Chapter 12. The Awoken Assembled......................... 270
Chapter 13. Nucleus of the Destroying Plague........... 287
Chapter 14. No Death in Service to the Plague........... 316
Chapter 15. A Stroll Through Darant......................... 337
Chapter 16. Lake District.. 355
Chapter 17. Big Po's Ultimatum............................... 367
Chapter 18. To the Frontier!................................... 382
Chapter 19. The Lakharian Desert............................ 401
Chapter 20. Awoken Undead................................... 423
Interlude 3. Yemi... 453
Chapter 21. Nergal's Summons............................... 467
An Afterword From the Author................................. 499

Book 1 and 2 Recap

Planet Earth, 2074-2075

OUR PLANET'S POPULATION has reached 20 billion, one-third of whom are noncitizens: those who are considered to be of no value to society, therefore having no right to enjoy the creature comforts of civilization.

The UN Department of Education requires every teenager aged 14 to 16 to spend an hour a day in Disgardium. Having made a mistake while generating his character which resulted in leveling problems, Alex Sheppard quickly loses all interest in the game. For over a year, he spends the obligatory hours sitting on a bench next to the sandbox tavern in the company of Eve O'Sullivan, a girl next door who has a crush on him.

His parents are about to get a divorce which would result in lowering their civil status (where "A" is the highest class of the world's elite and "L" is the lowest, reserved for the dregs of society). This would affect their income so badly that they wouldn't be able to pay for Alex's further education, shattering his dream of becoming a space guide in the world where

Disgardium Book Three

Mars colonization has become reality and the orbit of Venus is about to be moved.

Now Alex is obliged to play Disgardium - if only to pay for his own studies. He chooses Scyth as his in-game name.

In order to preserve the game's balance and disarm any imba players, Corporation Snowstorm which owns Disgardium has come up with a policy of "Threats". Any player whom the artifact of True Flame identifies as a Threat can be expelled from the game by performing a simple ritual. The Threat's eliminators would then receive a reward based on the Threat's potential while the expelled player gets a reward based on his or her current level. This makes any Threat elimination much more interesting for potential eliminators (or "preventers", as they prefer to call themselves) at an early stage before the Threat gets the chance to properly level up.

The Threats themselves have to focus on leveling, trying to survive undetected for as long as they can, simply because the reward they receive is based on their current level where "A" is the highest Threat class and "Z" is the lowest.

In a reversal of fortunes, Scyth becomes a class-A Threat. Several things coincide to bring him to the top: the curse he receives from an NPC called Patrick O'Grady, the first human whose consciousness was digitized and transferred to the game, while another NPC Cursed Lich Dargo, a dungeon's boss, is in fact played by a noncitizen, a certain Clayton. Clayton used to be a space shuttle pilot who lost his citizenship after a life-threatening accident. Seeing the stubborn boy die time and time again without giving up, Clayton finally fakes his own defeat, allowing Scyth to kill him.

As a reward for killing the dungeon's final boss, Scyth receives the Mark of the Destroying Plague which endows him with the ability to safely absorb all damage received. Together with Patrick's curse, it allows Scyth to reach the unexplored area in the Mire and find the dying avatar of Behemoth, one of the five ancient Sleeping Gods.

Scyth makes friends with a group of Dementors: his classmates Ed "Crawler" Rodriguez, Hung "Bomber" Lee, Melissa "Tissa" Schafer and Malik "Infect" Abdualim. Scyth helps them to win a bet against Big Po, the leader of the Axiom, the #1 clan in Tristad's sandbox. Together they create a clan of their own: the Awoken.

The Awoken win the annual Junior Arena games by building a temple of the Sleeping Gods on the desert island of Kharinza. Their victory attracts the attention of the recruiters of the Preventers alliance which counts dozens of the strongest Disgardium clans.

After their Arena victory, the school bans Scyth and his group from Disgardium for eight weeks, forcing him to fail the Nucleus of the Destroying Plague quest. In his absence, the Destroying Plague finds a new herald: Big Po. When Scyth returns to the game, Big Po opens the portal of the Destroying Plague, planning to conquer Tristad. Together with his friends, Scyth manages to defeat the undead and eliminate the "Threat" of Big Po.

They're joined by Tobias "Crag" Asser, an unlucky ex-ganker who's now the favorite of Nergal the Radiant. His identity as a "Threat" has been uncovered, so now Tobias is forced to go into hiding, both in the game and IRL.

Tobias turns to Scyth for help and gets accepted into the Awoken clan.

Now the schoolkids' newborn clan will have to take on the entire world, virtual as well as real.

Chapter 1

Breaking Out of the Sandbox

"I'M ROOTING for you, Alex," Tissa said in parting. "We won't be able to talk, what with me being in the sandbox..."

"I'll let you know as soon as it's done, as soon as we break through and I leave Dis."

"I'll be waiting. Look after yourself. Good luck!"

The girl blew me a kiss and her hologram disappeared.

My parents had flown off somewhere, and the catdog AT and I were left to fend for ourselves. The pet, however, was thinking only of itself at that moment; so carried away with cleaning himself that it was as if he really was a cat, not just imitating one.

The projection of the Solar System on the wall gently hummed away, and if one zoomed in to look closer, one could see a column of colonization shuttles flying to Mars. Months of travel separated them, but on the map the shuttles formed a dashed line. *I'll be there one day too.*

Space... My dream to find the funds to study in university had almost become a reality, but there were a few 'buts' left. The winnings from victory in the junior Arena, the bet I'd won, the rewards for raising my potential to L and for eliminating Big Po — all this added up to over one and a half million gold. Unfortunately, the money was stuck in the game until adulthood. It wouldn't arrive until I'd passed the citizenship tests, which I had to wait two months for.

Incidentally, Tissa and Infect had already received their artifacts for neutralizing the Threat. As for what I'd receive, I didn't know yet. To find out, I'd have to at least log into Dis to start with.

I hadn't visited Disgardium since the Destroying Plague broke through to Tristad. In the meantime, the former Dementors and I celebrated my birthday in a small family restaurant on the coast of the Pacific. Eve was invited too, by the way, but she said she couldn't come.

The next day, once we'd recovered, we held a clan meeting with our new clan member taking part for the first time; Tobias Asser, also known as Crag. The former members of the Dementors, once kicked from the clan for ganking, kept quiet and didn't even react to taunts from Hung and Malik. They didn't go too hard on him. They knew how much Tobias would strengthen the clan.

Anyway, Infect had seen the battle machine he

could turn into the day before, gaining a seven-times boost to all his main stats. We swept away the remnants of the Destroying Plague's assault easily, as if we weren't up against powerful mobs at level thirty or above, but a mere rat pack from the cellar of the temple of Nergal the Radiant.

We had a meeting on the balcony of Ed's apartment and decided to go out into the wide world along with Crag. They're expecting one Threat, and if something happens, a second could slip away. Thinking a little longer, we finally realized this was the only option. If they met Crag right after character registration, then the only way to get him out would be to group up and jump with *Depths Teleportation*. Because he might just not reach the Darant town hall room which was the real meeting place.

We summarized our short-term plans. Infect was supposed to be coming out of the sandbox very soon, while Tissa would have to wait two more months. Until then, we decided to keep building our nearly finished clan fort, investigate the island and level up in zones that match our levels.

We thought about moving to the dark side but decided to stay in the light. Our kobold adepts were in this area, and Patrick and his new trogg friends were waiting in Darant. Dangerous to show your face there on the dark side...

I took a deep breath and slowly breathed out. Then I grabbed AT, lifted him up and gave him a peck on the nose. The catdog meowed in indignation. Went back to his spot and resumed cleaning himself.

Time to go.

At that moment, our clan noob Crag was waiting for my signal so he could climb into the capsule at the same time and enter great Dis after completing the adult registration procedure. "Let's go!" the message went to Tobias, Ed and Hung all at once.

Crawler and Bomber awaited us in the clan fort's tavern, ready to celebrate our breaking out of the sandbox. *We're waiting. Jump with the noob ganker right after you register,* Crawler answered. Bomber immediately chimed in. *Don't even think about leaving the guest room! There's a whole rally of those damn preventers out there!*

Throwing off my clothes, I approached the Altera Vita, my new capsule issued by Snowstorm for reaching class L, the maximum initial Threat potential.

They released the capsule in a limited-edition series. When they brought it in, dad shook his head in envy. I can imagine the dens of iniquity he'd love to visit if only he could use the capsule. The capsule used consumable cartridges to provide intravenous nutrition, hydration and first-aid. In addition, it could influence one's emotional state, and an active intra-gel stimulated the muscles and massaged the body.

If I wanted to, I could immerse myself for several days. If I had someone to swap out the consumables, I could do even longer, but such long periods of immersion weren't good for you anyway.

"Initiate immersion," I commanded.

"Understood, Alex."

In a capsule configured and trialed in test worlds, the immersion site was set to Disgardium by default. The intra-gel quickly filled up the space, the capsule took control of my body, and three heartbeats later I hung in a sterile vacuum of limbo.

A huge game world appeared underneath me, and the outlines of its six continents broke through the clouds.

Welcome to Disgardium, Alex!

You have reached an age threshold, Alex. Your character will be moved out of the sandbox!

You must regenerate your character.

Attention! Because you are a Threat, the game nickname **Scyth** *cannot be changed.*

Attention! Because you are a Threat, the game class **Herald** *cannot be changed.*

You can change your faction, race and appearance.

Deciding to change only my appearance, I enlarged the window with my character model. I saw that the system had updated my previous form of a fourteen-year-old boy; my face was rougher and harder, I was taller, my shoulders were broader.

Thinking for a moment, I dragged the age slider to the right, adding on another ten years. After a moment's hesitation I changed my eye color as well. My real eyes are green, but in the game they'd be blue. This avatar would be permanent, and as it happens, people take adults more seriously not only in the real world, but in Dis too.

All done.

Character successfully generated.

The system showed me the character profile and moved on to the final stage of registration:

Scyth, do you want to claim a reward for being online or do you prefer a permanent +5% experience bonus? You can change your choice at any time in the future.

I chose the second one, because 'payment for being online' could earn you no more than thirty phoenixes a month, and only if you practically lived in the game. Five percent to experience, on the other hand, was a big advantage in the higher levels.

I skimmed the profile to make sure everything was alright. At the same time, I changed my privacy options, resetting them to the defaults. Only my nickname, class and level remained visible.

Taking a deep breath, I confirmed the selection. My interface disappeared.

The Destroying Plague

I started to fall down, to the Latteria. The earth rushed up to meet me and I could make out the tall, colorful houses and broad streets of the capital of the Commonwealth. Suddenly, everything went black for an instant, then noise, light and smells crashed down on me.

Operation Breakout had begun.

* * *

The room smelled of dust and age, although everything looked clean. The high windows were overshadowed by the foliage of trees, not enough daylight got in, so lanterns burned on the walls.

In contrast to my first visit to Tristad, there were far more new players who had chosen Darant as their starting zone. Several hundred humans, elves, gnomes, dwarfs and other races of the Commonwealth bustled through the town hall's guest room, pressed up against the registration desks or just staring around and feeling their arms in awe. The latter were always new players, in Disgardium for the first time.

Looking around, I felt a cold sweat. A huge area the size of a hangar, filled with lively players of all species, ages and genders, all shouting over each other. But even among the crowd, some high-level players stood out clearly, those from the three top preventer clans: Modus, Azure Dragons and Excommunicado. How? How, in the name of all the Sleepers, did they get here? Neither Crawler nor

Bomber had said anything about this. Here they just saw noobs, and just calmly got their grade and walked out into the hall where they the preventers checked them by the fire of the *True Flame.*

I span my head trying to make out Crag but couldn't find him. Judging by the active avatar in the clan list, he'd already logged into Dis. Might be stuck on the character generation screen.

Artifacts of the *True Flame* flashed here and there around the hall. From level two hundred, the top players walked around the hall in pairs and scooped up any noobs over level one exiting the teenage sandbox. I don't doubt that on Shad'Erung, the continent of the dark side, the clans there checked for those defecting to the Empire. And the variety of neutrals in the capitals no doubt got checked too. The stakes were too high, even for the top players who were ready to split it among the whole Alliance of Preventers.

Alright... Time to calm down. I looked around for the *Depths Teleportation* icon and sighed in relief: it was active.

Now the important thing was for Crag to finally get there. I'd group up with him and take him to Kharinza, the clan fort. Gyula and his brigade of rough workmen had just finished construction...

"Noob, twenty-six!" I heard from afar. I'd been seen. "Hey, you! Stay there and wait your turn!"

The nearest group of preventers got distracted by an elf that was asking for more money for the right

The Destroying Plague

to check her wrist. Banger split off from another group and headed toward me, splitting through the crowd like an icebreaker. He was a gigantic lopher, part elephant and part man, at level two hundred and twenty. A rare race. Who would want to live in a lump like that, and with a long trunk to boot? But people still took it for the racial bonus — high *endurance*.

I took a few steps back and hid behind a broad twin bas-relief column. I wasn't completely sure, but it looked as if our worst fears had come true. Big Po, although unsure that I'd kept my Threat status, but surely burning with a thirst for vengeance, had shared his suspicions with the preventers. And they had somehow got access to the guest room from the Mayor of Darant. Fine. I'd thought about this outcome as well.

Flashing a glance around the other side of the column, I looked toward the exit. The stocky, bearded level-fourteen dwarf called Gonzo had already gone through the checkpoint and was now moving into the guest hall.

Imitation worked successfully. Great, now I was Gonzo the dwarf, tested in the fire of the *True Flame*.

I walked out from the other side of the column and confidently melted into the crowd. Where was Crag?

Banger from Excommunicado was heading to where Scyth was hiding. A hobbit pattered behind him with a minor elemental floating above his shoulder, distorting the air with its heat. Nether!

13

True Flame Spirit, level 224
Elemental
Tierz's pet.

I tried not to look worried and calmly headed for the far end of the hall, where the scribe tables stood in long rows. I'd register and then take it from there.

"Gonzo, wait!" I heard from behind my back.

I didn't realize at first that the shout was meant for me. I took another step or two out of inertia, then stopped and turned. The lopher Banger walked toward me, while his partner, the hobbit Tierz, was looking behind one of the numerous portals, trying to find the elusive Scyth there. The portals work only one-way to this side and only for new players, so logically, there was no way I could get through there, but the hobbit still checked it. Unsurprisingly without success.

"What?" I asked in displeasure. "I already went through the checkpoint..."

"Have you seen a tall man around?" Banger boomed, narrowing his eyes. His arms were as thick as my torso, but with human hands. Huge, monstrous, but human. "Um... Nick Scyth, level twenty-six. Rare class, too... Um... I forgot it! So, you ain't seen 'im? He was just there, behind the columns..."

"I saw him," I nodded and waved toward the far corner end of the guest hall. "He went to the scribes."

The Destroying Plague

"Ugh, damn him," Banger decided. "He'll get checked again after he registers anyway. Show me your wrist!"

The sudden order made my heartbeat faster, blood rushed to my face. The elephant-person turned to his friend.

"Hey, Tierz, come here, let's check this noob!"

The halfling was examining the wrist of a level six forest elf that had just come out of the portal. When he finished, he gave the pointy-eared player a gold coin and walked over to us. Looking around again in search of Crag, I decided to leave on my own. It seemed something had gone wrong. Taking advantage while Banger was looking at his colleague, I activated *Depths Teleportation*.

The falling sensation and the visuals that take place when you use that ability are pretty extreme. I'd compare it to jumping off the top of a skyscraper; the contents of your stomach rise to your throat, your heart beats a hundred miles an hour, your vision blurs... In short, it's an acquired taste. I instinctively closed my eyes.

Even then, I realized something bad had happened. System messages don't care if you have your eyes closed.

Depths Teleportation interrupted!

Unable to leave Darant Town Hall Guest Room without finishing the character registration process!

Nether! Everything that could go wrong had gone wrong. The worst of it was that the system still counted the ability as used, and the talent started its half-hour cooldown time.

Then Crag appeared! I would never have recognized him if I hadn't seen the nickname; the previously tall man had become a short dwarf. Artful waves in his beard, a tattoo covering half his face, his hair immaculately braided. It was obvious what had delayed him. He'd been giving his character a new look!

His appearance drew the attention of the Excos, and both moved to intercept. The elephantine Banger didn't seem quick on the uptake. He checked himself, turned around and barked out:

"Stay there, Gonzo! We'll check you and you'll get a gold coin! For nothin'!"

"I already got one, thanks!" I pulled out a coin with my free hand and span it before him for effect. "Or are you going to give me another?"

"Um... Nah, we won't give you more. It's never enough for you, noobs! But you're still getting checked! Got it?"

"Got it," I agreed peaceably. "I'll wait."

I was really in trouble! If they'd had a one-time-use artifact, they might have spared me, but with an elemental pet, these checks cost them nothing. I threw Crag a group invitation. He immediately accepted it and I began to think feverishly.

My clanmate started making all kinds of

excuses, playing a dumb noob that didn't understand what the hobbit Tierz wanted. The Excos couldn't use force on Crag, since Darant was a peaceful zone, and any aggression could send their reputation into the minus points. On the other hand, the network was full of conflicting information, but how it was in reality...

Play for time I wrote to Crag, then lost myself in the crowd. When the lopher turned, I was no longer Gonzo, but Rayman; a paladin at level three hundred and forty-seven, from the Azure Dragons. Yes, I took a risk, but it worked out. If I reached a scribe and registered, nobody would be able to stop me from grabbing Crag and jumping to Kharinza.

I bowed my head and crossed half the hall before I saw that I was about to be next to the real Rayman. I couldn't turn back into Gonzo — he was nowhere to be seen now. Turning around, I focused on Banger and turned into him. The trick looked normal to those around me — just someone swapping one equipment set for another. The name shows up only when you look close. In the meantime, Crag smiled stupidly while the hobbit Tierz explained something to him.

"Hey, Bang! What're you doing over here?" a tall elf in a green mantle hailed me, Koba from Modus. "The Exco inspection zone is over there. Where's Tierz anyway?"

He pointed to the far end. Fortunately for me, the real Banger was hidden behind a column at this point.

"Tierz is over there..." I copied Banger's manner of speech and intonation and vaguely waved my hand. "I'm... Um... I lost track of a noob, actually. He disappeared in the crowd. Just lookin' for 'im..."

"What?" Koba asked. "You let a noob get away?"

"Well, yeah. No problem, I'll find 'im..."

"Alarm!" the elf suddenly shouted into the signal amulet hanging around his neck. "Potential Threat! Cover the exit!"

The next instant, several soldiers from Modus gathered at the exit and dragged those leaving the room back inside. A gaggle of commands filled the hall, including from Koba's signal amulet.

"Entrance covered! We're locking down the building! Repeat all the checks!"

The elf kept hold of his amulet and asked:

"What's the noob's race, name and nick?"

"Um... One sec... Gonzo, I think. Level fourteen dwarf."

"Got it," Koba nodded and shouted into the amulet again: "Nickname Gonzo! A dwarf..."

I slipped through to the scribes and stood by the desk of the nearest free one, an elderly gnome lady in glasses and an extremely unhurried way of talking. After listening to her welcoming speech, hurrying her up and interrupting her, I finally got it through to her that I wanted to register.

And that's when I ran into a roadblock. As if it wasn't bad enough that Crag was flooding me with panicked messages and threats to give me up to the preventers if I didn't keep my promise, the gnome lady in front of me shook her head and said something. It was tough to hear her in the cacophony, but I noticed she wasn't hurrying to hand me a registration sheet.

"Sorry, what?"

"Switch to your true form before starting the registration procedure, young human!" the gnome said strictly, raising her voice.

She emphasized the word 'human.' A girl standing at the next desk shot me an interested glance. In the meantime, Crag stopped writing coherently and just spammed my direct messages with exclamation marks. Crawler and Bomber had joined him, realizing by our delay that something had gone wrong. Hung was swearing so hard that the chat window even blushed.

"Stop holding up the queue, ya big lug!" someone hissed from behind. "What're you doing here anyway?"

Now I'd drawn even more attention. I shot a glance over my shoulder and saw a little level one fairy called Mint floating in the air, piercing me with a gaze of displeasure.

"Sorry, kiddo." I stepped away from the desk.

"You're a kiddo, elephant boy!" she shrieked. "Stick that trunk you-know-where!"

Quickly slipping behind another column, I switched back to my true form. I heard blood bumping in my ears when I reached the newly vacant desk of scribe Ionescu and began the registration process, trying not to pay attention to the shouts from the other end of the hall. The bustle and chaos behind me grew, and I felt myself begin to sweat.

"They've caught a Threat!" a gnome standing nearby suddenly gasped in surprise. His eyes widened, he stared and excitedly clicked his tongue. "Woah!"

I heard shouts from all over. The people were watching as Crag was dragged from the other end of the hall. Tierz got his way after all and revealed Tobias's status.

High-level players all over the hall rushed to help the already strong group. I couldn't even see Crag himself now behind all the preventers clad in gleaming armor.

Crawler and Bomber had caved before the anxiety of the unknown and jumped to the town hall building in Darant. They already knew that a Threat had been caught. Rumors spread throughout the Commonwealth instantly.

Woeful messages filled up the clan chat — the guys had already mentally buried not only Crag, but me too. The city guard, high officials of the Commonwealth army and all the players were gathering outside the town hall. *Scyth, write something, anything!* Bomber demanded. *Who have they taken? You, or Crag?*

Without answering, I agreed that my character choice was final and not subject to change and handed the completed arrival sheet to the scribe Ionescu. He glanced at it and nodded in satisfaction.

"Welcome to Darant, Scyth!" the scribe said, stamping the form with a dull thud. "Next!"

Modus, Azure Dragons and Excommunicado loudly shouted across each other and had already started arguing about whose territory should be used to eliminate the Threat. The neighboring hall stirred with the sound of teleporters activating, and preventer leaders rushed into the hall. I saw Yary among them. A leader of Modus, he had invited me to visit him after the final of the junior Arena.

The leaders congratulated each other on the move, smiling and joking, and the junior ones stopped arguing when they appeared. It seemed likely that Tobias was about to be dragged away and taken somewhere where he could be quietly eliminated, with no witnesses. Crag filled my message inbox with demands to do something, anything at all.

All attention, eyes, and, I don't doubt, recordings of what was happening — it was all directed at the procession of preventers, so I calmly shifted into the form of the fairy Mint...

What? I looked down and saw that my legs weren't touching the floor! Of course, I'd turned into a damn fairy! That was why everything around me looked so big! With that thought, I soared up to the ceiling. Don't even ask how — I just wanted to go up, and I went up.

Depths Teleportation hadn't cooled down yet,

and there was no way to get Crag out without it...

"Hey, little one," I heard from below. "Come down, we need to check your status."

Tierz the hobbit from Excommunicado gestured for me to fly to him, offering a gold coin in his other hand. The little *True Flame Spirit* smoldered beside him.

Chapter 2

Plan B

WHILE I FURIOUSLY tried to come up with a way out, the hobbit's signal amulet buzzed. "Tierz, we've found the dwarf Gonzo and checked him. He's clean. Tell Banger he's an elephant, ha-ha-ha!"

"Got it, thanks. I won't tell Banger anything, he's already sick of your lame jokes."

"Alright, alright... Listen, the boys outside are wondering who we've taken. Is it really the guy with potential A?"

"No," the hobbit answered, frowning. "I can't tell you; the elders have forbidden it for now..."

Without listening to the rest, I seized the moment and flew to the end of the hall, where I started watching Tierz and what was happening with Crag.

The hobbit seemed to have gotten on my case for formality's sake. What threat could a level one fairy be anyway? Especially since he'd already found a Threat and relaxed. So, without bothering to look for me, he spat and joined his celebrating comrades. The sound of corks popping filled the hall. The Elvish sparkling wine was making the rounds.

Nonetheless, some preventers stayed at the hall's exit and kept checking everyone, even the level one noobs. Anyone who didn't need to be there was sent packing. Judging by the voices from the signal amulets, it wasn't just happening within the building, but around it too.

By then, they'd brought Crag to a registration desk and started processing him. I carefully flew closer and hid underneath a huge chandelier covered in lit candles, then messaged the guys to tell them what was happening. I decided to try and listen to what Yary was saying:

"Don't do anything stupid, kid," one of the Modus leaders said with an arrogant grin. "We know all about you: Tobias Asser, sixteen as of yesterday. You live, to put it mildly, in privation. Your parents are about to lose their citizenship. Do you want the same for yourself?"

"No," Crag shook his head. "But I won't get shit if you eliminate me. I just built up a little Threat, you can't particularly climb with that..."

"You'll climb, Toby," Yary clapped him on the shoulder. "Just not now. All in good time. We'll take care of your future..."

Crag grew thoughtful. Or he was waiting for me to do something. He held the registration sheet in his hands but seemed in no hurry to confirm it. The scribe waited patiently.

Crawler, level 31 mage, and his group (Bomber, level 31 warrior) want to join your group.
Accept? Decline?

I accepted the request and told them what was going on, hoping that the three of us could think of something. The answers came quickly:

[19:48] [Group] [Crawler]: I'm on cooldown too. But Bomb can get us all out. The important thing is for us to be close by, otherwise the teleport won't catch you.
[19:48] [Group] [Bomber]: The trouble is those damn preventers are chasing everyone off, and the guards are helping them! We're a way off the town hall.
[19:48] [Group] [Crag]: Do something!

Apart from the group chat, my direct message tabs blinked. I answered at once.

[19:49] [Private] [Crawler]: Scyth, get yourself out! It's too late for Crag! We'll help him level back up later.
[19:49] [Private] [Crag]: Scyth! You close by? What do I do???
[19:49] [Private] [Scyth — Crawler]: Stick to

the initial plan while there's still a chance. We have to get him out! Anyway, I doubt I'll pass their checks. It's still me inside here.

[19:49] [Private] [Scyth — Crag]: *I'm close. I can see and hear everything. Stay calm and stall for time, Toby. Depths Teleportation is on cooldown for now.*

With a slight hum, a *Dome of Silence* formed over the section of the hall around Crag. The mage had spared no mana in making it large enough to cover all the interested parties, and fortunately for me, I ended up under the dome too. And of course, I could have sat there until the preventers left, but I didn't like that idea. Crag and I were far from friends, but I'd promised to help him. Even his threat to give me up if he got eliminated didn't bother me. The important thing was keeping my word.

In the meantime, Yary continued trying to win Tobias over.

"Think about it. I can't speak for the other preventers, but I guarantee on behalf of all Modus that we will automatically accept your next character into the clan. And that means equipment, boosts, help with leveling up, a paycheck."

"Why are you messing around?" a gnome mage said, the level three hundred and seventeen Niu Lu from Azure Dragons. "You..."

Yary shot a glance at the gnome and he shut his mouth. Modus itself had respect, but its leaders commanded even greater respect and fear. Yaroslav-Yary wasn't the chief, but he was practically second after the clan leader Hinterleaf.

"Toby, this offer is available for ten seconds. We're going to kill you anyway, only on top of that, you won't get anything in real life either. You can forget about a career in Modus too. I don't want to brag, but you must know what we can offer..."

"Are you the ones that hired those inwinovas that wanted to kidnap me?" Crag interrupted him, raising his head.

"We don't work so crudely, kid. That was one of the losers who aren't here. Finish the registration! The time has come..."

I made my decision. I messaged Crag, told him to agree with all the conditions, that we had it all under control. Then, yet again thanking the game designers for the abundance of columns in the hall, I dropped to the floor behind the nearest and switched back to my true form.

"Hey, Yary!" I shouted loudly, emerging into full view. "Remember me?"

The preventers reacted instantly. I heard the ringing of weapons materializing, the flashes of spells preparing.

"Who the hell are you?" the gnome Niu Lu said, the first to collect himself. "A noob? That way!"

He pointed at the scribe desks beyond the perimeter. Fortunately, Banger wasn't there to recognize me. A gnome from the Azure Dragons moved toward me, but Yary stopped him, putting a hand on his shoulder and addressing me.

"Remind me... Where do I know you from?"

"The Junior Arena. Our team won the final, and you asked me to get in touch with you after I left the sandbox."

"I said that?" Yary asked in surprise.

Well, that made sense. For him, that was just a short episode from three months ago, after which I'd made no effort to be remembered, for obvious reasons. I knew his real age — well over forty — but the character, a Bogatyr-class human, looked fifteen years younger. Unlike many, Yary had kept his appearance.

"Yes. Apart from you there were Glyph from the Azures, Yagami from Mizaki and some other top player..."

"Some other top player!" Rayman grumbled, a human paladin at level three hundred and forty-seven. The same one I'd transformed into on my way to the scribe. "Get rid of him, we don't need him!"

Yary didn't like that. I don't know what his relationship was with Rayman, or with the Azures in general, the leading clan of the Asian cluster, but the right-hand of Modus answered defiantly.

"No, let him stay." He took a step and shook my hand. "Sorry I didn't remember you right away, Scyth. Stay close. You have potential, but Hinterleaf has the final say. I'll set you up a meeting..."

He turned to Crag, but before continuing to

pressure him, he turned back to me again.

"You ever seen a Threat being taken care of? Now's your chance." Yary glanced at Tobias. "Isn't that so, kid? Come on, Toby, don't drag this out."

I joined the group pressing Crag against the desk. He quickly turned around to glance at me, and I blinked fast. Taking a deep breath, Tobias confirmed the registration sheet. Thank the Sleepers, he hadn't forgotten to hide his allegiance to the Awoken, otherwise it would have all ended there.

"Welcome to Darant, Crag!" the scribe bellowed as if nothing was amiss. "Next!"

We left the town hall in a long procession. The crackling sound of preventers teleporting in continued in the square. Ordinary players were coming in too, but they were immediately escorted off the square. They complained, of course, but quickly calmed down when they got a coin or two. The preventers had to be given their due — they spared no expense in smoothing out public opinion. I remembered too well what a whole gold piece meant to a noob.

It seemed Yary had completely forgotten about me, but when he saw the minotaur — and clan leader of the Azure Dragons — Glyph appear and pay attention to me, he called me over and told me to stay close.

But then everything got messy. Since it wasn't possible to harm Crag in the heart of the capital, the preventers had planned in advance to perform the Threat-banishment ritual in neutral territory. After all, their alliance included not only Commonwealth clans, but also clans of the enemy Dark Empire. However, the precise location of the ritual was kept secret, and the leader of Modus, Hinterleaf, was preparing to open the portal there personally.

The royal guard cordoned off the square in front of the town hall. Apparently, based on the danger of the Threat, the authorities were working together with the preventers, creating as favorable a situation as possible for them.

The top players started summoning flying mutants, and one after the other they launched up beneath the clouds.

"Koba, take this guy with you," Yary said, turning to me. "Scyth, fly with him."

"Can you find space for two more? A couple of guys from my team are here too, but they got turned away."

Yary weighed something up mentally, then nodded.

"Alright. Tell me their nicknames, I'll give the order to let them through. They'll have to be quick though."

I watched my friends appear from thirty feet up, sitting behind Koba on his *Golden Gryphon*. Crawler ended up on a *Battle Hippogryph* with a beautiful elvish woman in the saddle. Bomb was less lucky. He found himself on the tail of a long, sinuous *Flying Snake*, which regularly threw him up and down in flight. It looked like the snake's rider was spurring the mount on and laughing, and that Bomber, somehow staying on by grabbing onto the saddle by his teeth and all his limbs, was a fine example of striving to survive at any cost.

* * *

None of us were able to grab Crag with *Depths Teleportation* in flight; the mounts were spread out too far apart. Even at the gorge where the banishing ritual was meant to take place, he was too far away, surrounded by high-level players. He was immobilized with a few control spells, and three battle 'stars' from Modus, the Azure Dragons and Excommunicado guarded him. Two leaders of the Children of Kratos also joined them.

A minute after we arrived, warriors from the other members of the Alliance started pouring out of portals, including neutrals and the Empire. I immediately recognized the mighty orc Horvac, the clan leader of the Travelers. His clan was the strongest among the dark factions, and he himself was so renowned for his eccentricity in real life that he never left the gossip column. Horvac, Glyph from the Azure Dragons, Colonel from Excommunicado and, of course, the head of Modus, Hinterleaf — these were probably the strongest players in the world. The Solo Adventurer Dek might have been catching up in levels, but in strength, opportunity and influence, he was no match. The very strongest was still the former

Modus member Mogwai, the druid animalist. That player, after reaching the *Resilience* cap, declared that he was tired of Dis and had decided to take a year off.

The gorge we flew into wasn't far from Darant, close to one of the Battlefields. It was getting dark, but the sheer mass of magic all around meant we could see as clear as day.

Officially, these lands belonged to the Commonwealth, but that was no barrier to representatives of other factions showing up there with impunity. Of course, outsiders would be subject to attacks from NPCs[1] in any territory, and if the level allowed it, then from players too. Global PvP was encouraged, and not only with the chance of equipment dropping from defeated opponents (even bags with one-hundred percent protection against losses were no guarantee), but also with *Marks of the Valorous* and *Honor Points*. The Commonwealth considered hostile even neutrals who belonged to neither of the strongest factions in Dis: the Commonwealth and the Empire.

And now the gorge was packed with top players from the Alliance of Preventers, which included ten clans: four from the Commonwealth, four from the Empire and two from the neutrals.

The best of the best from billions of players swarmed, gleaming with auras and buffs. Their mounts and battle pets roared, shrieked, growled,

---

[1] An NPC, or Non-Player Character, is a character controlled by a program or artificial intellect, and not by a player.

chittered. Giant spiders and praying mantises, dragons and lizards, bears and walking trees, phoenixes and dire wolves, hellhounds, elementals, demons, succubi, golems, rattling gnomish tanks and gyrocopters...

Someone summoned a fifty-foot tall *Bronze Colossus*, and someone else responded with a *Tree of Life* just as large. The mass of people shrank back from the giants, and Crawler and I were pressed against the walls of the gorge. Bomber had been swept off to the side, where he was talking animatedly in Chinese to a girl from Azure Dragons.

Thirty paces from me, the leaders of the Alliance argued bitterly — something was wrong. Thanks to the strange acoustics of the gorge, I could hear them just fine.

"I demand that any superfluous troops be withdrawn immediately!" Horvac shouted.

"You say that after bringing your own here?" the gray-haired miniature gnome Hinterleaf answered harshly. He rolled his Rs, giving away his Russian roots. "Where is the logic? We have a saying for this where I am from — a guilty mind betrays itself!"

"The dark ones are definitely planning something!" Glyph declared. "And the neutrals along with them!"

The Colonel, a mighty goliath[2], gave some

---

[2] The goliaths are a race of gigantic intelligent humanoid creatures that prefer to live in tribes in nature (mostly in the

hushed commands to his officers. Another portal opened a few seconds later and Excos streamed out of it, no fewer than ten stars. Seeing this, the others activated too. Within a few minutes, the concentration of high-level players per square foot in the gorge broke the record for the entire history of Disgardium.

"Yes, Horvac, the allies are right," Yary said quietly, but I and all the others heard him just fine. Moreover, when he fell silent, so did the others. "We've been guarding the Threat, and that's why we brought more than the agreed number of stars with us. But our people were meant to leave the gorge as soon as..."

I got distracted before I could hear more. The familiar voice of the lopher Banger made me sweat.

"Tierz, look who I found!" Banger rumbled, pushing his way through to me. "I was wonderin' where he got to!"

Frowning, Hinterleaf clicked his fingers and all the leaders were covered in a shield of a nature I didn't recognize.

"Distract him," I whispered to Crawler, pointing out Banger with a glance. "They wanted to check me, but I slipped away."

I'd need to walk thirty paces to get close enough to catch Crag in my teleportation. I started trying to get closer to him.

Bomber wrote that all the arriving troops of the

---

mountains). The race's name refers to the biblical myth of David and Goliath.

preventers were buffing each other and forming battle parties, and not by faction, but by clan. A storm was brewing.

The pressure beneath the dome grew as well. Yary and Hinterleaf stood back to back. Glyph was telling them something while the neutral clan leaders whispered with Horvac and the heads of the other dark clans. The same was happening around Crag: five Modus members closed ranks with some Dragons, Excos and Kratos, defending the Threat from the rest.

This is our chance! I wrote to the group. *Let's push through to Crag. Whoever makes it leaves with him.*

The atmosphere of mutual distrust was rising to a point of no return. Accusations flew back and forth, and any spark could light the fuse.

And then the spark came.

"Scyth! Stop!" Banger shouted from somewhere behind.

I'm not sure exactly what the trigger was. I guess it was his attack. In a fantastic display of his somewhat poor intellect, the lopher threw a magic bolus toward me, thereby igniting what might be the most chaotic slaughter in the history of Disgardium. My legs were entangled with spells, but *Liberation* cleared them. I rushed forward, changed my voice and boomed out:

"We've been betrayed!"

The trick worked. The rank and file troops

behind me cast defensive auras and magic shields around themselves; flasks of battle elixir popped open all over the hall, flaming blades hissed, battle staffs crackled with energy. A veil of fire covered me — Crawler's *Fire Shield.* I felt great regret in that moment that I hadn't had time to hand in my quest and get Behemoth's rewards. Not only that, but I hadn't activated the crystal I got from Big Po, the eliminated Threat! Whatever happened, that would have come in handy!

I summoned my pet, the *Swamp Needler* Iggy, and ordered him to stay close. Banger's attack actually worked in our favor — the stats of all the group members flew up, multiplied by seventeen. My pet was no exception. I'd already gone through this during the outbreak of the Destroying Plague, when Crag, Infect, Tissa and I cleansed the streets of Tristad of the undead, so I wasn't surprised when I grew, became stronger, felt my shoulders broaden and energy boil within me.

Without getting caught up in the fight, I kept pushing my way toward Crag until I hit the impenetrable barrier of the dome. I was still too far from my clanmate. Judging by the minimap, Crawler and Bomber were far behind me.

Hinterleaf shouted something beneath the dome in the meantime, calming his allies down with gestures. Yary stood behind him, Glyph and the Colonel stood at either side. Two Children of Kratos pressed against the wall of the dome. They were a strong clan, but their leaders were known for their entirely non-combative talents.

It seemed Hinterleaf's entreaties had no effect. Horvac shouted something, and a cloud of toxic yellow smoke filled the dome. Fire and lightning flashed within it, and a few seconds later Hinterleaf's magic dome broke with a crystalline ringing, flying apart in a barely visible shower of glass, injuring those nearby. A fair share hit me; sharp shards pierced my chest and shoulders. I had to pull them out, tearing my flesh.

"Plan B!" Yary shouted into his signal amulet. His voice boomed throughout the gorge. "Plan B!"

Hinterleaf, an illusion mage, created ten copies of himself and left them to help, while he himself blinked to a small cliff above us and raised his arm, baring his teeth in a sinister grin. He held a black scroll in his hand.

Everyone started fighting, but all with the same goal — Crag. All present wanted to kill and eliminate him as a Threat, and they no longer cared about the Alliance or clan leadership. The victors would write the story.

The aftereffects of mass spells flooded every inch of the gorge. The ground beneath my feet shifted, turning into a mire. Venomous predatory plants grew from the rocky surface. The air burned with frost one moment, then melted armor the next. Ultrasonic waves from a tower summoned nearby tore off chunks of equipment and flesh, ripping space itself. One of the feet of the monstrous colossus crashed down mere yards from me, crushing several players at once. The snaking branches of the *Tree of Life* strangled everyone they could reach. A few different types of mist scorched my nostrils, throat and lungs, and I held on only thanks to Crag's talent. The debuffs started stacking up perilously, but I only had another ten feet to go.

In the fury of betrayal, everyone fired off everything they could against friend and foe alike. Expensive scrolls and last-chance weapons were spent in their dozens and hundreds. Nobody saved their ultimate abilities — top players died trying to take with them whoever they could.

Gnomish tanks fired off cannons into the crowd. One of the shells flew into the melee around Crag, and the people there thinned out. Someone had placed an *Invulnerability Bubble* on Toby himself, and that saved his life.

The light players around him had beaten back both the dark ones and the neutrals alongside Hinterleaf's illusions, then started on each other.

Yary used *Charge* to ram into the back of a former ally from Children of Kratos, waved his two-handed sword to cleave someone else in two, then shielded Crag with his body. A mage standing nearby opened a portal. With a dull squelch and its structure sparking with veins of blue and green light, the portal swallowed up Yary, Crag and the only Modus fighter still on his feet. The mage who opened the portal didn't make it in, stunned by a rogue from behind, then exploding in a shower of blood.

Hinterleaf, sure that his boys had escaped with the Threat, threw a couple of deadly area-of-effect spells into the crowd. But there was far worse to come.

"Armageddon!" the Modus clan leader shouted.

The black scroll in his hand crumbled into soot and dust and he disappeared from the cliff.

The sky lit up with blinding light. As the meteor fell, its growing roar burst eardrums and shook brains. I cast *Stone Skin* and rushed toward the portal.

At first Bomber got covered in the crumbly, rusty flakes of something poisonous and huge, and neither his increased defense nor his legendary ring helped him, because the colossus stamped on him immediately after. Crag's boost disappeared as soon as they carried Toby through the portal.

My view of the glimmering passageway disappeared upwards, and I suddenly fell flat on my face. Someone had cut off my legs with a poleaxe, slicing my life down to a few percent and leaving a *Bleeding* debuff. Hearing my heartbeat heavy in my ears, I crawled to the portal. Only my extremely high *Resilience* kept me hanging on. I don't know what I was hoping for. I was too used to my undead curse, so I had no healing potions. And nowhere to put them anyway.

There were about six feet left to crawl to the

portal. I knew I was going to die. Didn't have a clue where they'd revive me: I wasn't bound to Darant, hadn't really had time. And I doubted they'd return me to Tristad.

Acid burned my vocal cords. I couldn't waste any time chatting, so I just hoped that Ed wouldn't let me down. In vain.

Crawler got caught in someone's spell and failed to get out of the impact zone. Then he got *Fear* cast on him and the effect made him run clean away from the portal. A few moments later, his avatar in the group interface flashed red for the last time, grinned out a skull and turned gray.

Someone's leg flashed from the side and I jerked out my hand and grabbed it. Its owner dragged me forward and a little to the side a step or two before he realized someone had grabbed him. The heavy metal toe of a boot struck my chin, wiping out the last of my health. A fraction of a second before that, I activated *Ghastly Howl*. It didn't work because of the level difference, so then I set Iggy on the attacker.

The meteor from Hinterleaf's *Armageddon* crashed into the center of the gorge. All color faded; all shadows filled with the blinding light of a nuclear explosion. I was ripped from the ground in unimaginable heat and thrown through the closing portal at an insane speed.

Chapter 3

Saving Private Crag

*I*N BIG DIS, there were a few types of portals.

The *Return Stone* ability was given to everyone and could be used once a day. It could be used to return to your bound place. The authorities and the freight guild put up large stationary portals with a fixed route in the cities. Personal ones could be made with skills, like we did, or scrolls. Dimensional mages could use another kind of portal. Anyone could walk through one of those, not just a member of your group or clan. That was the one I'd gotten into.

I flew into it alive, but I flew out of it dead.

Player Han Ro dealt you critical damage (Bleeding): 2647!
Health points: 0/6474.
You are dead.

Reviving in 10... 9...

The death was confirmed at the exit from the

portal. That ticking, critical *Bleeding* finished me off. It occurred to me that if Crag was nearby and could cover me with his talent, I'd have a chance to survive. But it looked like I was out of the talent's range.

I'd died with the worst luck, falling face down on my stomach. That meant in the ten seconds before my revival, I had no way to look around and see what was going on. There was also the question of where exactly I'd revive without being bound to anywhere. In the Darant graveyard? That would be bad, and it meant Crag was done for. Or...

Or just at the nearest graveyard. And that, from what I understood, belonged to Modus and was in their castle.

Hinterleaf said something nearby.

"... a very bad idea, Yar!" "You have to understand..." he paused. "Who's this?"

"A corpse," Yary noted, kicking me with the toe of his boot to turn my body over. "It's that kid Scyth, the one I was telling you about. Captain of the champions of the kids' Arena this year."

"The ones who beat our boys in the final? We'll deal with him later. Invite him after all this is over..."

I'd revived where I'd fallen so many times that I was surprised to find myself at another place when I crossed the threshold between worlds. I was in a rear courtyard, between a high wall topped with guards with their backs to me outlined against the dark sky, and a magnificent castle. Its walls seemed to be encrusted with diamonds and it shimmered, reflecting the starlight.

Death penalty: —3900 experience.

The air whispered and Iggy revived nearby. Swearing, I recalled my pet. He'd be more of a hindrance than a help here.

Switching into _Stealth_, I looked around. Tombstones surrounded the respawn point, most likely as decoration rather than real burial places. A nearby pool reflected the starry night sky and the local moon Geala. I heard splashing and the croaking of frogs coming from the pool. From somewhere far away, barely within hearing, came voices.

There were several tombs in the small graveyard that were covered in grass and flowers, and right before me stood a beautifully decorated crypt. It looked like a substantial, even unassailable stone structure with neither windows nor doors. Why would Modus have built it? Maybe to revive leaders when the castle was attacked; they might have spare sets of equipment or a hidden tunnel entrance in there that could take someone outside the walls.

The important thing was that there was nobody around, not counting the guards on the walls. I hid behind the crypt in case they turned, and I started thinking. First, I made sure that Crag was alright. His icon in the group was active, his health full. True, he didn't answer my message — they might have put a _Silence Seal_ on him.

A notification flashed up. Seeing that I'd turned up, Crawler wrote that he and Bomber had revived in Kharinza and were heading to the Darant city graveyard to meet Crag and me there if we died. It turned out the preventers had foreseen that possibility too, setting up a perimeter around the graveyard in case the Threat died.

Crag was nowhere to be seen, and I faced a dilemma: go searching in my own form or in another. The first option seemed risky. If I pulled Toby out with *Depths Teleportation*, I'd reveal myself and they'd be after me. For now, the preventers didn't see a threat in me — perhaps Big Po didn't betray me, otherwise Yary would be using very different words.

The decision made itself. The voices from afar got louder, and a large group of players appeared from around a corner of the castle. I sprawled out in the grass behind the crypt and watched.

They walked along the wall and, reaching the stairs down to the basement, they split up. One group stayed at the entrance, the other took Crag inside. I didn't know why, but Tobias still hadn't been eliminated. It looked like they were delaying it. He was walking on his own, but some sort of collar glowed on his neck. Maybe it blocked his abilities, I didn't know.

Suddenly I realized that I knew nothing at all, and the thought stung bad. I could have far better spent my eight-week ban and the time after, before I left for big Dis, instead of going on dates and moonlit strolls with Tissa.

The Destroying Plague

Five took Crag into the cellar, and three came back up almost right away. That meant two were left guarding him. The ones that came back up joined the remaining group and ran back. I took on one of their forms.

Soon they all hid behind the corner — there was something happening there, but I couldn't see what it was. The sky above the castle on that side suddenly lit up with crimson flashes.

Nether. Whatever was happening, all would be talking about it tomorrow, and I needed to help out my clanmate.

I stood up and walked confidently toward the entrance to the cellar. Thankfully, the door, which was set a little below ground, wasn't locked, and the hinges were oiled. I opened it slightly and slipped inside, finding myself in a poorly lit tunnel that led downwards.

I walked down the stairs and glanced around the corner. A straight corridor leading off in two directions. There was nobody in the left-hand corridor, but I saw the shadows of two intelligent creatures.

A few torches along the passageway flickered and smoldered dimly, making the guards' shadows dance on the walls, and submerging the space itself in half-darkness. Just one torch, the closest to the guards, burned brighter than the others. Thanks to that and my night vision skill, I could make out that Crag's guards were standing by a closed door. Berstan the bandit and ice mage Kara. Both were above level three hundred. I didn't doubt that they had advanced control skills.

I could try to use *Lethargy* on one of them, but there was a high chance it would have no effect due to the level difference. I could just walk up looking like an ally and take Crag away into the depths. That was the easiest option, and the best decision was often the easiest.

I checked everything carefully. Health: one hundred percent. *Depths Teleportation* to Kharinza was off cooldown. My profile showed the forest elf Isanor, a level three hundred and forty-six druid from the Modus clan. I'd approach, sweet talk them, and leave with Crag. It'd take less than a minute.

I walked out into the corridor and turned right, moving quickly as if in a hurry to report something. Fifty feet from them, Kara shouted to me.

"Forgot something, Isa?"

"Yary summons you," I answered, approaching. "At once! I'll stand guard."

"Did the Alliance decide to attack after all?" Berstan the bandit exclaimed. "Damn it, I knew it! Come on, Kara!"

I approached quickly. Fifteen feet left to Crag's cell.

"Wait," the mage stopped his partner, grinning.

He stretched out his hand, palm forward, the space around it condensed and then a stream of frost hit me. I froze stiff at once, but I could still hear Kara talking fast into his signal amulet.

"Hey, Hinter! "Guess what, we got an attempted kidnapping here! We caught some noob, but he's a strange one...! Nickname? Scyth... Yeah, right next to 'threat.' And you know what? He looked like Isanor! The spitting image! Got it. We'll wait..."

The ice mage Kara's voice got quieter, turning into an unintelligible murmur, and at first, I thought it was because of the frost. It wasn't just my hearing that went, but my vision too — everything I saw with my hazy sight lit up as if someone had turned up the brightness and contrast to maximum, then broke into blocks and disappeared.

Spontaneous Divine Revelation activated!

My heart tried to beat its way out of my chest, even when I realized that everything happening in the corridor was the result of a passive class ability. Jumping back from the entrance to the corridor, I froze on the stairs. I heard the voices of guards in discussion downstairs.

Suspicions began to form in my head regarding what exactly *Divine Revelation* protects against. It first activated when I was accused of killing the town drunk Patrick, killed by Atiyakari, a headhunter from Axiom. Judge cannon sentenced me to a trial by battle, and according to the killer and the bogus witness, there was no way out of that.

The second time was when Big Po infected me,

promising that my death would be permanent for the character. Then Snowstorm covered up what he'd done. Several hundred infected and killed, which meant losing their characters, had quickly received soothing messages from the developers. I got the information first-hand; plenty of guys from our school were victims. They didn't get their characters back in the end, but both their gear and their progress were compensated. Spells had to be leveled up again from nothing, but the perks the developers gave outweighed the drawbacks. Players were even given short-term soulbound artifacts that multiplied the experience they'd earned.

And now a third activation. Again, predicting that I'd lose my character. Who had something to lose from the death of Scyth and the elimination of a Threat? The Awoken and I, of course, but that's irrelevant. Snowstorm? Those folks had supported me in everything so far, but they have nothing to do with the Herald class and its skills. That conclusion was clear from the class and ability descriptions and from the anonymous messages from someone from the corporation.

Which meant that there was only one option more or less possible option: the Sleeping Gods. Most of them were atrophied and almost in a coma, but for Behemoth, I was the only way to get out of the nightmare in which he was stuck. But the question was: who in all the nether were the Sleeping Gods? Really — who?

The Destroying Plague

All these thoughts ran through my mind in a couple of seconds, but right then wasn't the best moment to get deeper into them. More importantly, I couldn't get Crag out. That bright torch above the guards was definitely unusual. It was entirely possible that it was a *True Flame* or an artifact with the same effect, which would explain why Kara saw through my disguise.

I didn't know what to do. Somehow draw the guards away from the torch, run to the cell and leave for the depths? What if the door was locked, and the talent couldn't pull Crag out? What if there was something that suppressed magic and abilities?

The little alarm bell within me that had begun to ring softly back in the guest room of the Darant town hall had now turned into a cacophonous warning blare, entreating me to save myself while I had the chance. The cowardly Alex Sheppard, who avoided conflicts and had replaced his childhood friend for the popular among a class of hooligans, shouted selfishly that the alarm was right. I'd been lucky so many times that day. It would be crazy to try my luck again. I doubted that *Divine Revelation* would save me twice. I didn't know if the spontaneous ability had a cooldown or not, but no doubt it did, and a long one. Days if not a week.

Nether... The words of Crawler and Bomber added weight to my doubts. Both of them insisted that I get out myself. Infect and Tissa joined them too — Ed had left Dis for a minute to tell them what was happening. The developers had blocked communication between us and the sandbox, and we didn't see each other's messages even in the clan chat.

That was hard. I remembered what was on the line. And how Tobias behaved toward me, how he almost betrayed the hard-working non-citizen Manny to the city guard for spilling a glass of ale. And I didn't care.

I didn't care for cowardice. I sat on the basement steps and kept thinking feverishly for a way to escape with that damn Tobias 'Crag' Asser.

* * *

Hearing a dull rumble and cannonfire from siege weapons, I leapt to my feet. The entire building shook, dust falling from the low ceiling.

Standing up quickly, I rushed out onto the street. The ground beneath my feet shifted, and a humming noise joined the explosions. It grew, everything around vibrated, and then suddenly became very quiet. An opaque defensive dome had surrounded the castle. Like a giant fountain, it streamed upwards from the castle's central tower and poured out in magic waterfalls around the perimeter, beyond the walls. I could barely see the stars at first through the matter of the portal, then they faded entirely.

I'd never seen anything like it before. All around

The Destroying Plague

the sphere cannonballs, arrows, lightning strikes and fireballs broke up silently as they hit it. Had the Alliance clans abandoned by Modus come to take vengeance?

I didn't notice my legs taking me to the main entrance to the castle. It looked like all the clan's fighting members had gathered there: several hundred players and roughly the same in pets and mounts. Not a one of them below level two hundred.

They looked at their clan leader. Hinterleaf separated from the group of leading officers and climbed onto a catapult. He came to Dis as an adult with means back when the game's founding fathers were still alive, and there were under a million players. A year later, Modus was founded.

The illusion mage's snow-white mantle shimmered with blinding light when he started talking, and his magically strengthened voice boomed from all directions.

"Brothers-in-arms! Modus!"

"Modus!" the crowd shouted in unison, raising clenched fists.

"Time presses. Beyond the walls stand not only the forces of the Alliance, but also their jackal sidekicks. Our enemies," Hinterleaf pointed at the closed gates, "are already splitting the loot and distributing our property among themselves. Your property!"

"They're done for!" someone shouted from the front rows.

"Perhaps," Hinterleaf agreed. "But I believe this is the first time in the clan's history I haven't known what to do. The officers are divided, and I have decided that you have the right to know what is happening and which decision we need to take. As you all know, yesterday the Alliance took a class-D Threat in Darant. As planned, the elimination was intended to take place beyond the frontier. I planned to open a portal through which one member of each Alliance clan would travel. But... we were betrayed. It is hard to say who began first, and that no longer matters. The fact is that they treacherously attacked us at the assembly point. If it had been just the dark ones..." the clan leader laughed bitterly. "Our opposition against the Travelers and the other dark ones has too rich and bloody a history to expect anything more. We had a plan B for that outcome. But then our own stabbed us in the back! The Azure Dragons, Excommunicado, the Children of Kratos..."

"Those dumb rich kids?" a centaur standing nearby asked in surprise, taking off his helmet and scratching the back of his hairy head. I was surprised by anyone choosing such a race — controlling six limbs must be difficult. "What beef do they have with us?"

The backbone of Children of Kratos consisted of rich youths that weren't above spending their parents' money on boosts and equipment. It was a strong clan with a rich history, a kind of elite club for citizen children at category C or above. In many ways, they played just for fun and rarely got involved in open battles and conflicts with their equals, let alone anyone stronger.

I listened to Hinterleaf again, at the same time searching for options and waiting. I knew one thing for sure: something was about to start, and in the ensuing chaos, I'd have a chance to pull Crag out.

"Alright, I'll get to the point. We failed to determine the nature of the captured Threat. The boy won't engage and refuses to talk, but we did learn something. This isn't confirmed, but it seems like he strengthens the group he's in. Strengthens it a great deal. Do you understand? With such a partner, and we can't accept him into the clan for obvious reasons, we will be capable of much. Just imagine it — perhaps with him, we'll finally be able to break through to the Valley of the Winged Terror or even reach Meaz! The boy must agree, as it will allow him to further develop his potential. We will offer him a share of the loot and a fixed rate for being online..."

The Modus clan leader seemed to surprise not only me, but his clanmates too. Hinterleaf's reputation as a treacherous, cruel and authoritarian leader didn't match with what I was seeing. Unless these games of democracy were a part of another plan.

As soon as I thought of that, Yary interrupted the clan leader. The knight stood up next to the leader and took off his strangely shaped helmet with a blade at its peak. A shadow crossed Hinterleaf's face. Maybe the old man really was giving way. That must be the source of the conflict with his own officers, masked as it was under 'differences of opinion.'

"I doubt we'll get out of here at all with the top clans on our tail. My people, that which our dearly respected clan leader has said — it is utopia. We won't be forgiven for such a trick. Nor for solely terminating the Threat. There's a reason we're called Modus. We value covenants that take the interests of all sides into account. That's how we reached the top, by solving problems not with weapons, but with words. Who is in favor of letting in the Alliance's envoys, to solve this misunderstanding and deescalate the conflict?"

"They can't pierce the *Righteous Shield*! It regenerates faster than they can damage it! They could bring the entire army of the Commonwealth here and still break their teeth!" Hinterleaf bellowed. "We will reinforce ourselves with mercenaries..."

"Blackberry, what's the situation with the mercenaries?" Yary interrupted, addressing the officers.

The tall figure of an elvish woman in leather armor, with a short crossbow at her back, stepped forward from the group. Her long legs ended in black boots with wings.

"All mercenaries above level three hundred were engaged this morning," the girl answered loudly, raising a few feet off the ground so that everyone could see her. "The client has not been disclosed, but it's likely to be the Travelers."

"You see?" Hinterleaf shouted triumphantly, although the new information contradicted his words. It seemed like he was more interested in winning the argument with his officers for the majority vote than in solving the conflict with the alliance. "The dark ones decided to betray is long ago! And now one of us is ready to compromise? To subjugate ourselves and serve up the Threat on a silver platter?"

"That's an exaggeration," Yary stated. "Hint, you're our leader. We'll accept whatever decision you make. You know that. But I beg you, be reasonable! We can't hole up in this castle and hide from the world! We're getting reports that our mines and plantations are under attack too. Our new castle at the frontier is under siege, and it doesn't have a *Righteous Shield* artifact! We're already losing before the battle has begun! No clan has ever won in a battle against everyone else. And that's what you're leading us into!"

Hinterleaf chewed his lip as if choosing his words, took a deep breath and spoke gloomily.

"You don't even know what you're refusing. To the nether with it! Enough words! We need to make a decision. Who is in favor of keeping the Threat for ourselves? Regardless of what we do with it."

He cast a dark gaze across the clan. Not a single hand was raised. The Modus leader nodded disgustedly.

"Nether take you, weaklings. Call in the

emissaries, one from each Alliance clan."

Yary gave the required orders. Two stars ran to the basement where Crag was being kept. The emissaries demanded that they be shown the Threat, to ensure it was still intact.

I braced myself and messaged Tobias to tell him not to listen to anyone, that we'd be leaving soon. You never know, he might decide it was all over and just turn his coat.

In the meantime, the Modus soldiers formed into a defensive battle formation in case of unforeseen surprised from the besiegers. Regardless of the discipline that reigned in their ranks, I managed to slip through the darkness closer to the spot where Crag should be brought through.

First the defensive dome disappeared. Then the gates swung open, opening the way to the emissaries. Each of them was mounted on a winged mount and could have flown across the moat and walls, but they came in across the bridge in a column: Glyph on his *Winged Tiger*, Horvac on his *Ghost Dragon*, the Colonel on his *Burning Phoenix* and all the rest. The eyes wanted to shy away from the gleam of all that legendary equipment. There was at least a billion gold walking across that bridge.

In the meantime, Crag's marker appeared on the minimap. The countdown was down to seconds.

They were supposed to be bringing him by not far from me, but I still kept pushing forwards to get as close as possible. Thirty feet, twenty-five, twenty...

The Destroying Plague

Damn! They turned fluidly and now were moving away from us. My heart, already beating fast, began to thump fiercely in my chest. I rushed to get closer, pushing through the crowd. I saw a gap and went for it, paying no attention to the shouts of displeasure and jabbing elbows.

Someone got particularly annoyed and tripped me up. I fell, my chin struck the pavement and my vision swam. Crawling, I swore under my breath. There was a palisade of legs around me. I jumped straight onto all fours, headbutting knees and calves, losing all sense of direction and realizing that I'd lost...

The depths icon lit up, turned active, but I didn't have time to activate the ability — the range broke again. And then Crag, as if sensing something, stopped. Lowering my head, I took on the form of Horvac, who was riding into the castle. The crowd yielded to the emissaries.

Jumping up, I took a step, another... and activated *Depths Teleportation*. Three heartbeats later, we appeared at Kharinza right at the entrance to the Temple of the Sleeping Gods.

The figure of Behemoth materialized inside. I nodded to the divinity and looked at Crag. He fell to the ground and sat down, dropping his hands onto his knees. A grubby smile lit up his face. I crouched down next to him.

We did it! We're at the temple! I wrote to the others. Crawler and Bomber soon teleported in a few feet away. Trixie, Manny and Gyula ran at full pelt toward us, waving their hands in greeting. The little man struggled along, trying to keep up, and shouted something.

"Damn, where are we?" Crag asked.

"Welcome to the future clan fort of the Awoken!" Crawler declared triumphantly.

"We're home, Toby," I whispered, falling onto my back. Myriad stars flickered, celebrating the end of an important mission. "We're home."

Interlude 1

Wesley

AFTER GRANDPA DIED, leadership of the large Cho family went to Uncle Joe, the older brother of Wesley's father. That had happened three years ago, back when Big Po was still called just Wes, and he hadn't yet come up with his nickname, Polynucleotide. The uncle then called the father to talk, after which everything changed for Wesley.

His father suddenly stopped eating at dinner, put aside his chopsticks, loomed gloomily at his wife and switched his gaze to his son.

"Your uncle Jonathan isn't going to help us anymore," he said. "If you still want to get into business, you'll need to win a scholarship. The family won't pay for your studies."

His father didn't explain Uncle Joe's decision, but Wesley knew that business wasn't going well in the family. Since that conversation, everything just got worse. He gained weight due to a corrupted nutrient exchange, and physical training carried as much weight in school as academic knowledge.

Wesley reflected. Back then he was only thirteen, with a little under a year left until he could play Disgardium. While his friends enjoyed childish VR worlds, Wesley tried to imagine his life and who he wanted to become. And the more he thought, the more he realized that he needed to make a career in Dis. He couldn't win a chance at a free higher education, that was clear.

Then he did what he loved the most — he planned. Many strove to progress, make money and forge a career in Disgardium, and to this day it was still a gold rush — there were still many unexplored lands in the game, and that meant chances to get rich quick. But few achieved success. Wesley decided to figure out why.

First, he studied how the best players in Dis had begun. All of them had a hardcore, even fanatic manner of playing. They'd spent all their time in the game from the first day they hit the sandbox.

But many did that, and not all of them achieved significant success. Something more was needed. That 'something,' as a rule, was a kind of in-game advantage: a rare ability, a unique artifact, generally anything that led to abnormally fast progress.

Wesley, thorough as he was and used to weighing up the risks and striving toward his goal step by step, derived a plan. The first part of his plan concerned the sandbox; he wanted to create a top clan and achieve domination, which meant storing up

The Destroying Plague

resources to make progress in big Dis. There were multiple options for the second part — Wesley decided to return to them when he was ready to leave the sandbox.

He brought his cousin Scott in on his plan, who'd started in Dis four months earlier. Scott was kind of a silly kid, so Wesley treated him as if he was younger. The cousin accepted Wesley's superiority and took inspiration from his ideas.

Wesley prepared a detailed leveling program for his cousin, which, if followed, would give both cousins a full set of equipment when Wesley arrived in the game, along with weapons and the ability to immediately take combat quests without bothering with social ones.

Scott didn't have much imagination. A couple of days before his fourteenth birthday, he decided to ask his cousin about his in-game name.

"I'm going to be Polynucleotide," Wesley answered.

"Poly... what? That's so dumb!" Scott shook his head. "What about Predator? Or Angel of Death? What kind of nick is that, Wes?"

"I chose it for its uniqueness. There isn't a single Polynucleotide among billions of players. I don't want to just another Wesley, or Angel of Death or Predator, because it's easy to get lost in that crowd. A name should be memorable."

"What does it even mean?"

"It's a biopolymer. Forget it, just remember that

it's from chemistry."

As it happened, Scott was so impressed by his cousin's originality that he called himself Polynuclear.

Each time his cousin played, Wesley studied the videos from his game and corrected his plans. And although Scott didn't do everything the way he was told due to his forgetfulness and inattention, in the end it all worked out. Wesley started in Dis with *green* equipment and weaponry.

Another Po soon joined them — Pocketrocket, Scott's best friend. He had some doubts at first that Wesley was worthy of leadership but calmed down when he lost to him in a duel in spite of a two-level advantage.

In math classes, Wesley met Irina Katznelson, a tall girl with a long nose and huge blue eyes. A head taller than him, she stooped to make it easier for them to talk.

In one of their instance runs, that time the Crypt of the Temple of Nergal the Radiant, they were looking for a fifth group member and found Sanji, also known as Atiyakari. They didn't know each other in real life, but the future bandit proved himself a skilled damager and joined their company.

And then there were five. More than enough to unite into a clan. Wesley loved math and the hard sciences, so he called the clan Axiom. Irina supported him and the others didn't object.

Soon the clan gained strength in Tristad, taking the most hardcore players it could find under its wing. Under Wesley's control, they managed to get into the top one hundred leaderboard in their first year based on their Junior Arena score, and higher level team members invited him to join their groups, acknowledging not only his leadership and talent as a tactician, but his skill as a PvP fighter as well.

The Dementors were too independent and selective to join Axiom, although Wesley kept trying to lure at least Hung from there. As for the Night Stalkers, the second strongest clan in the sandbox, he'd managed to negotiate a merger. JJ didn't argue with Wesley's leadership. His budding romance with Marishka stopped him from being online around the clock. He was at the mercy of his hormones.

The first part of the plan was done. There was still half a year left until the next part, until Wesley left the sandbox, and he didn't doubt that unforeseen problems would crop up there too.

That stage meant farming achievements. A new instance had opened in the Olton Quarries — Evil from the Depths — and Axiom was focusing chiefly on that. Uniting with the Night Stalkers allowed them to claim the instance, the full completion of which became a mere matter of time — they were missing a little damage, and that problem was solved when the main static members leveled up. Another dungeon nobody had yet completed, Nest of the Swamp Needlers, was delayed due to permanent debuffs. Every percentage of health was important for Murkiss.

For the first time in all his experience in Dis, Wesley allowed himself to relax a little. They organized a party in real life, and there he saw Irina with a new perspective. Overcoming his shyness, he asked the girl out on a date.

Now, months later, the boy realized his mistake. Not because of the girl, no, he liked her as much as ever. It was because he'd lost his concentration as a result of their developing relationship. *Focus on your goal!* his father had always told him, and Wesley had always followed that rule. His father had always been considered a loser in the large Cho family, but he didn't want his son to repeat his own mistakes. His low citizen status and neglect from his brother Joe were the results of his father allowing secondary things to distract him. He'd spread himself too thin. He hadn't focused. Wesley promised both his father and himself that he wouldn't repeat those mistakes.

Punishment came at once. He was flying to his first date with Irina when he got a call to tell him that a stranger had made his way into Evil from the Depths. Alex Sheppard, also known as Scyth. A name that Wesley ended up hearing more than once.

Things only got worse. Axiom lost its First Kill, first in that instance, then in another. It failed dismally in the qualifiers at the Junior Arena, losing the bet to Scyth for the legendary *Arena Master's Horn*, for which Wesley had had big plans. There wouldn't have been any bet at all if Big Po hadn't decided to go through some Triad acquaintances to hire those inwinovas to teach the Dementors a lesson...

The only silver lining of the following months was the First Kill on Bloodsucker, a strange rare spider that suddenly appeared instead of Crusher the wolf. They'd each received a *Spider Egg* then, which provided a battle mount. Some small consolation also came from the election victory for the Tristad city council. He became the first player to achieve anything like that, and he got an achievement and access to forbidden areas in the city.

Then there were plenty of strange occurrences. As Wesley analyzed them, he became more and more sure that Scyth was to blame for all of them. They studied his routes for several days. Atiyakari and Greykillah, the clan's top stealthers, sometimes tracked Sheppard's movements, but there was no way they could go up against his ability to jump all over the sandbox. Then Wesley made the decision to take Scyth as soon as he appeared in Tristad and check his Threat status. And that day, a Threat came from an unexpected place.

Tobias Asser, the failed ganker Crag, demolished the guards Axiom had placed at a new instance without much effort. Aphrodite was with him, but he doubted she was the problem. According to Atiyakari, the girl just showed her presence, although her damage was impressive.

While the whole clan rooted around to find the

guy, one of their own leaked info on Crag to the preventers and got paid a pretty packet for it. Enraged, Wesley nearly disbanded the clan in an attempt to find out the traitor's name. On the other hand, they still had a chance to eliminate Crag themselves.

But then the next day, something even stranger happened. Detrovay and Annamassy abandoned their post at the Sarantapod Hive. They'd just up and damn well left, since apparently Wesley himself had dismissed them! But he'd been at school! Unfortunately, the pair hadn't thought to record what they'd seen, so he didn't believe them. He decided instead that they were just feeding him excuses after they missed someone sneaking into the dungeon.

That was probably the last straw. He went nuts, shouted at Detrovay and Annamassy in front of all the officers, and kicked them out of the clan. Before that, JJ had already left Axiom with his guys, and the new wave of conflict divided the clan. Wesley flipped out, losing control of the clan and the trust of his members. Even Scott and Irina didn't support their friend. "Big Po has lost face," his father would have said, and those thoughts burned his soul.

All the following days, Wesley stubbornly wandered the outskirts of Tristad, trying to find the Threat on his own. With a *Torch of True Flame* clutched in his hands, he scoured all of Gloomwood, the murlock lands, the shoreline of the Bottomless Ocean and the edge of the Mire, all the while seeking

The Destroying Plague

Scyth or Crag. He had no doubt that one of the two were Threats. Maybe even both. In any case, Wesley was ready: he had *Full Petrification* and *Invulnerability Bubble* scrolls to help him subdue anyone he needed to. As to how he got them in the sandbox, that was another story related to his relationship with the Tristad Archivist and his friend from Darant, a high-level mage. A little flattery, a unique chain of investigation quests and the maximum reputation that came from it, allowing him to get these powerful spells.

In Gloomwood, he ran into the giant zombie wolf Punisher. By then, the level seventeen local boss wasn't a problem for him. Wesley got a First Kill and a strange ability, *Mark of the Destroying Plague.*

The skill seemed impractical at first glance, just a one-percent invulnerability procc. Along with an undead transformation. But a little later, he realized that it was enough to just wait for the ability to activate, then just not let it run out. A sudden notification that he'd received a Threat status with potential L confirmed it. Wesley laughed like a madman then. He'd been hunting Threats, then turned into one himself.

The hysterics passed and his calculating mind kicked in. He didn't sleep a wink that night. He tossed and turned, thinking up his plan of action, options for leveling up his new ability, and of course, for keeping his status secret. He gathered his officers the next day, accepted his mistakes and declared that he was leaving the clan. They tried to convince him to stay, but he'd already made his decision. His future would be built elsewhere. Anyway, he didn't want to risk his Threat status.

Wesley chose a small island a couple of miles from the continent to farm on. He got the idea to use *Exhaustion* right away. With that debuff, the undead curse wouldn't disappear even out of battle. The island was full of nagas and tritons, teeming with *Giant Crags* and *Flesh-Eating Turtles* at level twenty-five and above. But the main thing was that there were no people. He could level up to his heart's content. Once he reached the shore, he set a respawn point by the murlock instance so he wouldn't have to run far to recover his *Mark* activation, then he started implementing his plan.

Day by day, spending all his time there apart from when he slept and went to school, he boosted his level, his abilities and his *Mark*. However, the growth of the first and second soon stunted — the mobs got too weak. Still he didn't stop. He kept leveling up the chance of the undead curse activating. That meant dying repeatedly, which was tedious, but he believed it was worth it.

It turned out it was. A little time later, a messenger of the Destroying Plague appeared and gave him his first quest: infect a critical mass of citizens and open a portal. Apart from that, the messenger declared Wesley a *Herald* and told him the story of his predecessor, who had failed to live up to

The Destroying Plague

the Nucleus's hopes and had been deprived of his status. Wesley wasn't surprised when he learned it was Scyth.

Alex freaking Sheppard. The one that shot him down in his moment of triumph. Wesley had opened the portal, almost captured Tristad and prepared to become a legate of the Destroying Plague. And exactly then, that damned Sheppard had appeared with his flaxen-haired girlfriend, crowd-controlled him and eliminated him as a Threat.

And he'd been so close to victory! He'd raised his Threat level and was preparing to hand in the Nucleus's quest, certain that his potential would grow with his new talents. He was so upset that even the Snowstorm rewards were scant solace. He'd almost won millions, then got only a consolation prize. Wesley was crushed.

He fell into a depression for weeks and didn't use his capsule. Why hide it? He even thought of suicide, understanding perfectly that chances like that were one in a million, especially with such a high potential. The fact that four Threats had appeared within a year in their sandbox, counting that fool class Z necromancer, was a digression from the norm. It was even more offensive to realize that he'd lost his status too, after that idiot Scyth and the necromancer. And only that pathetic ganker Crag through some miracle, at first not even hiding it, managed to stay afloat.

Today they called him to the school principal.

"Cho," the man said, drumming his fingers on the table. "Ignoring the recommendations of the Department of Education, who have now sent you three letters, is not the best idea on the eve of your citizenship tests. It is my duty to convince you not to miss the required hours in Disgardium. It may negatively affect your citizenship!"

"Alright, Mr. Fultz," Wesley answered. "I won't skip it anymore."

As he sat in the flier, his decisiveness grew. He had no intention to return to Dis and live a drawn-out life as an ordinary player. Even if he did have the legendary *Bone Horse*, given as if in mockery by Snowstorm along with money and a little gear. That wouldn't make him unique. There were hundreds of millions of players like him, if not billions. No, he'd take another path.

It seemed he was the only one to put two and two together. There were many people in the multitude of videos of what happened in Alma'arasan Gorge, and later in the Modus castle. One of them was Crag, as prisoner of the preventers. Wesley also noticed Scyth, although Sheppard only took part in the events in the gorge... The fake Horvac in the Modus castle courtyard and Crag's escape — these were familiar tricks. Very similar to the time when certain 'heroes wishing to remain nameless,' took the First Kill in the Sarantapod Hive.

Sheppard was definitely hiding something. He hadn't stopped being a Threat after losing the Mark of the Destroying Plague. The more Wesley thought about it, the more convinced he was.

There was no question of whether to give up to the preventers. That was the least that Wesley could do to knock that arrogant bastard down a peg or two. But what would that give to Wesley himself? The financial reward and legendaries interested him, sure, but he wanted to try something else. After all, he could contact Modus any time he wanted. It was worth starting with something else.

With something Wesley considered himself a professional at. Good old blackmail.

Chapter 4

Home Sweet Home

*L*OOKS LIKE SOMEONE *from the top clans decided to use Crag against Modus,* Crawler wrote in the clan chat while I examined the fort. *Hinterleaf accused the Alliance of betrayal, but the fact that Horvac's twin disappeared with Crag is the news of the day! All Modus's castles are under siege, and even the preventers have gotten involved!*

That was to the good. While the strong fought amongst themselves, we'd have time to catch our breath. I decided to start with a quick look at the Awoken lands and a meeting with Behemoth.

The builders had finished the level one clan fort a few days before. There were no problems with the budget, or with the legality of payment — we made contracts with each of the workers. Crawler solved the problem with the miners in the same way.

The mine was part of Awoken's territory as soon as the fort was built. Considering the zone's high level, the resources in it were rarer, which meant more valuable. Gold, mithril and thorium ore, for example, weren't sold in hundreds of bars like copper and iron, but in stacks of ten because of their cost. And they were worth more than a hundred gold a stack.

The problem was something else. Manny's miners didn't have enough skill to mine rare ores, which practically forced us to make short-term hire operations for minerals based on their craftsmanship grade. All the adepts of the Sleeping Gods were mining the available metals and working three shifts at Klondike — which was what we called the clan mine.

Crawler, as my right-hand man, paid a contribution and applied to register the mine. It happened to be yesterday, after three days without other pretenders appearing (there actually were some, but none could declare their rights — the coordinates weren't given to such shady companies), the guild of miners gave us an exploitation license.

That allowed us to employ miners, at the same time giving them separate bonuses. That obvious trick allowed non-citizens among the adepts of the Sleeping Gods to increase their income severalfold, and now rumors spreading through all Cali Bottom, and that drew more volunteers to us. *Unity* also increased their stats, which sped up the process and got us more resources.

Our main limit was on the number of adepts. There were now sixty-nine of us followers of the Sleeping Gods. We'd need to build a second temple to raise the limit. The sewer troggs won over by Patrick O'Grady in Darant were also waiting for this. I just had to get through to there to meet the first priest and his new friends.

So, I didn't delay my meeting with the god, after which I planned to get to grips with the Snowstorm rewards. To tell the truth, I was burning inside with anticipation and excitement to dig through the loot!

There was some more great news; a small tavern had sprung up there, where I had a private room with a chest just like at the Bubbling Flagon. I'd left the crystal that dropped from Big Po in storage there.

Courtesy of Bomber, the tavern was dubbed the Pig and Whistle. The adepts of the Sleeping Gods got free service there on the clan's dime. Would that policy change? I didn't know. We had no plans to take on new members due to certain, ahem, circumstances, and the clan treasury was healthy enough to feed and water the current membership.

I had plans to walk around the fort in daylight to examine it and think about upgrades.

But my first task was to deal with Behemoth's quest. Without the usual invulnerability of the undead curse and *Plague Energy*, I felt extremely uncomfortable. Especially considering what was happening in the wider world. Also, there was still a Montosaurus of unknown level wandering Kharinza.

The guys were waiting for me in the tavern, which was run by Steph, the younger sister of Gyula.

The Destroying Plague

We knew her from the Bubbling Flagon. Back there, the woman had been an ordinary washgirl, but she'd picked up some things from the chef, Arno: she'd learned *Cooking* and even leveled it up to expert. She'd heard plenty of good things about me, but this was the first time we'd met.

"How should I address you, Stephanie?" I asked.

"Oh, however you like," she said shyly. "Kids your age call me Aunt Steph."

And it was settled. She got really upset when I didn't try her freshly baked *Sea Devil Soup*, a scorchingly spicy shellfish soup. Bomber wolfed his down and eagerly took my portion.

Leaving our tavern, I walked down the fort's only street and in a couple of minutes reached the temple. I stopped there and stared a while, impressed by the structure's magnificence. I appreciated the work of our chief builder Gyula with fresh eyes.

The temple looked imposing in spite of its small size. A few slabs laid in a pyramid had stood here since ancient times and served as the building's foundation. The builders cleaned them up, pulled out all the grass and underwood. They added a few other smaller slabs, bringing the total to thirty. The result was a kind of triangle with the peak cut off. Carved cobblestones were laid on its surface, each with the symbol of the Sleeping Gods, a closed eye in a triangle. Looked like that appeared after the temple was opened and consecrated to Behemoth.

The temple itself was on the very top slab — with a sloping roof on six columns. The divinity's face grinned on its front; just like on the altar within, only far larger.

Hurry, Herald! a voice boomed in my head, drowning out my thoughts. *Hurry!*

I jumped up all the steps to the top and found myself face to face with Behemoth. His avatar hadn't changed since our last meeting — still the same three-dimensional human body with a hippopotamus head.

He hadn't spoken to anyone in my absence, not even with the only priest of the Sleeping Gods in Kharinza, Manny, and materialized only a second before I arrived. It seemed he'd somehow tracked my movements with *Depths Teleportation*, although that wouldn't be hard. After all, we got that talent from the final boss of Evil from the Depths, Murkiss, a scorpion mutated by the breath of the Sleeping Gods, whatever that meant.

"Mission to prevent the Destroying Plague from overwhelming Tristad successful, Sleeping God!" I reported, jokingly standing at attention.

I finally felt at ease and was in a playful mood.

"At ease, Herald," Behemoth played along with me, to my great surprise. However, the tension emanating from him in waves quickly brought me back to reality. "You have proven yourself worthy..."

Suddenly, the god drew me to himself, embraced me and slapped me on the back. That was something new. His blackened plate armor gave off intolerable heat, and I tore away, jumping out of his monstrous grasp. The god reacted with understanding.

"Forgive me. You humans are extremely gentle creatures. Fragile. You can exist only in one narrow range of temperature!

Hmm... First 'at ease,' then a reference to humans (humans, not 'intelligent life of Disgardium!') in this context... The farther into the forest, the thicker the trees, as my uncle Nick used to say. I never did understand what that meant, but he always brought it out when events developed unexpectedly, and new information didn't explain anything, just made things more confusing.

In the meantime, Behemoth pointed his piercing gaze at me and spoke.

"I received vile emanations from the parasitic creature that calls itself the Destroying Plague, from Tristad, then they suddenly stopped. You closed the portal and destroyed the creature, but many days have passed since then. What delayed you?"

I thought for a moment. How could I explain all the twists and turns of our exit from the sandbox, and the preventers, to a virtual entity, even if he was a god? But I had to, otherwise I wouldn't even get a quest completion message, let alone rewards.

"Are you aware, Sleeping God, that the strongest people of this world hunt those such as myself and my teammate Crag? They are of the opinion that we represent a threat to all intelligent life, and headhunters get very valuable rewards for hunting us..."

"Crag? You mean that little dwarf that appeared here with you? The nature of his power reeks of the droppings of the Radiant," Behemoth almost spat the name. "I had to hide my presence in his eyes as soon as I saw you two in the deep paths. We cannot allow the false god to learn of us too soon."

"Is everything really so bad? Nergal is the one that gave Crag his power, after all. And it helps make us stronger..."

"It is borrowed power, Herald!" the Sleeping God grumbled. "Nergal is not a god who demands nothing in return. Every request made to him and every ability he grants will multiply Crag's debt, and the false god will surely demand repayment."

"When?"

"When you least expect it! I have seen plenty of Nergal's deeds in my dreams. On his path to power, he shrank back not from sacrificial offerings, nor from connections with the elder demons and the rulers of the Nether."

"Are you sure? He's a god of Light!"

"Light is blinding. There is light that kills all life. Any element can be dangerous. We will return to this conversation. As for Nergal's gift, I must speak with your friend and study the pattern of the weave. I will see what can be done, but do not hope for too much too soon — my powers are still too weak."

The Destroying Plague

The Sleeping God turned his head to the side, listening to something. Mentally figuring out the direction, I realized he was looking toward the clan tavern. Having clarified something for himself, the god nodded and snapped his jaw in front of me.

"Continue your tale, Herald."

"We call those headhunters Preventers. They're heroes, the strongest warriors in the world. They started checking everyone who arrived in Darant, and we barely managed to get away."

"You were on the edge, Herald. The backlash of the *Aversion* was so strong that even my sister and brothers felt it."

Suddenly, I understand that he was talking about *Divine Revelation*. It seemed the effect of this passive skill, placed into the game's core many years ago, worked differently for every Herald depending on which divinity was their patron. So, my *Divine Revelation* was courtesy of Behemoth? That was worth thinking about.

"Then you should understand why I was delayed. First, I was waiting for Crag, because he could only leave Tristad today according to Commonwealth law. He can't travel through the Depths himself..."

"You are so sure of him that you risked yourself?"

"That no longer matters, Sleeping God. He asked for help when we were fighting off the Destroying Plague together. I agreed."

"You acted correctly," Behemoth said softly. "And have earned a reward!"

Placing both hands on my shoulders, he gazed into my eyes. I froze, unable even to breathe. My shoulders burned and streams of energy flowed through me, the power, will and wisdom of the Sleeping Gods, but little of it stayed: two divine talents.

Sleeping God Behemoth mission complete.

You successfully prevented the capture of Tristad by the Nucleus of the Destroying Plague, slowing the influence of the Nether in Disgardium.

Rewards:

— *Sleeping Invulnerability skill*
— *Sleeping Vindication skill*

Experience: +15000.

Experience at current level (26): 33650/36400.

Your reputation with Behemoth the Sleeping God has increased: +1000.

Current reputation: trust.

Your reputation with Tiamat the Sleeping God has increased: +100.

Current reputation: affection.

Your reputation with Kingu the Sleeping God has increased: +100.

The Destroying Plague

Current reputation: affection.

Your reputation with Abzu the Sleeping God has increased: +100.
Current reputation: affection.

Your reputation with Leviathan the Sleeping God has increased: +100.
Current reputation: affection.

The reputation bar with the other Sleeping Gods was almost full. Another point and it would reach *friendly*. If everything kept going well with Behemoth, there'd certainly be no problems there. Another quest or two and my reputation with him would reach *honored...*

Having finished the reward ceremony, Behemoth retreated and fell silent while I got to grips with my new abilities.

Sleeping Invulnerability, level 1
This ability's level is always equal to the number of active Sleeping God temples.

Absorbs 20% of any incoming damage. The remaining damage is split between all group members in proportion to their total health. A character without a group takes all the unabsorbed damage in full.

Sleeping Vindication, level 1
This ability's level is always equal to the number

---

of active Sleeping God temples.

Damage absorbed by Sleeping Invulnerability stacks up in the altar of the main temple. This is vindication.

Vindication can be cast in an area or aimed at a specific target.

Range (depends on Perception): 230 feet.

Unlocked a new stat: Vindication.

The maximum Vindication you can accumulate depends on the number of Sleeping God adepts.

Volume: 169,000.

A new black bar appeared in the interface. So that was the color of vindication... Well, it wasn't an undead curse with *Plague Energy*, but the potential was much greater! Without giving me time to study the rewards, Behemoth spoke again.

"With every temple you build and dedicate to one of the Sleeping Gods, the power of your abilities will grow. When each of us gains in power, your invulnerability will become absolute. And in contrast to the parasitic creature and his twisted undead curse, the invulnerability will not turn you into a walking corpse!"

Emitting streams of smoke, or perhaps steam from his nostrils, the Sleeping God laughed.

The Destroying Plague

---

* * *

That evening, I never did quite get to going through my rewards for eliminating Big Po. Behemoth and I spent around another hour examining the options for completing his quest.

Second Temple
The Sleeping God Behemoth desires that you build a new temple in any of the places of power he indicates, and that you consecrate it to a Sleeping God: Leviathan, Abzu, Kingu or Tiamat.
Rewards*: unknown.*

What could be so hard about that? We had builders, money for using stationary portals, and I could hide my true image. The problem was elsewhere: all the places of power suitable for building temples except one were on other continents.

Players had claimed only three of them, calling them Latteria, Shad'Erung and Bakabba. The first two were huge and separated only by the narrow Thunder Strait. They were the most explored and were occupied by the Commonwealth and the Empire. Those two largest factions of the light and dark races were divided not only by the strait, but also by expansive stretches of Unexplored Lands.

By its nature, the neutral playing faction was never united. They comprised people who chose races that belonged neither to the Commonwealth nor the

Empire. Geographically, they were spread across both continents, and those lands hosted the fiercest inter-factional conflicts on the Battlefields.

On Latteria, the Lakharian Desert was still unexplored, stretching across the frontier. On Shad'Erung — the Ursai Jungle. The greater part of these lands was not only teeming with high-level mobs, but their environments also tried to kill people. The Unexplored Lands constantly constricted as the maximum level of players increased, along with their abilities to strengthen their defenses and resistance. Conquered lands were taken both by NPCs and clans, but it happened very slowly, and here is why.

In the desert, even with maximum resists, players quickly baked as the heat debuffs stacked up. Sooner or later, they reached such levels that a single tick could kill you. The same happened in the jungle, only instead of heat, players died from poisonous fumes. Not to mention the aggressive flora, fauna and magical beasts, of course. Any mob in those lands could take out a whole group of top players.

As crafting grades increased, and elemental resistance along with them, the lines of the frontier retreated, but each time everything depended on the next rank — the key factor in the entire system of abilities and moves. Once, by eating soup in the swamp of the Mire, I reached the maximum possible level of *Resilience*. But that was just the cap for rank zero. As soon as my level got over one hundred, the limit would lift. I'd need to level up my skills all over again, but the first level of the first rank would be stronger than level one hundred of rank zero.

In all of Dis, nobody had ever reached rank four in a single ability, because not even any of the top players had reached level four hundred. The animalist druid Mogwai, who reached three hundred and ninety-eight and took a break from Dis, was still number one on the worldwide leaderboard.

As for crafting, crafters could reach only rank three in their profession, with the corresponding grade of Grandmaster. Great Grandmaster required rank four.

The only Great Grandmaster I knew of wasn't a crafter, but a specialist in hand-to-hand combat, Oyama. A mythical individual who long ago went to meditate and never returned from his long travels through the astral plane.

As soon as the crafters broke the threshold of level four hundred, they'd be able to create stronger potions and defensive items so that players could more easily withstand the aggressive environments of unclaimed zones. Then the frontier line would shift once more.

There, beyond the frontier in the Lakharian Desert, was one of the places of power that Behemoth had marked. And it was the easiest to access.

The others were spread around places just as far away, just as inaccessible to me as to everybody else.

In Bakabba, the third conquered continent, the

goblins called the shots. There were portals to Kinema, the capital of Bakabba, in Darant and Shak, the capital of the Empire, but to get there you had to complete a ridiculously long quest chain from the Goblin League to increase reputation with them to *honored.* I didn't have anything to do there anyway, since those green little creatures had already built their own temples to their greedy gods in all the places of power.

Another few places were on the three remaining continents. Only there was no sense in going after those.

The snowy continent Holdest spread across the South Pole. The craft of global shipbuilding hadn't yet reached the necessary rank even to sail there, not to mention conquer its lands. As for flying mounts, they got *Exhaustion* — they needed to rest on solid ground too. The gnomish airships could fly there, but the storms and vicious high-level creatures who dominated the skies over the ocean made such journeys suicidal.

Meaz, a small continent in the southern hemisphere, was covered in an impenetrable magic veil, and no player had ever managed to get through it. The entire game community had tried every which way to find the key to those lands, but in vain.

As for Terrastera, it was called hell on Earth, or rather in Dis. Creatures above level one thousand filled that dwarf continent's coastal waters, skies and land. Not to mention its active volcanoes that regularly covered the place in lava, ash clouds and acid rain. With the current rate of level growth among players, it would take thirty years at least to conquer Terrastera.

One of the places of power was at the floor of the Bottomless Ocean to the east of Shad'Erung. I'd heard of underwater kingdoms, but nothing specific — they were hidden to players too, for now.

That meant that the only realistic option left to us was the Lakharian Desert. With that not particularly comforting conclusion in mind, I left Behemoth and wandered over to my friends in the tavern.

* * *

"Don't worry, I hid well," Crag chuckled. Beer foam decorated his rich braided mustache. "They didn't get Crag; they didn't get shit! But you know..."

He dropped his head, faltering. Finally, he gathered himself and burst out:

"I really thought I was done for! In that guest hall, and while we were flying to the gorge, let alone in the gorge itself. I didn't see a single chance. I was ready to accept their offer... But then when they dragged me into that castle jail... He broke again, speaking in fragments. "What I mean is... Thanks... Thanks for not abandoning me! You especially, Scyth! I remember our... disagreements. I figured you'd have an ironclad excuse for just leaving on your own. But you... Damn! I'm sure I'd have just left if I were in your position."

"All in the past," I said. "Are you sure they won't find you in real life?"

"Yup. And I doubt they'll look for me here either..."

Crawler shook his head in disagreement. It was unusual and even a little funny to see him in the body of a gnome. But his choice was a good one, since gnomes had the best racial bonus to intellect, the most important stat for mages. Next to Crawler the gnome and Crag the dwarf, Bomber looked like a real giant, having chosen a titan as his character. Now he could use a shield at the same time as a two-handed sword, and also had solid bonuses to his defensive skills.

"For the moment, sure," Crawler said. "Kharinza is lost among thousands of tiny islands. But if someone decides to take a closer look at this zone, then believe me, they'll turn it upside down. They have ships, flying mounts too. As soon as they figure out where to look, they'll find us."

"Nah, I get that," the dwarf said in agreement. "I mean in real life. The school stuff is solved, I switched to home-schooling. And I hunkered down so far into the sticks that the Eye isn't even there."

The Eye was the name for the orbital crime identifier. It worked effectively anywhere in the world, at least according to the authorities.

"Where's that?" I asked in surprise.

"I paid an old inwinova lady cash in advance for

three months. Had to go into my savings. I'm out of money now, but that's no problem. In the meantime, I'll pass the citizenship tests and then I can transfer my earnings from Dis into real life."

"The old lady won't give you up?" Crawler asked, echoing my thoughts.

"The granny doesn't see shit, doesn't go online, just watches TV all day. She's a strange one... She feeds me from her supplies too. I have simple tastes, I'm living off UNBs[3]. I can eat tasty food here anyway!"

Crag sank his teeth into a boar rib in confirmation of his words. It looked tasty, and I followed my clanmate's example.

"That's you sorted," Bomber chuckled. "How about you, Scyth? Those preventers have some sharp knives in the drawer. They'll put two and two together and realize that someone stole the Threat out from under their nose."

"We still have time," I answered, not entirely certain of my words. "What's the news there, by the way?"

"Modus has lost all its castles but the main one," Crawler answered. "Other leaders have joined the Alliance, but not all. Some of them teamed up with Modus. But that's all speculation from journalists. Sooner or later the clans will come to an agreement and start digging. And when they realize that none of them captured Crag, but some third party... Eh, let's move on to some good news."

---

[3] UNB — Universal Nutrient Blend.

"You mean the fort?"

"Not exactly," Crawler smiled mysteriously, exchanging a glance with Bomber. "The miners found an instance!"

"What?!" I jumped up from the bench in excitement. "Here, in Kharinza?"

"Yup! Basically, while you were running rings round the preventers, one of the workers in the mine got attacked! Yesterday the digging operations reached a large cavern, but everyone was too afraid to go deep in. We were preparing for your breakthrough, so we didn't handle it right away. But today, zombies and skeletons started wandering out of it. We're too weak to deal with them for now — their levels start at two hundred. So this morning we lured the undead outside and put them under Monty. The workers collapsed the passageway pretty thoroughly, but I saw with my own eyes a portal to an instance deep in the cavern! What do you think about your new talents, Scyth? Think with them and Crag, we can complete it?"

"First Kiiiill!" Bomber sang, drumming his fists on the table.

"I don't know..." I thought for a moment. "If the mobs inside are above level two hundred, then no way. The level difference is too high, I doubt we'll even scratch them. Even with Crag's buff. And we can't grind like in the Mire for now. Only twenty percent of the damage gets stopped, the rest will get split between the other group members like I said. If I'm solo... Then there's no chance at all. Twenty percent damage absorption is less than what Bomber will give with his armor, parry and dodge stats."

"The key thing in the skill description is 'in proportion to their health,'" Bomber noted. "I'm probably the fattest here, so most of the damage will go to me if Scyth is tanking."

"With Crag, we'll all be fat," Crawler mentioned. "But Scyth is right, we're gonna have a rough time."

"But we need to try. I feel sure that *Sleeping Vindication* won't miss. It was like that with *Plague Energy*. We'll see. Right now it's more important to figure out what to do with the preventers in real life. I can't relocate like Tobias, so I want to apply to enter a program to protect underage children. Remember when they offered that to us all in tenth grade?"

"That's when they put a nanochip in you that constantly tells the police your lifesigns, precise coordinates and other stuff like stress hormone levels in the blood? And they see everything through your eyes too?"

"'If you think your life may be in danger...'" Bomber quoted Mr. Kovac. "Well, why not, it's an option. I doubt the preventers will directly break the law. And if they try to pull off something like what Big Po did to us, the police will be there in minutes. But that's before the citizenship tests. What about after?"

"Hey, Alex!" Manny called out to me.

He and Trixie, Gyula and the others sat at the next table discussing something, but apparently, they were listening to us too. Meeting Manny gave Crag a good dose of embarrassment, but he still managed to apologize for the incident in the Bubbling Flagon. The miner brigadier accepted the apology.

I turned around. There was something strange in the gaze of one of the unfamiliar workers, but I forgot about it right away.

"Yes, Manny?"

"We can hide you."

"Where?" we all asked in unison. Even Crag's ears perked up. It seemed life with the old inwinova lady wasn't all peaches and cream.

Manny left his group and sat at our table with his pint of beer. He took a theatrical pause, swigged his beer, wiped his lip and started talking.

"Alright, kids. I don't know what they teach you in those schools, but not all non-citizens are all that poor and miserable. If you think anything changed in society when citizenship categories were introduced, think again. There are still those that break the law."

"Hold on, Manuel, the Eye tracks everything!" I said. "And any crime for a non-citizen has an automatic sentence of death!"

Ed and Hung smiled. Manny bared his teeth too.

"Nah, pal. You just parroted what they tell you in school. Which is a kind of, let's say, idealistic parallel reality where there's no crime, or if there is any, then there's always an inevitable punishment. Maybe that exists somewhere, but not in the Zones."

The Destroying Plague

I'd heard about the Zones, areas declared unsuitable for life. Cali Bottom was in one of them, with its higher than average radioactive substances in the soil, buildings and atmosphere. It was in those environmentally dangerous places that the government put up cheap high-rise warrens for non-citizenships. Affordable housing for any non-citizen. No job? No income? Don't worry, you can take out a loan to live in an anthill. Can't pay back the debt by the time you're thirty? No problem, we'll make you pay it off in the lunar mines or with your own organs.

The world had reached a point at which human labor was cheaper in some places than robot energy. Nobody was in a hurry to do work like that, even desperate non-citizens, so the powers found another way to get the workers they needed. Vagrancy was outlawed before I was even born — you weren't allowed to be homeless. If you get caught without a roof over your head, you had one destination — a recreational zone. I don't know who had the sense of humor to give that name to labor camps from which none return. There are also rumors that scientists and pharmaceutical companies experiment on the poor, but there was no confirmation of that online.

The point is that if you wanted to live somewhere, even in Cali Bottom or Gaian Basin, you had to pay. Even something small, like the room in which Trixie and her grandpa lived, cost thirty six phoenixes a month, but you needed a capsule to legally earn in Dis.

You could rent a non-citizen type capsule at Snowstorm if you had a registered place of residence. And if you spend at least twelve hours a day online, you don't even have to pay for it. But could you call that living? Spending half your life on hard labor in Dis, another third on sleep, and the rest of the time in a crowded closet, living off universal nutrient blends. As far as I remembered, Cali Bottom didn't even have sidewalks. The residents went out for walks on the roof. The kids spent their time there too, deprived even of a basic education and unable to go into Disgardium until they came of age.

"The Zones have their own laws, Alex," Manny continued. "The authorities don't get involved there, they don't care. The police? Ha-ha, don't make me laugh. At first they tried to send mech cops in there, but after our boys put down a couple of the rustbuckets, they stopped. To the authorities, all Cali Bottom and the lives of its people," Manny raised a finger, "are worth less than one police mech."

"What does this have to do with Scyth?" Crawler asked impatiently. "You suggesting he hide with you guys?"

"Maybe let me finish and find out," the miner brigadier said in annoyance. "What I'm getting at is that your rich kid players don't venture into the Zones. The Eye doesn't work there either. And if you have money, then you can set yourself up a nice life with us. Diego Aranzabal lives in our neck of the woods. A bastard and a half but made a nice living off kidnapping. Not personally, of course. All kinds of drug addicts work for him, stealing citizen kids and demanding ransoms. If they get caught, they don't give up Diego, because they don't know his real names. If it all works out, then Diego gets tens of thousands of dark phoenixes."

That was the name of the cryptocurrency created in opposition to the official one. But something else bothered me — why was Manny talking about all this so calmly?

"That monster should be turned in! You know where he lives?"

"Alex..." Manny frowned. "He pays off high officials in the police and the peacekeepers to protect him. They have their own families too, and high fences won't stop the Damned — sooner or later one of them will get through.

The Damned was a name for certain desperate non-citizens. They were used for a guaranteed assassination, in exchange for a promise of support for their families. Another city legend that just became a reality for me. I remembered flying into Cali Bottom so carelessly... What an idiot I was!

"And anyway..." Manny continued. "Get rid of one monster and another rises to take his place. At least this one isn't insane. He returns his victims alive and unharmed. If the families pay, of course. Anyway, you won't prove anything. Like I say, the police don't care! And this isn't even the point! The point is that inside the high-rises, the rich inwinovas build whole palaces! They buy up one, two sometimes even three whole floors at a time through phantom buyers. They knock down the walls, break through the ceilings and end up with mansions that would make your class A citizens blush! I haven't seen it, but I've heard that Diego even has an eighty-foot pool in his! The less said about his lovers the better. He has a whole harem — half the girls in Cali Bottom dream of getting into that circle. Also, he has fighters in spades. Every resident of the anthill is at Diego's beck and call, and they all have a gun. If he whistles, the neighboring buildings will come to help too. And Diego is far from the only one..."

"So you're suggesting we hide with you?"

"Well, you don't need a palace. But Gyula and I have already figured out a way to help you. You, and therefore us. Along with our families, there are around five hundred of us. We could use the same strategy to occupy a floor or two of one of the new buildings in the south of the city. Believe me, Gyula and his boys know how to build not only in Dis!" Hearing this, Gyula nodded, but remained at his table. "They'll be able to fix it all up so that nobody can get close to getting in. Sorry that I'm sticking my nose in, but your boys were saying that Snowstorm showered you with a pile of money. What I mean is, you can afford it. If not in Cali Bottom, then there are plenty of other zones like it in the world..."

"Life expectancy in zones like that is under sixty," Bomber said in a mentoring tone, raising his hand and quoting Greg the teacher yet again. "The risk of cancerous illnesses... Oh, the Nether with it! It's a great idea! I'm up for it! Manny, you gonna teach me to talk to your chicas? I want a harem like Diego!"

"Dumbass," Crawler chuckled. "But the idea is cool, I like it. Scyth?"

I was thinking of Manny's offer from all angles. I decided to delay the decision.

"There's no point talking about this before the citizenship tests. The money is frozen in Dis anyway..."

Someone rose from the next table and approached us with an erratic, shuffling gait. Feeling safe, especially while in a group with Crag, I paid no attention, continuing to think over Manny's idea.

"The Destroying Plague says hello, traitor!" an unfamiliar voice rasped.

Something pierced me in the neck and an icy cold quickly spread through my body. The sharp pain took my breath away, and I started gasping for air, unable to breathe in. Everything got numb, I lost sensitivity.

Rick the miner (Ricardo Salazar) dealt damage to you: 0.
Health: 67262/67262.

You are infected!

"What the hell, Rick?!" Manny shouted. The

voices sounded as if far away. I heard the roar of a flying fireball and a scream of pain from a stranger burning alive.

I smelled the sweet stench of rot. I retched and felt sick. Then I started to collapse to the floor. I felt as something inside was twisting, wrapping up my guts, and my mouth opened in a soundless scream from the pain. Zero damage couldn't cause pain like this! It had to be the debuff! I read its description with my darkening gaze and went cold.

Infection
You are infected with the plague of the dead. After death, you will become a vassal of the Destroying Plague.

—1% total health per second.

The Nucleus of the Destroying Plague had found a way to take vengeance after all.

Chapter 5

Fort Kharinza

THE BOYS DIDN'T immediately realize that the *Infection* ticks were hurting them too. We were all in a group, and Crag's *Nergal's Wrath* reacted to the attack, but the debuff didn't care about my suddenly increased stats — my health was dropping in percentages.

I didn't realize this when the mess started with the emissary of the Destroying Plague in the form of the worker Ricardo. We checked the damage logs and invulnerability mechanics later, the next day. *Sleeping Invulnerability* blindly absorbed a fifth of the damage and split the rest among the group: me, Crag, Crawler and Bomber. In spite of the latter's boasting, my health wasn't much lower than his due to the bonus stats from the adepts and for achievements. Thankfully, my friends were quick.

With my *Infection*, I had no control over my body, so I told them in the chat to take me to the temple. The Sleeping God was our only hope in this situation, since there were no heals, and the cheap health potions Bomber was shoveling down my throat weren't winning the battle with my dropping health. Amazingly, I was so used to the Destroying Plague that I didn't even panic about losing my character. I just decided that since a deity had attacked me, then another might protect me.

Behemoth felt something was wrong himself — he met us on the temple stairs. They handed me to him, and he took me to the altar, but left the others at the threshold. A little later I realized why — he didn't want the adepts to see his weakness and vulnerability.

Carefully, even gently placing me on the stone floor, he pressed on my stomach a few times hard, as if trying to resuscitate a drowned man. Behemoth pressed and pressed, and I lost count of the presses and the time, focusing my darkening consciousness only on my remaining health. The bar slowly diminished, and the damage was no longer splitting among the group. There was no group now — my clanmates might have left on their own to avoid dying, or maybe Behemoth disbanded the group to avoid mixing up the Destroying Plague with Nergal's gift and the magic of the Sleeping Gods.

And it worked. Behemoth was literally pushing out the sickness. I felt nauseous, and a stinking, tar-like liquid with streaks of brown and green began to stream from my mouth, and then each breath brought forth clouds of oily soot and smoke, sent them streaming into Behemoth's nose and mouth.

The Destroying Plague

That went on for a minute or two, and when it stopped, my body started to obey me again. The remnants of my weakness prevented me from sitting up. The Sleeping God sat nearby breathing heavily, hoarsely. I touched his shoulder in concern, but he shrugged my hand off and gestured for me to wait.

The debuff hadn't gone anywhere, but something in it had changed:

Infection
You are infected with the plague of the dead. After death, you will become a vassal of the Destroying Plague.

The life bar slowly crept upwards. But the ticks hadn't gone anywhere — they'd just changed their victim. Behemoth shivered every second, shook. I couldn't see exactly whether he was losing health — the god didn't have a health bar. But if such a creature was experiencing pain so great that he couldn't hide it, then that definitely meant something.

"We do not have much time," he finally broke the silence. "It would not be difficult to get it completely out of you if you were an ordinary human. But you are extraordinary! You are the former emissary of this parasite! Its structure is interwoven with your energy signature, and to break them apart would be to kill you."

"But I watched that horrible stuff come out of me..."

"The parasite cares not what it eats. I simply gave it another source of nourishment, a little bigger, and it switched to me, while still remaining in you."

"So I can't die..."

"You cannot. I know that you are aliens from another world and can revive in Disgardium. Death is never final for you. But you cannot die — the parasite has attached your soul fast to your body. If you die, you will not revive, the parasite will take over your body, and I will lose my Herald."

"Are there any ways to get rid of it?"

Behemoth opened his mouth, his body shook, his legs bent. I helped him keep his balance by putting a shoulder under his arm just in time. He coughed heavily and spat out something anthracite and sticky. An acrid stream of smoke swam up from the stone floor.

"There are..." he answered. "Tiamat is well versed in such weavings, and for her it will not be difficult to get the parasite out of you, I am sure. But she is too weak to materialize in this world."

"How long can you hold it back?"

"My strength is fading. Too little energy, Herald," the god wheezed. "Too few adepts. Our *faith* is falling. We're spending everything to resist the parasite. The Destroying Plague. We have enough energy for six days. I fear that in such a short time, you will not be able to summon Tiamat."

"What happens then?"

"The parasite will kill you. But first it will

transform my imprint in this world.

"Sleeping God... These six days... Can we somehow extend them?"

"As I said, the balance of our influx and outflow of *faith* is negative. However, the presence of dedicated adepts near the temple, their prayers... That should reduce the losses. The effectiveness of *faith* of the undedicated is not great, if you gather enough of such intelligent creatures and allow them to pray here... That too may help.

"I know what to do, Sleeping God."

* * *

A minute before midnight, the system warned me of a forced exit from Disgardium. That was no surprise — we weren't allowed to spend too much time in the game on weekdays because the citizenship tests were so close. We'd gone out into the big adult world, but still lived by child's rules. We would become formal adults only after the citizenship tests, regardless of whether we were successful or not.

So we didn't have time to discuss everything that was happening in Dis and all our plans. We'd stopped all communicator chatter for fears of our safety, so I went to sleep in a complete mess. I tossed and turned for a long time, racking my brain for ideas, and then I couldn't help it — I got up and wrote an angry message to Snowstorm. I remembered that the victims of the Destroying Plague in Tristad were given hefty compensation, and as for me, Behemoth was right, I wasn't an ordinary player.

At school, I exchanged whispers with the former Dementors, but heard nothing concrete — they were still planning to hold a clan council in one of the family restaurants where the Awoken was born right after lessons. The whole school seethed with yesterday's events. Nobody knew anything specific, and the wild theories of the other students made us laugh.

Aaron "Robolover" Quan stood out in particular. He was going crazy over two things: Denise Le Bon and Modus. The boy compensated for not being the most active player with the successes of 'his' clan — he supported them as if a football team. Anyway, Aaron confidently claimed that he had access to a secret section of the Modus clan forum and knew the exact reason for the war with the Alliance of Preventers: a woman. Or more precisely: Denise Le Bon, over whose heart Hinterleaf and Horvac were warring.

"I bet Denise is the whole reason," Ed confirmed with an impassive face when Aaron went to him for support.

"The problem is that she wants Glyph," Hung added. "I read about that on the Azure Dragons fan forum. The info is solid, a Chinese guy I know confirmed it, a friend of someone from the clan..."

The answer from the developers came in my last lesson. It was laconic: everything was within the

The Destroying Plague

bounds of gameplay, there were no additional rewards after the loss of a character since I'd already received them for my current Threat level. No anonymous messages from that highly-ranked member of Snowstorm came afterwards...

After lessons, we applied to enter a child protection program. If we didn't hang around in dangerous regions, then we didn't have to worry about our safety thanks to the officials that were assigned to us. After the citizenship tests, which would also mean our exit from the program, we planned to move to Cali Bottom and set up a clan base there.

Tobias was waiting for us in the Chinese restaurant on the shore. He was in disguise, but it seemed to me he was trying too hard, apparently inspired by the appearance of his dwarf: he wore a curly beard, a mustache and a baseball cap. Considering that he'd also completely shaved his head, the boy was drawing more attention rather than less. But it was hard to recognize Tobias in him, he'd done a good job there.

"I used some cream to grow my hair quick. What do you think?

We kept silent, holding back our smiles, and Tissa gave him two thumbs up.

A waiter came, took our order, left. Ed glanced at me. I nodded and he spoke.

"Remember me telling you about that worker that got bit in the mine? Here's the thing. He was the

---

one that infected you. I logged into Dis this morning to talk to Manny. According to him, the man claims to remember nothing. Just remembers sitting at the table, eating, drinking, talking and... boom! He's standing by our table and burning alive. Bullshit, Alex. Either he's just lying to avoid punishment, or he got a quest from the Destroying Plague..."

"Or he really doesn't remember it," I said. "You keep forgetting that everything we see and feel in Dis comes from the capsule. It interacts directly with the brain, imitating tastes, smells, pain and pleasure. You think temporarily blocking out memory and taking control of the body is a problem for it? If the Destroying Plague is something like a deity or a strong creature, then it must be controlled by a powerful AI. And it may well have certain access privileges to interactions with players..."

I didn't have time to finish the thought, because everyone started talking at once. A hectic discussion of what had been said began: from direct laughter to bashful supposition. In the end, we decided to temporarily suspend the mine worker with pay. He could level up his skills elsewhere until we'd eliminated the *Infection.*

Then we moved on to discussing our plans, and Ed took the floor again.

"We can put aside our initial idea of holing up in Kharinza and calmly leveling up while we wait for Malik and Tissa. We have new challenges now. It's obvious that we badly need a second temple. Tiamat will be able to heal Alex and give him immunity from the Destroying Plague."

"And the only place for a temple that we might be able to reach is beyond the frontier," Tissa said quietly, dropping her head. This inaction weighed on her, as she was used to being in the center of the fray. She couldn't even write to us. "And you guys will probably have all the fun without me..."

"Damn, we planned to go to the frontier after the sandbox, and now we are!" Ed laughed nervously. "You remember? Back when Axiom wasn't giving us room to breathe?"

"There's something I don't understand," Malik spoke up. "The temple spot is far from the frontier! Even with maxed out resistance potions, we won't get there... Even if we quickly get into the forties and buy mounts, we still won't make it. Land mounts are too slow, and we're way off flying mounts. And then we'll still have to build the temple!"

"The temple will wait," I interjected. "If we get to it at all. Right now we need adepts, all the adepts on the island."

"Manny has already spoken to his boys. The workers are going to alter their shifts to put more people on the island at a time. They'll go to the temple to pray. I don't know how you pray to the Sleeping Gods, but I doubt words are that important."

"That's not enough. Our brave honorary citizen of Tristad, and also first priest Patrick, is in Darant right now. He wrote that he'd gotten acquainted with the city sewers..."

"Where?" Tobias asked in surprise.

"In the sewers. Nether knows what he lost there! Anyway, he met some troggs there. They're supposedly desperate to become adepts, but we can't take them yet because of our limit. But! They'll help us extend the delay on Behemoth's debuff too. Especially if they pray at the temple. That's why I'm heading to Darant today to find O'Grady."

"Your imitation skill isn't a panacea," Hung objected. "The preventers will definitely predict that, I bet they're already patrolling the streets with *True Flame*."

"I'll be careful. Next. We have renegade kobolds among our adepts," I continued, glancing at Malik and Melissa. "And we're very lucky that you guys are still in the sandbox!"

"Kobolds! Right!" Malik brightened up. He'd been worried too that all the fun stuff would happen without him and counting the days until he could go out into the big world.

"I've sent you the coordinates of the spot where I met them. If you don't find them there, search nearby. Together you can send the whole tribe to the base."

"They're mobs..." Ed said doubtfully. "Infect and Tissa are nothing to them, they might attack."

"I'm nothing?" the girl frowned. "I'm a priestess of the Sleeping Gods! They'll do what I tell them! Or I'll banish them and give them to anathema!"

The Destroying Plague

"Woah, woah," Hung chuckled. "Don't go to them with an attitude like that." If you start giving commands, they'll definitely aggro! We have few enough adepts as it is, so you'd better take off your crown..."

Urgent matters now discussed, we moved to our leveling plan. The higher our levels in the desert, the greater our chances of success with Behemoth's quest.

Ed brought up a holographic map of the continent's habitable lands and demonstrated two options for farming routes through the locations: one with Crag in the group and the other without, just in case Crag didn't want to risk it.

"I'll be there," Tobias said impassively, digging around in his teeth with a finger. "I get the impression we won't be able to level up on the island — either a dinosaur ate all the mobs or there never were any. And we can't get through the instance we found in the mine, right? I won't go out into open spaces, don't want to risk that, but instances are fine by me."

He wasn't saying anything new. We were already planning to pull him straight out of the depths into the instances. There were problems with choosing dungeons; plenty were under the control of clans, but there were enough public ones too, they were just scattered across the whole of Latteria. That issue was solved by getting to a spot once, then we could go back there every day.

"With Alex's new skills, you can easily skip level

thirty instances and move up to the forty pluses," Tissa added. "If *Vindication* ignores armor and doesn't miss, mathematically our Herald will be cracking bosses like walnuts. There isn't a single boss in that level bracket with over a million health. More or less depending on the party size."

"We don't need to take any senseless risks," Ed objected. "Have you forgotten? Alex can't die. We need to test everything out in dungeons at our own level, then decide."

"Agreed," I said.

"Then Hung and I will start traveling to the first planned instances. Portals will beggar us, and we can't use mounts yet..."

Ed's words reminded me that I had a *Ghost Wolf Summoning Scroll* waiting for me.

"...which means we'll be traveling by gnomish airship. Takes longer than portals, but it's a lot cheaper."

"Alright," I nodded. "Tissa and Malik will search for the kobolds in the meantime and convince them to relocate. I'll deal with the rewards for Po, then portal over to Darant..."

"Ugh, I don't like that!" Ed interrupted him. "Maybe I should be the one to find Patrick?"

I shook my head. Dis had broken my last character, forcing me to avoid conflicts. I didn't feel like cowering behind my friends' backs this time, waiting for them to do something.

"What about me?" Tobias asked. "Just chill at

the base? Boring..."

I barely kept myself from answering more harshly.

"Toby, the most influential people from two separate worlds are hunting you! And you're bored! Do something! Level a profession!"

"Just don't take fishing," Hung advised. "The monsters in the water here'll pull you in with your rod..."

While he pontificated on the peculiarities of national fishing in Kharinza, I thought back in reverse chronological order: fishing, the *Golden Fish* (caught by Hung in the Mountain Dams), our first joint campaign and the reason for the clan's creation — our dispute with Big Po. Some links in the chain were dim, giving way to a gleaming legendary. I moved from the comm to my character profile, opened the chest tab and brought up the description for everyone to see:

Arena Master's Horn
Legendary
Unique item.
Accessory.
+20% to all group stats.
Use: Summons ogre gladiators to fight for you until the end of the battle. The ogre's level is always 3 levels above the summoner's.
Cooldown: 24 hours.
Only for the Bard class!

Chance of loss after death lowered by 100%.

"Listen, Malik, you'll be coming out soon..." I said smoothly. "Could you change your class? What about switching to bard?

Silence reigned for a few seconds. Hung slammed his fist down on the table and swore. Ed and Tissa got what I was driving at right away and laughed. Only Tobias, having missed our bet with Axiom, glanced back and forth from one face to another and waited for explanations.

"Well I'll be..." Ed said thoughtfully, chuckling. "With Crag's talent, plus twenty percent to stats on top... That is a hell of a boost! And it's passive. We just need a Bard in the group!"

Malik leapt up from the table and backed off, shaking his head.

"No, no, no... No! You can't be serious, Alex? My daggers are scalable... My epics... My boots! The boots from the treasury? No, no, no... No! Me? A Bard? I'm tone-deaf! Hung, come on! Back me up!"

"You know, brother Malik..." Bomber said thoughtfully. "You haven't really been a thief once in your life either..."

* * *

Our little Pig and Whistle would grow in time into a full-fledged tavern as good as the Bubbling Flagon. But to explain why we had to build something small if

The Destroying Plague

the fort would have to be expanded anyway as our population grew, I'll have to explain a little about how building works in Disgardium.

Along with any other profession, construction was heavily simplified. Remember how I 'cooked' food, and you'll understand roughly how much the developers went again realism. All typical buildings had their own so-called schematics, like cooking recipes. After 'studying' a schematic, the builder could build it. Just like in cooking, to construct buildings you need ingredients, meaning materials like blocks or wood.

You could mine stone but couldn't build anything with it right away; you had to process it first. The quarry worker mined stone; the stonemason gave it shape. It could be 'processed' into blocks, slabs, bricks, cobblestones for sidewalks, whatever — the main thing is that you couldn't do anything without a leveled-up stonemason. Like with metals — unprocessed ore also served as a trading item, but it couldn't be used anywhere in that form. It could only be used when made into bars, which required knowledge of *Mining*.

Stone buildings were built without cement, wooden — without nails, but any building required a certain amount of resources. This many steel bars, this many copper, this much sand and clay, which was also added somewhere.

After gathering all the required resources in the necessary amount, the builders started the work.

Their speed depended on their crafting grade and the number of workers at the construction site. Next, magic got involved.

As Gyula explained it, if all the conditions were met and the resources were distributed properly, the system invited him to 'Start construction' of a specific part of the building, and then the process started when he confirmed it. Blocks connected solid to each other, transforming from several game items into a single whole, for example a 'Level 1 Tavern Foundation.' These parts then meld into just 'Level 1 Tavern,' taking their place in the world of Dis and taking on new properties such as durability and structure wear.

This meant that Snowstorm, on the one hand, was making everything easy by departing from realism, and on the other — making a bunch of different professions essential. I knew some of this already, and heard some from Gyula, but it was important to gather all the information and organize it to understand how to further develop the base and what we'd need to do so.

In daylight, the clan fort looked... different. Just a few buildings constructed along an improvised street that wasn't even paved. A tropical downpour that had been falling on Kharinza all night had transformed the trampled pathway into a muddy mess. With each step, my leg sank up to the knee into the sticky, slurping soup, reminding me of my trials in the Mire. The air was full of fumes and smells.

The Destroying Plague

"Sorry, boss, we got a serious lack of woodcutters," Gyula explained, wiping the sweat from his brow. "Some of the boys have taken on the craft, but they need to level it and level it..."

The air was so thick with fumes, you could almost cut it. The chief builder gave me a tour around the fort to tell me what had been done and what was left to do. He started with complaints.

"Nobody has a high enough profession for it, or we'd have put a road down long ago. And the stone situation is terrible! That damn reptile, the Nether take him, he's gotten cocky! She's a dumb beast, but even with chicken brains she can figure out where to get food. She's stopped even moving away from the mine, and why should she? The island is lifeless, it's not that easy to catch stuff in the sea, and we're here, right under her nose."

Crawler spoke of how he witnessed the Montosaurus hunting. The hunter became the hunted, captured in the tentacles of a gigantic kraken of unknown level. The reptile barely got away, and then didn't show up at the mine for a long time while she licked her wounds somewhere. But Gyula was right, and his boys' heroism was under no doubt — non-citizen capsules didn't dull pain. Every day in this deadly lottery, one of them died in the truest sense of the word. It was a good thing that the reptile's attack was fatal, and the character's death instant.

"I'll talk to Behemoth," I promised Gyula.

"Alright," the builder nodded. "There's something else too. Our boys saw some Sharks patrolling around Cali Bottom. They don't land, so they might just be tracking anyone who flies in."

"I'll keep that in mind."

Sharks were unavailable to non-citizens. Sure, now they were civilian fliers, but previously only the military used them. They're easily upgraded to full-scale battle vehicles; have huge durability and they can capture ordinary fliers. That might mean that Cali Bottom was closed to us for now, because the Sharks could belong to the preventers. After the events in the gorge, a fragile peace barely remained intact in their Alliance, alongside an unbridled desire to capture not only the escaped Crag, but also the unidentified A-class Threat. Horvac was cleared of suspicion right away because all of Modus had seen him enter the castle gates just as Crag was kidnapped.

The street led from the city's only gates to the temple. Buildings towered along either side, and a low palisade around the height of a man surrounded it all. It wouldn't protect against Monty, and it seemed of doubtful value before the undead appeared in the mine, but now...

The first building on the right was the as-yet empty barracks for NPC guards. I still hadn't hired any yet. Across the street, opposite the barracks, was the humble tavern, built using the same schematic as Tristad's Bubbling Flagon, but a third of the size.

Next came the merchant stalls on the left side

The Destroying Plague

of the street. They too stood empty. There wasn't much point in building them, but they were an integral part of a level one fort, just like the houses along the right side. After that came the headquarters and the vault. Crawler and I controlled access to both buildings through the clan control panel.

After that was just empty space, intended to eventually become a central square in front of the temple. I'd seen something similar in Tristad at the temple of Nergal the Radiant, and that place was always packed.

Overall, it all looked poor, miserly and homely, but in fact, the fact that it was all ours took my breath away! Especially since the island was big. We had enough space for everything.

A small graveyard had sprung up behind the temple and I'd set it as my respawn point. Not a particularly useful act given that my next death in Dis could be my last.

"We need to do something about that beast," Gyula complained again about the Montosaurus. "We're sticking to the temple, but if we grow, we'll need more space. The beast hasn't been bothering us, something holds it back, but it's no longer entirely safe behind the palisade."

I nodded and he spoke of a planned upgrade to the fort:

"We're a long way from a castle for now, but at level three, the fort will transform into a small fortress with a citadel and bastions. If we dig a moat..." Gyula paused to daydream a moment, then shook himself and continued. "To tell you the truth, it's beyond my current *Construction* grade. In the future, the clan castle will fill this whole area, and the temple will be at its heart."

"What do we need to upgrade? Resources? If we're missing something, we can buy it in. We have money."

"I'm afraid you can't imagine how much it might come to, Alex," Gyula shook his head. "Fort level two costs around two or three hundred thousand gold just in resources we don't have. I've studied the schematic. We'll get a blacksmith, a sawmill, a fishing post, all kinds of gardens. Again, a stone fence. Some of our guys will change their profession to something more useful for everyone — we'll be able to provide for ourselves... if we can do something with that overgrown reptile!"

"The Montosaurus and money..." I made a mental note. There was no point in dealing with all this until I'd dealt with the *Infection* and the second temple. "Anything else?"

"Yes. Even with all the resources, it's not that easy to upgrade a fort. There are requirements, and one of them is... We need residents! Look at the control panel, there's a Population bar. Our population is a joke right now: no garrison, no merchants, empty houses... We don't count as permanent residents."

"Do we need humans specifically?"

The Destroying Plague

"Doesn't matter. Any intelligent creatures..."

"You'll have your residents, Gyula. And far sooner than you think..."

* * *

After the tour around the fort and my conversation with the chief builder, I looked in on Behemoth. The temple was empty.

The Sleeping God didn't appear right away. Once he did materialize, he said that holding back the parasite was taking up all his resources, and forming an avatar cut down on the already small amount of spare *faith*. When I asked him to deal with the greedy dinosaur, Behemoth said that he couldn't meddle so directly in the affairs of mortals, then said something strange; that the deus ex machina limit was reached, whatever that meant, and I'd have to figure this one out on my own.

With those parting words, I visited the headquarters, a small building with one room, the fort control crystal flashing weakly at its center.

All its abilities were duplicated in my interface, but it wasn't just decorative. The developers had added the crystal to allow forts to be captured. In big clans with castles, the crystal was deep within the labyrinth of the clan vault, protected by the strongest defensive artifacts, traps, golems and its own guards, but our level of carelessness apparently broke all the records. Just walk in and capture us...

I placed a hand on the crystal. It was barely warm — a sign of very low mana. The more mana, the longer the crystal would resist capture.

Welcome to the Kharinza fort control panel, Scyth!

Owner: clan Awoken.

Level: 1.

Population: 0/100.

Structures: Headquarters, Vault, Tavern, Stables, Barracks, Houses, Cemetery, Merchant Stalls...

Bonuses (only for members of ruling clan):

+2% damage and defense within fort.

+1% damage and defense outside of fort.

+10% recovery speed of health, mana, vigor and class resource within fort.

+5% recovery speed of health, mana, vigor and class resource outside of fort.

Being within the fort for at least 3 hours adds the Rested buff:

+50% experience gained for 1 hour.

I'd heard stories of raiding groups missing literally half a percent of damage to finish off a boss. Considering that, an extra percent of damage was a nice bonus. *Maybe we should bring the workers into the clan. Increased vigor could come in handy to them,* I thought. But that would be a big step. I put the

The Destroying Plague

thought aside for later.

Leaving the headquarters, I went toward the tavern. It was time to deal with the Snowstorm rewards.

I got caught in the rain halfway there. One moment the sun was shining down from a cloudless blue sky, the next — boom! It covered over with clouds, rumbled with thunder and began to pour. I closed my eyes and stopped, spread my hands and raised my face to the sky, feeling the heavy drops land on it. My lips spread into a smile on their own. My parents couldn't wait for the citizenship tests, which were scheduled less than two months from now, so they could divorce. My entire life would be in the past, and I'd have to move to a new home. Preventers of all stripes were hunting me, not to mention the Destroying Plague. Even with a million gold in my in-game balance, I still wasn't sure I could get even a small portion of that money — Snowstorm had changed their own rules too often for me to trust them. Oh yes, and Scyth had only a few days to live, a week at the most, after which *Infection* would finish him off.

And I still just stood and smiled...

In my private room, drenched to the bone, I opened my chest and took out the large, pear-sized *Rainbow Crystal*. It constantly changed color depending on the lighting and angle. My hand barely held it — it was heavy for its size.

Tissa and Infect got similar ones, but they'd

used theirs and gotten entirely unexpected results. They already had experience of eliminating Threats: the unfortunate class-Z necromancer from Tristad, and Crawler himself, previously Nagvalle, eliminated by Infect and Bomber. In both cases, the crystals were smaller than a cherry and opened a portal to the Bandit Treasury, a small cave ten by thirteen feet in size, with rewards lying on the floor.

Big Po's crystal was different.

Tissa used it first. It was destroyed after activation, which was to be expected. But it opened a portal not to the little bandit cave, but to the Treasury of the Forgotten Emperor, full of gold, precious gems, artifacts, weaponry and equipment.

Once inside, Tissa jumped for joy. Knowing her, I expect the cave shook from her excited shrieks. At first the girl decided that it was all for her, but then common sense struck, and she figured there was some kind of catch. She wasn't wrong.

Snowstorm hadn't changed and had even found a way to turn rewards into a game within a game, a battle between greed and restraint.

The rules were simple: the item stats showed up only when you held the item. If you held an item for longer than ten seconds, then it was considered that you chose it and could no longer refuse it; to refuse meant to be banished forever. At the same time, Tissa had no visible timer, nor indicator to show that an item she took could be her last. An attempt to pick up several items at once led to them all collapsing into dust.

In the end, Tissa managed to get out with two pieces of gear: a legendary set ring for a healer, and a *Bottomless Mana Potion* — after which she was ejected from the treasury. She'd spent twenty minutes inside, fastidiously inspecting each item. While reading the description on the ring, the timer ran out and the legendary became her choice, whether she wanted it or not. The girl learned of this rule only after the fact. Thinking that she'd probably get more than a couple of items anyway, she couldn't refuse the flask of infinite mana.

And that's when it all ended.

Infect opened the portal later and then couldn't go in, seeing only a message that the location was temporarily unavailable.

After waiting for his girlfriend and cogitating on her instructions, he entered the treasury, intending to be exceedingly careful. Everything went well at first. Infect didn't take too long reading the descriptions, mercilessly suppressing his urges and throwing away items he liked, rushing to go through as many as possible in the hope of finding something truly outstanding. He dreamed of a scalable legendary or even divine item, or ideally — a legendary flying mount.

So, he crawled among the gold and jewels, which he didn't risk picking up, for a whole forty minutes. He soon got lucky — some top-range scalable legendary boots fell into his grasp, amazing ones! When equipped, they left a frozen trail behind Infect, slowing enemies by 30%! Perfect for kiting bosses and mobs! Back then, he hadn't the slightest inkling that the clan would ask him to switch from Thief to Bard.

But disappointment immediately displaced his joy. As soon as he took it, the treasury closed, ejecting the thief back to where he came from. In essence: forty minutes and change for one piece of gear. According to Infect, it was totally unjust!

It was tough to judge from his friends' experience exactly how the treasury determined you'd had enough. Did time spent there play a role? The number of items taken? Their value in the eyes of the system? Or something else?

I had no idea. I took solace in the fact that at least I hadn't used the *Rainbow Crystal* yet. Considering our new circumstances, I hoped I could find something useful there.

I also realized why the preventers were willing to unite into an alliance to catch higher-class Threats — I suspected that as the potential increased, the treasury level grew exponentially.

The *Righteous Shield* artifact that protected the Modus castle was no doubt from the same treasury, if not a better one.

Big Po's potential was probably L, like me before I met Behemoth. And I couldn't even imagine what could be gotten for me or for Crag, with his D potential.

The Destroying Plague

Attention! Do you want to activate the one-time-use artifact Rainbow Crystal?

The item will be destroyed permanently after use!

"Yes, activate," I said.

The crystal collapsed into fading multicolored dust, and right before me, growing from a tiny gleaming point and tearing space as it went, a golden portal emerged to lead me to the Treasury. I took a deep breath, trying to calm my rampaging heart.

I hoped I'd be in luck.

Chapter 6

The Treasury of the First Mage

RAVELING BY PORTAL was far more comfortable than by the depths. There were no side effects or unpleasant sensations: you enter, the light shimmers, and a new location appears beyond the veil.

I stood and waited for a while until my sight adjusted to the dim gloom of the treasury. But, glancing at the floor, I began to realize that something was different than how it was with Tissa and Infect. There was no pile of gold, no gleaming jewels — just a worn black and white tiled floor reminiscent of a chessboard.

Walls stood at either side an arm's breadth away, with another at my back. The ceiling was a meter above my head, reflecting the floor in black and white cells. The narrow corridor before me stretched twenty or thirty paces ahead and ended in a stone slab with large symbols carved in it.

I summoned my pet as I walked, just in case. He'd done well in the undead invasion of Tristad, leveled up and got the ability to inject *Binding Toxin* from a distance. I commanded Iggy to check the corridor and he chittered in response and went off to do my bidding. Nothing happened while he flew to the end and back — the corridor was clear.

Remembering the time limitation in the treasury, I quickly inspected the corridor's walls and didn't find any traps or caches in them. I headed to the end of the corridor.

Only when I got closer did I make out a lever set into the wall. My hand automatically reached for it, then froze halfway there — there was a purple glow around the handle. Hmm... I paused for a couple of seconds, then pulled on it anyway, but it wouldn't budge.

Then I took a step back and started studying the symbols on the slab. It looked almost like cuneiform: sticks, arrows, triangles and circles. Without knowing the language, it seemed impossible to understand. My internal timer began to count down the second minute of being in the treasury, which contained neither treasure nor anything else. My light stroll for rewards had turned into some idiotic puzzle quest.

I suddenly noticed movement in my peripheral vision and my gaze shifted. I saw that some of the symbols before me had turned into familiar letters:

Nobody is perfect!
Who are you?

The phrase sounded familiar but shed no light on the matter. Did it mean this place would give me what I needed? I'd like to believe that. Who was I?

"Scyth," I loudly stated my game name.

No reaction.

"Alex."

Nothing again.

I felt each symbol with my fingers, found no hints. I stopped and thought. I'd heard of instances and raid dungeons with puzzles like this in. These were often the very things that got raids stuck on a first playthrough, not the boss difficulty...

Alright, so who was I? Born Alexander Kieran Sheppard. I'd officially shortened it to Alex at age twelve. My parents got pretty upset.

In Dis I was Scyth, the initial of the Sleeping Gods, a Herald. Chief of the Awoken clan.

None of the above worked. I'd spent almost a quarter of an hour there but hadn't even gotten to so much as a crappy *green* item. I imagined how Ed and Hung would laugh after thinking me such a smartass all these years. To tell the truth, I hadn't felt so stupid for a long time.

I paced the corridor, tried to use force and unloaded a combo at the stone slab — it was useless. *Use your head, Alex!* I thought. *Nobody is perfect! Who are you? I mean, who am I?*

The Destroying Plague

Who is perfect? Nobody. Nobody is perfect.

"Nobody..." I didn't notice myself starting to think aloud. "I'm nobody!"

It worked! I heard the screeching sound of stone against stone, and three square blocks shifted a few inches out from the slab. Flashes of flame danced along them, and then shining words appeared: "Path of Glory," "Path of Strength" and "Path of Courage."

"Choose wisely, hero," the walls echoed. The voice that spoke the words sounded hoarse and unnatural, as if the language was foreign to it. Alright...

Why was all this different for me? I started puzzling over it feverishly, wryly thinking that I should level up my *Intellect*. Why was this happening? Was it because I was the one who took the final blow and performed the banishment ritual? Or was some other factor at play? What did I have that the others didn't? Sure, my Threat status. Maybe it was having an effect? Well... Maybe. Some trick of Behemoth? No, not likely. Some stats? My charisma and luck were through the roof thanks to my class. Luck? But I hadn't yet seen that my version of the treasury was better than that of my clanmates.

Right now, I had to pick a certain 'path,' which, logically, would determine what kind of rewards I'd get.

My needler chittered something and cantered back to the start of the corridor. Turning around, I realized that I was being rushed: the rear wall had started moving toward me. Slowly for the time being, but Iggy's chittering was getting louder. I needed to decide before I was squashed in this giant Scyth-squeezer.

Well, I had no thirst for glory, good or bad. Strength could come in handy, but I wasn't doing too badly on that front as it was...

Iggy whined at the edge of ultrasound, casting about in between me and the moving wall, which was speeding up, moving at maybe three feet a second now.

My time was running out. I interrupted my thoughts and pressed firmly on the block reading Path of Courage. A narrow strip of light soundlessly ran down the slab from top to bottom, leaving an entirely different surface with a fading glow behind it.

The slab changed, transformed into a gate made of a dull blueish metal. It seemed semi-transparent, but I couldn't make out what was behind it, and that was the least of my concerns.

I quickly returned to the lever in the wall, pulled on it and it gave way. The wall moved toward me from behind with an ever-louder roar, threatening to crush us, but the gate opened soundlessly. The approaching wall sped me through and crashed into the spot where the gates had just been, closing off my way back.

When the dust had settled, I saw a spacious hall with a high ceiling and snow-white, sparkling marble walls. It was absolutely empty. It was a hundred paces across and as many again long. The floor was checkered just like in the corridor. The high sky-blue dome of the ceiling evenly suffused the hall with soft light. When I looked closer, I saw a vertical line in each floor tile, flawed as if scratched on by a claw.

What now...?

The answer came quickly. Giant letters appeared in the air before me, seemingly made of stone, and they weren't a part of my interface.

The Treasury of the First Mage
Path of Courage

I barely finished reading it before the letters exploded and sent stone shards flying, but not even one reached me. A moment later the shards hung in the air, and then, gaining more and more speed, returned to their places, again forming text, this time something new:

To the brave will be given!
May the walker take 99 steps!

The letters trembled, shook and exploded again, this time turning into a disappearing dust. Whatever happened next, this was a far cry from the ordinary procedure of rewarding players.

"Walker on the Path of Courage! First step!" a severe male voice declared triumphantly.

It seemed to be coming from everywhere. There was little human in it — vowels were swallowed as if the speaker's vocal equipment was incapable of making such sounds.

"Get ready just in case, Iggy," I slapped the needler on his spiny back and started moving forward.

The pet happily rumbled in approval. He was a good fighter and always ready to go.

In the meantime, a gleaming vertical line about ten feet tall appeared in the air in the center of the hall. Expanding, it took on the shape of a portal and spat out something shriveled and wrinkled that looked like a hedgehog. Having done its job, the portal folded up into a point and winked out.

Momentum rolled the 'hedgehog' a few feet in a ball, then it stopped. Extending long needles, it turned around and straightened, letting me get a good look at it: a three-foot humanoid with a long, sharp face, a plated cuirass strapped to it to protect its chest and stomach, a buckler[4] in its hands and a twisted blade outstretched.

Hedgehog Warrior, level 27
Elite

Blearily narrowing its little red eyes, the hedgehog, no doubt the result of interspecies relations

---

[4] A buckler is a small shield up to 18 inches in diameter, usually metal and round.

between a desperate goblin and a hedgehog, saw me and growled angrily. A few seconds later, he was rushing to attack me, his round shield and blade held forth, his little legs beating. Iggy rushed ahead to protect his owner, his needles bristling.

The needler's *Binding Toxin* caught the hedgehog ten feet from me just as I was stringing my bow. I didn't want to fight a hedgehog barehanded. Infected by the toxin, the mob stumbled and fell to the floor, immediately taking an arrow to the neck.

You have damaged Hedgehog Warrior: 2893.
Health points: 36107/39000.

"Hey! How do you like my *Enhanced Quickshot*, Warrior?" My habit of talking to mobs hadn't gone anywhere.

As I approached it, I lost a few more arrows into it, including an *Explosive Shot*, then finally hit it with a *Crushing Hammerfist*, taking off the shell that I'd taken for a cuirass. Amazed that this wasn't enough to finish off an apparently ordinary elite, I gave it a *Combo*. The mob's defense was crazy. It cut my normal damage in half.

Hedgehog Warrior killed.

Experience: +900.
Experience at current level (26): 34550/36400.

The body started to twinkle, and I hurried to check the loot.

*You got **1000 gold**.*

Not exactly what I wanted, though generous. That was a lot of experience, but no wonder — the location was obviously unusual.

I rose, the hedgehog's corpse disintegrated, and two new vertical lines emerged in the air in the hall's center, auguring the opening of two new portals. But I had no time to swear at the strange treasury and even stranger mechanics of handing out rewards for Threats. Two new hedgehogs, their sinister spines bristling, had begun to rise.

* * *

Maybe this was a feature of my chosen Path of Courage, or a new idea from Snowstorm, but I'd spent over an hour in the treasury without getting kicked out.

After two level twenty-eight *Experienced Hedgehog Warriors*, which gave me two thousand gold each, three naturally appeared at an even higher level. With them, the *Mother Hedgehog Warriors*, I struggled. My health bar after the previous battle was a little under ninety percent. It wasn't regenerating, which forced me to be careful. Thankfully the mobs only attacked in melee range, so I kept my distance

The Destroying Plague

and kept using *Stunning Kick*, *Paralyzing Shot*, Iggy's similar *Binding Toxin* and his *Deadly Chirp*. At the same time, I kept my *Vindication*. It (the resource) was available — the *Infection* debuff had ticked up to twenty thousand while the guys were taking me to Behemoth. But I could only add to it by getting hit. That wouldn't be a wise move in this situation.

I sent the well-beaten trio of hedgehogs running with a *Ghastly Howl*, finished off the first one while the others ran around in *Fear*, and when the effect ended and the mobs returned, I knocked one out with a *Stunning Kick* and the second alongside Iggy. I didn't have any problems dealing with the last hedgehog.

The trio did manage to hurt me, though. It was a good thing I'd leveled up and my health had recovered. Ten thousand gold clinked into my backpack to join the other coins. I hurriedly invested my stat point into *Perception*, increasing the range of *Sleeping Vindication*.

Immediately after that, without a moment to catch my breath, another portal opened. Only one, but wider and larger. A level thirty *Hedgehog Guardian* noisily bounced out, a boss around the size of a small mech tank, with a hundred thousand health.

The guard made me sweat. He only dealt physical damage, but unlike the previous fighters, but he was twice as large, heavier and a couple of his attacks forced me to move quicker.

Spinning in place, he chaotically shot out metal spines in all directions and there was no way I could dodge them. All I could do was cover myself with *Stoneskin* and turn around, hiding my head to protect my eyes. I should have forgotten about my days of total invulnerability and gotten myself some good equipment! I was used to strolling through instances naked...

The guard's other special attack could have one-shotted me if I hadn't leveled my *Resilience* so high: the boss rolled up into a ball and rolled toward mc as fast as lightning. I couldn't just dodge — he easily changed direction and hit me with his spines, a glancing blow, but it still tore my armor and flesh. Elites might be twice as strong as ordinary mobs, but bosses were bosses; they dealt insane damage.

All my experience of fighting mobs depended on the invulnerability of my undead curse, and old habits die hard — like my habit of attacking bare-handed. After releasing a combo on the boss, I couldn't stop when he gathered himself into a ball bristling with needles. It was bad enough that I lost more health than I gained with *Lifesteal*; I also felt such terrible pain that I swore not to attack enemies like this again with my fists. It was one thing to hit the smooth surface of a shield or breastplate, and another entirely to slam your fist into a sharp and bony needle. I badly needed some plate gloves!

All this led me to a moment in which I panicked. I had less than a third of my health left, my

The Destroying Plague

Destroying Plague debuff hadn't gone anywhere, and I was far from willing to die and risk my character for the sake of gear, even super-legendaries. But I had no way out. My retreat was cut off, and even *Depths Teleportation* wasn't working.

Things looked dire, but Iggy and I beat away at the *Hedgehog Guardian* — in the end I couldn't resist, and fired an arrow charged with *Vindication*. Like Tissa guessed, the damage from the energy of the Sleeping Gods went right through his defenses; the boss died, generously dropping three thousand experience. Now the only problem was that my *Vindication* was at an extreme low — not enough to kill even a single mob.

Local achievement unlocked — Treasury of the First Mage: Path of Courage!
Achievement progress: 1/99.
Only heroes may enter the Treasury of the First Mage, and only the strongest in spirit among them choose the Path of Courage. The first guard is defeated, and you have opened your heart to the spirit of the treasury. From now on, each subsequent Step on the Path of Courage will be rewarded generously.
Reward: *+1% to damage against the guardians of the treasury and their minions.*

This was the first time I'd encountered a multi-stage achievement like this. I understood the mechanics, but I still wondered; would all the rewards be local, and the damage increase linear, just adding a percentage for each Step, or would I get something more serious as I went along?

After looting the boss, I realized that something more interesting had dropped from it than from the previous mobs:

You got a **Basic Magic Transformation Tome.**

At first, I was overjoyed, but then realized I was still thinking in terms of the sandbox. In Darant, anyone could buy magic tomes if they had the money. Magic was the same as skills in Dis: theoretically you could learn everything... Practically... There was no point in it, especially if your class wasn't predisposed to the corresponding stats.

Simply put, even a warrior that joined a guild of mages, Nergal followers or another school, could study a tome of basic light magic. That would let him heal himself in battle, but at a certain point the effect of that healing would be tiny relative to his total health. He wouldn't be able to level up the skill enough because his stats wouldn't allow it.

As for the cost of basic magic tomes, they varied from ten to fifteen thousand gold — I'd gotten as much from the *Hedgehog Warriors*. So, my first item reward from the treasury didn't exactly impress me. I wouldn't have even called it a reward.

And here's why. The tome ended up not in my backpack, with its unhappy three free slots that I'd carefully freed up for my loot. No, it went to the *Treasure Hunter's Bag* that had apparently appeared out of nothing. It had no material incarnation; it was just an icon in my interface.

Treasure Hunter's Bag
Divine
Soulbound to Scyth.
Capacity: *99 cells.*
In the days when the One Ocean washed all the world and struck the first created continent, the First Mage of Disgardium created this created this spaceless immaterial bag specially for his treasury. Every treasure hunter that has ever broken in and dared to steal anything at all has received such a bag, and once they died, they were doomed to become its guardian.
Effects: *disappears along with its contents after death in the treasury or will be permanently soulbound to the player if they get out alive.*

I couldn't believe my eyes. What? The bag's name was showing up red! Divine gear! Considering my class penalty, it was just a stunningly essential gift! Epic chests of similar capacity cost upwards of a hundred thousand gold, and this was divine quality too! Holy... All I had to do now was get out.

An invisible bell tolled once. The ringing echoed endlessly throughout the hall, bouncing off the walls. No new portals appeared, but the gates behind me opened. The far wall of the corridor was back to where it should be. The veil of a portal glittered next to it.

Nothing else was happening except that my life had started to recover, and a lot quicker than it should have done. A minute or two later it reached the max, only now the upper limit was at ninety nine percent! The last little sliver of it was red, and I saw an explanation in a row of debuffs I'd gotten:

Curse of the Treasury
The stuffy air of the Treasury of the First Mage is affecting you.
—1% total health.

It looked like I had the option of leaving with what I'd gotten or staying to try my luck and let the games continue until I either left or died. The main thing that bothered me was — what would happen if I died? Would *Infection* activate?

This version of the treasury relied on the player's greed, giving them a choice after each Step: take something and leave, happy with what you got, or risk everything you already got to try and get more?

The second option was the obvious choice for me. The divine bag was a great reward on its own, of course, but from what I understood, it wasn't the main reward, but just the packaging. And the basic magic tome and sixteen thousand gold... If I was honest, I'd hoped for more.

"Walker on the Path of Courage! Second Step!" I heard from beneath the hall's dome.

The Destroying Plague

The gates slammed shut. The squares on the floor changed — instead of one line in the corner of each, two lines were now etched. An angular point of travel magic appeared again in the center of the hall.

The portal it turned into was darkened with mist and spat ash and sparks out from the other side, after which came a cloven-hoofed and horned mob:

Satyr Tormentor, level 28
Elite

Covered in matted fur, unarmed and unarmored, it seemed this creature needed none of it. My first arrow clattered harmlessly off his chest. The damage logs didn't even update. The cloven-hoofed creature ignored *Binding Toxin*, fired in a fine sticky stream from Iggy's stinger.

Stamping his hooves, he emitted a staccato bleat, pierced me with his gaze and waved his arms. It was obvious why he was unarmed: his horns, tail and talons extended and filled with mist. The tip of his tail shined with a dull metallic gleam. The satyr bowed its head, stamped a hoof and, bleating something threatening, began his charge.

And this was just step two of ninety-nine? At that moment, preparing to apply *Stoneskin* and to counter the hoofed creature with a charged *Combo*, I sorely regretted that I hadn't entered the treasury before *Infection*.

At least then I wouldn't be afraid to die.

Chapter 7

Path of Courage

T HE DRAWN-OUT BATTLE with the hoofed satyr minions was tough. I didn't have enough *Vindication,* and the miserly drops of *Health* I was getting with *Lifesteal* from my *Combo* weren't helping. My arrows didn't harm the demons, and my hand-to-hand damage was badly reduced. If it weren't for Iggy, I might not have lasted the three rounds. The needler fired from his machine-gun stinger, not forgetting to periodically implant larvae in the satyrs and give them a debuff to cut down their total health.

A quarter of an hour of constant mayhem, constant walking on the edge and a bunch of burnt-out nerve cells — but I survived. In no small part thanks to my speed advantage, moving twice as fast as the mobs.

The finale of the second Step was the appearance of the guardian:

Satyr Guardian, level 31
Boss

The Destroying Plague

It seemed the mob's levels were changing to match mine. The second guard was level thirty, then I leveled up and the enemy's level also changed. But there was another option: the guard at each next stage would be one level higher. I didn't like that option at all, because it would turn advancement into an unachievable mission. Although, it fit perfectly with the reward limitation that Infect and Tissa encountered — they dangle all the stuff you *could* get, but in the end...

This boss didn't start the battle right away. After emerging from the portal, the satyr carefully looked around, then studied me with his gaze. Bowing his head, he chuckled — his upper lip peeled back and bared large horse teeth.

In the meantime, I was trying to figure out what his special abilities were. If he was a melee fighter, like the previous satyrs, then I had a chance... If not...

No. The guard struck his palm with his fist, beginning to enshroud himself in armor. His already impenetrable fur was covered in black scales, forming into full-fledged armor. The clawed hands of the hoofed creature flashed with fire, finally dashing all my hopes.

A mage after all. The satyr attacked, starting with a bunch of fireballs. Several small, walnut-sized balls of plasma shot at a speed that gave me no time to even think of dodging. Protecting me, Iggy threw himself in front of them. His pre-death squeal ravaged the ears with a *Deadly Chirp*. The satyr froze, and I used this to close the distance. I released a few arrows as I ran, aiming for the boss's bare head. One hit, landing in his face. The needler's stun still hadn't worn off when I extended the effect with a *Stunning Kick* and desperately loosed my entire arsenal on the boss.

The satyr recovered from the stun, pulled the arrow out of his cheek along with a good part of the cheek, leapt up and kicked me full force in the chest with his hooves. All the air went out of my lungs. I was thrown thirty feet, not to mention the damage — my health bar turned yellow. Rising up, I waited for another fireball to hit me and turn me into a human torch, or for something else to happen — any kind of trickery. But after hundreds of deaths in the sandbox, I had no fear of pain. Especially since I still had some surprises for the satyr.

Clenching internally, I somersaulted to the side away from a path of fire, took some exploding fireballs to the chest, paying no attention to the burning and flames, tied the guard's legs with a *Slowing Shot* and fought fire with fire with an *Explosive Shot*. The shot hit the satyr in the stomach and knocked him off his feet, but didn't even damage his armor.

Working my bow as I ran, I dodged a clawed arm cutting through the air, jumped to avoid a hoof, and struck with *Hammer*. The satyr's elongated face twisted, he took a step back to maintain his balance and I struck his turned-back leg with a *Combo*.

The Destroying Plague

The satyr's limb flexed and he fell to one knee. The mob blocked my next strike and suddenly grabbed hold of my arm, turning my wrist to himself.

"Wait…" he bleated, panting and swearing fiercely. "Azmodan's cock take you! I swear on the Faun, this is Behemoth's seal! How did you get it? This is the mark of the Sleeping One! How? Who are you?

He released my arm and rose, showing no aggression. He ran a finger along his torn cheek and the edges of the wound merged. His large nostrils flared in greed. The satyr was waiting for an answer.

"I am Scyth, initial of the Sleeping Gods…" I answered, surprised by the mob's behavior. "And you are?"

"Flaygray is my name," he said. "What do you seek in this hole forsaken by all the gods, Scyth?"

"This is the Treasury of the First Mage, right?"

"The First Mage?" the satyr asked in surprise.

"Um… I don't know his name. I don't even know who he is."

"No wonder. I was possessed centuries ago… Or rather, a couple of sinister and frivolous fiends dragged me here, pulling me from my long frolics. 'We'll clear out the treasury and be rich until the end of our days,' they said. Heh. We got stuck here forever. Even in those days, none remembered the name of this 'First Mage,' except that he was called by another name — Rascal. They said he was a good-for-nothing. Haughty, greedy, boastful. The gods punished the cretin and sent him to the Nether.

I noticed that I was out of combat, which hadn't happened since the very beginning of the second Step. And not only had the satyr's name appeared in his profile, but the color had changed too: the enemy red had turned to neutral yellow!

"As you say, Flaygray. What surprises you about Behemoth's mark?"

"What surprises me?" The satyr laughed. "I do not know your times, but in my days, that name inspired respect even in the most superior of demons! I never saw it myself, but I heard that Diablo and Belial turned the whole underworld upside down in joy when the Sleeping God disappeared!"

"He couldn't have disappeared. You know that, right?"

"Pfft... Of course not. But the new gods did such a number on the mortals that they forgot all about praying to the Sleeping Gods. And without faith, there is no god, any, um... god would tell you that. Well, thank you for sating my curiosity, Scyth. Shall we continue the battle? Who knows, perhaps one day I will get out of here and perceive Behemoth with my own eyes? By the way, you are nimble for a human! But that will not help you, I fear..."

Flaygray began to retreat, putting distance between us and starting to cast his fireballs.

"Wait..." an idea was forming in my head. "You said 'get out'? How? You're bound to this place..."

"Nobody has the right to bind a free satyr to

anything!" the hoofed creature stated proudly. "But my spouse... To the Nether with that witch! I have a contract, Scyth. When the guards grabbed me and my stinking demon drinking companions, they gave us a choice: die or serve as guards. As soon as I send ninety nine treasure hunters to the Nether, the contract will be complete. I will be free."

"And how many treasure hunters have you already sent to the Nether?"

"Um..." Flaygray faltered. "You will be the third. But those two, to tell the truth, are here too... Nobody wants to die for no reason, you know how it goes..."

"For centuries? Do you know how much time you're going to be here?"

"Listen, boy, math isn't my strong suit!" he said petulantly. "What business is it of yours anyway? For us guards, time does not exist. We awaken when an invader appears, and once they are dispatched, we go to sleep again. It's even fun!" he bleated, a note of challenge in his voice. "Now do you want to fight or not, thief?"

"And if another thief like me kills you?"

"Guards don't die, if you haven't yet figured that out. What Step are you on?" The satyr examined the floor under his hooves. "The second? Who was before me?"

"A hedgehog."

"The savage from Meaz? He has a bristling personality! And you defeated him?" the satyr asked doubtfully. He took a few more paces back.

"Yes. But he didn't talk to me, unlike you. I think I can get you out of here, Flaygray."

Focusing on the guard's icon, I sent him an invite to my group. I didn't know how an NPC would see that exactly, but I'd managed to group up with Patrick, and invite the kobold renegades to become adepts of the Sleeping Gods too.

"I suggest you join my party... And I'll introduce you to Behemoth too," I promised. "If you want..."

The satyr froze and his eyes glazed over. Was the AI trying to calculate this non-standard situation? Flaygray unfroze and then asked in a businesslike manner:

"What do you want in exchange?"

"Will you help me defeat the other guards?"

"That goes without saying!" he said in annoyance. "There's no other way out of here. How many years of my service do you require?"

"Um... None. Once we get out of here, you're free to go wherever!"

"No, no, no, Scyth, you won't pull the wool over my eyes!" The Satyr laughed and gestured threateningly with a clawed finger. "You aren't as simple as you seem, haha! You say you'll let me go just like that? No, there's definitely some trap there! What about a year? Would a year of my service suit you? Only I warn you in advance, I drink heavily and become very irritable when my mouth is dry."

"Deal!" I extended my hand to shake. "Then accept my invitation to my clan."

The Destroying Plague

The reason for him joining was obvious: the clan bonuses would help us in the next Steps, and some of the experience would go to the clan.

Flaygray, a level 31 satyr, has joined your group.
Flaygray, a level 31 satyr, has joined the Awoken clan.

Achievement progress — Treasury of the First Mage: Path of Courage — 2/99.
Reward: *+10% movement speed in treasury.*

Either this was a hint that I was going to need to run, or there was just no meaning in it and all these rewards were in the core of the location.

You got **Seed of the Flesh-Eating Tree Protector.**

The second Step brought me almost ten thousand experience in total, the same amount of gold and an unusual artifact that turned up in my bag on its own.

Seed of the Flesh-Eating Tree Protector
Epic
Of this seed, planted in blessed soil, a Tree Protector will grow. Releasing iron-hard and deadly mobile roots all around, it protects its owner and their

allies.

The extremely rare fruit of the Tree Protector have advanced magical effects and are used to make delicacies.

The fallen leaves of the Tree Protector are a powerful ingredient in alchemy.

The bark of the Tree Protector is resistant to fire and magic. With its high durability, it is often a component in the creation of shields and armor.

Gardener craft required!

Imagining this predatory tree in the clan fort, I grinned a carnivorous smile. I hoped one of Manny's people would want to retrain as a gardener.

* * *

We approached the third Step fully armed and fully recovered. Then we had to wait another ten minutes while my *Revive Pet* cooled down, but then we had Iggy with us. As soon as it appeared, the pet rushed the satyr and felt him for a long time with his antennae whiskers. The satyr murmured something in displeasure and Iggy answered with a short chitter and stepped off, now just darting jealous glances at our new ally.

All this time, Flaygray looked at the open gates longingly, but said nothing. Either he didn't see the portal glimmering at the end of the gloomy corridor, or he knew that he couldn't get out without me.

The Destroying Plague

The important thing was to figure out whether the guards' levels would increase with each Step. I decided for myself that if they did, then there was no point in risking it. But the next guard was the same level as Flaygray, thirty-one. A wordless stone golem that was immune to magic. The satyr's fire magic was useless, as were Iggy's abilities. But both of them found a way to help me: the satyr threw crushing strikes with his hooves, the pet fired volleys of needles.

The *Golem Guard* dropped my first 'dummy,' as I called them:

Belt of the Undefeated
Epic
Scalable
Use: binds to soul, taking on attributes according to owner's class.

Flaygray was distressed that I couldn't use the new gear. I couldn't drag the item out of my *Treasure Hunter's Bag*.

The next two Steps added a *Basic Levitation Magic Tome* and another 'dummy' — some gloves. Neither guardian — a fat ten-foot-high caterpillar and a bear-like creature — presented particular difficulties.

By the twenty second Step, I was getting sick of the monotonous battles, but there was no reason to leave the treasury: the mobs were still three levels higher, and the boss guardians — four. My skills and stats, boosted beyond my level, helped us to overcome the difference without difficulty. Especially with Flaygray's help; he proved himself a strong fighter. I talked and he burned our enemies from afar. All the skills I was using were leveling up, and it even occurred to me that after the treasury, when I got to Darant, I'd need to visit the archery and *Unarmed Combat* trainers.

By Step thirty-six, my bag was full of dummy items for every slot, including jewelry. There were some really awesome artifacts too, like *Bottomless Healing Potion*. Of course, I regretted again that I couldn't use it in the treasury.

That said, my achievement progress strengthened me with each Step. The rewards turned out to be non-linear: for example, after the eighteenth guard, the bonus to *base damage* jumped straight up to fifty percent. My *resistance* to all elements, my *defense* and *critical hit chance* also rose. The thirty-ninth Step unlocked a new promising stat: *+1% chance to stun opponent for 1 second when dealing any damage.*

The only thing that bothered me was my health, which was constantly dropping from the treasury debuff, so I put all the stat points I earned from leveling up into *Endurance*.

The forced exit from Disgardium that should have struck after midnight didn't happen. I got a message that "due to special gameplay conditions" I was able to spend as much time as I needed in the capsule.

The forty second guard was a reptiloid from a race of raptors. As soon as it appeared, I showed my wrist. What had piqued Flaygray's interest might work again. At each Step, before the fight and during, I tried to talk to the guard, promising to help them escape the treasury that had begun their prison. With the reptiloid, it was pointless.

"He doesn't understand you," the satyr bleated. "These reptiles died out long before my time. They didn't speak the common tongue in those days. Let me try."

Addressing the raptor, the satyr emitted a series of guttural, interrupted noises. The six-foot-five reptile reared up on its two powerful legs and listened with interest. He looked at me, nervously twitching his mighty tail. Turned his head to one side like a bird, then to the other and looked at the satyr again; then emitted a long, ear-splitting roar from its toothy maw.

"Go closer, raptors have awful vision," Flaygray said.

"What did he say?"

"He laughed. He doesn't believe that Behemoth would become your patron."

I approached the raptor hesitantly, keeping my eyes on his extended, curved claws. The creature's upper limbs had developed into full-fledged arms, and its hands allowed it to hold a short spear with a broad, serrated tip about as long as my hand. After showing him my wrist, I stepped back. The raptor squealed something and his name turned yellow.

"He agrees," the satyr translated. "Says he's willing to take a risk for the chance to see the abyss the world has fallen into while he vegetated here, since a Sleeping God has chosen such a weakling as you to be initial. To tell the truth, Scyth, I think the same. By the way, our toothy friend is called Ripta."

Ripta the Raptor accepted my invitation to the group and clan. We hadn't just gotten ourselves a deadly warrior, but also a tank. At that moment I believed for the first time that I could complete the treasury. Both Flaygray, who had gotten the same experience as me, and Ripta exceeded me in level, had the health bars of bosses, and therefore they took most of the damage thanks to *Sleeping Invulnerability*.

The gates opened again to herald another successful Step, the achievement ticked up another level, adding a percent to my dodge chance, and another item went into my bag.

Diamond Worm Cocoon
Legendary
Personal item.
Free pet.
Diamond worms are extinct underground monsters that grow up to a hundred feet long. With a very thick skin covered in diamonds, they easily burrow paths through stone, cliffs and volcanic rock.

The Destroying Plague

No predators or monsters dared to enter the territory of the depth worm, lest they themselves became pray when the true master appeared.

Attention! This type of pet belongs to the free category: it must be bound to a specific area.

To hatching: 0/10000 experience.

Could I release the worm in Kharinza? As long as it didn't eat all our miners...

Things started to go even quicker in the sanctuary. It took us only a few short minutes to send the minions to sleep, and we tore the guards apart faster than they could recover from emerging from their portals. It even got a point when I'd forgotten the last time I'd taken damage.

By the sixty ninth wave, I reached level thirty-three. I didn't expect any cooperation from the guard at this Step — it was hard to talk to an insectoid, a monstrous beast with four powerful lower limbs, a bag-like body and two upper limbs, sharpened and serrated along their entire length.

Colicoid Guardian, level 37
Boss

Using the strategy we'd worked out, Ripta rushed the boss, but as a surprise to all of us, Iggy overtook him. Firing at the guard like a bullet, the pet chirruped at us and then spoke to the mob. It answered. Iggy chittered something again.

Flaygray said something about Azmodan's cock and the Faun's ass and asked a question.

"Is your overgrown fly intelligent?"

"It never even occurred to me until just now," I answered in embarrassment.

Ripta lowered his spear, turned, screeched something at the satyr and then spoke to the boss, imitating the insectoid's chittering.

"The raptor understands the language of the colicoids," Flaygray explained. "He just gave the guardian the same offer you gave us."

The surreal sight of the raptor speaking to the gigantic insect continued for a couple of minutes, then Ripta said something to Flaygray and he translated:

"His name is Anf. He's coming with us."

* * *

The new member of the Awoken looked like a mixture of a spider and a praying mantis. The insectoid Anf's ability was to bind enemies in a spider web, which removed all risk from our task. Standing as far as possible from the center of the hall, I calmly leveled up my archery and talked to Flaygray. The satyr commentated on events.

"Oh, I know that triton! I fought with him when I was the treasure hunter..."

The variety of races among the treasury guardians had long since stopped surprising me. The

The Destroying Plague

majority of the creatures represented in modern Dis didn't exist in the places players hadn't yet reached. Like, for examples, the hedgehogs from the unexplored continent of Meaz from the first wave. Unfortunately, the other guards didn't react to my mark from Behemoth, and some even aggroed on me with a vengeance after I showed it.

As we approached the ninetieth Step, I stalled more and more, thinking about leaving the treasury. The debuff had cut almost all my health, but each time I wanted to stay. I doubted the next boss would kill me in one hit, and my new clanmates wouldn't let him hit again. Each of them, Flaygray the Satyr, Ripta the Raptor and Anf the Insectoid all accepted the conditions. I had no idea for the time being what I'd do with them for a while year, but all in good time. Time...

Dawn was already breaking in the real world, and I couldn't skip school on the threshold of the citizenship tests, so I stopped even looking at the loot. One of the memorable items added to my bag was the set legendary *Svyatogor's Chainmail*. At first I didn't even pay any attention until my thoughts hitched on the familiar name — I remembered Xan and Bill, guests at Eve's birthday party, discussing this set piece.

As I got closer to the end, I stopped even taking part in the fights. Ripta tanked, Anf tore open enemies from behind and Iggy and Flaygray shot from range. I got involved again toward the end, releasing a series of special shots from my bow. Sure, that kind of behavior was unlikely an example of courage, but the system paid no attention to that. It seemed courage was judged by the very fact of staying after each subsequent Step in the treasury.

The battle with the ninety eighth guardian, the *Nether Demon*, stretched out a little. The boss kept spawning little minions, firing off ranged spells and intelligently switching to attack ranged targets, stunning Ripta and Anf with a special ability: the air around the demon collapsed, the boss itself appeared next to one of us and the two meleers were quickly pulled into the free space, crashing into each other and breaking bone and chitin.

The demon almost killed me the one time it ended up next to me, but, praise the Sleeping Gods, I fired a *Combo* at it in desperation and compensated for some of the damage with *Lifesteal*, then, without waiting for him to hit again, I used *Lethargy* for the first time in the whole treasury. The boss had a chance to ignore the ability's effect, but luck was on my side. We finished off the demon before he could recover, using all the group's crowd-control abilities.

One percent — that was my maximum health when we came to the last Step of the Path of Courage. Everything that could go wrong did go wrong: a succubus appeared from the portal.

Succubus Temptress, level 36
Elite

The Destroying Plague

While the enchanted Ripta couldn't tear his lovesick eyes from her, seeing the ideal raptoress, the others, recovering from their surprise, attacked and successfully finished her off — the spawn of the underworld could only control one intelligent creature at a time. The next two succubi chose Flaygray and myself as their targets, for which they paid dearly: *Liberation* removed the control, returning the *Charm* to the succubus. The mobs came in turns.

With my heart beating like a drum, I awaited the next wave. Iggy ran rings around the opening portals to immediately attack with *Deadly Chirp* and *Binding Toxin*. I prepared to use my *Ghastly Howl* as it came off cooldown.

The three temptresses placed *Charm* on my allies just as my *Ghastly Howl* sounded out. One of the succubi managed to strike Iggy with her scathing whip, cutting off a wing. The pet fell to the floor, but the others woke up. The succubi stopped controlling their spells as they ran in *Fear* and fell easily to the group. I didn't hold back then — I let loose as much damage as I could. With my leveled-up skills, bonuses from the achievement and high stats in general, I gave the succubi some heavy hits.

The last portal unsurprisingly released a *Succubus Guardian*. I was ready for anything. Almost anything. Just not for what Flaygray shouted joyously at the start of the battle.

"Nega, you licentious harlot! You got stuck here too?"

"Flay?" the succubus said in surprise. "What the hell are you doing here, you pervert?"

The goatish satyr and the devilishly beautiful succubus hoofed toward each other, embraced and joined together in a passionate kiss. Some time later, coquettishly fluttering her eyeglasses and bargaining for the sake of it, Nega joined the Awoken and the last slot in my bag filled up:

Righteous Shield

Divine Artifact

Creates an impenetrable stationery magic bubble with a set radius. The effectiveness of the defense drops in proportion to the size of the bubble.

Fed by mana battery crystals. Ability to transform 10% of absorbed damage into mana to maintain shield.

Requirements: level 3 clan fort.

I smiled tiredly. Maybe not now, but in the future, the clan would be protected.

Stone letters arose with a crash in the center of the hall.

Glory to they who complete all 99 Steps!
May they turn not from the Path of Courage!

Achievement progress — Treasury of the First Mage: Path of Courage — 99/99.
Reward: *ability to make one achieved stat boost*

permanent for use outside of the Treasury.
  Choices available:
  +50% base damage
  +30% movement speed
  +20% dodge chance
  +20% parry chance
  +50% critical damage
  +10% critical hit chance
  +50% armor
  +5% chance to stun an enemy for 1 second when
dealing any damage

I collapsed the window, putting the choice aside for later. Only then did I realize how tired I was. It felt like my eyes were full of sand, my head was pounding and I desperately wanted sleep. It was a shame I wouldn't have time — it was time to go to school. My eyes passed over another message:

Achievement unlocked: First Completion —
Treasury of the First Mage
  The path opens to the courageous!
  Reward: *portal key to the Holdest continent.*

Holdest... The mere thought of that snowy continent in the South Pole gave me a chill. The key took its place in my backpack and I felt indifferent to it. To an item that all the top clans would kill for.
  Going through the loot, going through the rewards for the full achievement... Not today. I

yawned and looked around. Flaygray, Ripta, Anf and Nega all held their eyes on me. I hoped I wasn't wrong, that I really could get them out of there.

In the same corridor with the entrance, a portal glimmered behind the shut gates. I nodded toward it and led my motley company there. Anf chittered in excitement at Iggy, Ripta snorted nearby and tried to convey some thought to me, Flaygray and Nega walked arm in arm and built plans to annihilate the wine supplies in the nearest tavern...

My legs were barely holding me up, but I couldn't suppress a broad smile. Artifacts, gifts to friends, the investment in the clan's future, new allies — I felt immense joy and pleasure at what I'd done.

I just hoped Aunt Steph and the workers didn't have a heart attack when we appeared.

It was a great company: a human, a giant fly, an insectoid, a satyr, a raptor and a succubus. The deep paths of the Sleeping Gods were inscrutable!

Chapter 8

Patrick Again

ON AN EARLY tropical morning, in the square in front of the temple of the Sleeping Gods, before the eyes of dozens of builders and miners, the six appeared: five intelligent creatures and one semi-intelligent (although who knew?) gigantic scorpion fly. Us.

Having confirmed that all my newly acquired allies had successfully quit their previous place of service, and the class penalty on my inventory had broken its teeth on the divine nature of my *Treasure Hunter's Bag*, I breathed a sigh of relief. Twice. Then my jaw dropped: the guards' levels had changed. Flaygray the satyr was at level three hundred and fifty, Ripta the raptor — three hundred and seventy, the insectoid Anf — three hundred and ten, and the succubus Nega — three hundred and twenty.

"How?" I said, unable to restrain my surprise.

Nega chuckled and the satyr gave me a patient pat on the back.

"The Rascal fooled himself. He was so afraid

that someone too strong would come into the treasury that he put an *Equalization* spell on it. The treasure hunters were weakened to the point that they matched the guards, and the Rascal found some loophole that allowed him to make the guards always a little stronger than the thief. But the defensive spell had a reverse effect too, which is what happened in your case, Scyth. We all dropped to your level. Well, almost..."

"You got lucky, kid." Nega embraced me intimately and ran her tongue along her lips. "Now tell me, where can a classy lady whet her whistle around here?"

"What?"

"Where's the drink at?" Flaygray said, joining his girlfriend.

The succubus ran a long, sharp nail along my cheek and suddenly transformed into a woman of stunning beauty. A human. I felt my heart beating out of my chest and my trousers starting to get tight. This wasn't the sandbox. It was all adult here! My *Liberation* reacted immediately.

Control effect removed: Charm.

The succubus turned back into a demon again. With an attractive figure and outstanding virtues, but still with the same grayish, scaly skin, legs on hooves and charming little horns that broke through her mop of bluish-black hair. With relief, I realized that my appetite was fading. I didn't want to think about how ashamed I'd be to start stripping off in front of my workers...

"I'm feeling jealous, Nega!" Flaygray declared. He nervously looking around and suddenly fell to his knees. "It's him! He himself!"

"I swear on Azmodan's ass..." the succubus swore, turning after the satyr. "It's the Sleeping God?"

The raptor hissed something in awe, and the insectoid began to click his sharpened legs against the steps of the temple.

Behemoth, cutting a fine figure at the threshold to the temple, had taken on the same form he used for me. A nightmarish ten-foot creature: teeth, fangs, spines, tentacles and a multitude of steaming craters all over his body. This was no attractive and perfect god like Nergal the Radiant, no template of beauty and kindness, no, it was the image of terror and nightmares. It was no wonder that the rulers of the Underworld trembled so.

Leave, I will deal with them, the Sleeping God's voice whispered in my head.

For an instant, it seemed as if his figure wavered slightly. Looking closer, I searched for sights of exhaustion on his face and saw, for a fraction of a second, unnoticed by the others, that Behemoth's shadow disappeared. A couple of seconds later it blinked again.

I had to hurry in all respects — with gathering more followers, with the second temple, and to school.

I quickly went over to the workers nervously standing around nearby to explain the newcomers' appearance.

"Manny, Gyula..." I nodded to the familiar foremen. "Trixie, you're here too? Aren't you on the night shift? What about your grandpa? You're early today..."

"We try not to leave here in general," Manny said. "And old man Furtado sleeps most of the day. He gets insomnia at night, so I've moved Trixie to the day shift."

"Grandpa is resting," the dwarf confirmed. Knitting his brow, he pointed at the former treasury guards. They were bowing their heads before Behemoth while the god explained something to them. "Who've you brought? They look terrifying!"

"They are, a little. But they're with us now. These guys helped me a lot, be nice to them."

"Wouldn't be anything else with those," Gyula said quietly. "What do you think, can they handle our dinosaur?"

"I doubt it. But they can protect us from the creatures from the mine. By the way, the insectoid and the raptor don't speak our language. I don't even know what they eat, but explain to them through Flaygray, that hoofed guy over there, that they can't leave the fort. Take the satyr himself and the succubus to the tavern and try not to let Aunt Steph have a heart attack..."

Once I finished speaking, I left Dis, shot out of my capsule, got dressed and rushed to school. Being even five minutes late would go on his personal record. Forever.

My jaw ached in my lessons from constant yawning. I didn't say anything specific in response to my friends' hints that they wouldn't mind hearing about the rewards for the Threat. I dreamt of one thing only — sleep.

"At least say which artifacts you got; do you remember?" Tissa needled him.

"Nah," I answered with a yawn. "All kinds."

"If he doesn't remember, that means it's definitely more than three," Malik rubbed his hands.

I didn't tell them about the treasury, the Steps and the loot. Firstly, it wasn't safe, and secondly, it could cause unnecessary fuss. I'd take inventory, discuss it with the guys and decide what to do with the spoils. But I couldn't hold back my promising smile in anticipation of my friends' surprise and joy, and that gave me away. All the same, I didn't crack, and they didn't push too hard, understanding my fears.

I went home on autopilot, didn't even bother eating, and mom didn't insist. She shouted from my parents' room that there was food in the oven, and that she was feeling ill and wanted to rest. She asked me if I'd bring her some red wine too. I couldn't find any wine, just empty bottles.

I went to see mom to talk, but she said she had a headache and was concentrating on a TV show. Seemed like something had gone wrong with her lover

— either he didn't want to keep the relationship going or he refused to marry after mom's divorce, I didn't know. Nobody told me anything, and everything I heard was from scraps of my parents' arguments.

But dad had found someone too — he was always feeling great now. He'd stopped drinking, was smooth-shaven and held his head up; he whistled, joked and didn't even react to mom's venomous taunts. *Looks like he's with someone who makes him happy now*, I thought. My feelings were mixed. I was worried for my mom, angry at my dad and at the same time happy for him — he was moving on with life.

Fighting sleep, I took a contrast shower, gulped down some coffee and climbed into my capsule. I didn't waste any time eating, afraid that I wouldn't be able to help but fall asleep after that, and time was running out to help Behemoth with followers. Tissa and Infect had combed the whole area around Tristad where I met the kobold renegades but didn't find a trace of them. So the only hope was the sewer troggs. But they weren't that easy to find either — first we had to find Patrick.

Before jumping to Darant, I used *Cloak Essence* to hide not only all the information about myself, but my appearance too. Instead of me, people saw a blurry smoky silhouette.

There were no suitable candidates for *Imitation* in our fort. Crag was unsuitable, and Crawler and Bomber were out of view — the guys had flown by

The Destroying Plague

airship the previous day to the intermediary points on their path to the dungeons. If everything went to plan, they'd clear a path for us to a couple of instances for levels thirty and forty. Not the best place for farming considering my progress in the treasury, but it was too late to change it now.

I could have taken on the image of one of the non-citizens, but they wouldn't be able to move freely in the capital, and a worker appearing at the town hall in the city center wouldn't go unnoticed.

There was nothing unique about hiding information on yourself. Those assassins had a similar talent, and scrolls for hiding your character were sold openly, so I wasn't taking a risk by appearing in Darant incognito.

My first impression of the Commonwealth capital was fuzzy; I was only able to view the city from a bird's-eye view. Darant stretched out for many miles around, dotted with idyllic gardens and poor slums, aristocratic palaces and mage towers, crafting districts, rows of merchants and stores for any wallet. At the city center, surrounded by a royal park, canals and walls, the castle of king Bastian towered. It was entirely impossible for an ordinary player to get in there.

Bastian the First was the gloried offspring of Rant the Unifier, who bent all the human kingdoms to his will. Bastian went even further, uniting humans, elves, gnomes and dwarfs into the Commonwealth, not to mention another dozen or so smaller races.

This happened just when the world of Disgardium was opened to players, and therefore everything that happened before Bastian could be considered legend and myth thought up by the game designers. However, the AIs themselves that played the important rulers of the world didn't see it that way, perfectly 'remembering' everything that happened before the 'undying' appeared. That definition was no longer applicable to me. My character's death could be its last.

Appearing in the town hall square, I barely dodged out of the path of a mounted knight and knocked a high official off his feet. As soon as I'd apologized to him, I had to hide behind the corner of the building from some patrolling preventers.

There I had a chance to look around. The square was still teeming with my enemies. Ed had searched on the secret forums and explained: they weren't sure that an A-class Threat like Crag would emerge from the sandbox, but they hadn't stopped checking newcomers.

I hadn't seen such a mob since the times of Glastonbury. Except in New York. Dozens of races, ranging in level from one to three hundred, players, locals, mounts and pets... My eyes darted around. Across the street were banks and guild buildings, with players constantly streaming in and out. I noted one of them that I considered a potential candidate.

Shelestina, Elf, level 33 Hunter

The Destroying Plague

It was probably pointless to use the word 'beautiful' when talking about elvish girls, but Shelestina was certainly that. She had long legs clad in hunting trousers and knee-high boots. She wore light chainmail under her leather jacket and a silver diadem instead of a helmet. A white owl called Boo sat on the elf's shoulder, apparently a battle pet.

Imitate Shelestina, level 33 elvish hunter?

I'd almost agreed, preparing to run from my spot far away from the original, when the system asked me another question:

Your battle pet Iggy has an imitation available.
Imitate the snowy owl Boo, Shelestina's battle pet?

Chuckling, I accepted the suggestion. Iggy had been seen in the Arena and was fundamentally linked to Scyth in the minds of fans. Until we finished with our business on the continent, the swamp needler would now be a snowy owl.

* * *

Being the first priest of the Sleeping Gods, our honorary citizen of Tristad wasn't in the clan, and determining his location was problematic.

Understanding this, I spoke to Behemoth before I jumped to Darant, and he placed his palm on my chest, imprinting me with *Search of the Fellow Believer.* That meant that an arrow in my interface constantly pointed out Patrick's location. The map showed the first priest's marker in a tavern on the edge of the capital. I paid ten gold for a cab to take me there to save some time. The prices in the capital were daylight robbery...

Ping! The icon of a new message flashed in my interface. Who could that be? Damn! News from Snowstorm. I opened the message with a growing sense of unease.

Dear Scyth,

We are proud to invite you as the winner of the Junior Arena to the yearly Distival 2075 ball, which will take place next Saturday, on April 13, 2075.

This year, the ball will take place in the Burj Khalifa building in Dubai. The event begins at 19:00.

Outstanding players of Disgardium are presented with the honor of attending Distival. Congratulations, Scyth, you are among them!

You will find information on your tickets, hotel and the event program in a separate message.

Best regards,

Amanda Royce, VIP Client Department Director, Snowstorm Incorporated.

The Destroying Plague

I hadn't heard anything from Crawler and Bomber, so they must not have read the message yet. Or maybe they didn't get one? There was still time. We could discuss it when we next met.

Collapsing the window, I returned to the achievement given for completing the treasury to pick up my reward.

I discarded the bonuses to *armor*, *dodge* and *parry* right away, considering the possibilities *Sleeping Invulnerability*. The *movement speed bonus* was good, but I ran twice as quickly as mobs even without it, and the extra thirty percent didn't make a lot of difference. I thought about the pluses to basic and *critical damage*.

In any case, I dealt well enough with mobs at the same level as me, and against those with superior strength, I could use *vindication*. It was good because it ignored the enemy's defense stats and levels, but there was a downside to it too: the harm was equal to the energy put into the strike. And in this case, the *critical damage* chance approached zero. *Vindication* didn't crit.

So, discarding one after another, I ended up choosing *+5% chance to stun an enemy for 1 second when dealing any damage*. Even if it worked only once per battle, the stun might interrupt a spell being cast, open up the opponent and give me the chance to get the initiative.

Imba *dodge* and *critical damage* stats, and extremely high *accuracy* were good only with enemies at an equal level or lower. The penalties when fighting against high levels, both players and mobs, would cut all these stats down for each level difference by ten percent.

As for duels with equals, even then it was no simple matter. My twenty-ish percent chance to dodge would be cut in half, for example, if I successfully evaded an attack. The effect was called *diminishing returns*. It worked only against physical attacks and it prevented you from dodging more than five or six hits in a row.

In battle against magic, you needed another stat entirely: magic resistance, and it was a separate stat for each element. I didn't have that, because it wasn't a default stat for humans to have, but was added by equipment. All I had was my *Stoneskin*.

I'd already split my stat points equally between *perception* and *endurance* back in the treasury. The first, which among other things influenced a range of second-degree stats, increased the effect radius of *Sleeping Vindication*. The second increased my survivability. For level thirty-nine, my stats looked more than good.

Another level and I'd be able to use the *Whistle of Summoning*! I imagined cleaving through a fort on a *Legendary Ghost Wolf* and my smile stretched from ear to ear...

"Out of the way!" a viking on a giant white bear roared, almost overturning our cart.

The driver expertly avoided the collision and

sent some quiet curses the way of the level three hundred viking.

My thoughts interrupted, I looked at the map — we were only a couple of blocks away from Patrick now. I used that time to look at my loot from the treasury, but there wasn't enough time to check it all. The system balanced the goodies — most of the loot consisted of epic scalable 'dummies.' That was good, it meant I could outfit the whole clan. I had over a dozen magic tomes — Crawler and I could go through them.

Something that surprised me even in the treasury was that some of the artifacts needed identification. From what I remembered, the Magic University in Darant could handle that for us, but it could wait. The names of the artifacts with hidden properties were intriguing: an accessory called Balancer, a ring called Elemental Concentration, a trident called Thunderbearer... and I didn't even know if they were legendary or not! Neither the items' quality nor their properties showed up.

"We're here, boss," the driver said.

Thanking him, I climbed off the cart and headed for the tavern Gracious Courage. As I understood by the public going inside, it was a relatively popular place among legionnaires and veterans of the Commonwealth army.

* * *

I found Patrick in his most natural state — thoroughly drunk at the bar. He was making noise, demanding more beer be poured after the foam settled, and not even for himself, but for another customer. The reason for his righteous became clear immediately. Patrick was fishing for a free drink. But the gray-mustached veteran didn't treat the First Priest of the Sleeping Gods to so much as a glance, sipping from his glass with melancholy. Patrick tried unsuccessfully to hypnotize the fighter with his gaze, but the man had incredible restraint.

"A reminder to all customers — the pet battle is starting out back very soon!" someone's voice declared to the whole room. "Sign up! A week of free drinks to the winner! "Place your bets..."

I loitered at the bar all this time, not yet resolved to speak to Patrick. Some players were having a noisy feast a little further from him, and not knowing O'Grady's reaction in advance, I didn't want to risk approaching him.

I pushed between him and the veteran and ordered two ales. Iggy plopped down from my shoulder, reduced to the more polite size of an owl. I ordered him some meat. Didn't I mention that needlers are carnivorous predators? Pets needed food not just to restore their health and vigor, but to grow too. Each time they ate, they got a little experience boost.

The Destroying Plague

Patrick saw us, measured me up with an interested glance and broke out into a craggy smile.

"Nice weather today... eh..."

"You can call me Shelly, Mr. O'Grady," I answered. "Can I get you an ale?"

"I don't know, I don't know," Patrick shook his head playfully. "I have so much to do! And I have a beautiful wife and kids waiting at home..."

The barman put two perspiring glasses on the bar. I took them, threw Patrick an "As you like" and headed for a free table. It turned out hard to find one. I had to move into another room, smaller and without a stage.

"Wait, Shelly!" Patrick protested desperately. "You know I'm an honorary citizen of Tristad, right...?"

The relapsed town drunk ambled after me, noisily musing that a glass of cold beer wouldn't get in the way of his plans, and his wife probably wasn't waiting at home, she said she wanted to go shopping with a friend after all, and the kids... hmm, the kids... They'd find something to do with their nanny. By the end of his journey, it turned out that there were no kids at all, and Patrick wasn't even married, he'd just gotten tongue-tied when he saw such a beautiful girl, which I most certainly was, and...

"Shut up, Patrick. Scyth sent me. Remember him? Don't say his name aloud, he's a wanted man."

I sat at a table and ordered Patrick with a glance to sit opposite.

He gulped, narrowing his eyes at the beer. I nodded and he grabbed a glass. Quaffing noisily, he half emptied it and sat back in his chair in satisfaction. Then his brows went up and the drunkard excitedly cried:

"Sc..."

I kicked him in the shin.

"...scallywag, he was, a scallywag! My boy! Where is he?"

"He says hello. What happened, Patrick? You gave up drinking and went to meet Jane!"

"My beautiful Jane..."

A couple of glasses later, showering tears, snot and drunken revelations, he explained that Jane had married some high society mage and ran off for an expedition beyond the frontier. Patrick tried to talk her out of it, but the girl didn't recognize him.

"She forgot me..." the drunkard laughed bitterly.

I thought that was unlikely. It was hard to forget someone you never knew. But now wasn't the time to deal with the puzzles of Patrick's personality.

"A sad story," I commiserated sincerely. "Scyth told me to take you to him. The Sleeping God has need of his first priest. He also mentioned the sewer troggs. Where can I find them? I have a message for them."

"The troggs..." Patrick said sadly. "They left."

"Where exactly? Do you know where to find them?"

The Destroying Plague

"Their chief Muvarak said on parting that they were heading for the Stone Rib. In Darant they were thought of as subhuman and cleared out as much as possible, but they left them alone as long as they kept to the lower levels of the sewers. Everything got worse when something woke up there, down in the depths. The troggs were in a trap: undead attacking from beneath, the Darant guards from above. One dark night they broke out and went north, through the wastewater ponds..."

While he spoke of the sad fate of the sewer troggs, I studied the map. The Stone Rib was found in the Windfall zone, designed for players between levels forty and fifty. A few instances, a couple of raid dungeons, five or so clan castles. Where would we find the troggs there, and was it worth it? And how would we get them to Kharinza after? We couldn't move in the Depths, even in groups. Patrick said that there were almost a thousand members of the tribe. That would need a *Large Raid Portal* like the one that the Modus mage created in the gorge.

"Your bird is fun, Shelly." Patrick switched his attention to my pet, who had apparently copied not only the appearance of the owl, but its habits too: standing on the table, Iggy tore at some meat, grabbing it in its talons and swallowing it down, throwing his head back. "How's... the boy doing?"

"He asked you to join his clan. He said that such an experienced fighter and soldier like you would be very useful. Apart from that, there's a tavern in the clan fort with unlimited booze for members. Want in?"

Patrick's eyes widened when he joined the clan and saw my true form: I'd used the same option as Infect, allowing us to see each other in stealth. Understanding came slowly. Patrick rubbed his eyes for a while, then tried to focus his gaze, but his pupils moved to the sides. When the drunkard finally realized it was Scyth sitting before him, he launched a wave of curses, accusing me of putting too much on him. But when he saw me put a finger to my lips, O'Grady nodded, looked around and seemed to sober up.

"Straighten out yourself and your business, Uncle Patrick. Today or tomorrow my guys will come for you and you'll be able to get to the base. The Sleeping Gods need..."

"Just look at this!" a huge hand dropped down on O'Grady's back. "There you are, you old alkie! Guess you thought we'd gone on a campaign and you decided to crawl out into the light? Big mistake!"

Three soldiers in Commonwealth army uniforms surrounded our table. All were in plate armor, with helmets in their hands and claymores at their belts. Patrick pulled his head into his shoulders. Centurion Walsh, one of the soldiers, at level two hundred and eighty, pushed me along the bench and sat opposite Patrick.

"Sorry, elf girl, we got words to say," he said without even looking at me. "Ain't that right,

The Destroying Plague

O'Grady?"

The soldier's traveling companions, their armor clanking, moved another bench over and sat down.

"Alright," the drunkard whispered, looking at the table. Only now did I realize how withered and old he looked. "I got nothin', Walsh."

"We ain't talking about money!" the man spat. "You owe me a lot more than just money. You shamed my honor, and I won't allow that! I swear on Nergal, you'll die in the mines!"

"What did he do wrong, Centurion?" I asked.

"This don't concern you, sharp-ears!" Walsh hissed. "Better get out of here before we take care of you too!"

"For what?"

"For hanging around with this fool! You're sitting here, drinking like old friends... It's very suspicious! Ain't it, boys? Let's check this elf girl? Maybe the boys from the watch'll dig something up on her too?"

The centurion's soldiers jumped up and moved behind me. They took me by the arms and began to lift me up when Walsh gestured for them to stop.

"Not just yet. We'll deal with her later," he said, before turning to Patrick again. "Alright, you old rogue, you outplayed me in the Arena. The damned leveler cut me off from my usual combat style and I had to fight old-school. That's fine, if we had ten more fights like that, you'd be six feet under. But what you did after... No, you bastard, Centurion Walsh doesn't forgive things like that. Finish your swill and you can forget about the taste of ale until the end of your life.

"Listen here, centurion!" I didn't like what was happening, and I raised my voice, but it didn't exactly sound threatening in my elvish form. "Patrick O'Grady is a war hero and an honorary citizen of Tristad. It so happens that I know him well and want to help him out. How much and what does he owe you?"

My high *charisma* and convincing skill seemed to work on the centurion. He scratched the back of his head, frowned and said:

"Fifty thousand gold!"

Patrick finished his ale, choked, coughed for a while, then shouted at the top of his lungs:

"You've gone mad, Walsh! Insulting a soldier of the Commonwealth out loud means half a year of community service or a fine of five hundred gold!"

"Add to that the slander and libel you spoke against the lady of his heart, alkie!" Walsh growled, bringing his fist down on the table. "Swimming naked in the fountain! All the debts you built up in the district! The flowers you picked in the royal garden and tried to sell at market! Every petal was worth a hundred! And you carried off armfuls, you bastard!"

"I'll pay it all back," I said.

"Peanuts," the centurion waved away my offer. "The main thing is his idiotic propaganda! Do you know, elf girl, that your friend was inciting honest folk to turn away from Nergal and side with the Sleeping Gods? He should be punished as a heretic! I think the

Inquisition would be very happy to put the rascal to the question, and then to the torch! In the name of Nergal!"

"In the name of Nergal and all the new gods!" legionnaires echoed from all over the tavern. It turned out everyone in the building could hear Walsh's speech.

"I should have left with the troggs..." Patrick sighed sadly.

"That's another thing! You hung around with those barbarian monsters. With pagans!" Walsh finished his accusatory speech. "But all this is nonsense. The boys from Tristad spoke well of you, and we would have swept it all under the rug. But I can't forgive you for Olivia."

"What happened with Olivia?" I asked, realizing that she must be the centurion's love.

Patrick blushed and muttered quickly:

"Nothing. Nothing at all..."

"Nothing..." Walsh said bitterly. "All you did was kiss her and grope her breasts. In front of everyone! Do you know that I'd proposed to her then, O'Grady?"

Nether! My quest to reform Patrick hadn't gone anywhere, but even without that I felt some responsibility for the old crank. And gratitude too, of course — everything I'd achieved in Dis started with him. So I went into my inventory and pulled out the required amount of money in thousand coins.

"Here's fifty thousand. This is for Olivia. Can

my friend Mr. O'Grady and I leave now, Centurion Walsh?"

Rising sharply, I pointed Patrick to the exit with my eyes while the centurion gazed at the gold.

Walsh frowned, picked up the coins and answered.

"Alright. I forgive him for offending my bride. I have no more grievances against O'Grady."

"Let's go, Patrick," I said.

"I don't think so," the centurion snarled. "I said I forgive him for the insult against Olivia, but this lowlife has done a lot more than that. I'm afraid I don't have the authority to write it all off. Take him, boys..."

Walsh's men began to lift Patrick from the table. The first priest of the Sleeping Gods didn't resist, just stared helplessly at his empty glass. Then, while they were escorting him past the bar and I was following, he turned and whispered soundlessly:

"Sorry."

My eyes went dark, my legs buckled. I smelled death. My throat roiled and I barely kept myself from throwing up. The shadows of the legionnaires and Patrick were lost in the crowd. My health points had dropped to a single sliver. Suspecting the worst, I opened the debuff description.

Infection
You are infected with the plague of the dead. After death, you will become a vassal of the Destroying

184

The Destroying Plague

Plague.
  —1% total health per hour.

If my health was dropping again, that meant something was wrong with Behemoth. Nothing too bad so far — the regeneration was still much higher — but it was an alarming sign. I coughed heavily, suppressing my churning stomach. Shaking my head, I rushed after Patrick. His marker was already at the tavern exit.

I'd already caught up to them and was thinking of a way to get the first priest out of this when the message icon flashed up with a ping. I automatically glanced at it — it was from Yary. He was all I needed right then!

Where did you go, young Scyth?
  Not changed your mind about joining Modus? If you're in Darant, we can talk at the Elvish Garden. I'll be there all night.
  Yary

I told him I wouldn't be able to meet today — was stuck in an instance. I got an answer at once. *Then I'll see you at Distival. You got an invite, right?*

Well, I'd deal with this later too. The important thing now was getting Patrick out, finding those damn troggs and getting Behemoth the faith he needed.

I rushed out of the tavern and shouldered my way through crowds of passersby to catch up to the legionnaires.

"Centurion Walsh!"

"What now?" he asked, frowning.

"You said the watch was ready to give Patrick a clean slate for his service. Right?"

"Let's say so."

"And you forgave him the personal insult. Are soldiers of the Commonwealth truly no longer men of their word? Is their word not stronger than oak?"

Walsh took a deep breath and exchanged glances with his men. Then he barked a quick order and the legionnaires ran further along the street at a light jog. Taking advantage of the centurion's momentary inattention, Patrick approached and spoke quietly.

"I completely forgot! Chief Muvarak of the sewer tribe left me this..."

The drunkard stuck a hand into his vest pocket. Instead of a pile of garbage, nutshells and sand, he pulled out something like an amulet on a string: a faded leather triangle with a fringe and a seal impressed on it.

"This is a charm. It shows the path to the tribe totem. It can help you find the troggs in the Stone Rib."

I took the trinket. The seal upon it was faded, rubbed, but still recognizable as the gaping maw of a bear.

"I can handle the mess I've gotten myself into," Patrick said. The honorary citizen of Tristad looked me in the eye, and his gaze was hard. "Find Muvarak..."

"Listen here, sharp-ears!" Walsh joined the conversation. "Your involvement in the fate of this heretic is extremely suspicious. The boys are fetching the watch and the inquisitors, and I hereby order you in the name of King Bastian the First to stand..."

Damn it, O'Grady! I thought before activating *Depths Teleportation* straight to Kharinza. Along with the honorary drunkard of Tristad.

Interlude 2

Melissa

AS HAD BECOME custom recently, we decided to fly in the same flier after school, but Alex refused at the last moment.

"I'm falling asleep," he said, yawning widely. "You guys go, I want to sleep on the way."

Melissa thought of keeping him company, but Scyth still had things to do in Dis. Essential things, everyone understood that. She hugged Alex and kissed him. The boys were embarrassed by this public display of affection. They couldn't get used to the fact that Tissa, 'one of the boys,' was now Sheppard's girlfriend. Hung emoted a facepalm, Malik rolled his eyes. Ed just turned away, waited for them to finish, then touched Alex's shoulder.

"Everything going to plan?"

"Yes. I'm in Darant, I'll find Patrick, talk to his troggs, and if they agree, bring them to the base."

"Good. Hung and I will blaze some trails and come back to the fort. Then we'll discuss what to do next. We have good news and bad news. The good is that the desert debuff works based on a percentage of health, which means it kills all players of all levels and resistances equally. The bad news is that we're barely a mouthful to the mice there."

"There's another option apart from the lands beyond the frontier..." Alex muttered, sitting in the flier. His sleepy voice was barely audible.

Melissa saw him enter a destination and switch the autopilot on. Alex waved his hand in parting and his flier took off, leaving Melissa with the boys on the landing pad.

"What did he mean?" Malik asked in confusion.

"You know him," Hung shrugged his shoulders. "He's a quiet type. He won't tell us until he tests this 'option' of his."

"That's what I don't like about it..." Malik sighed, jumping into the flier first.

The orb-shaped aircar made of super-strong transparent plastic took in all four passengers and gently lifted off. The compensators kicked in and the fast take-off to a thousand feet, into the atmosphere layer designated for civic air transport, was barely noticeable.

They didn't talk about the game as they flew, fearing that someone could be listening in. They had nothing else to talk about except the upcoming citizenship tests.

When the flier landed on the roof of a building and the girl rose from her seat, Malik asked her:

"Are you going straight into Dis?"

In their years of study and friendship, it had become a tradition that Melissa was dropped off first. Not just because she lived closer, but also because of her dad. He demanded that her daughter fly home straight after school — while the head of the family earned money in his cheap old capsule, all the housework was hers.

"First I need to make dinner, then tidy up the house," she answered. "I'll meet you in the tavern, Malik. I'll message you."

After her mom died, her dad found it harder and harder to maintain his citizenship status. Mom had been good at ideas, and her colleagues respected and valued her as an expert sociologist. But her ideas were too... dangerous. So, when she died some at the top sighed in relief.

But dad... After mom's death, it was as if he was adrift. He drank, went on benders in drinking establishments, got into fights, and in the end, he lost his job as a corporate lawyer. That sobered him up and worries over his daughter's fate brought back his prudence.

Nonetheless, every year on the day before the attestation for his category, he became irritable, got nervous and desperately studied new laws and legal cases. His lack of work in his specialty reduced his value for society, but his qualifications compensated for it slightly. As did the royalties from Tissa's mom's scientific works. It wasn't much, but it was a big help in maintaining the citizenship of her close relatives.

The Destroying Plague

That said, this couldn't go on for long. In the last two years, they'd dropped a category. Give it a little more time and her dad, if he didn't find work, would lose citizenship. And Tissa along with him.

She'd pass the citizenship test of course, but how long could she support her status without a higher education? At twenty-one, they'd give her a category... Or they wouldn't, instead declaring her useless and stripping her of her citizenship. Dis could help. The government took fast progress in the game as a sign of determination and the presence of important qualities. But she was unlikely to achieve anything significant there within five years without a Threat as a friend.

She recognized that Alex's success would be her success too. It would give her choice in the future — they'd already spoken a lot about this, deciding in unison to dedicate a year after school to Dis, and then to join university together. Even if they didn't manage to finish their studies before they fully came of age, they'd get a delay until their diploma. And the money earned from eliminating Big Po should be enough for all the Awoken to pay for their studies...

"Dad, I'm home!" Melissa shouted.

Throwing off her jacket, she walked into the living room In the bedroom, her dad was just leaving his capsule — one of the two installed in the home. The other one used to belong to her mom, and when Tissa reached fourteen, a new temporary one from the Department of Education wasn't required.

"How was school?" her dad asked, emerging from his room. He was already dressed and looked tired.

"Same as usual. Mr. Kovac went crazy and dumped a bunch of written assignments on us, and the other teachers did too. I don't know what to start with and how to finish it all in time. How was your raid?"

Her father, or rather, his character, a knight at level two hundred and sixty, was part of a small group of mercenaries. Not the coolest, and, to put it plainly, not the most successful. But yesterday they'd had some luck — a rich couple hired him and a few other warriors to finish some achievement and get some gear that dropped from a specific boss.

"Annoying customers..." her dad muttered. "They think that just because they hired us, we're their damn servants!"

"Did you wipe?"

"Yeah..." her dad's face darkened. "That rich little upstart aggroed a patrol right before the boss. We had to start over again! Lost a bunch of time and some of our payment! It's a good thing that the epic they wanted dropped right away at least, the chance wasn't a hundred percent..."

"But the wipe was the customer's fault, right?" Tissa asked in surprise.

"We missed a point in the contract," he said in annoyance. "Any wipe means minus five percent. Damn them anyway! Even after the penalty, we made some good money, flower."

Tissa walked over to her dad and hugged him. He stroked her hair.

"I ordered some fresh groceries with the contract money. Want to make dinner? I'm starving!"

* * *

After the memorable final in the Arena, Tissa was invited to several clans, not counting those to which all the Awoken were invited.

The girl caught the eye of the Damsels, a non-combat clan that specialized in monetizing their members' looks. The clan hadn't achieved any particular success in its in-game endeavors, but was still considered one of the richest due to its careful positioning. The Damsels were invited to high-class balls and rich private parties, both in Dis and in the real world, and used them to promote their private brands and show the girls' lives in both their guises in real time. The main requirement for joining was being naturally beautiful. Any hint of plastic surgery meant a refusal. Another important aspect was that the Damsels' in-game images had to match their real ones.

Perverts, Tissa had thought then.

You could create any appearance in Dis, but the rich types didn't like to be tricked even in a game. The Damsels satisfied that demand.

She'd gotten an invitation of an entirely

different sort from the White Amazons. The ochre witch was impressed by Tissa's game skills, which were a perfect match for the unspoken racial requirements reflected clearly in the clan's composition. A blond-haired, blue-eyed white-skinned girl, tall and beautiful, the champion of the Junior Arena, the only girl among the boys — a tasty treat.

My dear, come have a drink with me in a wonderful cafe... the ochre witch had said to the priestess of the Sleeping Gods. *We'll have a great time!*

Tissa ignored the offer, but Elizabeth, as the leader of the White Amazons was known, was a persistent type. Around a month ago, she'd met the girl on the school landing pad and convinced her to talk.

Stunned by this attention from a lady of luxury, a C-class citizen among other things, Tissa agreed. Instead of a 'wonderful cafe,' Elizabeth took her to her place in a flame-red Ferrari Falco.

They flew over half an ocean at supersonic speeds and landed on an idyllic beach on a tropical island. The automatic security system set up around the aerial perimeter requested that the driver identify herself. Once convinced that Elizabeth had the right to land, the turret gun barrels lowered. A police drone nonetheless approached and took the biometric details of the guest, the underage Melissa Schafer, with dependent citizenship status K.

Being in such a respectable district for the first time, the size of the houses and grounds belonging to

The Destroying Plague

high-category citizens astounded Tissa. All around were golf greens and miraculous lakes glittering in the sunlight, complete with swans and pink flamingos. The uncrowded streets were lush with greenery. The girl couldn't hold back a cry of joy when she saw a reindeer fawn calmly walking down the sidewalk. She was even more surprised that one of the streets of this clean and gleaming town belonged to the White Amazons.

"One of these houses could be yours, my dear," Elizabeth noted.

At her fifty years, she looked no older than twenty-five — obviously plastic surgery, or possibly a youth procedure undergone on the Moon. Melissa had studied all the information available online about Elizabeth.

They spent the whole day together — conversation with the Ochre Witch was captivating. A little later, some other Amazons came to visit Elizabeth, and the evening flew by for Tissa in warm and friendly company. They all seemed to be just as caring and honest as Elizabeth... Tissa didn't want to fly home to her sad little district, to the depressing and gloomy anthill apartment building, and she had a ban in Dis, so she was overjoyed when Elizabeth invited her to stay the night. Elizabeth herself called the girl's father, introduced herself and got permission to give Melissa lodgings. It probably helped that Elizabeth magnanimously gifted a legendary spear to her father — she logged into the game personally and sent it with her best wishes.

Her father, not knowing Scyth's status, was glad of his daughter's new acquaintance. Both he and the Ochre Witch were certain that Tissa would join the White Amazons as soon as she left the sandbox. Who would have refused? Elizabeth promised to pull the right strings to get Tissa a higher education remotely, without harming her game career, something in the sphere of sociology or virtual world design. She promised to get her a job, high status and in the end — the right to live on an idyllic island in her own two-story house.

The girl didn't tell her friends the details of Elizabeth's offer. Alex didn't even pay any attention — they all got offered like that, some more, some less... But the seed of doubt had been cast.

After the events of recent days, it had grown. Because of what he'd done, it had been immensely hard for Scyth to get out of the sandbox. Tissa didn't trust Crag and wasn't sure that he wouldn't betray them at the first sign of a threat to his own benefit. And now the Destroying Plague debuff...

It'll all be worked out before I leave the sandbox, Melissa reassured herself. And if it all went to hell, she'd take the Ochre Witch's offer. And the guys... The guys would get it. That was why they were friends.

The Destroying Plague

* * *

As always, merrymaking and laughter drifted out of the Bubbling Flagon. After the death of Tashot, Chef Arno and a range of other key NPCs in the area, reinforcements arrived from Darant: some retired foreman bought the tavern, a veteran of the Commonwealth army. A fat lady took the chef's spot, and new priests with suspiciously high levels came to attend the temple of Nergal. Chief Councilman Whiteacre had survived, but half the members of the city council had turned undead. New members had to be elected. Apart from that, the city watch had been almost entirely changed, and for the sandbox their levels of over one hundred looked strange.

The tavern's new owner declared a tournament in the rear yard, a bard on the stage sang some desperately sad song and fell under a justifiable hail of apple cores and chicken legs. Infect was behind the bar.

"We going?" Tissa asked, approaching her clanmate.

"Give me a minute," he answered indistinctly, chewing on some boar jerky. "You know you can't eat like this at home. Oh, look who's here!"

Tissa turned and saw Aphrodite, former neighbor of Alex. Eve O'Sullivan, spoilt, empty-headed and sour-tempered trash.

One of Hung's multitude of cousins had studied with her and told of the girl's tricks. *Apologize at once!*

she'd demanded one time from a teacher that had criticized her. *Your citizenship status is lower than mine, I won't let you speak to me in a tone like that!* The girl treated everyone beneath her citizenship category like shit even before she got plastic surgery. Once she bought more beauty, she got even worse. It was strange that Alex had been her friend for so many years.

Eve swept over to a table by the stage, hanging on young man's arm. Tissa didn't recognize him. Feeling Tissa's gaze on her back, she glanced over her shoulder, immediately turned around and said something to her boyfriend. He laughed and cast a passing glance at the priestess of the Sleeping Gods.

"I don't have much time," Tissa said, hurrying Infect.

"Just a sec, let me finish my drink..." He started chugging down a glass of beer.

They ran into Rita Overweight outside the tavern. *Like some kind of rally of Alex's exes*, Tissa thought. The tradeswoman was in a hurry, but she stopped when she saw the pair.

"Hey! What're you guys up to out there?"

"Out there? Where?" Tissa asked in confusion.

"In the big world. Alex threw me the descriptions of a couple of pieces of gear, asked me to get him prices on the black market. What've you been farming? Raid instances?"

"Who do you see before you, Mega-Extra-Overweight?"

"Um... you."

"Exactly right. I'm in the sandbox, just like you! Infect and I aren't there," Tissa shook her head, "and we aren't farming shit."

"Got it," Overweight said, pursing her lips. "Alright, well... bye."

Infect remembered himself only when she'd already walked away.

"Hey, wait! What artifacts were they? Over..."

Tissa hissed in his ear:

"Don't make a fool of yourself!"

"What?"

"She knows and we don't? What the hell?"

"To hell with it. Let's jump?"

Tissa nodded, and an instant later Infect took both of them to where they'd ended their search the previous day. They'd roamed practically the entire base of the Nameless Mountains but hadn't found a single hint of the renegade kobold camp. It was good, at least, that the mobs caused no problems — Tissa and Infect had reached level twenty-eight during the assault of the Destroying Plague.

"Where are we headed?" Infect asked.

"I don't know," Tissa shrugged. "We could go a little further south and go to the other side..."

"I wanted to ask..." The boy faltered.

"What?"

"You and Scyth are serious, right?"

"Of course!" Tissa burst out. And hurriedly turned around to hide her emotions.

"Have you already...?"

"None of your business!"

This was too much. Friend or not, Tissa had no plans to talk on that subject. She frowned and crossed her arms in annoyance.

They actually hadn't. At first Alex behaved too hesitantly, then he reached sixteen. Formally, he was of age and she wasn't. Understanding this, Alex stopped even letting his hands roam, and after his exit from the sandbox they were practically never even alone.

Tissa smiled as she thought of him. She'd always liked him, and not just for his looks; for his headstrong character, his self-confidence, his knowledge beyond what they were taught in schools. But there were plenty of people she liked, and Sheppard had seemed too arrogant for her liking.

It all changed in the last autumn, when he suddenly got passionate about Dis and became a Threat. The Dementors had no idea about that back then but stood behind the boy against Crag without having to discuss it. No matter how you span it, Sheppard was a friend, a classmate that they'd known since childhood. Tobias, on the other hand, was a creepy joker that had been forced out of the clan. By then, Melissa's serious interest in Alex was waking up, but even then, without realizing it herself, she spoke to him because it was necessary. The *First Kill* in the Olton Quarries was a coveted dream not only for Ed, but for all the Dementors.

The Destroying Plague

Then there was the business of Axiom, and Alex suddenly showed a new, unfamiliar side to himself. For Tissa, it was enough that he wanted to help the whole clan, not just her, and even if he hadn't made the bet with Big Po, it would have been enough for her. But Alex went even further and carried the Dementors to incredible heights that they'd only ever dreamed of before. And most of all — he gave them hope for a better future...

"What do you think, did I ever have a chance?" Malik interrupted her thoughts.

Tissa looked at him. His expressive eyes framed with long eyelashes were objects of desire for many girls, along with his open smile. But right now, Malik's gaze didn't have a single sign of his usual playfulness. *You had a chance, idiot,* she thought, but answered entirely differently.

"No."

"Why not?"

"You're like a brother to me, Infect. Let's leave it at that. I'm Scyth's girlfriend," she ended decisively, both for him and for herself. "And your friend. Agreed?"

Infect nodded thoughtfully and turned away. Tissa fell onto her back and stared at the cloudless blue sky. She picked up some grass and put it between her teeth. Infect lay down next to her, head to head. Minutes passed and neither stood up. Searching this huge area for the missing kobold tribe seemed like a fool's errand. Without mounts, constantly running into mobs...

"What if it doesn't work out?" Infect broke the silence.

"If what doesn't? If we don't find the kobolds?"

"With Scyth. He's always getting into scrapes. Wouldn't be surprised if the preventers get him tomorrow."

"He can handle it. And we'll help."

"Of course! But if not? What then?"

"We'll keep playing together. We'll level up a new toon for Alex, if he wants to play again. But I doubt that — he has enough money for his studies, and he never liked Dis much."

"Why is he always so lucky?" Infect sighed. "It could have been me. Or Bomb. Or Crawler..."

They had an old habit of using different names for different worlds. Probably so they didn't forget where they were.

"Stop it." Tissa jumped to her feet. "Come on, they're close!"

"What? Who's close?"

"I got a new ability! *Search of the Fellow Believer!* The kobolds are in a cave in that gorge we were wandering around yesterday..."

Tissa shared the map coordinates with Infect, buffed them both with *Light Feet* and they ran. The thief went into stealth in the gorge, and a couple of seconds later she heard him sigh.

"I'm going to miss this..."

"You mean the invisibility?"

"Uh-huh. I'll be like a clown, walking around with a tin whistle. I won't be able to fight or run if I have to."

The girl stopped suddenly. Noticing her friend's ghostly silhouette, she took him by the shoulder, looked into his eyes and spoke strongly:

"Have you forgotten why we're here? It's not for fun! I'd gladly change classes myself if the clan wanted me to! But they need a healer more."

"I'm useful too! I can see the unseen, scout, stun, disarm traps! I have the highest level, not counting Scyth's cheater abilities..."

"Less than what the legendary buff will give to the whole group. The whole group, Infect!"

The thief fell silent and sighed, offended. Tissa knew that he understood the need in changing classes, but she had no plans to support him in his imagined slights. A successful clan didn't discuss the leader's decisions, especially when they were made unanimously.

They continued walking in silence. Once they reached the spot, they stopped. There was no indication whatsoever of kobolds in the cave. There weren't even ashes from fires, a permanent feature of the rat people, who believed that fire awoke their intelligence. That was why they had an eternal love for candles — every kobold wanted to have a little fire with them always.

The thief slipped into the cave first as a silent shadow.

"Psst!" the girl heard from inside. "They're here."

Tissa raised her head high, straightened her shoulders and walked inside proudly as befitting a priestess. Squeezing in through the narrow and winding passageway, she saw shadows dancing along the high cave walls.

"Stop, human!"

Narrowing her eyes, the girl saw a rusty blade at her throat.

"I come in peace. Who is your leader?"

Two kobolds emerged from the semi-darkness: a tall one with a huge paunch and a short one, gray and hunchbacked. The second limped, leaning on a crooked staff. The limper narrowed his watery eyes, looking into Tissa's face.

"May the Sleeping Gods never wake!" she cried.

"And may their sleep be eternal!" the old man responded.

"And may their sleep be eternal!" the whole tribe repeated in unison, their words echoing off the walls.

"Bow..."

Tissa could have sworn that she heard Behemoth. The chief of the Grog'hyr tribe, Shaman Ryg'har and another eleven kobold renegades, clanking in dirty broken armor, fell to their knees before the priestess of the Sleeping Gods.

A little time later, the tribe joined the populace at Kharinza, and Tissa and Infect returned to the sandbox before *Exhaustion* could kill them. They didn't see much in their three seconds in the clan fort, but they realized something was happening there.

Chapter 9

A Still Unconquered Herald

ABYSS TAKE ME, where am I?!" Patrick brayed.

The fleshy, stinking paw of a monster covered in welts and blisters and seeping slime grabbed air instead of the first priest's shoulder as he jumped away. The clumsy creature, as if assembled from different parts of dead men, lost its balance and stepped past on inertia. I waved away an untimely notification about an upgrade to *Depths Teleportation* and whistled, assessing the mob's level and class.

Sickening Rotter, level 239
Elite

Casting a glance at the fort, I felt a cold sweat forming on the back of my neck. We'd jumped into the height of a local plague zombie apocalypse. The undead moaned all around, and rotters and skeletons wandered the fort's only street, but most of the mobs were furiously attacking the temple. Something prevented them from going beyond the foot of the stairs, some invisible barrier.

Get to cover, now! I heard Behemoth's voice but was already starting to recover on my own. I dragged Patrick toward the temple, trying to think of a way to break through the screen of the undead. I dropped my elvish girl disguise as I walked — there was no point in keeping it now. Along with the false image, I shook off the stupor that had been growing from my second day without sleep.

Crag, level 26 warrior, and his group (Ripta, level 307 raptor; Anf, level 310 flayer) invites your group (Scyth, level 39 herald; Patrick, level 26 warrior) to join them.

Just in time! I accepted the invite without thinking. The presence of Anf and Ripta was comforting, but also perplexing: why weren't they just sweeping away these small fries, over a hundred levels beneath them? And where were the satyr and his girlfriend?

Over a dozen of the living dead blocking the path to the temple turned around when Patrick and I started running and jumped into a gap between a skeleton archer and a raised corpse. *Ghastly Howl* had no effect on any of them. No surprise, but it was worth a try. Although, possibly thanks to the ability, the skeleton missed its target. Its arrow glanced my ribs, taking off a chunk of flesh and I flew bleeding into the cover of the temple.

Without a doubt, even such a hit from a far superior mob would have killed me instantly. The logs showed that the archer's damage exceeded my health many times over, but the effective damage was split mostly between the insectoid and the raptor. Nonetheless, even with the protection of the Sleeping Gods, my health was cut by more than half.

Our people were crowded on the temple stairs. The workers watched the undead in horror as they tried to break through the barrier only a few feet away. I doubted many of them had seen anything like this... Although, what could be more terrifying than the Montosaurus?

Crag elbowed his way through the miners and builders and helped me to get to my feet. He looked me up and down with interest and chuckled.

"Did I imagine it, or were you just an elf girl?"

"Not now, Toby! Tell me what's happening. Where's the Sleeping God? Where are all our new allies?"

"A free tavern in a protected fort," Patrick muttered nearby. "I didn't expect this from my boy!"

Manny and Trixie helped him up, greeting him like an old friend. The dwarf kept saying 'Uncle Patrick is good,' and struggled to embrace him with his stubby arms.

"The first priest should go up into the temple," Crag noted. "Behemoth is struggling to keep the barrier up. Anf and Ripta can't leave his side, they're sharing their energy with him."

"You've met them?"

"Yep. Flaygray introduced me to them and Nega," Crag chuckled and blushed. "The satyr and the succubus got stuck in the tavern when it all started by the way... Where the hell did you find them? They won't tell me anything. Flaygray even said I should ask the master my questions. Meaning you! How..."

"Stop. I'll explain everything later, now isn't the time."

I shook Trixie's hand and greeted Manny. Then I asked:

"Why didn't you leave Dis? You can't work like this anyway..."

"Do you think we just don't care, Alex? We know that the god needs everyone right now. If the temple falls, you'll die, and then all this is over. No. We'll be here to the end..." Manny waved his pick over his head in fury. "May the Sleeping Gods never wake!"

"May their sleep be eternal!" the miners echoed in response.

I don't know who first started that. Probably not Behemoth himself, and certainly not me. It was probably by the hand (or tongue) of Bomber or Crawler. They must have dug something up from the game mythology.

"Cultists," Crag said, smirking.

Patrick hugged everyone. The workers greeted him gladly and behaved as if with an old friend and drinking buddy. Which is probably what it was.

"I'm so glad to see you all, old friends!" the first priest shouted. "I so hoped to see you again!"

"Scyth, it wouldn't hurt to send him to the Sleeping God," Crag noted, nodding upstairs. "He needs more support; he's collapsing under the pressure."

"Mr. O'Grady," I said, distracting Patrick from the workers. "By all the Sleeping Gods, into the temple, now! Our god needs support!"

Grabbing him under the arm, I dragged the obstinate priest up the stairs. Judging by the smell, he was still drunk. Crag kept pace with us and continued his report.

"Basically, the satyr and his girlfriend are holed up in the tavern with some of the workers. They can't get out for some reason. We haven't had any news from there since Behemoth put up the shield."

"Where did the enemies come from? The mines?"

"Something like that. The undead broke out of a closed mineshaft. There were three lich bosses in the lead. The miners ran to the fort. They were quick enough, nobody got hurt. The undead ran after them, but later it became clear that the temple was their main goal. It all happened really fast; it hasn't even been an hour! Fortunately, the Montosaurus appeared and made mincemeat out of some of the undead. The dinosaur bit the first boss in half and ate him. But two others got into the fort: one is sieging the tavern, the second — the temple…"

I sent the unhappy Patrick into the temple and stopped outside.

"If Flaygray and Nega are in the tavern, then why didn't Ripta and Anf stop the assault? They're over level three hundred!"

"You think they didn't try?" Crag said. "They almost died protecting the temple. That lich is a hell of a warlock. He took control of the raptor and made him attack his own. The mantis held him back as well as he could, lost an arm for his trouble, but managed to drag Ripta behind the shield. The lich's spell broke. The Sleeping God healed them a little and brought them in to help maintain the shield. They're inside, see for yourself…"

A terrible picture was revealed in the temple's hall: the god, this time in the form of a huge man with a hippopotamus snout, stood hunched, his eyes closed, and arms raised, as if holding up something incredibly heavy. Beads of black blood seeped from his pores. Nearby, the insectoid and raptor lay flat on the ground, not moving. Their health indicators showed that they were alive, but badly injured.

Behemoth closed his eyes slightly for a moment, and the weight of the whole world came down on me that very second. My knees bent, but I somehow stayed standing, wheezing. Crag and Patrick grunted when I grabbed their shoulders.

I will not last long; I heard the Sleeping God's voice in my head. *The invasion must be stopped!*

Patrick fell to his knees and began furiously praying. The pressure lifted slightly.

"Crag, call your workers, have them do the same!" I said.

Toby nodded and disappeared. I looked around feverishly. How could we get out of this?

Bomber and Crawler weren't in the fort — they were still traveling to the instances, and they wouldn't have been much use here anyway. I didn't bother writing to them, so they wouldn't jump in and get into trouble. Thoughts swarmed in my head, but none were of any use. My gaze passed over my skill panel, hoping to catch on some idea. I saw the icon of the gold bag. That was it! The artifacts from the treasury!

I opened the bag and begin to pick through the items, sorting them by usefulness. The *Diamond Worm* wasn't going to work; it had to be fed *experience,* and anyway, judging by the needlers, it would need to grow first. The *Flesh-Eating Tree Protector* had the same problem. And there was no gardener in the fort to plant the tree and look after it properly. The unidentified artifacts were useless — I hadn't made it to the University of Magic to identify them. The high-level gear was unusable due to the penalties. I could put them on, but the bonuses wouldn't work and my stats would drop to abysmal levels. What else? The magic tomes, although nice, were useless. There was no magic flute to save the day, nor a bard to play it.

Nothing that could help us fight off the undead attack. Except...

I had four guards at level three hundred and above, a patron saint of my very own and the killer talents of two top Threats! The puzzle tapered off to solving a single problem: uniting all the guards in one spot to boost them with Crag's talent, cover them with *Sleeping Invulnerability* and kicking some dead ass.

I remembered that *Depths Teleportation* had leveled up. I opened my profile and stared at the skill description. It changed a little with each level-up. Now let's see... There it was!

All I had to do now was prepare: assess the enemy's strength and reequip. The twelve levels I gained in the treasury made all my old equipment obsolete. The *Burning Shot Bow* that I'd been so proud of looked great at level twenty-five and was good enough at thirty, but now any *green* piece of gear at my level would be better.

In the meantime, the space of the hall filled up with Sleeping God adepts from the non-citizens. They surrounded the god and began to pray. I heard English and Spanish, Portuguese and Polish, Chinese and Russian — the poor knew no nationality. I couldn't translate their prayers, but somehow, I knew that for Behemoth, the words didn't matter. The pressure on his shoulders finally lifted.

"What now?" Crag asked, returning.

"The influx of faith will support Behemoth and give us a little time, even if it isn't much. So first we'll assess the enemy's strength."

"And then?"

"And then we'll suit up and go fight."

* * *

There were around fifty mobs roaming the fort above level two hundred, and two bosses. I knew the mobs well from the cellars of Nergal's temple in Tristad — each had killed me a hundred times. *Skeleton Warriors, Skeleton Archers, Broken Skeletons, Brainless Zombies,* two *Foul Queases* and three *Sickening Rotters.* The last ones differed in their creation method: the queases were sewn together from body parts, whereas the rotters were raised from rotting masses of corpses in which bones still swam and innards could still be seen, with bloody veins and blackened ligaments. *Cursed Liches* at level three hundred and six led the onslaught.

One after another, I activated the 'dummy' epics from the treasury for each slot and collected enough to activate all the bonuses:

Unconquered Herald Set

Epic

Scalable

Consists of 16 items: knuckledusters, quiver, bow, helmet, necklace, shoulderpads, chestplate, belt,

---

pants, boots, gloves, ring, bracelet, earring, cloak.

4/16 Unconquered Herald set bonus: *damage taken reduced by 5%.*

6/16 Unconquered Herald set bonus: *5% damage reflected back to opponent.*

8/16 Unconquered Herald set bonus: *5% chance to reflect damage taken to the enemy in full.*

10/16 Unconquered Herald set bonus: *Thorn Aura (deals 300% base damage to all enemies within 30 feet once every 3 seconds).*

The armor was the color of ultramarine, and it looked unusual. Almost like plate, but without the grandeur of military armor, it looked light and weak, as if made of foil. But all the joints were perfectly matched — I kept complete mobility. A silver-gray cloak covered my back, a mithril earring hung from my ear. The epics were guaranteed to scale, so they'd always be current and would add to my stats even as my level went up.

I particularly liked the set's weapons. The knuckledusters span my whole forearm: a vicious sharp thorn ran from my elbow, while broad metal projections on my knuckles provided the main power. Now my *Hammerfist* was the best meat tenderizer ever!

The new bow had a longer range, more power and a higher rate of fire than my old epic. The set quiver added attack speed and stored up to nine types of ammunition. I was still shooting *Strengthened*

Steel-Tipped Arrows, but I could get a nice damage increase if I used better arrows. All I had to do was reach the weapon store.

All the set items were soulbound — only I could use them. Separately, they were nothing special: each added a bonus of around fifty points to main class stats, in my case — *charisma* and *luck*. In general, in terms of health and damage, I'd even lost out a little. The sandbox epics increased my *strength*, *agility* and *endurance*. It was a good thing at least that apart from the pluses to the two main stats, the set items upgraded secondary stats too: bonuses to ranged and critical damage, accuracy and crit chance...

For example, my plate helmet:

Unconquered Herald's Mask
Epic, Unconquered Herald set item
Scalable
Plate armor.
Armor: 127.
+26 charisma.
+27 luck.
+19% attack speed with ranged weaponry.
+12% accuracy.
Durability: 900 / 900.
Sale price: 650 gold coins.
Chance of loss after death lowered by 90%.

Simply put, I was crazily charismatic and devilishly lucky in this set.

The Destroying Plague

Crag, who had observed my transformation with his mouth agape, was surprised when I offered him gear too, but he didn't refuse. Two 'dummies' was enough to replace his *blue* helmet and shoulderplates. All the rest of the boy's gear was epic, gotten by farming sandbox instances that were a breeze for him. We decided to keep the rest until the clan was assembled and distribute it by need.

Then something strange happened. I felt a piercing and interested gaze on my back and turned around: one of the lich bosses was staring at me from beyond the defensive barrier, but I was getting used to that by now. Crag was rooting through his interface, throwing on gear, and not looking at me. Everyone was in a trance in the temple, even Patrick. Behemoth stood with eyes closed. His avatar flickered more and more often, threatening to disappear completely. But the gaze wasn't from there. When the presence disappeared, the following appeared in my logs:

Luck increased by 500. You have caught the interest of Fortuna, the goddess of luck.

Your reputation with Fortuna, Goddess of Luck, has increased: +100.
Current reputation: affection.

I hoped Behemoth didn't get jealous. He'd sing his song again: another new little god, of whom there are more than a small world with a limited amount of energy can afford; demigods, imagining themselves to be who knows what! Hands off my initial! Oh well, I'd deal with that later.

Once I was done with the equipment, I checked my *Depths Teleportation* cooldown: 13... 12... 11... It was time.

Rising, I shouted to Crag.

"Ready?"

"Always, but for what? Even in this new gear and with my buff, we can't take these things out."

"We can't. And attacking the mobs ourselves would be dumb, I can't die. But we're not going alone. We're putting together a whole team of monster allies."

"You mean your new friends? But how? The praying mantis and the dinosaur have been unconscious since the undead broke free, and we can't reach the tavern. That lich over there will kill us without even having to move from his post," Crag pointed to a figure hanging in the air about a hundred feet from us. The boss methodically fired some brown smoking balls of some sort of magic at the defensive barrier, keeping his eyes on me always. "No chance, Scyth."

"We can get to the tavern another way."

Understanding lit up in the boy's eyes.

"The Depths? But they only send you to a random spot in the chosen location?"

"Before. It used to teleport you to any random spot, if only you knew the place. Then it became possible to fix a specific location. But at skill level ten, the choice got even more precise."

"One sec... So you can portal us right into the tavern?"

"Bingo. Now I have the ability to choose a specific place within a location. The guys mentioned something about this, but only in passing."

"Let's jump."

"Wait. Let's try bringing Anf and Ripta."

The boy nodded excitedly — he couldn't wait to try this venture. And he wasn't risking anything; even if he got Subthreat penalties, the rewards from his personal Threat would easily compensate them.

We returned to the temple, pressed our way through the crowd of the devout to Behemoth and spoke to the god.

"Sleeping God, I need help from Anf and Ripta."

"Without their support, I cannot hold the defensive barrier long," he answered, opening his eyes.

"You won't have to hold it long."

Without saying anything, Behemoth closed his eyes again. The insectoid and the raptor started coming to. Both their health bars were in the orange zone, but that should be enough for my plan. Especially since I planned to heal the guardians.

We helped them rise, and considering their huge frames, that wasn't easy. Then I tossed Anf the *Bottomless Healing Potion* flask. His health was lower than Ripta's.

"Drink," I said, showing with a gesture what I wanted from him.

The insectoid, who really did look like a gigantic praying mantis, grabbed the potion in his pincers and chugged it. His health bar started to rise. The insect's type reminded me of Iggy, and I summoned the pet. He appeared in his true form.

Anf returned my potion. Iggy restlessly ran circles around the insectoid and got some strokes as a reward. The needler chirped in satisfaction.

"Enough chatter, guys," I interrupted their friendly conversation. "Ripta, I'll let you drink too, fix your health. Only a little later, in five minutes."

I waved the empty vessel. The dinosaur seemed to understand, squawked something, and then Crag came and pulled out his own *Medium Health Potion*.

"Not much for your level," he said regretfully. "But better than nothing."

The raptor drank it and cheered up. The health bar crawled up from the orange zone, and the terrible wounds left by Anf's razor-sharp arms healed up. Behemoth's strength wasn't unlimited. We needed to hurry.

"Alright. Ripta. Anf," I pointed my finger at them and continued my speech, complete with gestures for better understanding. "We. Are jumping. To Flaygray and Nega. You. You. Me. Him. Them. Will fight.

The raptor emitted an abrupt, trumpet-like sound. Anf made do with a laconic chirp. I exchanged a glance with Crag. He nodded and I activated *Depths Teleportation*.

Good luck, I suddenly heard Fortuna say in my head.

Nether! It's a good thing Behemoth didn't hear her!

Chapter 10

The Worms Will Eat You From Within

I SUSPECTED that the Pig and Whistle clan tavern wouldn't survive an assault like this, and we'd have to rebuild it. We got there without any surprises, ending up by the same table I was seated at last time.

Casting a quick glance around, I saw that all the furniture had been moved to barricade the doors and windows. The undead were still trying to climb and break their way in, but they got stuck and blocked the entrances for the others. The puddles of blood, bone shards, smoke, soot and sickly-sweet smells weren't creating a particularly positive atmosphere. Halloween was half a year away, damn it!

"Glad to see you, boss!" The succubus curtsied, picked up a bottle of dwarfish brandy from the floor and took a long swig. "I know a little of the language of the dead. Our undead guests have said a great deal of interest about your good self..."

"Not here, Nega!" Flaygray interrupted his girlfriend. His voice shook and he was barely keeping his poise. "The lich tried to convert us to his side, but I sent him to Azmodan's ass with great pleasure. All the same, he managed to tell us a thing or two. And Nega, I must admit, almost agreed..."

"Agreed? Forget it, we don't have time..." I started saying, but then fell silent when I saw nobody was listening to me.

Nega rushed to a far window blocked up with tables, grabbed the skull of a twitching skeleton, pulled and tore the head from the body. The body kept moving, but the succubus didn't bother finishing it off. She smashed the skull against a wall and turned to me.

"'Agreed' is a strong word," she threw, continuing her enlightened conversation. "I just asked about the conditions. Then I explained to the lich that I was busy for now, but maybe, after my contract with the boss... Ow!" she cried as a tiny fireball from the satyr hit her in the ass. Nega's tail twitched nervously as she rubbed her scorched buttcheek. "Flay! You old lech!"

"No negotiations behind the boss's back, got it, you little witch? Sorry, Scyth, she's still young..."

Ripta drowned out Flaygray's voice — the raptor shrieked aggressively and rushed over to a far corner, where a zombie was already rising after falling down through the ceiling. A few waves of the spear laid the creature's spirit to rest with all its health points. Anf excitedly scampered around the room in search of an enemy, found the unfinished skeleton and started crushing it into bone dust.

Nega watched him and chuckled drunkenly.

"Fine. I'm guilty! Punish me! Spank me, boss!"

Without a pause in her speech, she snapped her whip at a level two hundred and seventy *Brainless Zombie* that had broken through the barrier. Still laughing, she approached the struggling creature and mercilessly smashed its head in with an elegant hoof. Worms wriggled out of the skull and the succubus wrinkled her nose. Iggy, interested in the worms, flew over to this unexpected lunch. Then, after waiting for my permission, he started chowing down. I didn't watch.

Crag stood silently; his eyes glued to the succubus. Judging by his attempts to tear his gaze away, this boy from a very religious background was struggling with temptation. And it was winning.

In the meantime, Flaygray ran to one of the windows, glanced through a gap for a second and fired a few fireballs out onto the street.

"Damn lich," he swore. "Ugh, I hope he comes to me in the afterlife! I'll pull out his soul!"

"I'm afraid you won't meet him again. He's linked to the Destroying Plague..." the succubus answered.

"He and his master are upstarts! Where did this Destroying Plague come from anyway? In my day, we didn't have anything like that in the Underworld."

I opened my mouth again to shift the conversation to something constructive, but the succubus spoke first.

"Alright! If the boss doesn't want to spank me, and Flay is more interested in that gross lich's ass, then maybe..." Nega took another swig of brandy. Her gaze swept across Anf and Ripta and stopped on Crag. The succubus crooked a finger at him. "Come to me, boy."

"I don't think so." I grabbed the enchanted Tobias and shook him by the collar.

The undead had stopped trying to press through all the cracks, and the lich hadn't yet raised the fallen ones. Maybe he had a cooldown on that ability? I took advantage of the breather.

"Flaygray, why haven't you pushed through to the temple? These dead guys are no match for you!"

"It's not that simple," the satyr said darkly. "Nega almost killed me. The lich took control of her."

Only now did I notice that he had less than half his health, and long wounds covered his body. As if from a whip. The succubus looked almost unharmed. It seemed Flay had decided not to attack his old flame. The same as what happened to Anf and Ripta. It was so unlucky that they happened to be split into pairs!

"But he's a lot weaker than you, and now there are six of us. Where are the others? Aunt Stephanie, the miners?"

"The people are upstairs. This is no place for them," the succubus answered soberly. "The lich really isn't that strong. Physically. His power is in something else — as you've realized, he can take over other minds. I have the highest defense against such magics, but the power that bastard has... It's something else. Tell me, boss, if it happens again and one of us kills one of the group... would that sit right with you?"

"That won't happen. Crag isn't just any ordinary guy, Nega. His talent will give us a huge boost. Even if the lich does take control of someone's mind, the others will focus on the enemy. Dead lich and living ally."

"That changes things!" the satyr rubbed his palms together. "Because the lich's curse cannot be removed. I barely managed to get out of there," he added. "The humans helped me with the barricades, but Nega got in and hurt many people. When she finally came around for some unknown reason, I was on my last legs..."

I guessed the lich got distracted when Patrick and I appeared. If I'd been a minute or two late, the tavern would be cleansed, Flaygray would be dead, and the undead raid would have unleashed its entire strength on the temple barrier.

Ripta emitted a series of noises as if someone had blown into a whistle several times. The satyr nodded to the dinosaur and spoke.

"Now that we're all together, I swear on

Beelzebub's belly that the lich will learn the true fury of the Underworld!"

"Don't anger the Sleeping Gods," Nega hissed. "What's the plan, boss?"

The map showed the whole fort with the enemy markers. Three dozen undead and one lich were attacking the temple's protective barrier from all sides. Another lich had the tavern surrounded with a little over twenty skeletons, zombies, a rotter and a queaser. A small group of undead had made their way inside through the back door, but they had no way through to the main hall — the door was locked and blocked with oak tables.

"The overall plan is this. We go out. We give that lich a beatdown. We put the undead out of their misery. We go to the temple and do the same there. But first, let's clear the tavern itself so the people upstairs don't get hurt."

By then, my *Bottomless Healing Potion* had finished cooling down and I let Flay drink it. The whip wounds healed, and now our team no longer looked like a gang of cripples. Flaygray had even sobered up.

While Crag and I took apart the blockade at the back door, the others stood at the ready. After freeing up the space, I pulled the latch open and quickly jumped back. The door flew open and the dead began to pour into the tavern with a dull moan. I glanced at one of them and calmed down.

Ancient Skeleton Warrior, level 247

A piece of cake for my team of monsters, I thought, and... was wrong. There were too many of the zombies and skeletons — we couldn't handle all of them at once. Only Flaygray among us had area of effect spells, but his *Wall of Fire*, which threatened to burn down the whole tavern, just set the undead on fire. The building filled with smoke and the stink of burning meat. Smashing through the doorway, a queaser forced his way into the hall.

"Scyth, get back!" Crag shouted.

Retreating, I activated *Ghastly Howl* and started shooting arrow after arrow into the zombies in the hope of slowing them down at least a little. The ability didn't do much, as expected, and the arrows uselessly glanced off or clattered away, dealing no damage.

Three skeletons were hanging off the satyr, a *Sickening Rotter* was crushing the praying mantis, the succubus and the raptor were locked in desperate close combat. Crag kept himself to the side — if he died, we'd lose his buff.

A dozen or so of the mobs grabbing onto the guardians died, but rose again immediately, revived by the magic of the dead. And once revived, they changed their tactics. They stopped focusing on the guardians and, stubbornly ignoring the strikes raining down on them, they pushed through toward me. And one of them made it.

I trusted my theoretical calculations, but when the legless skeleton at level two hundred and seventy nimbly crawled toward me, I still got scared for a moment. The pain was tolerable, and the damage took away less than a quarter of my health. Dangerous, but not deadly. The important thing was to get out of the way. The next second, a double fireball from Flaygray killed the legless skeleton.

In the hellish cacophony of screams, chitters, growls, groans, the whistle of split air and the crack of broken bones, I heard a rustle behind me. Turning around, I saw that the undead that Nega had killed were rising.

Everyone regrouped on me, treading on the bodies of crawling zombies.

"This plan isn't working, boss," the succubus said, breathing heavily. "We need a new one."

"They'll rise again, no matter how many we kill." I looked at my allies' health bars. Nobody was badly hurt. "Let's get outside. We'll kill the lich, then the servants will be easier to take care of."

"All the same!" Flaygray bleated, smashing another skull. "If he takes control of one of us..."

I didn't know who he was more worried about: himself or the succubus. But I went through the strategy again to calm the satyr down.

"Whoever he takes control of, the others have to break through to the lich. Once we kill him, the control will fall. He needs me, so I'll go first. If he tries to take over my mind, he'll break his rotten teeth on it."

The satyr conveyed the plan to Ripta, who

passed it on to Anf. Swinging and pressing the undead back, the seven-foot raptor and the almost as large insectoid threw aside the barricades covering the main entrance and burst out onto the street. The rest rushed through the open doorway. Beyond the threshold, we stood in a circle, back to back, and started approaching the boss so that I was always the closest to him.

The lich was sat by the barracks on the other side of the street. He reminded me of Dargo, the main boss in the instance under the temple of Nergal, who the late Clayton had played. A mantle like an upside-down tulip covered his body, with sharp petals spreading out in all directions.

Cursed Lich Koshch, level 306
Magical Creature
Boss

Koshch floated, not touching the ground with his blackened bare feet. When he saw me, he hissed something and I couldn't tell if everyone heard him or if his voice just appeared in my head.

"Apostate... Traitor..."

He disappeared, then appeared again right in front of me. His extended bony fingers grabbed me by the head, pouring tons of death magic damage into me. His blackened fingernails sank into my skull, crushing the bone and pressing toward my brain. I screamed from the hellish pain, but he wasn't

The Destroying Plague

actually doing that much damage — almost all of it was split among my allies. Their health was much higher than mine, and along with Crag's buff...

"Pathetic, weak mortal!" the emissary hissed. "You cannot withstand the might of the Destroying Plague!"

My *vindication* meter was quickly rising, but it wasn't necessary. My party members threw themselves at the emissary of the Destroying Plague all at once. Nega struck the boss with her whip, tearing off half of his rotting face; a series of Flaygray's fireballs burned a whole in his chest, and the lich's clothes caught fire. Stunning him with a strike of his powerful tail and interrupting his spell, Ripta pierced the lich with his spear, and from the back Anf attacked him with his sharpened saw limbs. My *Combo* missed, as did Crag's sword strike. Koshch turned and took control of Nega's mind, choosing her as the strongest. The succubus looked at me. Her icon disappeared from the group list.

"No!" screamed Flaygray when Iggy leapt to my defense and attacked Nega.

"Hit the lich!" I roared. "Flaygray! The lich!"

Nega swung. Her long whip with sharp needles all along its imposing length struck my back, tearing away skin, flesh and bones. Then Nega pulled the whip back...

Through their combined strength, the guardians finished off the boss before my health fell into the red zone. The battle didn't last long, but they were the longest ten seconds of my life.

The Cursed Lich Koshch is dead.

Groaning in pain, I gulped down the health potion and asked Crag to pour some on my back. My damaged flesh hissed and smoked, and the wound drew closed. I sighed in relief, but it was too soon to relax — the dead were approaching behind me, even without their boss.

The second lich wasn't nearby, so it was easier to fight the creatures off. The liches might be able to maintain control over a limited number of minions, which would explain why the mobs had split up instead of crushing the barrier together — the officers of the Destroying Plague identified the dangerous enemies and prevented them from uniting.

Anf and Ripta, our melee fighters, took on the skeletons. Nega beat everyone within sight with her whip, while Crag finished off or tried to finish off some undead set alight by Flaygray. My *Thorn Aura* showed its worth, constantly firing without missing, but the damage had harsh diminishing returns, and the mobs took mere scratches — I noted this while automatically firing at the walking dead.

The *Foul Queaser* was the hardest to deal with. The Destroying Plague had upgraded the mob, and it had learned how to cast corpse venom *DoTs* and cruel slimy worms. It sounds funny, but the worms were at level two hundred, and only Flaygray's *Wall of Fire*

The Destroying Plague

kept them from reaching me.

In the end, neither Crag nor myself got experience — our team members were too high level. For every level above the mobs, the game applied a ten percent experience penalty. Any player more than ten levels higher than a mob deprived the whole party of experience. Given the level difference between my guardians and the lich and his minions, nobody got anything.

Once we'd dealt with a portion of the Destroying Plague's raid, we looked around. Scraps of flesh glistened all around, bones gleamed, and puddles of disgusting grime steamed from the queaser and rotter. On the spot where the lich died, who dissipated after his final death, some dust still remained. Ghostly smoke rose from it and snaked toward the temple. Either Behemoth was absorbing its energy, or this lich's life force was seeping into the other one.

Judging by the map, the second boss, feeling something amiss, was already assembling squads and moving toward us. From where we stood, we could see them marching down the street.

"Damn, no experience, no loot," Crag complained. "This is bullshit, Scyth!"

"We'll head to a normal instance at our level someday soon," I reassured him. "The weekend is coming up, we'll have time to farm and level up, don't worr..."

The popping of torn space heralded the coming

of a group of new guests. On the street, right between us and the remaining undead, the kobolds appeared. I also saw the figures of Tissa and Infect blinking in the crowd.

Seeing me, the girl waved her hand, describing a hanged man, and disappeared along with Malik, not waiting for death by *Exhaustion*, which killed faster than the torrid heat of the Lakharian Desert.

My familiar kobold renegades milled around in confusion in the middle of the fort. And judging by the rapidly approaching living dead, they only had a few more heartbeats left to live.

I was the first to run to them. I took out another skeleton archer close by with *Sleeping Vindication* before he could loose an arrow at a kobold , and stuck myself between the kobold chief, who was eagerly rushing to his death in battle, and a rotter. Hitting the thing was pointless, but I still tried a *Stunning Kick* before commanding:

"Grog'hyr, move your people over there! Now, hurry!"

I pointed the chief toward the approaching monsters: the hoofed satyr, the succubus demoness, the seven-foot raptor and the giant insect. The old shaman's jaw dropped, and his eyes widened.

"Those are demons!"

"They're our demons, Ryg'har!" I took an arrow while protecting the shaman. "Come on! Hurry!"

The tribe chief handed out the required clouts round the ear and barked orders to get his tribesmen to move, personally showing them the way. The other kobolds trotted after him.

I retreated too, fearing that the advancing undead might have enough total damage to kill me. Especially since my health still hadn't recovered from the attacks from Koshch and Nega. I doubted it would recover before we were done.

My allies stopped when they reached me.

"We can't get through to the lich without a fight. Think we can take them?" Flaygray asked.

"I have a better idea. I'll try to draw them off, you go for the lich. I think he'll chase me."

"Alright," Flaygray answered.

"Another thing. Get someone to escort the kobolds to Behemoth, he's having a tough time."

Using my speed advantage, I started kiting the undead toward the tavern. Stretching out into a scattered chain and ignoring the other enemies, the dead men shambled after me. A second lich spurred them on, twin to the first.

Cursed Lich Shazz, level 396
Magical Creature
Boss

I stopped in my tracks when I saw his level. When I checked his stats from the temple steps, he was the same as Koshch. Had the death of the first lich strengthened the second? My confidence in a good outcome reeled. Now the boss was stronger than my guards, and by a long way. How would we deal with it?

My thoughts ran feverishly while I ran in zigzags, laying a route: rounding buildings, firing slowing arrows (all missing) and hoping to needle the undead to death with *Thorn Aura*. By my humblest estimates, that would take days of constant kiting.

Constantly looking around, I saw Crag leading the kobolds behind the barrier, the guardians surrounding Shazz and the lich beginning to fight them. At first everything was going well, and the boss's icon burned a constant red, showing that he was under ceaseless attack.

A lot of the hits missed the boss. Even for Nega at level three hundred and twenty, the boss was too much. But the lich was taking significant damage from Crag's talent. Just as I was thinking that we might get through it, everything changed: Nega's icon turned red and disappeared from the group.

Under the lich's control, the succubus enchanted Flaygray and the satyr quit the battle. I didn't see the rest, because I'd run to the fort's exit, and the three-dozen undead in a chain blocked my view.

A large red inscription appeared in the center of my field of view:

Crag, level 27 dwarf warrior, has died.

Did the succubus take Crag out first, knowing

the value he added to the group? Couldn't fault the lich for his strategy.

Crowded out by the undead, I was forced to retreat from the fort. And in the end, I ran, because something even more terrible joined the common walking dead. *Bone Hounds*, assembled by magic from the skeletons of the dead, and *Plague Vectors*, gray blobs that took no physical damage. I'd encountered them in Tristad during the assault.

The hounds were at least as fast as I was, and as soon as I saw them, I made a run for the jungle as fast as I could. Pushing my way through the undergrowth and trees, tripping over roots, I ran and wished with all my heart that the guardians succeeded and managed to get behind the barrier if they started to smell burning.

The next notifications that appeared in my field of view a few seconds later finally crushed all my hopes:

> *Ripta, level 307 predator, raptor, has died.*
> *Anf, level 310 flayer, colicoid, has died.*
> *Flaygray, level 305 adventure, satyr, has died.*

The *Bone Hounds* silently followed somewhere behind me. My *vigor* was into the yellow zone, but I kept moving. Then I got a last message:

> *Nega, level 320 temptress, succubus, has*

died.

A triumphant whisper carried on the wind:

"Worthless traitor! The worms will eat you from within!"

The sickly-sweet smell of rot filled my nostrils.

Chapter 11

Walking Dead

THE SKY WAS ALMOST completely obscured with stormclouds. A tropical downpour could start at any moment. The air thickened and seemed almost tangible, making each breath a challenge. I would have winded myself after ten minutes of running like that in real life. I knew that for sure from my physical education lessons.

In Dis, thanks to my leveled-up *endurance*, I lasted a lot longer. But running is pointless if you don't know where you're running to, and you can't stop. Breathing deeply and heavily, I started to feel sick. The sweet smells of the jungle (flowering plants, raw earth and damp wood) added to the stink of the rotting undead corpses.

I heard the hounds' bones crunching as they chased me into a thicket, and along with my heart beating its way out of my chest — my real heart, in real life — my panicking brain ran through my survival options at the same feverish rhythm. One of those ideas — doable, though risky — was using the

Montosaurus. The huge boss, who had already eaten one lich just because it felt like it, was wandering the island somewhere. Introducing him to the second dead warlock would be a great solution. For everyone except the lich and his master, the Nucleus of the Destroying Plague.

With that thought, I found the tallest peak of the mountain range in the north of Kharinza, oriented myself by it and started to move with more purpose: I changed my direction and moved toward the mine. By Manny's words, the dinosaur now wandered there constantly, having realized that there were always snacks to be had around the mine. The miners made peace with this, drawing lots at each shift to decide who would die. The unlucky man wolfed down an anesthetic — the strongest dwarven ale — and went to distract the monster, clearing the path into the mines for the others. They returned from their shifts the same way.

"You will serve, mortal," the lich's voice whispered.

The echo in the jungle created the sensation that the undead were all around, but the minimap convinced me otherwise: the walking dead were stretched out in a chain, and the boss closed it, ever crying:

"Traitor! Accept your fate!"

His insistent challenges distracted me, messed with my head, but I stopped paying attention to them and tried to concentrate.

The Destroying Plague

Was it possible that what was happening was just another modeling of the future from *Divine Revelation*? Unlikely. It was probably still on cooldown.

Could I leave the game just by pressing the Quit button? No, not in combat, that wouldn't work. An emergency exit from the capsule? My character would be considered killed if I was in combat when I did that. Not to mention that the temple of the Sleepers and the civilians would be without protection. Even with the help of Patrick, the workers and the kobold tribe, Behemoth wouldn't be able to hold up the barrier for long. The treasury guardians...

If Crag stayed in the group after reviving, then Flaygray, Nega, Anf and Ripta had just disappeared as if they'd never been. My heart clenched painfully at the thought that I might not be able to bring them back. Ordinary mobs respawned, but not them.

Refusing to believe in the finality of their death, I opened the clan member list. Scyth, Crawler, Bomber, Tissa, Infect, Crag, Patrick. Period. My eyes stung. I saw the dead guardians not just as NPCs I barely knew. Flaygray had seemed far more alive to me than some human beings. Nega, who had protected the civilians in the tavern out of nothing but good will. Ripta and Anf, ready to sacrifice themselves if only they could help Behemoth hold back the undead onslaught and protect the miners... No, they were alive. And I was proud to call them my friends...

The chat icon flashed. The notification sound

was lost in the drawn-out roar of the dinosaur from the direction of the mines.

[18:09] [Clan] [Crag]: You OK, Scyth? All the undead went after you, the fort is clear. Should I come help?

[18:09] [Clan] [Scyth]: You can't get through to me. I'm going to try and kite the lich to the dinosaur. Stay close to Behemoth. How is he?

[18:10] [Clan] [Crag]: Flickering. He doesn't speak to me, I'm not even an adept.

[18:10] [Clan] [Crawler]: What's going on over there? Bomb and I are ready to jump to the fort!

[18:11] [Clan] [Scyth]: Don't even think about it. If I fail, we'll need you in Darant.

Forcing my way through the undergrowth, I jumped out onto a rocky open space. The mountains towered above me; their northern cliffs lapped by the waters of the Bottomless Ocean. The dinosaur stood at the entrance to the mine with its tail to me, looking inside the mine. Too used to its evening meal, that overgrown lizard!

A huge hundred-foot hulk, blue-black in color, with an undetermined level and sixty million health — let's see how the lich would stand up to this.

I looked to the side — about sixty feet away were the rocky elevations that I'd used to hide from the Montosaurus before. The ore in this spot broke through the surface, and it was there that we'd gotten

The Destroying Plague

our first resources for building the temple. Taking a few paces toward the beast, I estimated the distance, stopped and looked around. The undergrowth rustled. The Montosaurus turned its head, let out an earthshaking roar and began to trample its way toward me.

I mentally counted to three and threw myself along the undergrowth to the shelter of the crevasse. The Montosaurus snapped its jaws only inches from my back when five *Bone Hounds* leapt on it from out of the bushes. Naturally, I didn't see it — I was running as fast as I could to jump into the crevasse before the dinosaur used *Icy Roar*.

I fell into it just as the Montosaurus sounded out its earsplitting roar. My muscles immediately froze, and my body stopped obeying me under the influence of a *Terror* debuff. I could still hear everything: a crack, a dull thud, a crackle — and the bone shards of one of the hounds flew by above me. Several red marks disappeared on the minimap, with just one large one remaining — the Montosaurus.

My *Terror* debuff ended and I dared to take a look outside. The dinosaur was chewing the bones left from the hounds. The map showed that four *Plague Vectors* were approaching it. Those didn't take physical damage.

I heard the Montosaurus's noisy breath. It stretched its head toward the forest and froze, listening to something. The black dots of the *Plague Vectors* emerged from the undergrowth and the dinosaur emitted a throaty rumbling sound like a cough. Then, fire!

A stream of bright white napalm streamed across the ground, pouring over the newly arrived enemies. A moment later, they died. Within thirty seconds, the lich boss had lost all his *Bone Hounds* and *Plague Vectors*!

Next from the woods came a *Sickening Rotter* and a *Foul Quease*. Paying no attention to the dinosaur, both of them walked efficiently toward me. As if not believing its luck, the Montosaurus froze, cocked its head and assessed the quantity of food in front it, then caught up to both of them in one step.

Crushing the rotter underfoot, it grabbed the quease in its huge maw and swallowed it whole, growling deeply. Then, holding the rotter in its claws, it tore off its upper section, snorted in surprise and spat it out. It coughed again, rubbed its face with its arm — maybe it didn't like the taste of the slime — and sprayed out a string of flame. Nothing but a smoking crater remained of the queaser, and the Montosaurus itself sharply moved from its spot and trampled away toward the ocean, the ground shaking in its wake.

Another couple of minutes passed while I chewed through what I'd seen and accepted that plan A had failed, and plan B would need at least a little calm time. Then the first skeletons and zombies began to emerge from the forest.

The Destroying Plague

---

* * *

Even at such a hopeless moment, I unwillingly thought of leveling up. *Stealth* was useless against such high-level enemies, but I still switched it on. Even a split second of not being seen by undead over level two hundred played its role:

Stealth level increased: +4! Current level: 71.

Chance to remain unnoticed to enemies increased to 71%.

Immediately after the notification, the first skeleton that shambled out onto the rocky ground saw me and moved to intercept, its bones rattling. The magic that prevented it from decaying weaved its way in a fine, barely noticeable stream through the air into the depths of the jungle, like a thread leading to the puppetmaster.

Stealth check failed! Seen by Skeleton Warrior!

With my speed, the skeletons and zombies shouldn't have been a problem. Without waiting for these guests, I left the gorge that had now saved me twice and ran away, cutting a path through to the fort. I'd reunite with Crag, and if Behemoth's defensive barrier was still active, I could rest and do something else to save us.

I had two real ideas in my head and one suicidal one. The first required money, lots of money, Crawler and Bomber in Darant, and... luck. A lot of luck. The suicidal idea was to ask for help from Yary, one of the Modus leaders. A most foolish thought, but it was a way of choosing a lesser evil and dying another day. I wanted to leave that crazy option as a last resort.

As I ran, I mentally wrote a message in the chat:

[18:24] [Clan] [Scyth]: Crawler, Bomb, I need you in Darant. Now! Also: does clan mail work instantly? How long does it take for items to deliver?

[18:24] [Clan] [Crawler]: Understood. We're jumping to Darant. Mail is almost instant for a level 10 clan. Ours delivers gear in 30 minutes.

[18:25] [Clan] [Scyth]: That'll do. Here's what I need: I'm going to send you some unidentified artifacts, I need you to identify them at the University of Magic. Bomb, you need to get to the mercenary guild and find out what's what there. A special condition: we only want max level NPCs.

The mercenary guild was famous for its soldiers of fortune keeping their mouths shut. Everything they learned during their missions stayed between them and their clients. The reason for that wasn't just the astronomical penalties and the guild's flawless reputation from its business on all three inhabited continents. There were also certain divine oaths involved. The guild's mercenaries couldn't break their silence even if they wanted to. But I believed that player mercenaries weren't bound by their oaths outside Disgardium, so I decided it was better to hire locals. Those would keep their mouths shut even if you hired them to depose King Bastian the First.

I sent Crawler the Balancer, Elemental Concentration and Thunderbearer as the most suitable for this situation judging by their names. I doubted that the slotless artifacts Isis' Blessing or Ebis' Inspiration could help in battle, but I sent them too. The rest of what I hadn't gone through from the treasury, not counting the 'dummies,' was various kinds of class legendaries or high-ranked epics unsuitable to any of us and requiring no identification. Apart from that, I put one million gold into the mail, leaving myself only three hundred thousand and change.

The clan treasury remained untouched: betting it all, frivolously hoping to make it back in the short term and depriving myself of the chance to study in university was idiotic. I doubted we'd meet another Threat to get us rich so quick again.

[18:26] [Clan] [Crawler]: We're in Darant. Let's do it. Hold on there.

Somewhere in the distance, I heard the trample

of the Montosaurus. I listened hopefully, thinking about whether it was worth dragging the chain of enemies back to the monster, but decided not to risk it. It could tear me to shreds with the same success, and if it did then neither artifacts nor mercenaries would help me. It was a good thing that there was only one supermob on Kharinza. If there were normal ones here, I doubted we'd be able to set up our base and mine ore so easily. Their level would probably be much higher than ours.

I didn't run full-pelt to the fort, instead trying to buy time. I led the chain of mobs in zigzags, periodically activating *Stealth* and leveling it up by eleven points in total. The most important thing was not to fall prey to arrows from the *Skeleton Archers* and to keep at least fifty feet away. They didn't fire over that distance for some reason. Bomber let me know in the clan chat that my package had reached its target.

[19:01] [Clan] [Bomber]: You didn't tell us you were a millionaire, Scyth! We split the cash.

As I ran through the forest, I awaited news from the boys and hoped Behemoth was getting a breather. While there were no enemies, the Sleeping God was saving his energy for the protective barrier and spending his strength only on neutralizing the *Infection.*

But Crawler and Bomber needed time to get to

the required places. Darant was huge, its streets winding and filled with people. At least the University of Magic and the Guild of Mercenaries was in the center.

I ran through the jungle, exchanging messages with Crag, gaining ground on the mobs, going into *Stealth*, then taking to my heels again when they detected me. The lich was silent when he lost me from view but spat his threats again as soon as his minions found me. The initial shock of the death of the guardians had passed, along with my sense of hopelessness — we had a plan, and we followed it.

When I tore away from the dead chain once again and laid down in a small ravine, Hung contacted me again.

[19:11] [Clan] [Bomber]: Alright, I'm at the guild of mercenaries. It's more complex than we thought — turns out not just anyone can walk in and use their services. The whole range is available only to people who have a high reputation with them. You also have to sign a basic contract, either on behalf of a clan or personally. I think it'd be better to sign it on behalf of the Awoken, the clan's reputation with the guild will affect everyone. I need more authority, Scyth.

Opening the clan management page, I gave Bomber the right to sign contracts on behalf of the clan, and a couple of minutes later he gave me the low-down:

[19:14] [Clan] [Bomber]: Alright, we can't hire soldiers for inter-clan warfare, for eliminating hostile players, for... Long story short, we can basically only hire locals and only against hostile mobs. I think the Destroying Plague and his guys match those conditions, right, Scyth? The maximum available levels for hiring right now are: 360-370. The cost: 50,000 per soldier per hour. Hmm... And another condition: if the enemy's level exceeds the level of the mercenaries, the minimum number of troops you can hire is a battle star, five intelligent creatures. What level is that lich?

Quarter of a million gold for a star per hour? That was a year of university! That kind of money could buy a premium-class flyer! I whistled.

The lich immediately replied with a piercing whisper.

"The worms will eat you from within, traitor!"

"They've already eaten you!" I couldn't resist shouting in response. "Corpse!"

Crag answered Bomber in my place, indicating the boss's level. Tobias also entered the discussion, but mostly to drop dumb jokes and generally fail to take the situation seriously. It seemed he was getting bored among the adepts praying to the Sleeping God in the temple. Having learned the lich's level, Bomber was silent for a couple of minutes, then wrote:

[19:17] [Clan] [Bomber]: So how many mercenaries are we taking? The minimum is a star

---

given the boss's level. We have enough for two. If we need more, I'll need Crawler's money.

Would a single squad be enough? Theoretically, with Crag's buff, it should be. Even if the lich took control of one of the mercenaries, the mobs were still at level two hundred. We could hire two stars to make it a sure thing. An hour should be enough to grind the lich and his dead minions to powder. But a quarter of a million into the wind? If we profited from selling the artifacts even after identifying them, then the mercenaries... In our case we wouldn't even get experience for the undead, let alone loot.

[19:18] [Clan] [Crawler]: Our reputation with the University of Magic is zero. I planned to study there, but at first, I had no money, then there were other things on my mind. The cost for us to identify one artifact is 450 tons of gold, Scyth. That means there's only enough for one artifact. Decide which. You know better what you guys need there.

I froze, shocked by the cost of simply identifying an artifact. You could buy a top-range legendary for money like that! No wonder the Darant University of Magic was flourishing.

Behind me, thirty feet away, the approaching zombies groaned. I set off into a run again, jumping over weeds and strange red vines hanging from tree to tree, and remembered something Nega had said about a certain balancing spell. Then I weighed all the pros and cons of hiring two stars of mercenaries. Then I ran through the names of the artifacts in my head again but basing my decision on names only would be foolish. How could you understand based on the name 'Mark of the Destroying Plague' that it was one of the most imba things in the game? My only hope left was that Fortuna would help me.

[19:20] [Clan] [Scyth]: Crawler, identify the Balancer. Let's see what it is. If we're out of luck, then we'll hire two stars.

For the next five minutes, probably while one of the university mages was identifying the artifact, I felt terribly anxious. My *vigor* was in the red zone, and I felt a crushing tiredness descend on me again. Two days on my feet without so much as a nap, and now a lich with an undead army at my heels. The boss's brains must have completely rotted away, since he was repeating the same thing to me over and over like a wind-up toy.

But my wait was worth it.

Crawler's next message filled me with hope.

[19:25] [Clan] [Crawler]: Jackpot, Scyth! Check out the description!

The item's name burned red — it was divine quality!

The Destroying Plague

Balancer
Divine
Bracelet.
On activation: on damage, balances the target with the attacker for 5 seconds.
Cooldown: 24 hours.
Chance of loss after death lowered by 100%.

I gasped when I saw the imba bracelet that was now in my treasury. Just one star would be enough with such a *Balancer*. Sure, the lich was strong, extremely powerful, but what could he do against a harmonious team of five professional mercenaries almost equal to him in level? Especially strengthened by Crag's talent? And with the *Balancer*?

Exactly. Nothing at all.

* * *

The sun was almost hidden behind the treetops. The downpour never did happen. A thick veil of moisture hung in the air.

Crag and I stood at the temple, watching the undead rampaging below, beyond the shield. The lich Shazz, his arms outstretched, seemed to be channeling all the strength of the Destroying Plague to try and destroy Behemoth's shield. Muddy, gray-green flows of *plague energy* streamed into the barrier. Three dozen zombies and skeletons added their damage to the already buckling shield at the same time.

"When you were hanging out with these guys..." Crag nodded at the dead, "were you the same?

I found the most decayed zombie and pointed at it.

"Sometimes I looked like that. Or even worse. It all depended on how long I'd had the undead curse.

Having seen what was happening, Crag and I went back into the temple. Someone was piling the bodies of the dead guardians by a far column. Maybe Behemoth had ordered them brought to the temple, or maybe it was at the workers' own initiative.

While I ran, the god's avatar hunched, faded and dwindled — the Sleeping God was flickering, unable to hold back my *Infection* and maintain the barrier and his avatar at the same time. Fortunately, there wasn't much longer to wait. Crawler had almost met up with Bomber, who had hired a battle star of mercenaries.

I approached Behemoth and spoke to him.

"My friends... Flaygray, Nega, Ripta and Anf... Are they gone for good?"

The god's avatar did not speak, but I heard his voice in my head: *Tiamat can bring them back. They did not become true followers of the Sleeping Gods, but they believed with all their heart. Their battle is not over.*

Sighing in relief, I decided to help Behemoth with my presence for at least a few minutes until the reinforcements arrived. I sat in lotus position and thought: *How do I pray?* Behemoth answered that the words didn't matter; only faith in the Sleeping Gods mattered. Patrick was sitting nearby and looked almost asleep, but his lips were moving soundlessly. Maybe he was praying, or maybe he was just dreaming of drinking some tasty elvish wine. In any case, Patrick was no example for me.

I turned my head and listened to the murmuring of Aunt Stephanie.

"We seek your protection, Sleepers. Scorn not our prayers in our grief but keep us from all danger forevermore. Just and terrible Behemoth, lifegiving mother of all Tiamat, fierce Kingu, ruler of the ocean Abzu and the mighty Leviathan! Patrons and creators of our world may your sleep be eternal, and may you never awaken!

The words didn't matter; the faith mattered. Did I believe in the existence of the Sleeping Gods? Hell, yes, I did. Just as I believed in their might and that all Disgardium was the product of their dreams given material shape. And may their sleep be eternal...

So, I sat and lost track of time, not even noticing myself begin to whisper unconsciously. I felt my thoughts incarnating as *faith*. It melded in with the flow from all the adepts, streaming to the altar, and from there to Behemoth in interwoven strands of invisible energy. There was something mystical in it, without the usual logs and system notifications that accompanied actions and steps — the digital gods of the virtual world demanded no words or rituals; only true faith.

I didn't hear the clap of the portals or notice my clanmates arrive with the mercenaries on the temple steps, so I gasped when Crawler touched my shoulder.

"We're here, Scyth. Take the artifact."

He extended a black bracelet toward me, so black it swallowed light; fine as a wire, but heavy. I took off my gloves and vambraces and pulled it onto my wrist. The bracelet gripped me, sinking into the skin of my arm.

Returning my equipment, I put the icon for activating the artifact in a visible spot. You could activate abilities in Dis either mentally or through a visual 'button press.' I felt like I could trust Crawler more now — he had every opportunity to take the item for himself and pay for his whole future.

Crag, Crawler and I went outside so as not to disturb those in prayer. Bomber and the five mercenaries awaited us: a tall troll, a muscular minotaur, a dryad whose green hair floated in the air as if something alive, a centaur with a long spear and a brown-skinned orc. Their level ranged from the dryad at three hundred and sixty to the orc at three hundred and seventy-five. A team assembled by Disgardium itself, based on the fact that all three main factions were represented: the Commonwealth, the Empire and the neutrals.

Bomber introduced me to the mercenaries.

The Destroying Plague

Nodding, the huge fierce orc, covered in scars and with a broken lower fang, took a step toward me and stretched out a hand.

"My name is Xerozok. Is this everything?" He pointed to the undead beating against the shield. I nodded and he continued. "The job looks trivial: we pacify the lich, the undead will weaken and become easy prey. Or first we will deal with the small ones. We will see. It will be done. You are too weak; you should stay out of this. If you wish to take part in the battle as the client, this must be negotiated and paid for separately. Extra effort will be required to protect you. Your friend," he nodded toward Bomber, "chose our cheapest deal. That means you can't expect any loot, and you must stay a safe distance away during the battle and not get involved. If you violate this condition and someone dies, the guild will bear no responsibility. Got it? I advise you think quickly, human, this is a short-term hire and we're on the clock."

"Understood. We accept your conditions, but I have a suggestion. We have to group up."

The orc's thick black brows rose. The dryad snorted. Limping, waving long arms that stretched beneath his knees, the hunchbacked troll approached us. Even so, he was two feet taller than me. Rings decorated his long, fanged face, and a red-dyed mohawk topped his head.

"If you're worried about combat experience, don't," he said with a thick accent, stretching out his vowels. "Nobody will get any exp for mobs lower level than us. You'll barely get crumbs even for the lich..."

"I'm worried about you. My friend Crag and I have divine talents that strengthen all our allies. The important thing is that the enemies attack first, not us. And as the customer, I insist on that. It will lower the risk and make you far stronger."

The orc frowned. His imposing lowered again and he nodded. He accepted the group invite and the rest of the star followed. Crawler and Bomber didn't refuse either, of course. I sighed with relief for the first time since the guardians died — at least I wouldn't die to a single hit now.

"There's more. We already killed one such lich and we're roughly familiar with its abilities. It can take control of other minds..."

I gave him a summary of all we knew. Xerozok nodded and spoke hoarsely.

"Stay behind the barrier."

He walked away to his own and the mercenaries conferred for some time. It looked like tanking in their group was the job of the minotaur, shrouded in massive rough plate from head to toe. He had no shield but did have a two-handed sword as broad as a shovel, which astounded the imagination. With a sword like that, you could cut that dryad in half just by stabbing her. Xerozok quietly said something to his team, pointed at the lich's minions, then at himself. It seemed like he was planning to go first and draw away the undead, so they didn't get in the way. The minotaur, troll, centaur and dryad were to deal with the lich themselves.

The mercenaries had no time to finish planning.

Cracks formed along the barrier, and a heartbeat later it shattered to pieces with a crack. Behemoth's defensive shield was down. I stopped feeling the Sleeping God's presence, and an instant later I felt sick — *Infection* had gotten stronger, and the damage was tolerable only due to the high-level mercenaries in the group. The workers, kobolds and Patrick screamed desperately in the temple, no longer with the divine protection.

The lich and his undead were running up the temple steps. Toward me.

"Remain at a safe distance!" the orc roared at us.

We jumped back and the mercenaries got to it. The dryad whispered a spell and roots sprang out of the ground, immobilizing Shazz. The centaur, standing closest to the enemies, raised his spear and ran through two zombies at once. The orc growled out a few commands and the mercenaries went into battle.

Feeling my heart thumping, I opened my profile for a second to check: we'd started the battle. Crag's talent hadn't activated.

The orc, crushing skulls with his heavy hammer as he walked, swept the undead off the stairs and descended on them at the foot of the temple in a

---

powerful deadly meteor leap. As the closest to the lich, he took a *Sprint* to the boss, but halfway there he tripped on some bony hands growing out of the ground and fell. Dead men's fingers immediately entwined his body, keeping him down. The centaur rushed to the leader's help: jumping into the advancing mass of the dead, he stove in a couple of rotting chest cavities with his hooves, threw his spear into the lich and started helping Xerozok get up.

The dryad stood on her tiptoes, stretched out, raised her arms and began to sing in an unfamiliar language. Waves of healing energy emanated from her in circles, hitting both the undead and her group: killing the former and healing the latter. The dryad twirled, slowly moving closer to the enemies. The minotaur towered like a cliff nearby, covering her fragile body.

Their ally, a troll shaman, broke into a dance without leaving his position, and ghostly copies split off from his body. Moving away from the troll, they built up to a suicidal speed and crashed into the enemies with a crunch.

A couple of minutes later, three dozen skeletons and zombies had turned into a mass of bones, scraps of rotting flash, severed heads and limbs.

The lich freed himself from the spear and bound the orc and centaur to the ground, lifted into the air and spread his hands. His crooked fingers fired off streams of *plague energy*. The skeleton bones began to form into the bodies of *Bone Hounds*, and the flesh and blood of the zombies gathered into three piles, melded together like mercury and made three *Foul Queases*. A *Plague Vector* formed from the remainder of the blood and piles of slime. The lich wasn't giving up.

The new mobs were higher level than the last ones. The queases were now at three hundred, the hounds — two hundred and ninety. The minotaur bellowed, shaking the columns of the temple, and drew aggro, but the undead moving toward him obeyed the lich's silent commands and changed direction toward me. Shazz hadn't lost hope of killing me. The Destroying Plague really had my number! I physically couldn't complete his quest, because I was banned, and my guilt was rather in the fact that I planned to sabotage the assault.

Realizing that the undead hadn't reacted, the minotaur closed the distance with one long leap, blocking the undead's path and striking the earth with his giant fist. The earth rolled in waves outward from his strike and paralyzed the mobs. In the meantime, the orc and centaur freed themselves from the dead men's hands holding them, severing and crushing to bone dust the limbs reaching out of the ground.

The centaur attacked first, piercing the frozen undead with his spear. Then the orc advanced. The dryad and troll attacked the ink-spot smudges of the *Plague Vectors* with spells. None of the new mobs died immediately, but a few hits and the first quease was down, then the second and the third. The centaur crushed the hounds to dust, and the plague vectors faded to the magic from the dryad and troll. The lich was left alone.

I prepared myself. During the battle, an idea formed in my mind; to leave the group when the boss's health got low, then shoot an arrow at him with the *Balancer* active and a maximum *vindication* charge. The stored energy should be enough to finish off Shazz and take my share of the experience, and maybe even achievements.

Having killed all the minions, the mercenaries assembled at the foot of the stairs and went into a combat formation: the tank at the front, the mages at the back covered by the meleers — the warrior orc and the spear-carrying centaur. Crawler was standing nearby.

"You are thinking the same thing I am?"

"For sure. We go out when the lich is at half health. Crag's talent didn't work anyway. We'll form our own group and attack with everything we have. The exp calculation system is a mess, so try to hit it at least once.

"I'll fire with my crossbow," Bomber said. "I don't think Crag or I can get near the boss..."

In the meantime, the mercenaries were getting stuck into the lich, surrounding him. Shazz span as if in a frying pan, dodging strikes, casting spells, immobilizing and spewing curses. His health slowly but surely fell. He would have already gone down if it weren't for the fact that he took off into the air as often as his cooldown allowed. He was almost untouchable there except by the mages, and he used the opportunity to regenerate by absorbing dead energy from the defeated mobs.

Crag estimated the distance to the fight and felt the need to say:

"I have throwing knives. But I need to get closer, their range is only thirty feet..."

"It's time," Crawler interrupted them. "Leave the group!"

The mercenaries had managed to pin the boss to the ground — the centaur's long spear pierced his chest, emerged from his back and thrust into the ground. The lich desperately tried to climb off it, trying to fly up into the air again. The minotaur leapt high into the air and brought his broad sword down on the extended thin neck of the dead spellcaster. It was a one hundred percent crit, but through some miracle, the boss's head remained on his shoulders. The blade cleaved through the collarbone and took off the left arm.

To everyone's surprise, Shazz didn't fall and expire. On the contrary, this let him free himself and take flight. Raising his arm, the lich span around himself. The long mantle in the shape of an overturned tulip sparked, scraps of cloth tore off, blackened and flew away.

"Watch out!" Xerozok the orc shouted. "Split

up!"

The minotaur, as the least quick of the lot, failed to make it in time. A scrap of black cloth, like an autumn leaf torn from the branch, gently landed on the tank's shoulder. His stunning, pain-filled wail carried all through the fort. The scrap of the lich's mantle snagged on his metal shoulderpad and it melted immediately, flowing away in burning droplets. The stink of burnt flesh filled our nostrils. The tank's health went down by a third, and the boss's area of effect spell sped up its action. More and more black flakes about the size of a child's hand broke free from the mantle and soundlessly span through the air in all directions with a misleading lightness.

We'd already set up a separate group, summoned our pets and were waiting for our chance to put Bomber under a strike. The legendary ring *Zuantewith's Valor*, which absorbed lethal damage, should save him. The warrior would survive, and we'd get Crag's buff. I was ready to press the *Balancer* and shoot an arrow charged with *vindication*. All that remained was to wait for the *Grave Storm* to end and the lich's mantle to stop throwing off deadly bombs. The mercenaries came to the same conclusion and amiably retreated to the stairs, waiting for the boss to finish. I saw the centaur trying to interrupt the cast by throwing a chakram[5], but it failed. The disc's blade just glanced off the spinning lich.

---

[5] The chakram (Sanskrit: circle, ring, disc) is a throwing weapon. It is a flat metal ring sharpened at its outer edge.

The Destroying Plague

The last sepulchral piece of cloth landed on Bomber as he walked down the stairs. The warrior's figure flashed with a magic bubble, which took the deadly damage. Hung survived and immediately returned to us. All our stats had increased by a factor of seventeen, and Shazz had less than quarter health left.

The boss summoned another forest of dead hands to immobilize the mercenaries, and, paying them no more attention, flew toward us. The lich pierced me with his dead eyes.

"Run, Scyth!" Bomber shouted. "We'll hold him!"

"No! We're taking this asshole out!" Crawler shouted furiously, losing his self-control. "Come on, Scyth!"

I didn't move from where I stood. Slowly, taking careful aim, I pulled back my bowstring, activated the *Balancer* and shot. The boss's level fell to mine, which meant that our hope of getting some experience and achievements from might be dashed — he'd die at the entirely mortal level of thirty-nine. But that didn't matter — the important thing was that the lich's health had dropped a lot!

It was as if time slowed: my arrow hung in the air, a fireball flew from Crawler to the lich, bomber's crossbow trigger was pulled, and Crag already had a throwing knife in the air. Our needlers were rushing to attack too.

Shazz immediately extended a hand to Crag

and, for the first time in the battle, used *Subjugate*...

I poured all the *vindication* I had left into the shot, almost forty thousand. For the level the lich had dropped down to, it should have been more than enough. That wasn't even counting the already high damage of *Explosive Shot*.

The arrow that pierced the lich's heart flashed and exploded. The flash of fire hid the action of *Sleeping Vindication:*

Crawler dealt damage to Cursed Lich Shazz: 1258.
Health points: 4941 / 56000.

Bomber dealt damage to Cursed Lich Shazz: 726.
Health points: 4215 / 56000.

Crag dealt damage to Cursed Lich Shazz: 1115.
Health points: 3100 / 56000.

You dealt critical damage to Cursed Lich Shazz: 49501!
Health points: 1 / 56000 (46402 absorbed).

Shazz survived. And I was very familiar with how he did it — the undead curse!

A strike from the minotaur a few minutes before this had taken off the lich's hood and bared his

The Destroying Plague

bald head covered in liver spots and scabs, and now I could see his evil smirk clear as day. His fine, bloodless lips parted, revealing blackened teeth.

"The Destroying Plague generously rewards its faithful servants! You know that, don't you, traitor?"

Crag, whose nick had turned red to show that he was under the lich's control, now blocked the stairway, covering the boss from the mercenaries. They'd managed to get away, but neither of our groups were fated to win this battle. The first strike against Crag by the mercenary group turned our clanmate's talent against us. The effect of the *Balancer* had ended, Shazz returned to his level and became seventeen times stronger.

Laughing, with a couple of movements of his hook-like fingers, the lich raised a few undead soldiers at his own level, covered the area around him with a slimy mass of *Devouring Plague*, which inflicted a deadly debuff, and threw a couple of balls of *Grave Worms* at the mercenaries. Strengthened by Crag's talent, the worms nimbly pinwheeled their way into flesh. The massive instant damage and the resulting DoT killed the mercenaries in mere seconds. Even the dryad, pulling out all the stops in her panic to heal the group, couldn't save her comrades.

Hearing the call of the Sleeping God, I rushed into the temple and shouted:

"Everyone logs out of Dis right now! Patrick, Ryg'har, take the tribe to the woods! I'll distract the lich!"

Suddenly, my gaze was drawn like a magnet to the droplet of protoplasm remaining in the spot where Behemoth had stood. Listening to the will of my heart, I bowed and touched it. The droplet pulled itself into my finger and I rushed to the exit to draw the lich as far away as possible.

As I ran out of the temple, I saw Bomber and Crawler die; I saw the needlers, Iggy, Alien and Whatchamacallit, flare up in black flame and collapse into dust.

I ran around the building and jumped from the top slab of the temple's foundation. The lich gave out a triumphant laugh, and a couple of seconds later I saw that my legs were rotting alive and dissolving in bubbling slime.

This is not the end, Herald, I heard Behemoth whisper. *The parasite is very confident, but he has miscalculated...*

The Sleeping God's voice cut off when I died. Hanging in a great nothingness and twisting in phantom pain, I read the blood-red text hanging in front of the black, utter abyss before me:

You are dead.

Infection effect: now that you have died, you have become a vassal of the Destroying Plague.

Initializing global event: Invasion of the

The Destroying Plague

Destroying Plague.

Character regeneration required.

Approximate regeneration time: 24 hours.

Initiated character race change procedure. New race: undead.

Initiated character appearance change procedure. New appearance: current, with alterations for features of 'undead' race.

Initiated character faction change procedure. New faction: Destroying Plague.

At the end of all these procedures, you will become a Legate of the Destroying Plague.

As founder of the Awoken clan, you will be invited to change the faction of all the clan's members. If any of the members refuse, they will be forcibly excluded from the clan.

Logging out of Disgardium.

This isn't the end! was my first thought. The next, with a sense of great relief: *I can finally get some sleep.*

Maybe I imagined it, but I felt the approval of the Sleeping God.

Chapter 12

The Awoken Assembled

I WOKE UP from a nightmare in which I became undead in the real world. It took me a while to come around and feel the edge separating the game from reality. It had been a long day. Hours of wandering through the Treasury of the First Mage, then Darant and my conversation with Patrick, the escape from the capital watchmen, the invasion of the Destroying Plague, the fight shoulder to shoulder with the guardians, the coming of the kobolds and the retreat into the jungle. Then there was the Montosaurus, the mercenaries, the invulnerable Cursed Lich Shazz, the Sleeping God...

I died! Behemoth lost his avatar! And the temple... Shazz had probably already destroyed the temple. The terrible finale weighed on me like death. Despair rushed in. Even the thought of the money saved for my university studies was no comfort.

The Destroying Plague

Through sheer strength of will, I cut through the panic and tried to collect myself, cutting off thoughts of Disgardium.

I was in real life. I was home, in my own bed. My eyes found the clock — it was approaching midday. I'd overslept for school!

Jumping up from the bed, I began to get ready in a panic until I realized that it was a weekend. Thank the Sleeping Gods! I can't imagine how I'd have sat through my lessons thinking about my character's fate. My thoughts returned to Dis.

Judging by the latest system messages, although Scyth had died, his game hadn't ended. But what was his role now? Changing faction, becoming a vassal of the Destroying Plague — what did it all mean? Would his divine abilities remain? Would my class still be the same, or would Herald switch to Legate? Was Legate even a class at all? I remembered the Emissary of the Destroying Plague declaring that very title as a quest reward. It might indicate a position in the hierarchy of Destroying Plague vassals and give new abilities. There was no point in guessing, it was easier to wait until the evening and log in. Then everything would be clear.

Someone knocked at the door and it swung open.

"Alex?" My mom's head peeked round the door. "You up? Great! I wanted to let you know I'm going away for the weekend. Dad isn't at home either... hasn't been back since yesterday. Breakfast is on the table; lunch is in the refrigerator. There's a pizza just in case. Behave yourself, dear. Oh, and another thing... Maybe you'll want to go for a stroll or to the movies with Melissa..."

She tapped her finger on her wrist several times, and my comm notified me that I'd received fifteen phoenixes.

"Thank you, mom." I doubted I'd want to go anywhere, especially to the movies. "When're you coming back?"

Mom shrugged and disappeared without telling me when she was planning on returning. A couple of minutes later, I heard the door closing.

I needed to sort myself out and think everything over well. My communicator had detected a change in the frequency of my heartbeat, realized that I'd woken up and given me a bunch of notifications of missed calls and messages. Without paying them any mind, I went to the bathroom to take a shower. I felt an urgent need to wash the mud of the jungle away, the touch of dead hands and the bubbling slime of the *Devouring Plague*.

An hour later, now that I'd wiped away the imaginary filth, recharged and had breakfast, I was fresh and full of energy. I sat at the table, drank some fresh coffee and listened to my friends. Or rather, their messages. If I said they were full of well-meaning calm and certainty in the future, that would be very far from the truth.

We need to meet, Manny wrote, and that was

far from the only message from him. In the last one he let me know that he'd given all the workers the day off, since 'dead men have occupied the fort and mine.'

Alix, call me back as soon as you wake up. I'm worried. Love you — that was Tissa's message. One of them. The ninth. The tenth succinctly reported: *I'm on my way to you.*

The last came from Ed, ten minutes ago: *We're all on our way to you.*

I didn't have time to finish my coffee. The door buzzed and my clanmates' faces came up on the screen, serious and frowning. Even the ever-smiling Malik looked crestfallen. My mood was no better, but I was still glad to see them; we were all still together.

I opened the door. Tissa threw herself around my neck, Ed nodded with a whistle, Hung said "Hi," with nothing but his lips. Malik clapped me on the shoulder and Tobias appeared behind his back — bearded, bald, in sunglasses and a panama hat. This guy was a true master of secrecy and disguise!

The guys all hovered outside the door, not knowing what to do. Apart from Tissa, this was the first time any of them had been to see me. Tissa looked guilty. She bit her lip, sighed and spoke first.

"Sorry for bringing everyone here, Alex. But I think this situation counts as an emergency."

"You did the right thing. Sorry for not answering, guys. I hadn't slept two days before all this. Yesterday I just fell out of my capsule, into bed and was out for the count. I only just woke up...

Um... Come in. My folks aren't here, so we can stay and discuss everything here."

I led them into the kitchen-living room. Under ordinary circumstances, I was sure they would have been looking around my house like meerkats, but right then they followed me like a funeral procession and sat down.

Tissa sat on the sofa. She looked a little lost and was dressed strangely feminine for her: not quite a dress, but not a formless gown either, but jeans that stretched over her long legs and a tight t-shirt that emphasized her curves. Hung Lee barely fit into an armchair and had to move it back so his legs would fit behind the table. Ed Rodriguez spread out in the other armchair, in shorts and vest as usual, outlining his powerful shoulders and biceps. Swarthy Malik sat bestride a barstool. He looked like a young man next to the other guys — narrow-faced, thin, with girlish long eyelashes.

Tobias milled around in his ridiculous disguise, dressed in cheap trash from Walmart. Eventually he just sat down on the floor and crossed his legs. Yeah, there wasn't a lot of space in our apartment. The boy's rumbled black t-shirt read "I need more personal space" with the Reality Distorters logo at the top, another game like Disgardium, only space-themed.

"Coffee?" I offered. "Anyone want anything to eat? Alright then. I'll start with the most important part: I didn't lose my character, or my Threat status.

Hung elbowed Malik in the side.

"I told you! Our Alex ain't so easy to..."

"Wait, Hung," I interrupted. "All in good time. I don't have enough information for a full picture. What happened after I died?"

"Crawler and I revived behind the temple just as you jumped and fell into the boss's AoE. Crag went down right after..."

"Yeah, the boss cut off control and fired off some crazy shit," Tobias confirmed. "Sent me to the respawn point."

"Did you revive?"

"No, it was my second death that day."

"Um... I don't understand..."

"In big Dis, you revive instantly after your first death just like in the sandbox," Ed began to explain. "After the second, you have to wait an hour to revive. After the third you have to wait twelve hours, then the counter resets. For Crag, it wasn't his first death that day, so he just logged out of the game."

"Let me tell you what we saw before we got out of there," Hung said. "All the workers used the emergency log-out. Only Patrick and the kobolds were left. They ran as fast as they could into the jungle, right into Monty's maw, but Ed and I caught up to them, hooked them in our *Depths Teleportation* and took them to Glendale. That little town where we leveled up before you left the sandbox. The residents there aren't particularly kind to non-humans like the kobolds, so we took them into some caves outside of town. As for Patrick... Well, you know him."

"He found a tavern and set up shop there?"

"Pretty much," Ed smiled. "I sent him a hundred gold, should last a while. Did you say something about coffee?" He glanced toward the kitchen with interest, smelling the aroma of freshly ground beans still wafting out. "Wouldn't mind something to eat too..."

"Yeah!" Malik and Hung echoed in chorus.

Crag's drooling face made it obvious that he wouldn't refuse some food either but was too shy to admit it. In real life, the boy seemed almost the complete opposite of his virtual persona: tense, timid, tongue-tied. In Dis, he transformed.

I stood up to heat up a couple of big pizzas and pour some coffee, but Tissa beat me to it.

"Let me," she said. "Save your stories for me!"

"Wow! Little Tissa feels like home at Alex's place!" Hung laughed. "So, you're all serious now?"

"I think we should get ready for some little Scyths," Malik shook his head in concern.

The atmosphere was cleared. Throwing jokes back and forth and mocking each other, we ate and I told them everything I saw after my character died, including the fact that the clan members now had a choice: to stay with me and change their faction, or leave the clan.

"What are you talking about?" Hung frowned. "We started this with you and we're with you until the end!"

The Destroying Plague

"I even prefer it this way," Tobias muttered. "This whole subject of the Sleeping Gods is so murky, and Behemoth..." I've never seen more nightmarish creatures.

"You think the Destroying Plague is any nicer?" Tissa giggled.

"No, but we haven't seen him," Tobias shrugged. "Maybe we won't even see him. What difference does it make? People play for different races; the main thing is leveling up."

"By the way, what's it like when you're being controlled by another mind?" I asked, remembering that I was a vassal of the Destroying Plague now. "You just watched without controlling yourself? How did it feel?"

"It's a weird feeling... You know, it's like you really turned into enemies to me! I knew how things were really, of course, but I felt totally different. Although maybe it just seemed that way. In fact, I lost control of my body. All the ability icons went inactive, so I couldn't have helped even if I'd wanted to.

His words didn't uplift me. If 'vassaldom' meant something like what Tobias experienced, the game was over for me. But I still held on to hope for something more. Behemoth's last words still ran through my head too. The deity was an in-game AI, at the end of the day, and he was sentient. He wouldn't have said such words to give me hope for no reason. He really might have some sort of plan.

We spent some more time discussing what the

faction change would give us, and the guys saw only pluses: unexplored lands, unique quests and abilities, rare achievements... The overall depressed atmosphere was replaced with excitement and passion. Which was possibly excessive, given that all our suppositions were based on the paltry couple of system messages I'd seen before I logged out of the capsule. In any case, the guys had cheered up. Infect had even started walking around the living room and looking at the family holograms with interest.

I noticed that Tissa, although she was smiling along with everyone, looked far from happy. It was clear why — what girl wanted to play as undead? Rotting, covered in cadaveric spots, surrounded by similarly disgusting characters? Not just on a monitor screen like in epochs past, but almost living it?

The guys' enthusiasm rocketed up when we got onto the subject of the *Balancer*.

"Imagine the achievements we can get when we start taking out mobs and bosses a hundred levels higher!" Bomber exclaimed. "And that asshole Monty is first on the list!"

"Hold on," I said, not sharing Hung's ardor. It seemed like he didn't know how the artifact works. "Yesterday, when I balanced the lich, he went to the same level as me. If the undead curse hadn't have worked and the lich had died, we'd have gotten the same amount of experience from him as a level thirty-nine mob. Well, alright, more since he was a boss. But you saw for yourselves that his level dropped..."

"You're both wrong," Ed said, rubbing his hands. He took out his communicator and brought up the description of the Balancer. "Look: 'on damage, balances the target with the attacker'! So, the mob becomes your level, Scyth, only when you deal damage. You hit, the system calculates the damage as if it's a mob of your level, applies it, then returns the mob's level."

"But I saw myself, even before I hit him, the lich..."

"It works in both directions!" Tissa shouted and smiled victoriously. "Right, Ed? When you were looking, Alex, the lich was attacking someone himself, right?"

"I'm proud of you, Melissa!" Rodriguez answered, imitating Mr. Kovac. "The lich cast Deadly Grasp on the mercenaries, those dead hands that came through the ground, remember? The ability binds them in place and deals damage." The lich was constantly dealing damage, then fell in level. For five seconds."

"So the mechanic for calculating exp in this case is unclear?" Tobias asked. "If the mob drops in levels and is killed in those five seconds..."

"We'll test it out," I said. "And even if we don't get experience, what stops us from dropping the mob's health to the minimum and then finishing it off with *Sleeping Vindication*?

"Only the fact that you might not have it anymore," Ed advanced thoughtfully. "If the Sleeping

God is gone and his temple destroyed by the lich, then you might have no divine abilities left."

"Plus, the whole system of bonus stat points for the adepts," Hung added. "Never mind, no point in guessing. We'll find out soon. Whatever the case may be, I'm with Alex."

"So, we're going to become undead now too?" Malik brightened up. "Then maybe I don't have to become a bard? Scyth can start using his old invulnerability tricks again and one-shot bosses, and I can still be a good old thief."

"Tobias?" I asked. "Are you with us?"

He nodded, inspecting his fingernails, and muttered something in approval. Tissa was silent so far, avoiding my gaze.

"Then it's decided?" Ed asked, looking at everyone. "We're changing factions and then working out a plan for our next actions after we figure out what the Destroying Plague wants from Scyth?"

"Wait!" Tissa lowered her eyes as if gathering courage. She made her decision and asked. "What then? Think about what we're losing here: all the cities will be inaccessible to us, we won't be able to show up in any populated zone without risking death! We'll never be able to go into any ordinary city! For our whole lives! Do you get that? No class teachers, merchants. I doubt we'll even have access to an auction house! The Commonwealth has its own auction, as does the Empire and the neutrals. I guess the Destroying Plague auction house will be separate

---

too? And who will we trade with? Each other? What if the new faction's zones are high-level? How are we going to level up? Are you sure Scyth will get his undead curse back? What if he doesn't?"

"You want to refuse?" I asked gently, taking her by the hand. "That's fine, and it won't change anything in our relationship. Especially since you and Malik are still in the sandbox. I can't imagine that it's possible to change your race before you go into big Dis."

"Actually, it's my birthday the day after tomorrow," Malik muttered. "And I didn't get an answer to my question; can I stay a thief or is it really important to you to have a personal bard with a guitar in your party?"

"Whether we're with the Sleeping Gods or the Destroying Plague, it changes nothing," Ed answered. "We can't go to Darant and just pick up some random bard, you know? I'm more worried about someone else right now. Tissa."

The girl took a sharp breath when she heard her name. Her shoulders drooped.

"I have to admit," she said quietly. "The White Amazons made me an offer that is tough to refuse. I don't want anything left unsaid between us, so I'll tell you all straight: I decided to agree. It's going to solve not only my problems, but just everything, even for my dad."

It seemed to me that she'd only just made her final decision. Having voiced her doubts, it was as if she'd cut off the other options. Yes, we'd earned a lot of money, a ridiculous amount, and we had great potential. And who knows, maybe that potential wouldn't go anywhere with the Destroying Plague but would only grow! However, you span it, the abilities of the Sleeping Gods were limited since we couldn't think of a way to complete Behemoth's quest and build a second temple. There was a reason the boys were so happy about the news of returning under the banner of the Destroying Plague — they remembered the miracles we performed in the sandbox with its help. Undead? So what? People played for races just as nightmarish, especially if you looked at the Empire. The new possibilities also inspired Ed, Hung and Malik, even Crag.

As for me, I was hoping I could fix everything. And the problem wasn't the creature that was the Destroying Plague, certainly a disgusting and unkind character. I could live with that. For me, it was more to do with betraying Behemoth, with whom my connection was more than just a part of the game. It was a silly thought, but I considered him something akin to an old comrade.

For Tissa, it wasn't all so categorical. Both Crag and I remained threats: eternally chased, hunted, living under the Damocles' Sword of the preventers. Tissa, as she'd admitted, wanted something else; stable progress, steady career growth in a clan, and, why hide it — her own share of glory. Her popularity after the victory in the Arena was starting to fade, and no matter how the girl joked, we saw how that bothered her. The rebel Tissa was hooked on popularity, and if it weren't for a direct ban from her dad, she would have gladly gone to be on the TV or network shows she got invites to. But Mr. Schafer had his own ideas about how all that would end and nipped it in the bud. Popularity like that was short-term if you didn't maintain it with new achievements — streams and demonstrations of gameplay. If she stayed in our clan, Tissa couldn't talk about her life in Dis because of my status. With the Amazons, she could say what she liked.

In the end she weighed up everything the Ochre Witch was offering. And to be honest, we understood her. Everything she'd been striving to achieve in all her days in Dis for the last two years had been offered to her on a silver platter. My uncle Nick used to love that turn of phrase. We were upset, of course, but at the same time we were just happy for our friend.

When the guys were leaving, Ed remembered something important. He stopped at the threshold.

"We forgot about Patrick! What if he turns undead automatically? He isn't a player! I'll log in before Scyth and take him out of the town. Just in case..."

They left and I took stock of our meeting: the Awoken had remained almost entirely whole, changed its faction, race, and, based on what we learned next, it would continue to implement its plan to achieve greater heights in Disgardium. And Tissa... I'd come back to her decision to leave the clan after the citizenship tests. Then her time would come to go out into the big world, and who knew, maybe something would change in the clan and her relationship with me.

After seeing my clanmates out, I thought I'd spend the next couple of hours on tenterhooks before I logged into Dis, but I was wrong. After lunch I got a call from Rita Wood, also known as Overweight.

"Alex, we need to meet," she said, and her voice sounded alarmed. "It's important!"

"Fly to my house," I answered and gave her the address.

Less than an hour later, she appeared at the door. At first, I didn't even recognize the girl — I was used to her virtual appearance in the sandbox. It had been two months since we'd last met in real life. Rita had changed — she was stretched out and thin. Her high cheekbones stood out on her once round face. I hesitated and she came in without waiting an invitation, hugging me and pecking me on the cheek. She followed me into the living room, but started talking as soon as she came in.

"A couple of days ago, you linked me the descriptions of a couple of legendaries and asked me to price them on the black market. I sent them to a trustworthy acquaintance. He's been in the business a long time, but his activities are... kind of illegal. If you know what I mean. Nobody works in this business without protection, and my acquaintance's protection is someone from Tristad. So, here's the thing..."

Rita glanced into the refrigerator and pointed at some soda water. I nodded, she took out the bottle, opened it and took a swig.

"One of the pieces of gear is pretty normal, at least among legendaries. Shamanic chainmail that enhances spirit magic. There were no problems pricing that, the average value is around a hundred thousand phoenixes. Less my acquaintance's fee, you'd get around seventy-five thousand for it. More or less..."

She fell silent to drink more water. Seems she got a thirst in her rush to get to me. I'd contacted Overweight because we needed real money. Phoenixes. I couldn't wait two months until the citizenship tests to transfer the clan gold into real money. After the escape from the Modus castle, we discussed where to hide from the preventers' persistent attention, and Manny suggested we fit out a base in Kali Bottom. Everyone liked the idea, but we needed money. That was when I remembered the artifact black market.

All trades in Dis were tracked, whereas through the black market, you could buy and sell items and services for real money. Well, alright, for cryptocurrency, since trades in phoenixes were also tracked. But for our idea, cryptocurrency was enough: we planned to use it to pay for our accommodation, and we could always turn it into phoenixes. In short, I

---

wanted to sell the legendary *Summoning Whistle,* or the *Arena Master's Horn* I'd won, but then I completed the treasury and chose a couple of legendaries that wouldn't be any use to the clan.

"So, what's the problem?" I asked.

"The second legendary. That's the problem. It's a chest item called Vestment of Irkuyem's Fury, and it turns out to be far from simple. It's part of a top set for druid tanks. The full set can absorb, for a minute, as many percent points of damage as health you lose. Can you imagine that? This set is the dream of any bear druid! Where did you get this, Alex?"

"Why does it matter where? That's awesome! Just imagine how we could sell it for!"

"You aren't hearing me!" Rita said nervously. "My damn trustworthy acquaintance is a Triad man! And he wants to know exactly where I got the info on this legendary!

Chapter 13

Nucleus of the Destroying Plague

T HE TRIAD HAD EXTENDED its roots throughout the world and absorbed many other similar structures. As of today, it united and controlled practically the entire criminal world. The Syndicate, Eastern European authorities, South American drug dealers, Yakuza, the Nigerian Death Squads — they'd all either been beheaded or destroyed or had willingly joined the Triad. Since then, the organization had gotten a lot of multinational fresh blood.

The Triad mostly consisted of non-citizens, and rumors persisted that the organization had a link to the government.

Naturally, the black market of Disgardium was also controlled by criminals. But that was only the tip of the iceberg. The Triad had extended itself in the game itself too, controlling many industries. Even

Snowstorm couldn't do anything about it.

What could you do with the Celestial Warriors clan? A good, flourishing clan which owned the entire resort city of Perfetto in the Empire's south, with all its gambling businesses with unlimited betting, brothels for any taste, restaurants where every chef was a grand master of cooking, an arena with famed gladiators and daily performances from world-renowned stars. And a few other little things: vineyards, breweries, idyllic gardens and famous people's villas.

Everything was possible in Dis. And that may be the reason that more and more citizens preferred to save money for a holiday in Perfetto, through a portal cast by a mage from the Celestial Warriors, make themselves at home in a hotel owned by the Celestial Warriors, and waste time and money in buildings belonging to the Celestial Warriors. Also known as the Triad. Even some in the top preventer clans belonged to it, it seemed.

So, Rita's concern was understandable. There was nothing unusual about the Triad's interest in the set legendary. What was annoying was their interest in its source. Rita could easily name me, but her feminine intuition told her that there was more than curiosity behind this apparently idle question.

"I said I didn't know who owned the item. That I'd met a representative of his, a middle-man, in a securoom..."

'Securooms' were miniature cryptoworlds. They

were often just buildings without doors and with a couple of chairs, or (guess why) a bed. These worlds were created at request, with a random algorithm. They had no physical location and existed only in the form of data in the operating memory of the two capsules of the attendees. There were no logs, no way to record events. Total isolation. Information was conveyed only between the capsules and only encrypted.

Rita wasn't making excuses, but I saw she felt ill at ease.

"This middleman, my acquaintance, asked too many strange questions! He doesn't know me personally; we only meet in securooms. Each time I generate a new appearance and call out a codeword agreed during the last meeting..."

"So, there's nothing to worry about?"

"There is, Alex," Rita sighed. "You can't sell the item until you decide to reveal yourself. You know what Essence Revelation does? Magical gear identification?"

Oh yes, after yesterday's events I certainly knew. But it seemed the girl had something else in mind.

"It identifies an unknown artifact?"

"You're talking about revealing the hidden properties of an item, and that too. But apart from everything else, Essence Revelation reveals information about all the previous owners. It's an expensive service, extremely expensive, but if you decide to sell the Vestment of Irkuyem's Fury, and the Triad buys it, then you're going to get a knock at the door. You see, this set, according to my acquaintance, drops only in one place, which you can only get to under special conditions. That's how he said it, 'special,' and looked at me like I was stupid. Tried to judge my reaction. It was news to me, so I hope my surprise seemed honest."

"Then let's just forget about this legendary and sell only the shamanic chainmail?"

"I revealed that one too. Now these two pieces of gear are linked in the eyes of my acquaintance, and believe me, he's already tracking all the auction houses of Dis for either item to appear."

It was important for the items to show up for sale, so as not to put Rita in a bind. If only I could get rid of their 'history' so that my name didn't show up among the previous owners... Never mind, I'd sort it out later, maybe we'd find a suitable spell.

"I still need money, Rita... Phoenixes. I'll see what else I can sell, only... Do you have any other contacts? Only not Triads."

"I can go to the market myself, without a middleman. Although then I'll have zero reputation and the same level of trust. "But listen..." Rita hesitated. "You only just got out of the sandbox a week ago, right? It's none of my business, of course, but where did you get top-end gear like that? And so much of it... Wait! Before you start stammering and lying, let me tell you what I think first. Alright? If I ask rhetorical questions, don't answer — I'm just following the chain of logic."

I shifted on the sofa, and not at all because the hem of Rita's dress rose when she tucked a leg underneath herself, and not at all because of her outstanding... beautiful eyes. Only the scene reminded me of a very similar one, with a conversation in the exact same place and on the exact same subject. Only with a different girl.

"First your fantastical ascent in the sandbox. A level one loser that couldn't find even five silver for gear, suddenly climbing up to level five in a few days. That could be explained by the support of your classmates, but a couple of months later, after creating your own clan and bringing in those nerd Dementors, who couldn't stand noobs, you won the global Junior Arena. I could name another range of strange events too, like the bunch of anonymous First Kills that crashed down on the sandbox, a few awesome epics you put up for sale, but I think I've made my point. And now it seems like you're trying to auction off the best items ever seen in Dis, and you're treating them as if you have a whole chest full..."

Rita's eyes widened and she gasped.

"Wait. Do you really have a whole chest full? Daamn! You really can't lie to save your life, Alex! You gotta improve your poker face."

"Don't try and trick me, Wood. Not a single muscle moved on my face!"

"Uh-huh, sure. Your ears are red, and

anyway... You... I won't say it directly... Long story short, you're special, right?" Rita was imagining something terrible and shuddered as she imagined a Threat. "I see by your eyes that the answer is yes! Gotcha!"

"What are you driving at? If you want to give me up..."

"I have too much respect for you. I like you, Alex! But even without that, I believe in a little something called karma. So, don't expect any tricks from me. On the other hand, I have some unique information, and as a professional merchant, I can't just sit and do nothing."

Rita said nothing for a moment but didn't get an answer. I'd become undead, a vassal of the Destroying Plague. If all the preventers of the world started hunting me, I could just go beyond the frontier and live there. At least I didn't have to fear the debuffs of the Lakharian Desert. And in real life I could hide with Manny, with whom, incidentally, I needed to speak and decide what to do next with the workers.

"Alright, Alex. Let's try something else. Don't answer anything and don't promise anything. Just keep in mind that you can count on me in your threatening," she smiled, "deeds and trades. And if it's possible, and I see based on the example of the Dementors that it is, I hope I can join your clan."

"Thank you for your frankness. I really value it and your understanding. As for the clan... I need to discuss it with the others."

"Alright."

Rita stood up and I showed her out. I apathetically snoozed in my bed before my log-on to Dis. Too much was happening.

* * *

Fort Kharinza welcomed me with the wailing of wind and a stench. The dusk sunbeams, piercing through the two peaks of the mountain range, covered the roofs of the untouched fort building with a bloody light.

Before, there had been an improvised graveyard with decorative tombstones behind the temple of the Sleeping Gods, but now the place had taken on the shape it had before my first time on the island: ancient stone slabs in the form of a truncated pyramid, with no structure at the top.

The ruins of the destroyed temple had been cleared in less than a day. Who did that? The lich and his rotting friends, no doubt. I saw a chain of zombies extending beyond the bounds of the fort, passing the last stones along the line. The dead men showed no reaction to me. Their boss Shazz was nowhere to be seen.

I didn't really know what to do. I tried to reach out to Behemoth with my thoughts but got no answer. All I could rely on was myself.

So, what did I have? Obviously, all this was

part of the script that had launched the global event — Invasion of the Destroying Plague.

Something similar had happened many years ago, when players were only just getting to level one hundred and unlocking the continent of Shad'Erung — someone found an injured orc on the shore. A ship of the Empire had crashed against the cliffs, and only the orc captain NPC survived. The player that found the injured orc launched a global event, and sometime later, it became possible to choose a dark race — orc, troll, ogre, minotaur, dragonite... That player, incidentally, was Horvac, the leader of the Travelers. The orcs held a conversion ritual for him, and he became one of their own. Horvac took his whole clan to the Empire and became a billionaire.

Apart from my character changing, nothing like that seemed to have happened this time. No notifications, news of a new faction on the game forums, nothing.

My interface was the same, except that the abilities linked to the Sleeping Gods were inactive; the grayed-out icons of *Sleeping Touch,* *Sleeping Invulnerability* and *Sleeping Vindication* did nothing when I tried to use them. My quest log said the same: Behemoth's quest hadn't disappeared, wasn't showing up as failed, but also wouldn't open — it was just a gray line in the list. The map continued to display the places of power where a temple of the Sleeping Gods could be built. A point had been added to them on Kharinza.

The Destroying Plague

I got disappointed when I opened the profile, however. Now that the sole temple had been destroyed, all the Sleeping God adepts had lost their *Unity* bonus. The divine passive skill itself hadn't disappeared, but also wasn't activated.

At least my class skills were still working: *Divine Revelation, Imitation, Lethargy, Liberation* and *Cloak Essence* remained available.

I looked at my body. I still had all my equipment except my boots. My feet looked human, but the dead flesh and deadly-pale skin confirmed it: Scyth was undead now.

I opened my profile to confirm:

Scyth, level 39 undead human
Real name: Alex Sheppard (hidden).
Real age: 16 years (hidden).
Class: Herald (hidden).
Clan: Awoken.

...

Hidden status: *L-class Threat with potential **A**.*
Hidden status: *Initial of the Sleeping Gods.*
Hidden status: *Legate of the Destroying Plague.*

I still had my class and Threat potential. The initial title was showing up, and that gave me hope that Behemoth would return. Without the Sleeping Gods, but with the Destroying Plague, my potential was only L — it had gone up to the maximum only

---

when I became the initial of the Sleeping Gods.

I stopped and listened again, trying to catch at least some sort of sign from Behemoth. Nothing at all.

Behind the pyramid of slabs upon which once stood his temple, I found the place of my death. The earth there was like ash turned to mud after a downpour and then dried out under the rays of the southern sun. And there were my boots, stuck in the mud. None of the undead had given them a second glance. I picked them up and put them on.

I saw a pack of *Bone Hounds* further down the street, right next to the tavern. After my conversation with Rita, I'd contacted Manny and suggested we meet there. The brigadier answered that he'd already died twice to the dead that day, so he could only log into Dis tomorrow. By then I should be able to figure out what awaits me in the game and what we could now do with the clan and the workers. We settled on that.

High-level skeletons and zombies roamed the streets without purpose. The mobs' yellow names showed that they were neutral to me. Something rumbled a little further out, beyond the fort gates, and I headed that way. The undead paid me no attention whatsoever, as if I'd become one of them. Although that was true, I guess.

I don't know why the lich Shazz left the fort untouched. Maybe the aura of the Sleeping Gods got in the way. He'd started building outside of it. A huge section of jungle had been cut down, about three hundred meters squared. *Foul Queases* were pulling

The Destroying Plague

trees out, squads of *Bone Golems* and *Plague Belchers* patrolled the edge of the construction site. The sheer variety of the undead made my head spin. *Cadavers, Hungry Corpses, Corpse Eaters, Plague Spitters, Blood Collectors* and *Meat Collectors*. The Destroying Plague's army at rest. Even if we'd survived yesterday, my defeat was just a matter of time.

Only now did I realize that the Destroying Plague was transforming the area; the soil around looked like what I'd seen at the temple, a pale gray sticky substance. An analogy flashed up in my mind: the terraforming of Mars, after which the planet would start growing plant-life, supporting water, an atmosphere; all the suitable conditions for life. Only with the undead it all happened a lot faster, and probably in the other direction.

The cut-down lumber was being stacked up by a huge arch still under construction, apparently moulded from the ash covering the ground. I didn't know who erected the arch. But when I looked closer, I saw some semi-transparent strings stretching out from the cut-down trees and seeping into the arch, and the green leaves lost their color, withered and fell into gray dust in the blink of an eye. The arch seemed to be steadily growing. So they used the energy of life itself as material for their magic? Or rather, of death?

I felt a vibration under my feet. The earth trembled and began to move. Ten feet away from me, in a fountain of showering dirt, a twenty-foot long *Fighter Worm* shot out of the ground.

Pale yellow and bulging like a maggot, the worm wiggled its long, rough whiskers, turning its eyeless wrinkled face toward me, then dug down again. This mob's level was two hundred and thirty-six, the same as the other undead around. That made me think that the Destroying Plague wasn't ready for serious resistance. One smooth raid from any top clan would crush this rotting army into molecules. And that meant that the Nucleus needed me more than I needed it. It was time to find out more details.

Impassively pushing the skeletons aside, I headed toward Shazz. I doubted any of his dead minions could answer my questions. The lich saw me but didn't react at all. He just kept floating in the air and giving his silent orders. Without him, everything here would probably collapse, and the brainless undead would just roam the island until Monty ate them all. Strange that I still hadn't seen the dinosaur...

"Life is death, Legate!" the lich extended an arm and pointed his three middle fingers at me.

Shazz's arm had recovered after the minotaur cut it off.

It seemed he was expecting some sort of response from me. In contrast to the Destroying Plague emissary who once appeared in the Bubbling Flagon and gave me a quest to capture Tristad, it looked like the lich was a former human. But his face showed no sign of emotion, just a passionless mask. Having received no answer, the lich continued.

The Destroying Plague

"But there is no death in service to the Destroying Plague! Legate Scyth! You have been given the honor of becoming a *Nucleus Speaker*. Follow me.

A window with a quest popped up:

Call of the Nucleus

The Cursed Lich Shazz wants to take you to the Nucleus of the Destroying Plague. Follow him.

Rewards:

— +10 reputation with Destroying Plague faction

— +5 reputation with Cursed Lich Shazz

— next quest in the Invasion of the Destroying Plague divine quest chain

The quest was accepted automatically. With no doubt that I would follow him without objection, Shazz floated through the air toward the mine. I walked after him, still looking around, and once we reached the untouched forest, I saw that the zombies and beasts had stopped working. The queases dropped their cut-down trees and the zombies wandered after us, occasionally moaning and howling. The skeletons meandered after them, their bones clacking. The undead, whose intellect exceeded that of the living dead, quickly lost interest in us: the hounds started fighting amongst themselves, the golems collapsed into dust.

The lich stopped. Gazing toward the construction site, he hissed something, raised a hand and clenched it in a fist. A trio of *Howling Banshee*

Lieutenants appeared around him. They looked nightmarish, with empty eye sockets, jaws full of fangs hanging low, and holes in their faces instead of noses. Their tangled long hair gave the creatures a caricatured similarity with human women, but the impression disappeared as soon as you looked at their bodies and limbs: their whip-like arms hung lower than their legs, which had knees that pointed backwards.

Shazz gave them a silent order and the banshees floated toward various parts of the construction site. An earsplitting shriek filled the area. The dead arranged themselves into a line and returned to their patrolling. The queases collected their dropped wood and dragged it to the strange vampiric arch. The piles of bones that had been the golems turned back into full-fledged mobs.

This was final proof that without the lich, this entire army was meaningless. Satisfied that order was restored, Shazz turned and opened his mouth.

"Follow me, Legate," he repeated and continued.

"Aren't you afraid for your minions, lich?" I asked as I pushed my way through the undergrowth. "There's a huge dinosaur that roams this island. You must remember it! It ate your friend, the other lich."

Shazz froze and slowly turned his head toward me. This looked pretty creepy considering his body stayed in the same spot and his skull turned a full hundred and eighty degrees on his neck. Some spark

The Destroying Plague

of emotion finally appeared in his eyes — interest.

"You are strong. Your will is mighty, Legate. Now I understand the decision of the Nucleus."

"So what about the dinosaur that ate your friend?"

"There are no friends in the Destroying Plague. Dersh is dead, but his death strengthened the other Legates. Koshch and I."

"Koshch... That's the one we tore to pieces, right? How does that work with your "no death in service to the Destroying Plague" thing?

"Dersh and Koshch lost their earthly forms, and their consciousnesses have gone to rest in the embrace of the Destroying Plague. When the time comes, they shall return. All shall return," he said, his tone matter-of-fact as if he was talking about the fact that he was a lich and I was Scyth. No excess fanaticism. He was just stating a fact. "As for the dinosaur, the beast-god's animal instincts are too strong. It felt the presence of the Nucleus and went to ground. It will not be a problem. When the time comes, it will join our ranks."

The Montosaurus avoided the ancient place of power where we'd built the temple of the Sleeping Gods. It might be the same thing with the Destroying Plague. Since the lich was answering my questions, I decided to press further.

"Where is the Nucleus? And what is it?"

The lich measured me up with his eyes.

"Follow me, Legate."

Pushing through the bushes — Shazz used his ability to move without touching the ground and swam straight through — I suddenly felt the presence of the Sleeping God, then heard his weak voice.

I have cordoned off your mind, Initial. Do not let them suspect that you are free. The mark of the parasite is supposed to wipe away your will and force you to fulfil their commands unquestioningly.

"What do I do, Behemoth?"

Collect information. Learn their plans. Think of... The voice faded with each word until it disappeared entirely.

I knew that Behemoth needed energy to exist in Dis, but I decided I'd have to wait until later to think of a way to help him. Right now, I just had to follow the lich. Our path was definitely leading us to the mine, which was exactly where the undead army had emerged from.

Soon I saw proof of that. We went into the mine, walking ever deeper and deeper, until we reached the collapsed section that had now been cleared. I remembered Crawler and Bomber telling me about it. This was where that worker got bitten.

The lich flew into the gap and I wandered after him, stretching out my arms and feeling the cave walls. I stumbled, fell and picked myself up, trying not to lose Shazz, who was giving off a barely visible ghastly glow. He ignored any attempts I made to get him to talk.

Ahead arose a small arch like the one being

built near the fort. Between the columns that joined above us, there was a weak spatial ripple. The portal that Crawler had thought an instance led to the Nucleus of the Destroying Plague.

"Follow me," Shazz ordered yet again, and disappeared through the veil.

* * *

Taking a step after him, I felt as if suspended in some kind of jelly. Time spent in the space between worlds stretched out into long seconds. I felt as if I was being checked, felt out with invisible cold tentacles, and let free only once they were sure I was one of them.

Falling out of the portal, I found myself in a massive room. The walls and ceiling disappeared in mist. The entire surface around was covered in slime and vibrated like a living thing. Where was I? The open map showed my marker where no other player had ever set foot — in the center of the South Pole. On the continent of Holdest.

I could no longer feel the cold now that I was undead, so I had no idea what the temperature was, but I didn't yet have any freezing debuffs. Maybe precisely because I was undead.

"Wait here," the lich commanded and slowly floated forwards.

I stayed where I was and, taking advantage of the breather, looked around. A strange body of water extended before me, filled with a bubbling matt slime, thick and viscous. At the center was an orb-shaped pulsating dark-green mass, covered in transparent veins and vessels. With each pulsating in-breath, a black liquid moved across it and erupted from the orb's surface. It seemed this was what was forming the pool of slime around it. Darkness stretched out behind it, and it was unclear whether the cave ended there or stretched on further.

So, this was it...

Nucleus of the Destroying Plague

The description showed no more information. I still didn't know what the Nucleus of the Destroying Plague was.

The lich returned to me and ordered me to follow him. At the edge of the plague reservoir, he grabbed me by the shoulder.

"Stay here," he ordered. The lich's quiet voice seemed too loud in this grave silence. "Move any closer and you will die. Nothing and nobody can withstand close proximity with the Nucleus of the Destroying Plague.

"What is it?" I pointed to the liquid bubbling away in front of us. "Is this the Destroying Plague?"

"All around you is the Destroying Plague." The lich spread his hand to indicate all the space around and pointed a hooked finger at himself. "As am I. And you. All of us are the Destroying Plague. It permeates through all here."

The Destroying Plague

Little particles of unknown origin floated in the air, like soot or dust. I didn't see any sources of light except the Nucleus itself, which gave off brighter illumination than the lich, but still with a deathly dullness.

There seemed to be some soundless dialog between the Nucleus and Shazz, and then the lich left us with a couple of parting words.

"Life is death, Legate!"

"There is no death in service to the Destroying Plague," I answered as he left.

I remained alone with the Nucleus. Behemoth ordered me to pretend and gather information. That was just what I intended to do. I knelt down and greeted my new boss.

"Greetings, ruler!"

"I welcome you, my Legate!" a powerful and harsh voice echoed through my skull. "You cost us dearly. Two of three remaining Legates fell so that you might join the Destroying Plague..."

"Who are the Legates? How does your hierarchy work?"

"I am the Nucleus. Those who can speak to me are Legates. The Legates are the strongest warriors in the ranks of the Destroying Plague, and they keep their minds and will so that they might rule over the lower circles of the Destroying Plague. They were nine. Nine Cursed Liches. The Nine in Despair, who found each other. Who arose and were victorious. Those who cast aside the personal and joined into one

---

inseparable whole."

"I don't understand you, my lord. You speak of nine liches. I've seen only three. Four, counting the one that the beast-god on my island destroyed. Where are the others? What did they do to become Legates? And why me? Will I become a cursed lich too? But I don't have any magic, I can't perform necromancy, I can't even..."

"Enough!" the Nucleus interrupted my speech so unceremoniously that a hellish pain flared in my head. "There is much for you to learn, but your first lesson must be discipline. Speak when you are spoken to and remain silent when no answer is required. Your indolent curiosity is inefficient. You will learn more when you prove your usefulness. For now, you are not yet ready. Approach! We must begin your tuition, Legate!"

"Um... But how? This... liquid... won't it kill me? Shazz said that nobody can survive your presence."

"You waste my time..." the Nucleus said in displeasure.

The tone and the voice sounding out in my head scratched at my brain itself. I'd disappointed the ruler! Terror gripped my body and I began to shake, but, realizing that it was a forced tremor, I quickly got a grip on myself.

Before I could even apologize, tar-like tentacles shot from the black slime, gripped me around the torso and dragged me toward the pool. I was thrown

The Destroying Plague

headlong into and a soundless wheeze ripped from my chest; the slime sank into my skin, seeped into my nose and mouth, covered my eyes.

I tried to flounder in deadly panic, but the sticky liquid was so thick that I couldn't move so much as a finger. My life started dropping fast — something was killing me.

"Remain calm, Legate. Leave all your fears behind. There is no death in service to the Destroying Plague. Take power!"

I obeyed and stopped resisting. When I realized that I no longer needed to breathe, my heart stopped trying to beat its way out of my chest. The swamp of the Mire had taught me how to behave in such a situation.

Stay calm, Alex, I thought. *It's just a game. It's just images in your head, created by the capsule's intra-gel as it connects to your brain. You're undead now! You don't even need to breathe! Sure, it's gross and disgusting, but nether, this crap is something like a god. Behemoth called it a parasite, but he said the same about Nergal too! You must be strong. Right now, and in general in Dis. Only then can you achieve your goal...*

I hit the bottom a few minutes later, felt it first with my shoulder blades, then with my whole body. It was hard, without silt.

The debuff *Presence of the Destroying Plague* took ten percent of my health per tick. Shazz promised that this would kill me, but I wasn't dying.

Opening my profile, I saw ludicrous bonuses to health regeneration. Maybe that was from the slime I was immersed in.

The Nucleus had stopped talking. Nothing was happening, and that brought me back to thoughts of my goal. Why was I here?

I'd started to take Dis seriously when I realized there was no other way to fulfil my dream of space. The money for my studies was already sitting in the clan wallet — what we'd gotten for realizing the initial L potential and eliminating the Threat of Big Po. If we added the value of the items from the Treasury, the *Summoning Whistle* and the *Arena Master's Horn*, the pile got big. Enough for all the Awoken to fully pay for their university studies and support themselves into adulthood.

A good education meant that you could look confidently into the future. After all, a university diploma was practically a guarantee of citizenship status above G. Interesting work in your specialization and a good career, premium-class accommodation... What else could one want? All that was already practically guaranteed. Especially since it looked like our paths would split after the citizenship tests. Ed wanted to be an expert in corporate strategic planning. Hung would love to try himself out at American football. Tissa could draw beautifully and was considering a career as an artist. As for Malik, his dream was to become a comedian.

Right then we were just playing, captured by

the thrill of it. Advancing our Threat level, getting cool positions in Snowstorm and pushing our way into the elite citizenship categories — sure, it was a worthy goal. But if we were serious, what chance did we have? Our Threat level was confined to the Sleeping Gods, and even when Behemoth was healthy, the chance that we could build five temples was only slightly higher than zero. Take away the Destroying Plague and what would be left? Let's say we put up a temple in the Lakharian Desert, although I had no idea how. Maybe if we leveled up super-fast and tried to get to Holdest... But how could our little clan resist the preventers? And they were just a small part of the game community. If Nergal and the other gods declared war on the Sleeping Gods tomorrow, then all the top players of the world would be advancing on our temples. And we couldn't defend them.

It occurred to me that if we relaxed and just let the inevitable happen, then it wouldn't even be that bad! It was fully possible that we'd even keep playing Disgardium, but just for fun. There was plenty in this world that was more fun to do than lying immersed in a pool of death itself — there were nightclubs to dance in, establishments to fulfil any dream, beaches to sunbathe on, delicacies to gorge on, and all of it without causing any harm to your health!

All we had to do was pass the damn citizenship tests and openly sell our artifacts and legendaries through the auction house. We could even get Rita involved so that she didn't have to spend her whole

---

life in Dis. *A spoon is dear when lunch time is near,* Uncle Nick used to say, and her altruistic gift of the *Large Bear Bone* with its tiny damage was the first gift I'd ever gotten in the game.

So, then what was the point in this torture? I didn't want to play as an undead! I was tired of running and hiding, I was sick of hiding my name, I wanted glory for my achievements. I didn't want to live in Cali Bottom and hide from every drone or flyer! What was the point? For a miserly chance of getting my Threat potential up to the maximum? Heh, I'd need to take over half the world for that!

"We will take over the whole world, Legate," the voice of the Nucleus interrupted me. Nether, could it read my mind?

Ability unlocked: Destroying Plague Immortality!

Destroying Plague Immortality level 1

If you are the only representative of the Destroying Plague in an area, then when you take lethal damage, you will be given temporary immortality: 100% of all subsequent damage is absorbed, 1% is converted into plague energy and stored in a reservoir.

The effect lasts until your health is fully recovered.

Plague reservoir volume: 100,000.

The Destroying Plague

New stat unlocked: Plague Energy.

You can use Plague Energy to increase the power of an attack in part or in full at a rate of one energy point per HP of damage.

Ability unlocked: Plague Reanimation!

Plague Reanimation level 1

There is no death in service to the Destroying Plague! You can breathe unlife into the dead. Reanimated skeletons and zombies will join the Destroying Plague and serve the Legate.

Chance of saving skills and combat abilities possessed in life: 1%.

Limitations: up to 10 servants at current ability level.

Cost to use: 1000 Plague Energy plus 1000 per day to maintain reanimation.

Unlocked ability: Plague Pestilence!

Plague Pestilence level 1

Infects the living with the Destroying Plague. After death, the infected arise from the dead and obey the one who infected them.

Only works through physically touching the victim. Only works on non-player characters.

Cost to use: 10,000 Plague Energy.

Seeing familiar abilities from a new point of

---

view, tripped up on the limitation in the description of Plague Pestilence: 'Only works on non-player characters.' If that was true, then how did Big Po infect so many players?

"Legate Polynucleotide developed his ability," the Nucleus answered. "He was a diligent and determined student. But, as you were able to prove, overconfident."

"Are these all the abilities you plan to give me? What's my task?"

"Prove your loyalty, Legate, and you will gain new knowledge."

My body began to rise to the surface and flew out like a cork from the plague water. I wasn't just pushed up, but also returned to where I was before by the same tentacles.

A quest window opened:

Stronghold of the Destroying Plague

The Nucleus of the Destroying Plague demands a stronghold near thickly populated districts of the continents of Latteria or Shad'Erung. Use the provided design to build it and erect a Large Plague Portal. This will unlock the path for the legions of the undead.

Rewards:

— 200,000,000 experience

— +1000 reputation with Destroying Plague faction

— +500 reputation with Cursed Lich Shazz

— Legate's Crown, an item of the legendary

The Destroying Plague

Destroying Plague equipment set
    — Abilities: Subjugate Mind, Plague Boost.

You got **Design: Stronghold of the Destroying Plague**

"I'm going to need allies," I started thinking aloud. "My old friends. Teammates. I'll need builders, resources…"

I filled my head with thoughts about where and how to build the stronghold so that the Nucleus wouldn't hear my true thoughts. Studying my profile, I ran into the *vindication* line. I didn't know how; maybe it because of the *Presence of the Nucleus of the Destroying Plague* debuff, but the resource had increased to a hundred percent, and the Sleeping ability icons blinked often, becoming accessible one moment and locked again the next.

"You are right to recruit all those you consider necessary," the Nucleus answered, and a new notification appeared before me:

Undead Transformation
You can transform anyone who wishes to serve the Destroying Plague into an undead. This will change their character's race and faction. All their other characteristics will remain the same.

"How much time do I have?" I asked, not seeing a deadline in the quest.

"We don't yet have enough power to fight against all the intelligent races," the Nucleus said. "As the herald, you must hide your true nature. And you must use this to develop your abilities and become stronger. Eras passed while I hid in this cave at the edge of the world. I waited patiently and am willing to wait even longer. Legate Shazz has shown initiative and begun building a stronghold on your former lands. That was an error — those lands are lifeless and will bring no value to the Destroying Plague but will strengthen the Legate himself. He will gain strength and wait for you to open him a path to the living. Kharinza saw many deaths in the time of the Departed, and Shazz will be able to raise one of them. When you open the portal for him, the lands of the living will shake!"

"You understand that I can't build a stronghold in inhabited lands? Like I already said, I'm no builder, and my allies aren't going to be allowed to stroll around the lands of the living unpunished now that they'll be turned into the undead. For that reason, I suggest we choose the Lakharian Desert for the stronghold. It's on Latteria. There's no intelligent life there, and I guess the deadly heat won't hurt people who are already dead.

"That makes sense," the Nucleus approved. "You may begin, Legate. There are followers of the Cult of Moraine in certain cities of the Commonwealth and the Empire. They pray to death and can provide you aid. Their weakness and cowardice give you an advantage: they will fear you more than the authorities. The strongest among them are Plague Necromancers. Find and recruit them! If you detect any traces of Moraine, find her. She will be your ally."

"Is she in the Destroying Plague too?"

"She is a goddess, foolish Legate."

I felt the Nucleus chuckle.

"Now commence. And remember that life is death, but there is no death in service to the Destroying Plague! We will transform the entire world! All mortals will achieve immortality!"

I imagined a Dis full of the walking dead, the full global zombie apocalypse that the Destroying Plague wanted to create with my hands...

Then I pulled out my bow, notched an arrow and spoke through my teeth.

"As you wish... my lord."

Balancer activated: chosen target Nucleus of the Destroying Plague lowered to level 39.
Duration: 5... 4...

Chapter 14

No Death in Service to the Destroying Plague

SHAZZ WAS STILL where I met him, managing the construction site. A mirror copy of the arch had arisen opposite, and between them, two sides of another strange structure had begun construction. When I appeared, the undead drifted away, and even a banshee lieutenant bowed her head as I passed.

The undead had cut down more of the forest, and the landscape around the construction site was starting to look like something alien. Shazz saw me and nodded.

"Life is death, Legate," I greeted him.

"There is no death in service to the Destroying Plague," Shazz extended three fingers.

The Destroying Plague

Answering with the same gesture just in case, I pointed to the arch growing out of the dead soil.

"What are you building?"

"It is a Plague Ziggurat. A concentrator of deathly energy. There is much of it here. The ziggurat will strengthen my legions greatly once it is built."

"So, when you complete your plan here, you'll be sending those legions to the continent?"

"That is the next stage."

"How did you get a portal through to here anyway? Why not do the same on the continent? Why did the Nucleus need me?"

"The Destroying Plague was spread long ago. Back when all the nine Legates walked Disgardium. But it did not take root everywhere. The living suppressed the infection whenever they had the slightest suspicion, burning both the bodies of the infected and any emerging vectors."

I remembered reading about the sporadic appearance of low-level undead instances.

"That which was left here, on Kharinza, remained whole and even grew. Later, when you came to the island, the Nucleus ordered the locals to open the portal. They had enough strength to do so."

"The locals? But when we were there, I didn't see anyone..."

"Because you are in the Destroying Plague. If you were a stranger, you would have ended up in the domain of an insignificant necromancer lich, instead of the abode of the Nucleus."

"So now everything depends on me?" I decided to try and squeeze as much as I could out of the situation. "At the will of the Nucleus, I will build a stronghold of the Destroying Plague in populated lands. I'll need resources and a workforce."

"I cannot offer you those that are bound to me, Legate," the lich answered without emotion.

"I don't need your dead men. The Nucleus gave me the power to turn allies undead. Until I do so, I don't want to see any of your minions any closer than three hundred feet from the fort. The same for the mine."

"In the name of the Nucleus," the lich nodded. "You have my word, Legate. But you will need forces. Accept as a gift..."

Shazz stretched out his hands and a transparent stream of *Plague Energy* swam toward me from the tip of his index finger. The bar began to rise and soon reached the cap of one hundred thousand. Apparently, that was a drop in the ocean for the lich, but I thanked him. My head span, and my legs became so weak that I almost fell. With a barely perceptible nod, Shazz summoned the banshees and gave them a silent order. The officers led all the undead away from the fort and the route to the mine.

Feeling terrible, I barely held on until the problem of the undead was solved, then stumbled out of the game. Waiting with difficulty for the intra-gel to drain out, I collapsed out of my capsule.

The Destroying Plague

* * *

I got a fever. The 'home doctor' couldn't establish a precise diagnosis. An injection of anti-inflammatory and temperature-reduction drugs made me feel better and I burrowed under my covers.

Soon Tissa called, then rushed over as soon as she heard I was sick. My parents still weren't back, so the girl stayed the night. No, nothing like that. She looked after me, we talked, then we watched a couple of films and went to sleep. She was gone by dawn, so her dad wouldn't get upset.

By morning I felt a little better and I set up a meeting in the game, inviting Crawler, Bomber and Crag so as not to waste time moving through the city and to avoid listening ears on the comms. I told Infect to wait for my signal and then jump to Kharinza with Tissa. They'd stay there two or three minutes and we'd be able to announce the clan's decision. I also invited Gyula and Manny, because it was best that they decided the fate of their characters will full knowledge of the consequences, full knowledge that they probably wouldn't be able to change their race back.

The entire clan assembled on an early Sunday morning, except for Infect and Tissa, by the ruins of the Pig and Whistle. Patrick brought Crawler and Bomber from Glendale, and right then he was sleeping off some drink on a stall that had survived opposite the tavern, staunchly gripping a half-empty bottle of something dwarvish and very strong.

I spoke about my meeting with the Nucleus and about our options. About the hierarchy of the Destroying Plague, about the legendary quest, the new talents. I shared everything I'd seen and heard, except how it all ended. And then I thought about how to keep them from learning too much.

"Judging by the fact that there was no global Dis-wide notification, I guess you changed your mind?" Crawler asked. "Hey, where're you going?"

"One sec, just need to check something..."

I left my friends to cast a glance over the area occupied by the lich and his army. As we'd agreed, none of the dead had crossed the invisible boundaries we'd discussed. I didn't doubt for a second that it would stay that way. I just needed to buy a couple of minutes to think things over again.

Walking back to my clanmates, I looked at their faces; Crag impassive, Crawler with a look of concentration, Bomber smirking. Gyula and Manny were tidying up the remnants of the tavern in the meantime, with the builder frozen at the front wall of the building, focusing on his interface. I'd have to talk to them later and separately.

"Scyth, don't drag this out. What happened next?" Bomber clapped me hard on the shoulder, but I didn't move a muscle. "Did you kill the Nucleus?"

"Kill? No. I was about to loose an arrow, but I heard Behemoth's voice in my head. He said only one word, but it was so loud that my head nearly exploded. *Stop!* he shouted. Hell knows. Maybe it wasn't even the Sleeping God, maybe I just imagined it. And now I don't know what I was even thinking. That damn lich became damn near invulnerable as the only Legate left. I got practically the same undead curse myself... How could I have thought I could kill that thing? Whether it's a god or just something like one doesn't matter. It isn't that easy to kill. And I bet it all! Long story short, I didn't shoot..."

"What did the Nucleus do?" Crag asked.

"Nothing. I don't think it can even see anything, and in my head all I said was 'As you wish, my lord.' Although maybe it doesn't even read thoughts and I was just playing it too safe."

"Shouldn't it have reacted at least somehow? You used the Balancer on it!"

"The mechanics of that artifact are weird anyway! Maybe the target doesn't realize that its level drops. We'll have to figure that out later. We'll experiment on someone, find out what the target sees and feels. The point is that the Nucleus seemed to kind of switch off after my words. The light went out around it, the cave fell into darkness. Nothing else happened, so I just went back to the plague portal and through to the mine here on Kharinza. I asked our colleague in our little sect," I pointed toward the Shazz, "to take his minions away from here. Then I staggered over to the tavern and logged out. Felt horrible, even in the game. To be honest, yesterday I didn't even want to go on. Especially since I needed to talk to you guys before doing anything..."

"Alright, let's make a decision already," Bomber said. "I got no idea what we've been doing the last few days. Where's our good old power-leveling? Grinding? Farming? We've laid our path to the instances, Infect is coming out tomorrow. A full party. Sure, no healer, but to hell with it. We can roll over everything with an invulnerable tank and our cheat Crag. What do we have to do to turn undead? If you don't transform us today, I'm leaving the clan."

"We'll all leave," Crag said darkly. "Let's at least look at the race description. The bonuses, penalties..."

I linked the description in the chat. To tell the truth, I hadn't even had time to look at it all in detail the previous day. I was more concerned by my meeting with the Nucleus.

Undead

A variety of creatures in the world of Disgardium that are raised after death through divine or supernatural forces. This name applies to all creatures that function regardless of their life having ended.

Spontaneously arising undead may be found all over Disgardium, usually in the form of wights or ghosts. The most well-known types of undead — zombies and ghosts — are people who have returned to life after death. They are usually bloodthirsty creatures incapable of rational thought and hostile to any living creatures they encounter in their path.

The living dead were used as a weapon of war

The Destroying Plague

in the time of the Old Gods, when the first self-taught necrolytes learned to reanimate the corpses of fallen soldiers in the form of skeleton warriors. Later, this knowledge turned into a new type of magic called Necromancy, which is banned both in the Commonwealth and the Empire. The neutral races also have a zero-tolerance policy for this forbidden magic.

The spirits of the living dead are poorly connected to their bodies. The dark magic that supports the undead state serves as a buffer that prevents the body and the soul from fully connecting. Therefore the undead do not feel pain or other tactile sensations from most physical stimulants, and it is also why Light causes the living dead such pain.

Racial bonuses

Ice or Flame, It's All the Same... — *+100% resistance to climate influences.*

Pour Me More of that Poison — *+100% resistance to poisons and your blood is toxic to all life.*

Will of the Destroying Plague — *full resistance to crowd control effects.*

Don't Breathe! — *you can spend an unlimited time underwater.*

Cannibalism — *eat the bodies of your enemies to restore 5% health per second.*

Tirelessness — *you need no rest and your Vigor stat is disabled.*

Racial penalties

Absolute Evil — the intelligent races of Disgardium feel nothing but hate toward you.

Murderous Light — +100% damage taken from light magic, and light healing spells deal damage to you instead of healing you.

I Can't Feel My Legs — movement speed on foot reduced by 25%.

This Is For the Living — -50% effectiveness of healing and mana potions.

What a Monster! — -75% charisma.

It Reeks — the persistent stench of rotting flesh emanates from you.

"Hey, at least we'll stick together," Bomber joked, reading the last one. "Ain't that a comfort. So, are we transforming into undead or what?"

"What about Infect?" I recalled Malik. "Let's call him?"

"What about him?" Crawler shrugged. "You can only be human in the Tristad sandbox. He'll have to make his choice when he leaves, and for now we can only talk about us. Seems to me like we decided everything yesterday... But we should tell him. I'll go call him and get him to jump here.

"Excuse me," Gyula approached and interrupted Ed. "Got a moment, Alex?"

The boys nodded in understanding and I followed the builder. He went out onto the street and headed for the sanctuary.

The fort looked lifeless and deserted. No

buildings suffered except the tavern and the temple, and the bodies of the undead and mercenaries were gone. The blood, too. Nonetheless, the atmosphere itself felt heavy. Even the air seemed stinking and vile, possibly because of the army of dead people nearby. And that was strange, because when I became undead, I stopped smelling anything or noticing dead flesh even though I left the character settings at default.

We got to the top of the pyramid which had served as a foundation for the temple that had still stood there two days ago.

"Do you see the ruins?" Gyula asked.

"Ruins?" I asked in surprise. "There's nothing left here. Just some garbage, but I think that was here before the temple too."

"Garbage..." Gyula sighed. "You're not a builder, so you don't see it. Yes, the dead carried something off, but only what they found. I see more. Almost ninety percent of all the building materials are left: wood, stone, sand... We can either 'mine' them or 'fix' them. I can restore the temple, or, since we're already on the evil team and aren't planning to do that, I could break it down for resources."

"Leave it as it is for now," I answered. "When the time comes to restore the temple, I'll tell you."

"As you say. Can I borrow a few resources from here in the meantime? I want to repair the tavern."

"I think so, yeah. The tavern is the heart of the fort, we need it..."

Chuckling, Gyula walked to the spot where the altar had been, took out some tools and started hitting the air with a pick. That's what it looked like to me. *So much for realism,* I thought.

The process of gathering resources interested me. I moved closer and saw that Gyula really was hitting the air. But the pick didn't reach the piles of garbage; it hit some kind of resistance, striking against something, and each strike gave off a definite knock. Well, if there was a non-spatial inventory in the game, and when you looted a rat zombie you got its carefully collected innards in your bag, then it wasn't a stretch to believe in invisible 'ruins' that only builders could see. It made sense the more I thought about it: I hadn't seen any ore in the mine, even when Manny pointed straight at it. Rocks and stones.

"When we first got here, were there ruins then too?"

"There were," Gyula answered. "But they couldn't be repaired, so I just mined them. I didn't have the design..."

"Which?"

"*Sanctuary of the Departed.* I dug through the auction house later out of interest, looked online — couldn't find anything with that name." Gyula suddenly stopping striking with his pick. "Alright, Alex... Step back..."

Moving me aside, he started taking apart the invisible ruins. Suddenly, a body appeared, lying on the ground where a pile of garbage had just been.

The Destroying Plague

"I swear on Behemoth's snout, that's... That's Anf!"

It really was the dead insectoid's body. And I was wondering where the guardians had gotten to! Even yesterday it occurred to me that the lich might have raised them and added them to his army, but I didn't see anything of the sort among Shazz's minions. What if...

I targeted Anf's corpse and activated Plague Reanimation, mentally thanking Shazz for the energy he'd given me.

Raise Anf, level 307 colicoid, as an undead?
Costs: 1,000 Plague Energy.
Cost to maintain: 1,000 Plague Energy per day.

Confirming, I got a new system message:

Preserve the mind of raised Anf, level 307 colicoid?

"Nether..." I whispered, feeling my lips curve into a smile. "Yes!"

* * *

An hour later, under a persistent light summer rain, the satyr, succubus, insectoid and raptor had all joined our clan meeting. *Dead*, with strips of flesh hanging off, rotting wounds and bones sticking out here or there, but alive! Gyula cleared the space by the altar alone, digging out all the bodies, and I spared no *Plague Energy* to raise all the former guardians.

"I've climbed out of the deepest ass there is," Flaygray muttered. He scratched himself desperately, although by all the laws of nature, nothing should be itching due to his dead nerves. "I don't even know where you've brought me, Scyth. We never agreed that I'd turn into this," he pointed at himself. "I'll be the laughingstock of the Underworld!"

"Stop scratching, Flay, I'm sick of it," the succubus grimaced. She was the best preserved of the bunch, but a part of her scalp was peeling, she had a hole in a cheek and a broken horn. You couldn't call her beautiful anymore. Also, the guardians had lost all their abilities, gaining instead the standard "hit-tear-bite" from the zombie arsenal. "You have a phantom itch and you're only making it worse with your claws. And unless you somehow missed it, you aren't going to any Underworld. We're bound to Scyth, sure as death, ha-ha..." Nega's laughter could be called hysterical if it wasn't so creepy.

Calming down, the succubus stuck her tongue through the hole in her cheek and winced.

"I don't think they'll let me into the Underworld Beauty Contest," she said. "And how do I drink? It all leaks out!"

"Does alcohol even work on these bodies now?"

the satyr asked doubtfully.

"I'll be trying out all my body's functions," the succubus said threateningly, looking at me. "Now I understand what that lich was telling me, boss..."

Crawler and Bomber had never met the living guardians — they were traveling to instances that day, and now they silently stared at them open-mouthed and stayed out of the way. Especially since Ripta and Anf weren't silent, and their strange chittering and shrieking only added fuel to the flames. To put it mildly, the guardians were very unhappy. Particularly when they learned that when my supply of *Plague Energy* ran out, they'd fall down dead again. There was also the question of where they'd go when I logged out of the game, but there was only one way to find that out.

I didn't know what it did; whether the need to be subject to their Legate or the authority (unlikely) of the clan leader, but when I barked out *Silence!* — they all shut up. Most of all I was annoyed by the soul-piercing vibrating chittering of the insectoid, so I called Iggy over and sent he and his senior almost-relative Anf to talk silently in a corner.

"The Sleeping God Tiamat can return you to your former selves," I said. "And give you life back. At least that's what Behemoth told me, and I'm inclined to trust him. So in the grand scheme of things, nothing has changed — we still need to build a temple in the desert, just like before."

Ripta emitted a short squawk and Flay

translated everything for him.

"Why not here?" Bomber nodded toward the temple. "You could consecrate it to Tiamat, right? She'll take off your Destroying Plague marker, bring back your human..."

"Under the lich's nose?" Crawler interrupted his thought.

"Who cares about the lich?" Bomber started arguing. "The mercenaries, the guardians, plus with Scyth here I doubt the lich will be invincible again..."

"No," I interrupted. "Just trust me, no. We needed two temples even before the undead invaded, and nothing has changed now. We're nobody without the Destroying Plague, and the Nucleus won't forgive a second betrayal. It'll take away all our abilities and put a debuff on us. Even if we can deal with that, restore Behemoth's temple, bring the god back, stop being undead and clear out the lich's army... We won't reach the second sanctuary, and since I have a portal to Holdest..."

"What?" everyone shouted at once. Even Crag sat up straight, widened his eyes and stopped yawning in melancholy.

"I found a lot in the treasury... Wasn't that clear from the armor? Or by the artifacts I sent you, Crawler? Let's figure out your faction change first, then start going through the loot. It would be very foolish to enter into a new confrontation with the Destroying Plague right now. We need to use the undead racial advantage. No climate or elemental debuffs can hurt us, you know? If we want, we can go explore Holdest, and nobody is going to be able to drag us out of there. But that's a plan B anyway, because I doubt we can deal with the mobs there. I suggest we all transform into undead. I'll change my appearance and lay a teleportation point next to the sanctuary in the desert. Then we can start work on the temple. If the builders agree, of course. As for us, we can go run through some instances and level up like we wanted to, plus try out the desert mobs. I just need to level up my one-shot ability first..."

Two clapping sounds suddenly rang out: Tissa and Infect had jumped to us. Crawler gave them a quick summary. Once he was finished, I quickly spoke — the guys from the sandbox were losing health fast as we watched.

"So, we've decided then? I'm transforming you into undead?" All you need to do is confirm it, then the character regeneration process takes a day. I'll do the same with the non-citizens. They're not in the clan, so we'll need to contact each separately..."

"That's all well and good..." Infect said. "But I don't know what I'm meant to be doing."

The thief was more nervous than anyone — he'd started chewing his lip and frowning. Tomorrow he'd leave the sandbox, and the boy was worried that he'd not only have to change his class, race and faction, but he'd also end up who knows where.

"Stay a human when your character regenerates, Malik. Head to the bard trainer, learn the class skills and jump to Kharinza. Then I'll transform you."

"Still with the bard idea?" the thief groaned. "God damn it..."

"Gotta go, Infect!" Tissa said loudly. "It's time!"

The girl blew me a kiss and took Infect back to Tristad. I cast a questioning glance at the others once again, and, seeing no objections, transformed Crag, Bomber and Crawler into undead. They disappeared from the game.

Then I spoke to the awake and sobered-up first priest of the Sleeping Gods. In the end Patrick just had to leave the clan, since he refused point-blank to become undead. Truth be told, I'd only invited him to the clan, so he'd recognize me. Patrick was scowling and frowning at the surroundings, occasionally gulping from a bottle.

The guardians didn't say a word, still silent after my command, but I saw Nega boiling over and Flaygray licking his lips as they looked at the bottle in Patrick's hands. I realized the problem and gave them permission.

"Speak."

An instant later I was already regretting it but didn't shut them up this time. Nega shouted curses in one of my ears, Ripta shrieked into the other, Anf traded chirrups with Iggy at a rapid pace. Only Flaygray behaved rationally. He approached Patrick, pointed at the bottle and said something. The old drunkard laughed, and soon both of them were embracing like old buddies, sitting on a stall and having a friendly chat, interrupted occasionally by lip-smacking gulps of their fiery drink. Nega watched them a while, then broke away to dig through the tavern ruins. She soon returned victorious, waving some surviving bottles of wine. Ripta also couldn't help himself and rolled a barrel of ale out onto the street, made a hole in it with his claw and set his mouth over the resulting fountain. Looked like the news made all the former guardians want to drink their fill. Well, that was understandable. I didn't try to stop them.

I still had to solve the problem of the non-citizens before I went out to the frontier. Inviting Manny, Gyula and Trixie, who'd just logged in, I told them of our need to build a second temple where no other race except the undead could survive at the current levels. I explained that if they changed their race, they probably wouldn't be able to visit the cities of the Commonwealth, which meant they wouldn't be able to find work with anyone but us. Sure, they could delete their characters and create new ones, but then they'd lose their leveled-up skills and the years of hard work that went into them. I showed the undead class bonuses to make them feel better. For the workers, Tirelessness was the deciding factor.

"Alex, tell me straight, do you have..." Manny hesitated and pulled at his hair. "Do we have a chance? Never mind that we'll look like dead men, that's nothing, I'm usually covered in mud as it is. I don't mind that we won't be able to taste food either..."

"Trixie loves tasty eating!" the dwarf protested.

"Don't worry about that," I smiled. "You can change that in the character settings any time. Snowstorm isn't stupid. They don't make unplayable races. If you want to drink, eat tasty food or... hm, do other pleasurable things, you can configure all that. As for our chances, I'd be lying if I told you they were high. The whole world will be against us very soon, and I have no idea what that's going to lead to. We're too weak and we're going to have to hide. A lot depends on how long we're able to hide and how much we manage to grow. But the reward is worth the risks. There'll be a lot of work, and we can mine rare ore, which means valuable ore. And you won't just make a paycheck, but also a cut of all our resource sales..."

The workers, and Manny and Gyula represented the interests of all Kharinza's non-citizens, didn't haggle. Initially I planned to offer them as much as half, but then I changed my mind. The clan had high expenses: equipping the fort, paying the miners and builders, buying materials for building the temple in the desert, security and transport through the continent... Long story short, we agreed to five percent of the total ore sales and I decided that we'd have to bring Overweight into the clan after all, to handle our trading. I'd also have to bring in her brother, Underweight, so we had someone to trade within the Commonwealth.

I didn't have time to discuss this with the guys, but there was still time before the girl left the sandbox anyway. Manny shook my hand for a long time. The brigadier was touched that they'd be taking a share. Those kinds of offers were too rare in a time when all the virtual corporations were squeezing the workers for all they were worth, and charging them even for their tools.

Toward the end of the conversation, when they'd already decided to log out to discuss it all in their own circle, I remembered something else.

"Trixie, you like mining ore, right?"

"Nah," the dwarf shook his head.

"Then do you want to be a gardener instead?"

Manny and Gyula looked at me doubtfully. I explained why we needed a gardener, showed them the *Seed of the Flesh-Eating Tree Protector* and waited for an answer in silence.

"So, the fruit, bark and leaves of this tree are really valuable?" Manny asked thoughtfully. "And it'll help us defend the fort too... Well, no question about it! Agree to it, Trixie!"

"How's he going to change his profession here?" Gyula asked pointedly.

"I can send him to Darant before he chooses the new faction. I'll jump there too, disguised as one of you. What do you say, Trixie?"

The dwarf blushed, feeling himself the center of attention of such respected individuals. To become a gardener, he'd need to abandon his mining profession, although fortunately he hadn't had time to level it up much anyway. On the other hand, the clan gardener would have a stable, high paycheck... That seemed to occur to him too. The dwarf smiled, gave me two thumbs up and spoke in pride:

"Trixie gonna be a gardener! Trixie gonna plant trees! Trixie gonna dig soil...!

Chapter 15

A Stroll Through Darant

T HE HIGH SUN burned so hot that even the shade of the white stone buildings didn't help. The surface of the streets was planned and polished to a mirror sheen by magic, blinding me and making me squint. The red-hot air stung my nostrils and throat. Uncle Nick once took me and my dad to a sauna. I remember feeling more comfortable there. If I'd been in my undead body, I'd probably have dried out into a mummy, but I'd turned into Manny and become a human. Unfortunately, the heat was the least of my problems.

After the quiet and deserted fort, Darant was full of colorful and eclectic crowds and chaos whose mysterious rhythm was impossible to match for an outsider.

Trixie and I barely dodged out of the way of a rushing cavalcade of top players, one of whom shouted as he passed by in a rumbling gnomish chopper.

"Out of the damn road, inwinova!"

I quickly moved onto the sidewalk under a hail of abuse, pulling the dwarf behind me. Trixie felt very uncomfortable and withdrew his head into his shoulders. It occurred to me that without me, he'd either get lost here or get into trouble. Especially with two thousand gold in his pocket for changing his profession and getting tuition and tools. A quarter of that money would probably have been enough, but I preferred to give him a buffer. What had he seen, except the roofs of anthill apartment buildings in Cali Bottom? And when would Trixie ever be in the Commonwealth capital again? Exactly, he was here for the first and probably the last time.

Taking him by the hand like a child, I dragged him to the nearest tavern. Firstly, he needed a place to stop for the night if he couldn't get everything done that day, and secondly... There were too many people on the streets to take on anyone else's guise without drawing attention, so I figured renting a room with a view of the street from the window wasn't a bad idea.

Considering the distance, going to the desert on foot was foolish, so I decided to first get to level forty, the minimum requirement for using a mount. I'd learn to ride one in Darant, find out the cost of common mounts and choose something basic. Maybe a riding donkey or ram like the ones the dwarfs loved to use. I decided I wouldn't bind the *Legendary Ghost*

The Destroying Plague

Wolf to myself just yet. Who knew, I might need money and I wouldn't be able to sell the mount if it was already soulbound. Apart from that, I wanted to try out my plague skills in combat.

To do that, I'd need an instance around fifteen to twenty levels above mine — the maximum for fast leveling while still being realistically achievable. Going into a harder dungeon made no sense: I'd constantly miss, and my plague reservoir wouldn't last long enough to kill the bosses.

I found a suitable dungeon in the Lake District, six hundred miles from Darant. Far away, but the main thing was that the instance didn't belong to any clans. If I went to an instance like that solo... at the minimum it would invite surprise and questions I didn't need.

Pushing my way through the crowd by the auction house, we passed the trade district and reached the three-story Lion's Pride, a big tavern where the highest city officials condescended to eat. The gilded statue of the king of beasts decorating the entrance moved; waved its tail, turned its head and opened its mouth in a soundless roar. *Sorry to burst your bubble, Mufasa, but in Dis you aren't even in the top ten strongest beasts*, I thought. *Monty eats guys like you in heaps. Even my Iggy probably wouldn't be scared of you...*

A smooth-shaven and muscular viking NPC in wine-red parade armor stood at the entrance, halberd in hand. He measured us up with an indifferent gaze but said nothing when I reached for the handle of the huge oak door. He didn't even think about helping. What was he even doing there? A level hundred viking was no use as a guard; the average player level had long since exceeded two hundred.

We entered the semi-dark of the hall. Ahead of us was the reception desk, to the left was a restaurant filled with voices, to the right — the hallway to the stairs leading to the guest rooms. A heavy bronze chandelier hung from the ceiling, and massive statues towered by the walls, showing all the races of the Commonwealth. The floor was covered in a rug woven of gleaming fibers that reflected all the colors of the rainbow.

Trixie froze like one of those statues at the sight of such luxury. He seemed paralyzed. I barely held back a grin; to me it seemed completely tasteless. The simple but cozy Bubbling Flagon was much more up my street.

The player woman fulfilling the role of receptionist didn't pay us any attention at all.

"Hello!" I said, walking toward her confidently. "We need a room, please."

"We don't serve workers," she said coldly.

"I have money," I took out a handful of gold and showed it to the woman.

She didn't even look at it.

"Bjorg!" she shouted. The door opened and the viking appeared. "Throw these two out at once! Why did you let them in anyway?"

The Destroying Plague

"You said I should let humans and elves in without discrimination, Helga."

"Humans, Bjorg, humans! Not smelly miners!"

Instead of waiting for the guard to use force, I quickly moved to the exit. As offensive as it was, the tavern was a private business and its staff had the right to decide who to serve and who not to. But this felt too much like the real world. It felt nothing like Snowstorm's advertising campaigns about everyone being able to feel like a king or a hero in Dis.

I dragged the still-frozen Trixie outside, opened my map and started looking for a more basic tavern close to the gardeners' guild, realizing that leaving the dwarf here alone would be like abandoning a village kid in New York. He'd survive, but his money probably wouldn't. And Trixie had the mental age of an eight-year-old.

"Hey, good folk," I heard behind my back. The viking waddled toward us and whispered slyly: "You need food or a place to stay?"

"Both, honored Bjorg," I said.

"Then head to the Jolly Bear inn. My brother Bjorn stands guard there. Tell him I sent you. He'll show you in."

The viking explained the route, advising us not to use any coaches. "They'll take you to the cleaners," he explained. "That's the capital for you, Nether take it!"

A marker appeared for the Jolly Bear on the map, but although Bjorg was an NPC, there was no quest. Just the little AI that was the viking Bjorg, feeling the need to help some poor visitors to Darant. And maybe earn a little for the trouble.

It was a long way on foot to the tavern, but it led through the same part of the city that held the gardener's guild. Thinking for a moment, we decided to move under our own steam, meaning I decided so as not to cause suspicion, and Trixie gladly agreed. He was all in his curiosity, spinning his jug-eared head with his mouth agape, expressing childlike wonder at what he saw.

"Look, Scyth! Look!" the dwarf took me by the hand and jabbed his finger toward a barbarian on a mammoth. He didn't have the words. "Wooow!"

"Yeah, Trixie, wow! It's a mammoth. And we should go around it so it doesn't squash us..."

We walked through twenty-two districts that way, and it felt like I'd seen one long display case of everything you could buy in Dis. Truth be told, the sight impressed me no less than Trixie.

We stopped for a long time by street musicians — some played solo and some in groups, but thanks to magic, none of them played over each other. Invisible barriers around each musician removed all extraneous noise. Then I couldn't resist buying some Eternal Ice Cream for myself and the dwarf. I got chocolate and Trixie got one that randomly changes flavor. It wasn't actually all that eternal; it lasted just one day, but *all* that day.

The long walk of fame also had moving statues

of the greatest heroes of the Commonwealth, and then we wandered to Worship Square, surrounded by three dozen temples of the most respected gods of Disgardium.

Toward midday we decided to stop to eat. There was a huge variety of restaurants and cafes to choose from in Darant, but some delicious smells from a mobile snack stand dragged us there by our noses. The fat mustached cook, who personally made all his food on an open fire, cooked us a Fiery Hot Dog, covered it in tomato and garlic sauce and Ursai mustard and wrapped it up in some magic paper that steadily disappeared as you ate the hot dog. We had elvish fizz to drink. Our lunch cost us nine gold in total. We'd have to spend a year completing social quests for that money in Tristad...

There were a few more street food stands next to the hot dog stand, in which I saw dishes I could have made myself, like *Apple Cider, Roast Goose Wings* and *Beef in Dragonbreath Sauce*. Remembering the late chef at the Bubbling Flagon, Uncle Arno, I promised myself not to neglect my cooking skill and to work on it as soon as I got some spare time.

Hot dog devoured, Trixie bounced in glee and pointed at the stand. "Wings! Wings!" The roast goose wings gave off a breathtaking aroma.

Sighing, I bought him a whole basket full. He tried one, his eyes widened, and he licked his lips. I pulled one out to try too, and then didn't even notice myself reaching for another. Trixie cast an agitated glare my way but said nothing. Nether, but those wings were delicious! Hmm, *Raw Goose Wings*, the main ingredient of the dish, weren't that expensive...

"You know what?" I said to the dwarf, chuckling. "I know how to make these wings myself! So, don't worry, this isn't the last time you'll eat them."

The thought of renewing my *Cooking* activities got even stronger when we walked past a cookware store. I stood there a moment studying the display cases and couldn't help but go in. At first, I wanted to buy everything, and my inventory was big enough. They had it all! Frying pans, saucepans, pots, portable ovens and stoves, knives and all kinds of accessories with generous cooking bonuses.

In the end I bought a *Universal Mobile Pot* (*+5% chance to invent a new dish*), a *Cook's Hat* and a *Chef's Apron* (in total, *+50 to cooking skill* and *+15% cooking speed*). I also bought some new cooking recipes, all kinds of herbs and spices, some balsamic vinegar and a special kind of oil for frying. My *Kaizen Chef Knife,* given to me by Oliver at the *Cookery Duel,* was still waiting for its day in the kitchen.

We'd almost reached the gardener's guild, but Trixie grabbed me by the arm.

"Scyth..." he said, licking his ice cream cone. "I want to stay and live here. Can I?"

What was I supposed to say? That this city would chew him up and spit him out? That he wouldn't last three days here before he got kicked out? Those were the terms for visitors. If you wanted to live there, you had to be useful to the city, make some contacts and pay your dues. At least earn the respect of the people. Otherwise, three days — then you got a Disturber of the Peace debuff and hello, Darant City Watch! Those guys wouldn't just throw you out of the capital, they'd also drop your reputation so low that if you broke just a couple of other rules, you wouldn't be able to go back to the city at all.

I grew up as an only child, but I had enough experience talking to my parents' friends' children.

"You know, Trixie," I said, coming to a decision. "You can't stay and live here because we need you in Kharinza. I need you. Without your help, the fort will be defenseless and ugly. This place is full of strangers, but Kharinza is home, with all your friends, right? But you know what? We won't turn you into an undead, alright? That way you can come here sometimes — with me or with one of the other guys."

At first his face twisted from tears he could barely hold back, but it smoothed out with every sentence, and by the end it held a smile. Some would have called Trixie's face ugly — it was pockmarked, his teeth were yellow and crooked — but it was sincere. I clapped the dwarf on the shoulder.

"Now let's go do what we came here to do."

Trixie nodded and started mumbling a silly song about dancing clouds, a grasshopper playing a violin and something about streams. I remembered meeting him for the first time on an anthill roof in Cali Bottom half a year ago. He seemed so angry and threatening to me then. The memory made my heart feel lighter. I realized that I was starting to grow up and think of more than just myself.

Surrendering to my whims, I dragged Trixie into the nearest tailor shop and bought him some nice clothes — without special bonuses, but with big pluses to *charisma*. At least people might treat him in a little better in Dis that way.

Then we finally reached the guild. The dwarf slowed down at every window for the rest of our journey, looking at his reflection. He liked what he saw. He drew his shoulders back and walked with me further until he stopped again to get another look at his impeccable outfit.

I watched him with a smile, waited patiently and thought that when all this was over, I'd need to finish Patrick's quest after all and 'make a man of him,' or whatever it said in the quest...

* * *

After Trixie retrained as a gardener, we spent a little time in the guild store picking out decorations for the fort. Everything, even the trees, was sold in seed form, and the range was huge. I downloaded the catalog and flipped through it with interest, noting a few defensive plants like *Fiery Wasabi*, *Windblower Clover* and *Explosive Grapes*.

The Destroying Plague

Flesh-eating Sunflowers and *Healing Aloe Vera* also caught my eye. The first shot from afar, piercing its enemy with seeds that immediately began to grow. The aloe vera's name speaks for itself. It was clear that these plants weren't particularly effective in the beginning, but their level grew as they aged, and looking after them with special gardener skills and fertilizer sped up their growth. We bought those too.

We also couldn't resist buying a rare set of clothes with impressive bonuses to stats and gardening. The dwarf outright refused to put the set on, saying it was work gear, and he was there to relax.

You couldn't call Trixie smart, but he was no idiot either. And he wasn't naive. The school of life in Cali Bottom had at least taught him not to trust strangers and to see them first and foremost as a danger. That was why I confidently entrusted him with our purchases, worth in excess of five thousand gold in total.

Expensive, but the Special Section of the store had even crazier prices with a bunch of zeroes! All our purchases were *green*, uncommon quality. We added some ordinary vegetable and berry cultures to the pile, along with some fruit trees. The climate was favorable on Kharinza, and in a week or two, I thought, the whole fort would be gratefully eating apples, pears, pineapples, bananas and mangos. Melons, watermelons and pumpkins also existed in this world, and we bought their seeds too, so Trixie

---

would have enough work for a long time to come. And Aunt Stephanie would be so pleased! She'd have plenty to add some variety to the Pig and Whistle's menu.

We put what we'd bought into the special, multi-functional *Gardener's Bag.* Not an epic, but like any crafting container, it provided almost one-hundred-percent security. *Almost,* because there was still a chance to lose a certain proportion of the contents. That was to provide motivation for those that would never play without PvP opportunities.

After this, we quickly walked to the inn that Bjorg had recommended, this time without getting distracted. Once he heard that his brother had sent us, Bjorn, an exuberant and noticeably soused viking in a horned helmet, took us to the innkeeper. Without asking us any questions, he gave us a key to a room which turned out to be tiny, but quite comfortable, with clean windows and neat furniture, along with a great view of the lively street.

I looked out of the window and saw the dwarf Gonzo, the same one I'd turned into in the guest room of the Darant city hall. Since our last meeting, the player had leveled up and was now hurrying to the red-light district, whose closeness was what made the street so lively.

The district of forbidden pleasures was wisely hidden from gentle eyes with a semi-transparent, space-distorting barrier. My heart sped up at the thought of what went on there. I shook myself of the idea to go and 'just take a look.' It didn't seem right. Maybe it even felt like it would be a betrayal against Tissa.

Nobody would be able to pick up Trixie today, everyone's characters were regenerating, so he had almost another full day to enjoy himself in the capital. I could guess how he planned to do that based on the foggy glances he threw toward the neighboring district with its alluring red glow, but I wasn't about to judge him.

In the end, I took on the guise of a hunter called Headshot, which seemed most suitable to my aims. He was a level fifty-seven human of middle height, around age thirty, with a close-cropped haircut and mismatched equipment that even included a low-level epic. Iggy transformed into the black panther Biter. I had yet to find out know how the flying needler would use his abilities in battle, or what that would look like for onlookers and the combat logs.

I didn't waste any more time. I gave Trixie clear instructions to not get carried away and waste clan property, to avoid gambling institutions, and under no circumstances to get up to the kind of perversions he was obviously excitedly dancing about. My instructions given; I left the dwarf's spartan room. If everything went to plan, I could pick up Trixie tomorrow after school.

I left the Jolly Bear and paused, trying to figure out which way to go. A player carriage stopped nearby; a common horse and a common cart that gave plus twenty percent movement speed. He offered his services and the price was right. It took twenty minutes of rough road for him to get me to the auction house, and he took fifteen gold for the trouble.

The viking was right; this city was a rip-off. It seemed like copper and silver weren't even in circulation there, all the prices were in gold! I really needed my own mount, and soon. The question was — could I buy one?

Thousands of players jostled under the high roof of the Commonwealth's main auction house. The place was four soccer fields big, and hundreds of NPC auctioneers all along the walls called out the names of exclusive lots. Considering the size of the market, this method seemed less than perfect, but it wasn't just for show — players present in person and shouting bids had the advantage. If nobody had been there, the exclusive lots would be publicly accessible to those who preferred to use the in-game interface for the auction house.

People like me. After my faction change, I wasn't sure I could use the Commonwealth auction house. Successfully buying the Eternal Ice Cream gave me some hope that my *Imitation* worked not only on a visual level. And I was right.

In Tristad, I had to take a catalog from the auctioneer to access the lots. Here I just clicked the relevant button that appeared as soon as I walked into the building. For the game system, I was human, not undead.

The first thing I did was buy a bunch of strong arrows with various tips: *venomous, freezing, burning, piercing, explosive...* I added some *Splintering Shots*, which were self-guiding and hit three targets at once. Having filled my quiver to the brim and spent several thousand gold, I started choosing a mount.

Firstly, I filtered out everything with a quality above rare. I needed something simple and unassuming. I'd have taken a horse, but that wasn't the best choice for the desert. *Lakharian Dromedaries*, one-humped camels, were better for riding across sand. Unfortunately, they were epic and very expensive.

I had to settle for a *blue* ostrich mech. The gnomish mechanical transport reflected the strange love of the little people for ostriches, but in contrast to the living birds, it had no penalties on rough terrain. Nine thousand gold... Expensive, but everything I'd spent that day I considered an investment. If I thought about it otherwise, I'd have just sold everything and quit the game.

Spotted Mechostrich
Rare
Mount.
+200% movement speed.
Once considered the height of gnomish technology, the mechostrich has become a popular

means of transport among all the races of the Commonwealth. It requires no food, water or maintenance.

The gnomes say that the mechostrich is made without a drop of magic, but then how does it restore itself and what is its power source?

Not a battle pet. Does not take part in conflicts. Hides head in the sand at first sign of danger.

Requires level: 40.

Requires riding skill.

I'd bought the mount, but I couldn't use it yet, so I hid the mechostrich's *Summoning Whistle* in my bag and headed to the stationary portals, which thankfully weren't far away.

The Portal Hall building was like a spaceport — the same kind of labyrinth of life, with passengers rushing everywhere. It looked a lot smaller on the outside than inside. Magic. Magic everywhere. It seeped into everything in Dis. Mana, the basis of any magic, was the breath of the gods, whose source of strength was faith. That was the trade, mana for faith; intelligent creatures gave the gods faith and the gods gave them mana. As the population and followers of gods grew in number, so too grew the amount of mana in all existence, and along with it, magic and spells became stronger and more destructive from year to year. I recalled *Armageddon*, that Hinterleaf had used. It appeared in the game not so long ago.

There were permanent portals, arches fifteen

The Destroying Plague

feet tall and thirty feet wide, leading to the largest cities of the Commonwealth — the capitals of the gnomes, dwarfs, elves and other races. To get to other destinations, you had to order a personal or group portal, which was far more expensive. The transport guild competed with the clans for every high-level spatial mage, giving them huge paychecks and offering them the best working conditions. As a result, those portals cost ludicrous sums.

It was cheaper to fly by airship or griffin. The first belonged to the same transport guild, while the Royal Griffin Airlines network belonged to Bastian the First himself. But in both cases the journey would have taken too much time; a day or more.

After queuing a while, I found myself face to face with a frowning goblin in a peaked cap.

"Destination?" he asked in a squeaky voice.

"The Lake District."

"Three thousand one hundred gold," the goblin said without skipping a beat.

A payment window popped up. Suppressing my desire to tell the goblin what I thought of his attitude and then go catch an airship, I paid the required amount. It would take me several days to fly so far. The goblin gave me a metal token with some small text flashing on it:

Destination: Lake District.
One-way ticket.
Take advantage of transport guild portals!

Instant, safe, reliable!

"Happy travels, Headshot!" the goblin grinned, baring sharp teeth. "Next..."

Chapter 16

Lake District

ONCE IN THE LAKE DISTRICT, I wasted no time; I headed straight for the instance called Abandoned Ruins of Dothleran. The recommended level was sixty. There were three bosses and packs of roaming human mobs inside. I should be able to handle it.

It took me an hour and change to get to the dungeon, but I made it before nightfall. The entrance was through some huge lopsided gates with a portal field stretched across them.

There was a group of players gathered at the respawn point. Judging by the fact that one of them was without pants and the other was in a shirt, they'd just wiped. An elf girl screamed at them, her voice breaking, until someone asked her to stop.

"We don't have enough damage!" said a thickset dwarf warrior in pants. The tank, judging by his full-length shield. "The healer's doing fine, I'm holding aggro, but we ain't killing 'em before enrage kicks in!"

"What are you implying, Garran?" the elf girl

turned on him.

"Three percent! Three percent!" the cleric wailed.

"You don't understand! I lost my coat! My epic coat! If only you knew how hard it was to get..." another player whined, an elvish archer.

He was almost crying, and the others looked crestfallen too. For a second, I even thought of offering to help them finish the dungeon. In the end I changed my mind and slipped past them to the gates.

In big Dis, unlike the sandbox, whenever a group of players entered a dungeon, a copy of it was created especially for them. But the rules were the same: if the group wiped, they lost their progress and had to start over. And the worst of it was that you had no way to get back any items you lost. They just got added to the dungeon's loot pool.

I couldn't go in right away. A warning appeared before me:

Attention!

You are trying to go into the Abandoned Ruins of Dothleran, intended for completion by a group of players with a minimum level of 60!

Your level (39) is beneath the recommended level. Are you sure you want to enter?

Ah, if only you knew how much money I spent to get here! I thought.

"Hey, dumbass!" the crying and depressed elf

archer shouted at me. "Where do you think you're going with your fifty-seven levels? And solo too?"

Looking around, I saw that the whole failed group had formed a semicircle, blocking my retreat. Had they decided to make up for their lost gear by ganking a lone noob? And I'd wanted to help them...

"Stop!" the archer shouted, but I'd already walked into the instance.

Now even if they followed me, they'd end up in another copy of the dungeon.

The instance was gloomy. Destroyed buildings loomed against a crimson sunset. The skeletons of burnt trees reached into the sky. The air smelled of wildfire. Stone blocks towered all around and I saw the foundations of buildings — there used to be some town here, but now fire cultists had set up shop in its remnants.

The first group of eight mobs stood nearby, but I paid them no attention for the time being. The cultists were arranged in a circle, arms linked, and heads bowed.

"Well, Iggy, want to have some fun?" I asked my pet, clenching my fists. "Stay behind me, don't get up close, attack from afar. If they attack you, run. Got it?"

My pet in his panther disguise growled his agreement. I took my bow in hand and began to approach the group of cultists.

"Intruder!" one of the mobs shouted at the top of his lungs.

The pack split into two groups of four: one stayed at range and shot me from afar while the other entered into close combat.

The first battle stretched out. At first I placed myself before the strikes of the enraged cultists, waiting with some anxiety for *Destroying Plague Immortality* to activate. The ability activated without issue when I should have died.

Then, sluggishly throwing out *Combos* and *Crushing Hammerfists* strengthened by my epic knuckledusters, I analyzed the logs. They appeared before me in full, displaying what was really happening and what others watching would see.

Iggy fired a *Needleshot* and missed. Yes, the damage was zero, but the visible part of the logs reported that it was a *Clawstrike* dealt by Biter. This was pretty transparent, of course, since it was impossible to deal melee damage from thirty feet away, but it was better than the logs saying that a panther was throwing around swamp needler larva. Just next time I used *Imitation*, I'd have to pick a pet with a similar fighting style to my own.

With my attacks it was easier, even in spite of the fact that I didn't have hunter class skills. A hunter would, of course, have used far more abilities in his rotation, but that didn't matter much.

While I was reading, I got cut with knives, stabbed with swords and shot all over with fireballs that tried to burn me alive. Nothing new. Although my *Resilience* was capped out at this rank and hadn't gone up, the *Plague Energy* I'd spent on raising and supporting the guardians was recovering. Long story short, I was spending my time profitably whichever way I looked at it.

My ordinary strikes often missed my target due to the level difference, but my skill levels and the *Unarmed Combat* skill itself grew as if on steroids. I was in no hurry. I'd need to spend a bunch of time to complete the instance just because even a full bar of *Plague Energy* was only enough to kill one or two mobs. No way around it with elites. It was far more important to level up *Immortality* itself to increase my plague reservoir's maximum.

After I managed to take out one particularly frisky cultist who stabbed me in the eye in a frenzy, I decided to see how he would behave in battle on my side. I activated *Plague Reanimation* on his corpse but didn't preserve his mind.

Mindless Zombie Cultist, level 61
Undead Human
Scyth's minion

An extra control panel appeared at the bottom of my view. That was interesting. I hadn't gotten that when I raised the guardians. Seemed like mindlessness required micromanagement.

The zombie pet stood nearby, drooling and growling, not getting into the battle. His eyes were empty and glazed over, although his dead hand still hadn't released the knife. Hoping that I wouldn't have to control the zombie's every step and using one arm to repel the furious cultists' attempts to take my head off, I started studying.

Although the crackle of burning flesh was distracting, to say the least. It broke my concentration, and the smells weren't helping either. Unable to stand the stink, I quickly went to my settings and lowered my threshold for touch, smell and taste to the minimum. The three senses switched off and I immediately found it easier to concentrate.

I looked at the minion icon. A row of commands extended from it: Stand, Follow, Protect, Patrol, Attack. Right, so it actually didn't need micromanaging exactly. The pet would decide when and which skills to use. Great.

Now that I knew what was what, I ordered it to protect me and the zombie woke up and rushed into the battle. The cultists, who hadn't yet attacked him, seemed surprised, then switched their target and started tearing their former colleague to pieces. That allowed me to get up and move a little further away. I noticed that my left leg had practically been cut off, but the magic of the dead held it in place, and it didn't cause particular discomfort — it was just visual effects.

The last thing I had to figure out was how my plague abilities leveled up. Counting the guardians, I'd already raised five dead people, but the *Plague Reanimation* skill had increased by just twenty five percent. The *Destroying Plague Immortality* progress bar still showed level one, with only a few points of progress. What played a role? Time while the ability was active? Number of activations?

I got an answer within a few minutes. When I killed another cultist with an arrow infected with plague energy, it boosted *Immortality* slightly, then the bar grew another percent on its own. I'd need to figure it out more precisely later, but it seemed like roughly a quarter of an hour for one percentage of growth at level one.

I'd gathered enough information. It was time to get to work. My zombie was in pieces by then, and the others switched back to me. The first thing I did was release a *Ghastly Howl*. My mouth opened in a snarl, visualizing the ability. It had no effect, but old habits die hard. Then I lost a plague arrow into the gown of a swordsman as he ran at me and attacked another with red tattoos on his face.

My smile grew wider with every second — pure, reliable grinding, oh how I missed you! I actively used all my moves from *Unarmed Combat* and *Archery*, leveling up both them and the plague skills. Everything was leveling up fast considering how far above me the mobs were, and I was getting a constant stream of experience.

It took me about an hour to deal with the first pack, but then the process sped up. I approached the next group of pyromaniac fire cultists with a group of six *Brainless Zombie Cultists*.

I gathered the mobs around me to gain *Plague Energy* but didn't release the zombies into battle until it was time. The game conveniently showed the aggro level of each group member, including the pets, so it wasn't hard to keep track of things. After the first kill in the pack, I could send the zombies in — the kill tripled my threat in the eyes of the mobs.

The third pack brought me up to level forty. I spent my points on my physical stats. Iggy also made gains. *Plague Reanimation* leveled up to two, but there were no visible changes in the skill. It did cost a little less energy, at least. *Destroying Plague Immortality* also leveled up, doubling the plague reservoir and increasing the conversion of damage taken into energy up to two percent. That would be a key factor in the clan's future leveling. The beasts in the Lakharian Desert had tens of millions of health, so leveling up *Immortality* was essential.

Putting down two more groups of cultists brought me to the first boss. As soon as I looked at him, I realized there was no point in trying — I wouldn't take down over a million health if I hit him for a year. While I saved up plague energy for my next shot, the boss would recover his health, and there was no other way for me to scratch him. Unfortunately, I retreated.

I didn't get any decent loot — just more scraps of *Silk Cloth*, a little gold and a couple of *green* pieces of gear. I didn't throw them away, remembering how hard our workers worked for every gold they earned.

The Destroying Plague

This stuff was crap, garbage, but still a monthly paycheck for Trixie in the days of the Olton Quarries.

I sacrificed the zombies wandering after me before I left, so as not to waste plague energy on them. It cost enough to keep the guardians alive... or at least lively. The zombies weren't much help in battle, they didn't deal much damage and there wasn't much use in them at all. Low level cannon fodder. I hoped that leveling up *Plague Reanimation* would let me raise more impressive beasts like the *Bone Hounds*.

With those thoughts, I stepped through the instance portal. *Immortality* still hadn't ticked off, but I still looked like a human, if an injured one — my health hadn't recovered yet.

"He's here!" someone yelped as soon as I appeared the gates.

I heard the patter of running feet and the clank of armor. I sighed sadly. These guys didn't look like evil gankers, just desperate loser. And each had ten thumbs if they couldn't complete the instance at level sixty.

"You spent a long time in there!" the elvish mage with the fine figure said. I couldn't help looking her up and down, but then I caught the girl's hateful gaze and took hold of myself. "Did you think we'd just leave?" she said.

"Guys, can we just go our separate ways?" I suggested. "I can guess what you want from me, but I'm not sure you'll get it."

"Listen, buddy," the priest said to me. "We've had a tough day, and now you've made us wait so many hours. Just give us everything you have and we'll let you live."

"What are you doing, guys?" the dwarf warrior rumbled. "That's not what we agreed! Listen, Headshot, three pieces of gear, our choice, and we won't touch you. Enzo needs your coat, he lost his epic inside. I need your pants, and..."

"Garran, what are you doing?" the elf girl interrupted the tank. "Are you nuts? Let's just take him down and it'll all be ours!"

"And who's gonna give me my epic back?" Enzo the elvish archer spat.

"Gear is important," I said, trying to calm the elf down. Epics were hellish to get for casual players like him. Some people saved up money in real life, sacrificing in the real world to make progress in Dis. This guy seemed like one of them. "What do you need a PvP flag for? Your nicks will go red, it's a whole thing..."

"This guy ain't wrong," Garran said, suddenly stepping back and raising his hands, trying to reason with the party. "Let him go in piece, since we can't come to an agreement..."

"Then why did we wait for him so long?" Enzo whined. "No, Garran, we have to get back what we lost!"

I couldn't retreat peacefully to the Kharinza tavern using *Return Stone*, they wouldn't have given me the five seconds to cast it. I could leave with *Depths Teleportation*, but... I was sick of running.

"What're you standing there for?" the elf girl snapped. "Get him!"

Flame shrouded her hands. Black smoke began to emanate from the priest. I didn't even twitch an ear when the rogue slipped behind me to cut off my retreat. Instead, looking at the elf girl and her sorcery, I spoke calmly.

"Your friend Garran is a little nicer than you guys. So, I won't take his stuff. As for the rest of you..."

A fireball seethed through the air and exploded, covering my chest in plasma. The archer drew his bow, the priest spread his hands in a spell. Glancing at his teammates, the warrior began a *Charge*...

My *Ghastly Howl* pulled the rogue out of stealth, and I finished him off first with an arrow to the throat. I added a little plague energy, of course. Then I took three more shots, enough to kill the archer, priest and the warrior Garran. The elf girl recovered from *Fear*, saw her comrades' corpses, went white and extended pleading hands.

"Don't kill me!" she begged uncertainly. "You got it all wrong! We just wanted to scare you..."

"Didn't work."

An adamantine arrow pierced the girl's stomach and the plague energy finished her off. I didn't take any pleasure in it, but let it be a lesson to the novice gankers.

I doubted they realized what exactly had happened. It wasn't their first death that day, so they wouldn't be back soon. Looting the corpses, I filled my bag all the way. I left Garran's things untouched as promised.

Then I went back to the Lake District, where I hid and watched out for a new disguise. Only then did I jump to Darant, to the Jolly Bear. Judging by the map, Trixie was still entertaining himself in the red-light district. I rented a room, left my character there and logged out.

The Lakharian Desert awaited me tomorrow.

Chapter 17

Big Po's Ultimatum

S PRING CAME to the city. The snows melted, the air smelled of the first green shoots, hot asphalt and earth. We walked onto the landing pad under the weak hum of flyers taking off and went to join the queue.

"What do you think, is Mr. Riordan on some strong drugs? Sulfuric acid rain, of all things!" Hung shook his head. He shrugged off his coat, took off his sweater and tied it around his neck. "And acid clouds too!"

"Yeah," Malik nodded in excitement. "And it's plus one hundred and twenty degrees! Horrible! Now I know where Snowstorm stole the Inferno from!"

The boys were discussing the last lesson in the colonization of the Solar System, in which Mr. Riordan explained why it was impossible to colonize Venus in the near future, unlike Mars, whose terraforming was just a matter of time. But as usual, even this topic got changed to Disgardium and the Inferno, a plane of the in-game reality unavailable to players and inhabited by demons. Flaygray and Nega called it the Underworld.

I missed Eve at times like that. She could discuss the colonization of the Solar System, expeditions to Jupiter and exciting news of distant space. In this company, I thought of the stars more and more rarely.

Tissa and I walked behind the guys. The girl was sharing her impressions of a new reality show that we just had to watch (and enter as contestants) together. I was shocked to hear that from her — nothing but Dis had interested her until recently. Although she couldn't do much in the sandbox.

"Hey, Alex," Ed called to me, turning and pointing ahead. "We have visitors."

"Yep," Hung said. "It's damn Big Po in person!"

The friends stopped. Our clan had only bad memories related to Wesley Cho, although, to give him his due, it was his efforts that led to the creation of the Awoken. Seeing me, the former Threat waved happily and walked toward us.

"Hey guys! Tissa, you look more beautiful every day!" Big Po smiled and behaved as if he was our best friend. "It's great to see you all!

I wasn't burning with a desire to talk to him, so I stood silently next to Melissa and observed the clownery from this former leader of Axiom. To be honest, I expected nothing good from him, and even the fact that he was alone didn't reduce my fears. Quite the contrary.

The Destroying Plague

"We can't say the same," Malik spat through his teeth.

"What do you want, Wesley?" Ed asked.

"Actually, I'm not here to see you. I need to talk to Sheppard." Wesley looked at me, still smiling broadly, but his piercing gaze meant nothing good. "What do you say, Alex? Got a minute for an old friend?"

I would have loved to refuse and tell him go to the Nether, but I knew he was a problem. I wasn't sure what kind yet, but his huge body and narrow, drilling eyes boded danger. It was better to know exactly what you were facing and be prepared than bury your hand in the sand like a mechostrich.

"Sure thing."

Wesley and I moved off to the side. For the next few minutes, he claimed that I was the one that pulled Crag from the not so strong clutches of the preventers, as it turned out, and he knew where to find him. Moreover, he didn't ask me to confirm what he said, understanding the consequences, but just laid out his conclusions. Once done, he got to the point.

"One million, Alex. I'm sure you got around that for eliminating me, if not more, considering my potential. It doesn't matter if you return my money in phoenixes or gold, I'm not picky. I'm sure in the end you'll earn a lot more if you increase your status..."

"Sorry, I can't listen to any more of this nonsense. Gotta go."

He stopped me, grabbing me by the arm and pulling me in.

"I'll fly straight from here to Moscow. You know what's there?"

"Uhm... The Red Square?"

"The Modus HQ, idiot!"

"I don't think they'll accept your application. And get your hands off me, Wesley. Those watchmen are already looking at us, in case you didn't notice. By the way, how did you get here? Actually, I don't care..."

The question was almost rhetorical, but he still answered.

"Axiom was a big clan. It had guys from your school too, so..." He suddenly calmed down and then smiled again. "You know what, you're right. To hell with Modus. I think I'll just go straight to San Francisco. The Triad is definitely going to want to hear about you...

He wasn't joking, and it was my turn to worry. The preventers were bound by public opinion — if they tried to pressure me outside the game, in real life, they'd get a reputation hit up to and including sanctions from Snowstorm. Recently, Ed and Crag and I had done a lot in that regard. They'd never use direct threats or criminal means. But the Triad...

"How come? Because of your conspiracy theories? You think they check information from every idiot that thinks they know something?"

"I'm no idiot," Wesley laughed. "I bought you all

the proof, and it's bulletproof!"

"Yep. Good luck talking to those gangsters."

I turned to leave, but a phrase thrown at me as I left forced me to stop and turn around.

"What do you think, Sheppard, will anybody care about the fate of some drug addict inwinova who randomly finds himself next to your mom or girlfriend?" Wesley glanced at Tissa. "You know those guys will do anything for fifty phoenixes, right?"

That threat was far more serious than everything so far.

"Listen, Wesley..." I paused, carefully thinking over my words. Crag's status was confirmed in any case, and it was better to speak only as if i was worried about Tobias's fate. "Let's get down to it. Even if we imagine for a second that you're right... Don't think I'm trying to buy time or anything like that, it's just that everything we got for you is stuck in our in-game account. We can't get anything from it until the citizenship tests. It's in your interest to keep your suspicions to yourself, because if the people you contact learn your information too soon, you won't get anything.

Wesley frowned. He didn't take long to think. Pulling me by the arm, he moved us further away from prying ears and quietly, barely audibly whispered:

"You know, all this is getting even more interesting. Crag is a Threat, that's a definite. You cover for him using your teleportation and imitation skills. There's a high chance that you're still a Threat too. I think you guys are cooking up something interesting. And either you are buying time to achieve something and then laugh at everyone from the top of Google Tower, or you're being strung along. I guess I'll risk... No, I *want* to get involved!" His eyes lit up as he barely held back his excitement. "I'm going into big Dis in the summer, and after the citizenship tests you'll not only have to compensate me, but also take me into the clan. If I haven't heard anything from you by midnight on the twentieth of June, my birthday, then I'll sell you both to the preventers and the Triad."

Wesley walked away toward a flyer, whistling and dancing. I couldn't say I was happy about his good mood. On the contrary, I wanted to run the guy down and beat the crap out of him. As if sensing my mood, Tissa gently took me by the hand and our fingers intertwined. Hung appeared on my other side and put his hand on my shoulder.

"Chill, bro, breathe deep..." he said, but his eyes tracked Wesley.

As we traveled, I used our ciphers to tell my friends what I'd heard.

"That's the best outcome you could have gotten," Ed approved. "We obviously won't be taking him into the clan or paying him. To hell with him."

"Why are you so sure he's not lying?" Malik worried. "He could give us up to the Triad today if he wanted!"

"He won't," Hung shook his head. "I know this

guy better than you. He can play dirty tricks, like when we all got beat up. But that time he just put the threat into motion — he warned that we'd have problems. If he's promised Alex he'll wait, then he'll do that. What does he lose? To be honest, we could have made extra sure he'd shut up if we brought him into the clan..."

"Hell no!" Ed interrupted Hung's thoughts. "What do we need him for? He's an asshole!"

"He has his head screwed on," Hung shrugged uncertainly. "Alex, are you sure you're going to have enough time for everything? What about you, Ed? You live for instances! And we need to build up the fort, along with the clan. Malik and I aren't going to have time for managing that stuff either..."

"Think about that later!" Tissa said. "We're all under protection! For now, we need to finally decide whether you're going to Distval or not."

She was planning to go, and had even ordered herself an evening gown, but the boys and I were still thinking about it. In the end I concluded that it would be more suspicious not to turn up. We were teenagers, damn it! We should be jumping for joy at getting an invitation, at the whole world seeing us! Especially since the dress code meant we didn't have to worry and could go in ordinary clothes. We weren't old enough for dinner jackets and didn't want to wear them either.

Ultimately, we managed to discuss another idea that came up when we were talking about how we were going to level up our characters.

"Do you know where we can farm rats, guys?" I asked.

"Well... In Glendale, just outside the city. There's a cave there that even has its own rat king," Ed recalled. "But why...? Oh, I get it!"

He exchanged glances with Hung, and they laughed. Malik's eyes passed between me and him in confusion.

"Explain!"

"What's to explain? Our buddy Alex wants a local rat Armageddon by infecting all those poor little critters with his plague crap!" Hung answered.

"Why?"

"To make *Roast Undead Rat Chitterlings*," I smiled. "Have you forgotten how I leveled up in the Mire? Plus one thousand percent to skill gains, bro!"

* * *

Arriving in Dis, I found Trixie and he and I went to the auction house to buy a gift for Malik's birthday. We'd figured out what exactly to get him in advance. He had a pet already, so I bought him a mount, a rare *Red Bear*. The bear cub wasn't red so much as light brown, but the merchant promised that it would get redder as it grew.

Along the way, I stopped by a merchant stall belonging to a player like Underweight and sold everything I'd picked up from the corpses of yesterday's gankers. The total value was unexpectedly high, and it paid for the gift.

Then we went to the city hall to meet Infect and welcome him to big Dis.

It didn't take long for him to appear, looking embarrassed and unfamiliar. Infect had remained a human but added a few years to his character and changed his appearance. It still looked like Malik's face, but the boy hadn't resisted in making a lot of improvements, as it were — he'd added an inch or two of height, made his shoulders broader, changed his eye color.

He told us that the preventers checked him when he arrived in the guest hall, but only quickly, and there were fewer of them than before. I gave him money for equipment and skills, then I jumped to Kharinza with Trixie, although he begged me to give him more time and let him stay with Infect.

By the evening of the same day, life in the Kharinza fort had begun to return to normal. After finally coming to their decisions, all the non-citizens had split into two groups. Those that wishes to change their race — all the builders and one group of miners — left to regenerate their characters. The others renewed their work in the mine. Shazz's undead didn't touch them.

There was no sign of the Montosaurus either. It occurred to me that there must be a reason the beast-god was hiding, but the workers weren't about to complain about it.

Aunt Stephanie and a couple of sharp girls from Cali Bottom had reopened the restored Pig and Whistle. Patrick, Flaygray and Nega were idling away their hours there too, resting before work in the desert began. As soon as I made a path through to the place of power, the guardians would have to move there until the temple was built.

Ripta and Anf needed no rest, at least not the kind the satyr and succubus preferred, so they were assigned to the miners to guard them just in case, and to help move resources to the clan storehouse. From there, the ore went to the miners' guild based on our contract. Crawler and Bomber were handling that.

While I was in Darant, the guys had gone to Glendale and brought the kobold tribe back from its outskirts. They ran away in all directions when they saw me, and it took some time to calm them down. I had to rely on the shaman Ryg'har's help, who saw the mark of the Sleeping Gods on me. The kobolds immediately fell to their knees and began to murmur prayers. Maybe I was just imagining it, but I felt Behemoth stir somewhere within me, feeding on the weak streams of faith.

I asked the kobold chief Grog'hyr to help the miners, and he gladly agreed. Kobolds were born diggers, after all. The clan would pay them in board, food and clothing for the ore they mined, since the kobolds didn't use money.

Trixie was childishly showing off his new outfit

in the tavern and was immediately the center of the workers' attention. His sincere and open admissions of the time spent in the district of forbidden pleasures caused a real furor, and even Flaygray listened with interest, dropping a sarcastic comment here and there.

Once finished with his tales, Trixie set about making the fort a greener place. He and Aunt Steph cleared the tavern's back yard so they could grow vegetables there and planned to plant some fruit trees. Trixie would put the defensive plants wherever Gyula told him. The *Flesh-Eating Tree Protector* would come when our gardener leveled up his skill at least to expert level. Otherwise there was a risk of losing the seed.

By then, Infect had already reached the fort and was strumming an epic six-string guitar. He bought the instrument at a bargain price in the Darant Music Hall, the class building for bards.

Infect played a few chords and sang us something rousing, although it had no effect on us since we were in different factions. In the future, though, his skill would come in handy: this specific song 'inspires bravery in the hearts of allies' and gave a five percent boost to all stats. The effect should get stronger the more he leveled up, too. Infect got himself some attacking skills on the guitar as well, which reduced enemies' healing and defenses, slowed their attack speed... Overall, it was a promising support class.

Infect reverentially accepted the *Arena Master's Horn* from me — his first ever legendary. Trying it out, he summoned two meaty ogre gladiators at level thirty-one. Since Infect was in the Commonwealth, an enemy of the Destroying Plague, the ogres attacked us, but the bard managed to call them off. They'd definitely come in handy for bosses.

Later we locked ourselves in the headquarters and started going through the loot. The first thing I did was lay out all the unused epic 'dummies.' There were over fifty of them left. I left it to Crawler to painstakingly figure out how to divide them up.

He did a quick inspection to find out who had what and which slots needed a boost, then gave out the set items so that each player at least had a set bonus from half a set. The bonuses from Crag and Bomber's warrior class sets, Infect's bard set and Crawler's mage set differed from mine, but they had something in common — a ten percent chance to reflect damage.

Crawler also ended up getting twelve magic tomes. He had to decide which branches of magic to level up along with his fire magic. The rest he'd leave in the clan storehouse — they wouldn't bring in much money, but they might come in handy to a newbie.

The non-slot artifacts Isis' Blessing and Ebis' Inspiration remained unidentified, along with the Elemental Concentration ring and the Thunderbearer trident. I kept them and the divine Righteous Shield. The Balancer was already equipped.

The Destroying Plague

In general, according to Crawler, artifact identification in Dis was like a lottery. Not every artifact was worth more than the identification cost. The usefulness of some of them wasn't always obvious either.

For several years, the owner of an artifact that broke up stormclouds couldn't sell it at the price he wanted. In any weather, even the very worst, Clear Sky drove away the clouds for an hour. Who needed that? But in Dis, as it turned out, everything had meaning. Somewhere in the Zeranda Mountains, a raid instance was discovered with a megaboss — the Vampire Patriarch. Not a single clan in the Empire could defeat him — the weather was always gloomy, and the boss regenerated faster than he could be killed. That was when someone remembered Clear Sky. At the end of a furious bidding war, the Travelers bought the artifact for five million gold. They successfully used it in battle with the boss, completely depriving him of his regeneration under the burning rays of the southern sun and got the first kill.

Entirely useless artifacts could also be found. What was the point of a flute that made flowers sing? Or magic powder that made everyone around burst into dance, except for enemies? In the end, we decided to put off identifying the ring and trident.

The remaining loot from the treasury was different kinds of legendaries. Almost none of them matched our levels, so two or three of the worst ones would go up for sale to raise money for the base in Cali Bottom, and the rest would go into the storehouse. Better to have than have not, as Uncle Nick used to say.

I also kept hold of the *Portal Key* to Holdest and the *Diamond Worm Cocoon*. I had plans for the worm, and as for the portal... It wasn't that I didn't trust the others, but its potential value could drive anyone crazy. In our psychology and sociology lessons, Mr. Wetmore explained to us that everyone had their price. It wasn't necessarily measured in money, but nonetheless, it was there. Would I have betrayed Ed Rodriguez for the chance to save my parents' marriage? I didn't know. I really didn't know.

Next, we went to the rat cave near Glendale to farm guts. We had to do that in two stages; first kill infected rats, then the raised zombie ones. Just as I expected, the raised rats were neutral to us, but that didn't stop our genocide. A double portion of guts and a *green* crown dropped from the king, a huge man-sized rat. The operation took less than an hour.

When we got back to the fort, I cooked some *Roast Undead Rat Chitterlings* and gave them out to the boys, saving a few for myself.

Evening was approaching and we could finally leave the island with a clear conscience. I sent Infect to regenerate, while Crag, Bomber, and Crawler, now all undead, prepared to farm a level thirty instance to which they'd already laid a path.

As for me, I was heading to Darant to jump

from there to the frontier.

"Good luck, Scyth," Crag said. "Try not to stand out. Sometimes you leap before you look. Think practically. Believe me, I know that better than anyone."

The former ganker looked nothing like the dumbass I knew from the sandbox. I didn't know what it was — if it was that he started living independently too soon, or our relationship to him, but he seemed... normal. A little self-centered, but calm, reliable and independent. Of course, he thanked me for the gifts, but he didn't bother haggling for every set piece like Infect did. Our undead guitarist bard argued desperately on the basis that he'd changed his class for the clan and come out of the sandbox later than the rest, so he needed to be better equipped. This trait in Malik annoyed everyone. Even his best friend Bomber broke down and cuffed him on the back of the head. We all cheered his reeducation attempt.

I left the fort to the sound of Patrick and Flaygray's wistful wailing. Those two were thick as thieves and drunk as skunks. They were sitting and hugging each other, swigging ale and filling the air with a song that reminded me of nails on a chalkboard. Even Shazz's *Bone Hounds* were moved. They gathered at the maximum allowed distance and, raising their heads to the darkening sky, snapped their jaws at Geala.

Chapter 18

To the Frontier!

*C*LANK, CLANK, CLANK went the metal claws of my mechostrich on the pavement. I was getting used to the movement in the saddle, but still feared to let go of the mount's neck. I'd fallen enough in my time at riding school.

You'll get the hang of it! my tutor had said on parting. That meant that the higher my skill level, the more comfortable the game mechanics would make it when riding the mechostrich. Thankfully, the progress bar was growing as I watched it, filling up by a percentage point every minute.

Upgraded riding skill: +1. Current level: 2.
You hold yourself better in the saddle. Movement speed while riding increased by 2%.

The notification came when I reached the Military District, having decided on Crawler's advice to take the *To the Frontier!* faction quest there, which was available to everyone. The forts on the edge of the inhabited lands required not only fighters, but workers too. Volunteers were given a discount on portals there, and on Commonwealth griffins and airships too. Nonetheless, the plan might lead to nothing; I was undead after all, even if I did have a human disguise.

The closest place to the place of power was Fort Vermillion, which I could get to through a portal. It was a small town founded three years ago on the edge of the Lakharian Desert. That was where I was headed.

In the Lake District the day before, I'd taken on the guise of Murphy, an elvish archer at level sixty-six. To be honest, I'd already forgotten that I was Murphy the elf. My friends had been calling me Alex or Scyth all day in the fort, so I didn't react at all when I heard the shout.

"Murphy! Hey, buddy!"

A heavy plate glove descended on my shoulder and I turned around. *Zoran, Human, level 68 Paladin*, the profile said. Looked like I'd got myself into trouble with my disguise, but I had nothing to lose by playing my role to the end.

"Zoran?"

It looked like the paladin was really pleased to see me. "Hah, you recognize me?" He hugged me and slapped me on the back. I heard the dull thud of metal on metal. "Damn, wow, what a meeting! How'd you end up here?"

While I was thinking of ways to wriggle out of

---

the situation and checking my *Depths Teleportation* cooldown, the paladin kept talking. It became clear that we'd met over a year ago in a random group and completed some instance together. Zoran had gained forty levels since then. Gradually it was revealed that we weren't friends. At least, the player I'd taken for *Imitation* wasn't in the paladin's friends list. That was why he was so happy to see me. It seemed this Murphy was a nice guy. Zoran remembered him for passing over some loot.

"You'll have to forgive me. To tell you the truth, I don't remember you too well."

The paladin answered that he only recognized me because his childhood friend has the same name, Murphy. We chatted for another couple of minutes, then I made excuses and started getting ready to leave. Zoran put a hand on my shoulder and asked:

"Listen, friend, what're your plans?"

"The frontier."

"So, you're going after *honor*? I've been planning to farm some too." The paladin stopped in thought for a moment. "How about we go together?"

Honor Points could be swapped for reputation with the Commonwealth or the races that belonged to it. They could also be spent on exclusive class gear sets. Unable to find a good reason to refuse the company, I reluctantly accepted.

"Alright. But first I need to pick up a quest."

Talking constantly, Zoran followed me to the quartermaster, who gave me the first in a long chain of quests. I had no plans to complete it, but the quest had no time limits or penalties, and I could always discard it.

Then we headed to the alchemist's store to buy a stack each of the best heat resistance potions. Another two thousand gold spent. I consoled myself with the thought that I didn't need the potions — I could sell them at the auction house to get my money back.

The paladin turned out to be an enthusiastic player — not hardcore, but still thirsty for progress. So, when I said I'd jump through a portal, he hesitated, but agreed to follow me.

"Lots of work in real life," he said. "Seems a shame to waste days of game time on an airship. Can have fun on them, sure, but can't level up."

We spoke while we stood in the queue for tickets. Actually, Zoran spoke for the most part. I asked what his job was that he could so easily spend so much money on a portal.

"Heard of the First Martian Company? Ha-ha, I guess not. It's a startup, I founded it. Don't mind the showy name, I just took it while it was still available. The company isn't earning money yet, but I have an investor already. I invented something, patented it and I get royalties for its use. Snowstorm bought it too, and they've already started using it to add something to their new capsules."

"What did you invent?"

"Heard of the neurointerface? I'm sure you

remember that ten years ago, immersion capsules only imitated immersion. Like in 5D films. The intra-gel changed the temperature so that the player felt warmth or cold. It got thicker and harder to imitate pressure on parts of the body. Still works that way now, but most of the interaction with your senses goes straight through your brain now. Why actually roast someone's ass if you can just send a signal to the brain...?"

"So, you invented that?" I was finding it hard to believe that the inventor of such a breakthrough technology, no doubt a very rich man, was wandering Dis in *blue* gear.

"No, of course not!" Zoran laughed. "I'm an ordinary neuronet architect, but a few of my theoretical projects could grow into something more. Just imagine your interface in Dis working the same way in real life! You look at a person and see their name, and your reputation with them. You can also look at your real body's stats, set goals and see them as a quest log[6]... And that's just the start! What do you think?"

"Sounds cool. I guess you're in the top citizenship category?" Questions like these weren't considered polite, but if Zoran wasn't lying, then he was a big deal in real life.

"Um..." Zoran faltered. "You're right about the category, but I didn't really get that myself. My family played a role in that. Doesn't matter what you do in

---

[6] Zoran is referring to the interface from the Level Up series.

our family, you get worldwide fame. My grandma Joanna was the best tennis player in the world in her time, and when she gave up sport, she achieved greatness in science. My great aunt on my father's side, Kira, is a Nobel laureate and founder of... Eh, never mind... I don't usually just tell people all this stuff..."

Zoran blushed, apparently deciding that he'd said too much and that it sounded like bragging. Was this all happening because of my high *charisma*, despite my undead racial penalty? But how was that possible? He was a player, not an NPC!

The paladin overcame his embarrassment and began to ask questions of his own. I really had to struggle to come up with a real life for Murphy. I didn't even know how old he was, or whether Zoran knew anything about him. Fortunately, it was soon our turn to buy tickets.

Even with a discount, the ticket to Vermillion cost me nearly six thousand gold — more expensive than a first-class flight to the Moon. Incredibly, the queues to the portal mages, of which I'd counted more than twenty, were even longer. The transport guild clearly wasn't going hungry.

I stepped into the portal first. As soon as I stepped out of it in the dusty and terribly stuffy guest hall at Vermillion, a local city councilor by the name of Westwood spoke to me.

"Welcome to Vermillion, city of the brave and stubborn!"

Zoran fell out of the portal behind me, and Westwood's attention switched to him. He repeated his greeting and got to the point.

"I see this is your first time at the frontier, Murphy and Zoran. Fair warning, it's hot here. Hot in all senses of the word. In the heart of the city, our mage softens the burning rays of the sun, but outside its bounds you'll have a hard time. I strongly recommend that you get some sunscreen made of jantak weed. When you finish with that, come back and I'll find you a couple of quests for the benefit of the Commonwealth!"

A quest window popped up in front of us:

Jantak Weed
Only cream made of an infusion of jantak weed picked by your own hand will allow you to withstand the extreme heat of the Lakharian Desert. Collect three bundles and take them to the local apothecary Hector Dagworth so he can make you some sunscreen.
***Rewards**: sunscreen made of jantak weed.*

I accepted the quest and saw a blinking warning:

Attention! In the current location, your imitated body should be subject to Burning Heat I (-50% health, mana and vigor regeneration; -5% health every hour).

Imitate negative effect?

388

Quickly accepting the suggestion, I looked at Zoran. It seemed he was already reading the debuff. The paladin drank his heat resistance potion and waited a couple of seconds to feel the effect. His eyes widened.

"Damn, Murphy, we need to go get some of those weeds as soon as we can! The resistance potion cut down on the debuff a little, but this is still going to be tough. This is nuts. And we're under a protective shield right now...! What are you waiting for? Drink while you still can!"

I wondered, would the reduced health from the debuff on me be imitated? Under Zoran's piercing gaze, I took one of the potions too, and *Imitation* invited me to change the way the debuff was being shown again. The hourly health reduction went down to a tolerable one percent. Nether, how did people live here? Did they go to sleep and not wake up? All you had to do to sentence someone to death was lock them in a room.

The paladin remembered something and ran after the councilor as he walked out of the room.

"Mr. Westwood! One moment!"

After a moment he came back, dripping sweat and scratching furiously, trying to poke his fingers through the joints in his plate armor to reach his skin. Unable to withstand it, he removed all his gear, ending up in light pants and a shirt. For the sake of my disguise, I did the same.

"Listen, Murphy," the paladin muttered.

"Westwood says there's some cooling fountain in the city. Sounds like just bathing in it nullifies the debuff. Want to go try it?"

"With pleasure!"

We left the hall. A tall shaman player at level seventy-six with the funny name of Ehehe was milling around outside. A round-faced man around forty years old, with a huge protruding belly, he stood in nothing but a loincloth, sweating and constantly wiping his brow with a handkerchief. He smiled broadly at the sight of us, showing jagged teeth. A strange appearance for a human character.

"What's up with this guy?" I asked Zoran vaguely.

"Looks like he believes in that unannounced feature," he shrugged. "You know, they say Snowstorm rewards you for using your real appearance by increasing your chance of getting rare loot. Or if you make yourself totally ugly, with some kind of physical defect like a limp or a squint, then it's all legendaries, they say!"

We reached the shaman and he spoke, his ingratiating smile still firmly in place.

"Finally! Been standing here all day, waiting for someone, anyone."

"Might I ask why?" Zoran asked, his eyes narrowing.

"It's all because of that damn jantak weed! It only grows in the desert, you can't buy it, you have to pick it yourself. I can't handle it solo; it needs at least two. You got the quest, right?"

"What makes you think we need the weed?" I butted in.

"It's obvious! Anyone who's been here at least once jumps straight to the tavern or here, to the hall, with a *Return Stone*. But you came out of the guest hall, so that means you came by portal. Only people coming here for the first time do that. The airships arrive in the morning, and there's no other way to get to Vermillion. It's a desert! Although I did know one fella that decided to save money and fly on a griffin — he didn't arrive alive. Or dead either, heh-heh... There are the caravans too, of course, but that wouldn't be your cup of tea at all."

Exchanging a glance with Zoran, I shrugged. The fat guy didn't bother me, since I was planning to quietly disappear in the desert and make my way to the place of power anyway. The paladin asked Ehehe a few more questions and found out why you couldn't gather the weeds on your own.

The jantak bushes were home to desert cockroaches, weak creatures, but numerous. They couldn't deal any damage to us because of their low level, but their bites gave us a one-percent penalty to movement speed. The effect stacked. And speed, as it turned out, was the most important thing in the desert. This meant that players in Vermillion had developed a way of gathering in pairs: one took aggro from the cockroaches and drew them away while the other pulled up grass. Then they swapped roles and repeated the process.

"What's to stop us from quickly picking some and running away?" Zoran asked.

"Have you seen people mining ore?" Ehehe answered his question with a question. "It's like casting, and any cast gets interrupted when you take damage. It takes a minute to gather three bundles of weeds. How're you going to pick them if the cockroaches are biting you all the time? They're immune to spells too. Those parasites are tough!"

"What about mobs?" I asked. "Cockroaches are one thing, but I bet there's plenty of other wildlife out there."

"The mobs here start at level four hundred. Snakes, worms, sand spirits and elementals, vultures, basilisks, scorpids, carbuncles, giants... You can run into a dragon or a golem, a hermit or tumbleweed. The last one is awful; it'll just digest you alive; you can't get out and it takes ages to die." Ehehe flinched. "If we get into trouble, nobody can save us. Be ready to respawn. Top levels can fight them, especially in a group, but we don't have a chance. So, there's one rule: if you see a mob, don't aggro it, avoid it, and if you attract attention, mount up and get out if you can. But some of the mobs out there... When you realize they're close, it's already too late."

"How come you haven't used a power-leveler?" Zoran asked with suspicion.

"It's expensive and... dangerous," the shaman shook his head in annoyance. "I've been hanging around here a week! Me and my teammate got ganked on the first day. On the second day I spent all my money on a high-level escort. Plus, I was glad that two at once would be going with me! I was so dumb. They didn't even take me into the desert, they just ganked me right outside the city. The next day was no better... Well, you get the picture! You see what I'm wearing. I want to finish this damn quest soon as I can do social quests. My whole progress plan revolves around *Honor Points...*

Zoran scratched the back of his head quizzically. We'd thought the shaman had specially taken his gear off because of the heat, but he had none left. Feeling bad for him, we agreed to take him with us and left the city council building together.

The road dust, stones, fences and walls of buildings — everything around was cracked and shimmering in the heat. The sweat on our faces evaporated faster than we could wipe it off. My traveling companions stopped in their tracks, getting used to the heat under the open sky — it was far cooler indoors. Making as if I was melting alongside them, I looked around.

Fort Vermillion had grown to the size of a town, but it was still far from the size of Tristad, let alone Darant. The buildings were crowded close together. The narrow streets barely had room for two carriages to pass. The sun was descending to the horizon and people were beginning to go outside. A riding turtle crawled past with its rider, its feet moving quickly. In the distance I saw a caravan of camels raising a small dust cloud. A single-humped camel lazily chewed some thorns in a stall across the road. It was one of those epic *Lakharian Dromedaries*.

"Everything dies down here around midday," Ehehe noted between gulps from his flask of water. "The debuff is dynamic, the penalties vary depending on the time of day and the shade. Life in the fort starts after dusk...

The fat man was in his element in the town. We took a shortcut through a tavern full of people into the backyard. From there they climbed over the fence and found themselves one district from the square into which the central street ran.

Ehehe pointed at a small fountain with high borders. Players were splashing around in the water. Nearby, some enterprising players and NPCs sold drinks and ice cream from open wagons on wheels. The shaman licked his lips and headed toward them, asking us to find a seat. He returned with a tray of six perspiring mugs of cold, frothy beer.

"Cheers," Ehehe said, offering us the tray.

Thanking him, we sat down on the stone border of the fountain. The shaman downed one of the beers in a single gulp, then started on the second at a civilized pace.

"Let's sit a while and then freshen up in the fountain," he suggested. "The heat effect is increasing, it's best we reset it. It's still tolerable in the city, but it'll be horrible as soon as we go out into the desert."

The Destroying Plague

"What about at night?" Zoran gratefully took a swig of his beer. His brows rose in surprise and he downed the rest in a few gulps. "That's the tastiest beer I've ever had!"

"It's local," Ehehe said with a certain pride. "Cheap, but tasty! As for night... Night brings other problems. Chills! I hope you stocked up on cold resistance? Jantak weed is rare, we'll need to periodically come back to the city to clear the debuff."

According to the shaman, high-level players had taken over a narrow strip at the edge of the desert, thirty miles wide at best. They hadn't gone any deeper, since the temperatures were even more extreme there both in the daytime and at night. Defensive potions and creams weren't any good out there. Plus, the mobs were over level five hundred.

We finished our drinks and bathed in the fountain, and when we got out, I suddenly felt an attentive gaze on me. I turned my head but saw nobody.

"What's over there, Ehehe?" I asked, pointing at a small, but high building on twelve columns with a sloping gilded roof.

"Fortuna's temple," the shaman chuckled. "She's the most worshipped goddess out here on the frontier. Even Nergal doesn't have as many followers. It's a good thing you reminded me, Murphy, ha-ha. You guys should look in there and get a blessing!"

We headed for the temple. The shaman explained what to do; we had to place a sacrifice on the temple's altar. It could be anything; an animal's innards, gold, equipment. The goddess took everything offered and gave a blessing in return based on the value of the sacrifice.

After queuing up for the altar, Ehehe the shaman went first. Thrice robbed and several times killed, he'd lost almost all his gear, so he could only give a handful of silver. Zoran went second. The paladin pulled out a bunch of all kinds of garbage that he hadn't had time to sell at a vendor. He added sword and a few gold coins. A blueish glow shrouded him. Smiling widely, Zoran moved away from the altar, whispering as he walked by:

"Don't be stingy, it's worth it!"

At the altar, I felt the familiar sensation of the unwavering attention of a higher power. I'd felt such invisible pressure before. It always felt different; heavy and warming from Behemoth, fleeting and burning at Nergal's temple in Tristad, sticky and cold from the Nucleus of the Destroying Plague. Right then I felt as if thousands of streams of champagne were pouring over me from head to foot, cooling and tickling my skin. In the hellish heat of Vermillion, it was like a gulp of water in the desert.

I stood by the altar for several seconds, hoping that the goddess would speak to me as she did during the undead invasion. But I heard nothing but angry complaints from the people behind me in the queue.

"Hurry it up, archer! Others are waiting!"

I pulled out some gold, then remembered the

two legendary pieces of gear that the Triad were interested in. My intuition told me that I could donate something of the exposed items — none would be the wiser, and they'd be unlikely to emerge again.

The people were getting more antsy and I caught movement in the corner of my eye; a priest of the goddess heading toward me. I couldn't make myself sacrifice the *Vestment of Irkuyem's Fury*, the legendary druid set piece. Blocking the altar from view, I put the second legendary on it, the shamanic chainmail. Someone in the queue laughed.

"Nobody cares about your garbage, noob! Move it along!"

Three seconds later, Fortuna accepted the gift. A deep purple glow infused me, and I walked away from the altar under envious gazes.

Fortuna blesses your endeavors!
+250 luck for 12 hours.

I had time to see the priest freeze, then start praying furiously. Some other notifications popped up:

Your reputation with Fortuna, Goddess of Luck, has increased: +1000.
Current reputation: trust.

Fortuna favors you! Accept these gifts from the goddess of luck:

+50 luck.

+5% chance to avoid critical damage.

+5% chance to detect invisibility.

+5% critical hit chance.

+5% chance to get a unique quest.

+5% chance to get upgraded loot.

Fortuna Smiles Upon You...

Fortuna, the goddess of luck, wants to get to know you better. Visit Fortuna's main temple in Kinema, which is on Bakabba.

Rewards*: next quest in the Wheel of Fortune divine quest chain.*

I accepted the quest and heard the goddess's gentle laughter in my head. *You're funny... dead man.* I heard the playful voice with perfect clarity. *Sorry, Fortuna, but there's no way I can get to the goblin continent just yet! Unless I swim across the whole ocean myself...* Fortuna didn't answer, and I put thoughts of her aside for a more appropriate time and rejoined my companions.

"What did you sacrifice?" they asked, but I just smiled mysteriously and shrugged.

In the end I 'admitted' that I'd been boosting my reputation with Fortuna for a long time and today her attitude to me moved to the next level. That caused a wave of vulgar jokes that I doubted the goddess would have liked.

Leaving the temple, we saddled our mounts. My

mechostrich rumbled beneath me, Zoran traveled on a regular horse, and Ehehe had an exotic *Desert Turtle* which was surprisingly quick. We soon left the bounds of the fort and found ourselves in the Lakharian Desert.

The sun was entirely hidden behind the horizon by then. It had baked every stone and every grain of sand all day, and rare decrepit plants swapped the day's gaudy colors for the charm of their night-time scents. It smelled as it only smells in a desert after many hours of hellish heat.

I could have left Zoran and Ehehe some time ago, but I was putting it off. For the first time in a long time, I was in the guise of an ordinary player with ordinary quests and cares. I swore on Fortuna's breasts, as Flaygray would have said, I was playing! Really playing, and I liked it.

Avoiding the shadows of mobs darkening the ground beneath the scarlet sky, we moved further and further out. In half an hour of careful riding, we ran into just one jantak bush — low, just up to my knee, with fat meaty leaves, seedpods and thorns. The system illuminated a couple of sprigs of weeds that could be picked for the quest.

I volunteered to be the first to kite the *Desert Cockroaches*. The shaman and paladin stood off to the side, and at their signal, I pulled at the flimsy bush, pulling it out with its long roots. Then I dropped it and started running. A stream of large, hand-sized cockroaches with oily gleaming sides flooded out of the sand.

Afraid of running into aggressive mobs, I directed my mechostrich back in the direction we came. I had to go quite some distance away for the horrible insects to finally retreat, but at least my riding skill leveled up again. By then, Zoran had written in the group chat that they'd collected the weeds and I could go back.

Halfway there, I saw the paladin's portrait suddenly flashing red. Someone was attacking him. I thought it might be the shaman's doing, but a couple of moments later both their avatars switched to skulls: both Zoran's and Ehehe's. They'd been killed.

Laughter from ahead of me made me stop my mechostrich sharply. I recalled my mount, laid down and activated *Stealth*. Nothing stopped me from just turning around and leaving. Night would fall in a couple of hours, when the timer should kick in and throw me out of Dis. I had more than enough time to reach the place of power. I doubted Zoran or Ehehe would have any issue with me. Anyone would have run away in my position.

But I wasn't anyone.

Chapter 19

The Lakharian Desert

THERE WERE TWO of them. A hobbit at level hundred and forty-two, a fairy one level below: a rogue and a mage. A sweet ganking couple. Laughing, they dug through the bodies of the dead and exchanged comments. Hiding in the dusk, I listened and tried to decide what to do with them.

Murphy, some gankers got us. Hide! Zoran wrote in the group chat. He'd already revived, but Ehehe was offline. Apparently, this was the second time he'd died that day.

"Damn, that guy was obnoxious," the fairy noticed. "No decent loot either, just garbage."

"Carol, you need to think outside the box," the dwarf chuckled. "That fool with his dumb nick led us to fresh meat. Look how rich this one is! So much gold dropped! Imagine what he still has!"

"Pfft, I could have lured the paladin out myself,"

the fairy giggled, taking flight above Zoran's corpse. "I'm a cute little angel, you know!"

Despite her size, the fairy looked alluring with her fine figure and her enticingly light dress. The dress must have been at least an epic.

They'd already finished collecting the loot, and I had to decide quickly if I wanted to fight them. A hundred levels of difference, and I only had enough plague energy for one... Ugh, Nether! Best to just do something.

"Hey, you!" I came out of the shadows, equipping my knuckledusters as I emerged. "You should find someone your own size to pick on."

"Hah, here's the third one, Carol!" The hobbit rubbed his hands in anticipation, then spread his arms, a cruelly curved dagger appearing in each hand. The ganker went into stealth and I heard out of thin air: "Lucky day for us, my girl..."

With my senses almost fully switched off, I only realized that I was being attacked when I felt a series of strikes in my back. My imitation ability spewed out fountains of blood, my health fell almost to zero, but, to the rogue's amazement, I didn't die.

Destroying Plague Immortality activated: *100% of all subsequent damage is absorbed, 2% is converted into plague energy and stored in a reservoir.*

"What the hell...?" the rogue said in wonder as he saw that his attacks weren't dealing damage.

The Destroying Plague

I turned to him, marked him as a target and nerfed the bastard.

Balancer activated: *the selected target Moyzo, level 142 rogue, has been taken down to level 40.*

My fist, shrouded in its plate knuckleduster-glove, flew beneath the ganker's arm and hit him in the nose, which literally exploded in a cloud of blood. The jagged barbs of the second *Hammer* in my *Combo* series hit him full in the cheekbone with the strength of a truck moving at full speed, and then a *Stunning Kick* followed.

Unfortunately, the stun didn't proc. The ganker grunted in surprise and breathed in sharply but didn't try to retreat. Especially since his girlfriend hadn't lost her cool and was already dropping her entire magic arsenal on me. He thrust a dagger dripping with poison into my neck; I jerked to the side from the force of it, managed to stay on my feet, and responded with a *Hammer*. The rogue took a step back, stunned and confused by what was happening, then dropped something at his feet and disappeared in a cloud of smoke. He had less than a third of his health left.

"What's wrong with this guy, Moyzo?" the fairy hissed and let loose a stream of filthy curses.

I didn't pay any attention to her yet, deciding to concentrate on the rogue while *Balancer* was still active. I stood in fire and clouds of smoke, but even through the distortion I could make out the attacking rogue's smooth movements. He spread both his arms wide and brought them together to strike at a single point. The daggers pierced my chest, turned, and the rogue spread his hands again, breaking my ribs.

"Die! Die! Die!" he screamed hysterically.

His favorite move, *Eviscerate*, worked well — a wide hole glistened in my chest, revealing my mutilated heart, and it occurred to me that I must be pure mincemeat inside by now. The move pushed Moyzo off balance and he instinctively thrust out a hand to catch himself as he fell. When the rogue froze in that pose for a moment, I released a second *Combo* at him, knocking his teeth into his throat and crunching his skull.

The entire fight with the rogue took five seconds, within the duration of the *Balancer*. I heard the fanfare of a level up, my health recovered, and *Destroying Plague Immortality* immediately disappeared. I jumped out of the fire, not letting it activate again. The next second, the fairy and I attacked each other at the same time; she with a *Plasma Charge* and me with an *Explosive Arrow* charged with plague energy.

Immortality prevented me from dying, but the fairy had no such luck. Her lifeless body fell to the sand. I stood for a few seconds, resting with my hands on my knees, recovering from the heated battle. The adrenaline rushing through my blood had nowhere to go and demanded action.

The Destroying Plague

I wrote in the group chat, told Zoran to come back. In the meantime, I looted the gankers and found plenty of interest. Snowstorm had introduced balancing mechanics which meant that player killers were far more likely to lose gear on death. Even bags with one-hundred percent chance of preserving their contents didn't protect them — *Killer's Curse* kicked in, and the more victims the ganker killed, the more gear he dropped. There must have been a pile of corpses at the feet of these two, because it seemed like they dropped everything they had, equipped and unequipped alike.

Going through the loot, I pulled out a few epics and put aside part of the gold. I decided to leave the rest for Zoran and Ehehe.

The paladin returned and stopped a safe distance away, frowning and surveying the battlefield. He took a few uncertain steps toward me. The spare set of gear he'd equipped didn't even have any rare items in it. It was all *green*.

"The world is just, friend Zoran!" I shouted in mock celebration. "Wouldn't you know it, a dragon flew in and finished off these two assholes!"

"Don't play dumb, Murphy," he answered darkly. "You killed them, right? The town chat is going nuts. The gankers raised hell, they're shouting about a Threat! Everyone is expecting the preventers to turn up! Who are you?"

"That so? Hmm, alright. I'm not Murphy, in case you haven't guessed. So, don't get mad at your

---

friend, he has nothing to do with this."

I activated *Cloak Essence*, turning into a smoky silhouette, and continued:

"If you run into Ehehe, give him some of the loot from the gankers. I haven't touched your gear or money. And... As for who I am, I'm a guy that just wanted to play for a day. It was nice to meet you, Zoran!"

I summoned my mechostrich, mounted up and headed southeast.

"Thank you!" I heard after a moment, the wind carrying the paladin's belated words of gratitude.

* * *

My lessons flew by, because Mr. Kovac was absent, there was no replacement to be found for him and we were let go early.

On the homeward journey, Ed and Hung told of their successes of the previous evening: they'd completed an instance designed for level thirty and had leveled up, and today they were planning to conquer a dungeon ten levels higher.

"You know, this isn't fair!" Malik claimed suddenly. "We're undead too, where's our *Immortality*?"

"Heh," Hung chuckled. "I'm a human too, like Horvac, but where's my space yacht?"

"As I was saying," Ed cast a disapproving glance at Malik, "today we're heading to a level forty dungeon. We shouldn't have any trouble even without a healer, with Infect's legendary horn and Crag by our side. What do you think, Alex?"

"I think I'd feel easier if you had Tissa with you..."

We decided that they'd farm this dungeon as long as they could, since they had no other routes laid. We didn't need more anyway; if everything went to plan, they'd be joining me in the Lakharian Desert the next day.

I'd almost put my foot in it the day before while running as fast as I could from the spot where I'd been found out. One of the scouts sent by the preventers saw me from the sky. I had to log out of the game.

So, I didn't know what to expect when I logged back into Dis. I appeared in the desert ready to use everything I had, but there was no need — this spot was too far from the frontier to set up twenty-four-hour surveillance. Considering the flight time and the powerful stacking debuffs of the desert, the preventers wouldn't have had enough people.

I rode my mechostrich for the next few hours, then continued on my own two feet. Yesterday I'd thought I could get to my destination in a couple of hours. Now I was laughing at my own naivete. It didn't occur to me at all that the mechostrich might break down, unable to withstand the attacks of a massive basilisk. I didn't think about the fact that my feet would get stuck in the sand, and I'd have to walk up and down high dunes. All that saved me was the movement speed bonus, which remained extremely high even with the racial penalty. I stubbornly moved toward my goal, the place of power where we could make a base.

The rare vegetation I ran into the day before had disappeared. Now there was nothing but sand all around. Few had been able to get so far into the depths of the Lakharian Desert. I'd crossed the civilized strip of its edge yesterday, but today I'd made my way much further in. A tail of dozens of aggroed mobs followed behind me.

Mist Harpies and *Stinking Vultures* dove at me, *Plated Scorpids* burrowed out of the ground under my feet, and after them came *Shai-khuludas*, colossal sand worms bigger than an aerotrain. *Tumbleweeds* rolled across the ground, truly nightmarish creations — like huge balls of twine hiding innumerable tentacles and suckers seeping acid. Groups of elementals and twenty-foot-tall basilisks moved slower than the rest and from time to time fell back until I aggroed other similar mobs. Most impressive of all were the *Hooked Mortens*, reptiles that leaped like frogs with a pair of ten-feet-long hook-shaped growths on their backs.

There was only a little left before I reached the place of power. I climbed another dune and froze, stunned by a howl that broke the sound barrier. The world slowed, sprays of sand flew at me and the howl turned into a lower sound, as if from a badly tuned trumpet. I stepped back, fell, and just in time too — a splayed hand with large, curved, hook-like claws flew just by my face, and a massive limb covered in chitinous shell passed above me. A little closer and I'd have been crushed and drowned in the sand. I somersaulted to the side and rolled down the dune, letting my momentum carry me to the bottom.

Lifting myself up, I looked back. There was a battle raging at the top. There was a squat creature, just five feet tall and reminiscent of a stingray with its broad, flat body. *Level 498 Hermit, beast,* the interface said. Bristling, the beast hugged the ground and then jumped sharply, attacking an armored monster of monstrous size, a mix of a megalodon, turtle and armadillo. That turned out to be a boss: *Sharkon, level 502 Underground Terror, beast, local boss.*

Striking with its legs a couple of times, the hermit jumped back. Its attack didn't penetrate the boss's armored face. The outcome of the battle was obvious — the boss would tear this upstart to pieces.

In its habits, the hermit seemed like a cat. It backed off, hissed, growled angry, struck its spiny tail against the ground and tried to dig its nails into its enemy. Sharkon ignored his attacks, came closer, moved its head out of the path of jaws clicking like a mantrap, opened its own mouth and clamped its jaws down on the enemy's body.

Awkwardly digging sand with its limbs, the hermit began a hollow scream. His skin shined slightly in the weak moonlight, and his life dropped into the orange zone. Sharkon shook his head and opened his jaws. The hermit crashed into the ground, fell a few feet down the dune on its back, but then immediately stood up in a single imperceptible movement. Its broad jaw shone with rows of triangular shark's teeth, almost the same as the boss's, only smaller and sharper.

Taking advantage of the fact that my train of mobs was only just reaching the foot of the dune, and the enemies at its peak hadn't seen me yet, I ran up and touched both of them in turn. *Plague Pestilence* successfully infected both the hermit and the boss.

The first mobs chasing behind me were reaching me by then. I took all my equipment off so that it wouldn't get damaged in the upcoming bloodbath, then ate some *Roast Undead Rat Chitterlings* to make my skills level faster.

The last thing I saw more or less clearly was a *Hooked Morten* preparing to jump at me. Preparing myself for the long nightmare ahead, I noticed its leg muscles clenching, and then I saw it firing toward me like a giant toad. I saw long triangular feet waving in the air, saw it extend its arms tipped with long claws. I waited until the very end, then infected the beast, dodged away from its lightning-fast strike and hit it with a *Crushing Hammerfist*. With surprise I saw the creature twist in the air, dodging the attack, then it froze and turned its face to me. *Damn, quick reactions,* I just had time to think before it all went south.

Next came the usual hell that I'd first

The Destroying Plague

discovered in Gloomwood, then successfully survived in the Mire. My body was torn, ripped, broken, chewed, bitten, burned by fire and acid, pierced through... I felt no pain, which was the main change from my previous experience. The calculation was simple: level up *Destroying Plague Immortality* as high as possible until the timer activated at midnight to kick me out of Dis.

Distantly, as if an observer, I checked for which weren't yet infected and touched them with *Plague Pestilence*. I didn't try to save any energy — it was recovering far quicker than I was spending it, so I used infected *Combos* everywhere, leveling up not only the series, but also the individual moves. The system reported nine out of ten hits as misses, but the insane level difference still sent my skill rocketing up. Even *Stunning Kicks* that I took lying down still hit targets. Game conditions.

The logs showed six-figure numbers of damage taken and absorbed, and my plague reservoir recovered fully in mere seconds.

Of course, I didn't hope to kill anything, since the health of each mob exceeded twenty million, and the fat boss had a lot more, not to mention his defense characteristics.

By that time, Sharkon had defeated the infected hermit and switched to the other uninvited guests. And the system gave me a choice:

Infected level 498 Hermit has died and

---

turned into an undead.

Bend the creature to your will? If you decline, the creature will act independently.

This time there was no option to preserve the creature's mind — it seems that only happened in cases when there was something to preserve. I accepted the suggestion — it was dumb to refuse a subject minion at such a high level.

In the meantime, Sharkon was drawing the ire of more and more of the still living mobs, and that bothered me — the more damage I took, the faster my ability leveled up, and I didn't like the idea of running again to pick up more mobs... Although the boss itself would stay anyway, right? Consoling myself with that thought, I continued entertaining myself.

I sent a raised *Zombie Hermit* off to the side before he aggroed anyone. I wasn't planning on losing such a powerful mob for no reason. All the other infected mobs that had died and reanimated went in the same direction. I didn't have enough fingers to count the variety of their species.

Apparently, their high level didn't just influence the growth of *Plague Pestilence*, which had reached level three, but also *Plague Reanimation* which activated when they became my subjects — the ability to raise minions had leveled up twice, extending the cap and increasing the size of my zombie army.

Plague Reanimation ability leveled up: +1.

The Destroying Plague

Current level: 4.

There is no death in service to the Destroying Plague! You can breathe unlife into the dead. Reanimated skeletons and zombies will join the Destroying Plague and serve the Legate.

Chance of saving skills and combat abilities possessed in life: 4%.

Limitations: up to 40 servants at the current ability level.

Cost to use: 1000 Plague Energy plus 1000 per day to maintain reanimation.

My first zombie of the day, the Hermit, a nightmarish mix of cat, stingray and weasel, turned out lucky; it kept its skills. This good news was a rare glimmer of positive emotions. All the rest, on the other hand...

The dead magic of the Destroying Plague never let the creatures finally grind me into powder or tear my head from my body, no matter how they tried. It calmed me to repeat my tried and tested mantra that this was just virtual reality streaming into my brain, that my body was nestled in safe intra-gel, and the slowly but surely increasing progress bars of my skills, which I kept my eyes glued to, gave some meaning to the madness. My unarmed combat skills reached the limit; level one hundred, after which I tried to shoot with my bow with the same goal, but I couldn't draw it in the mass of mobs.

When there were only four mobs left, along with

a thoroughly beaten boss leaking orange blood, *Destroying Plague Immortality* reached level nine, and my plague reservoir was almost full.

Destroying Plague Immortality leveled up: +1. Current level: 10.

If you are the only representative of the Destroying Plague in an area, then when you take lethal damage, you will be given temporary immortality: 100% of all subsequent damage is absorbed, 10% is converted into plague energy and stored in a reservoir.

The effect lasts until your health is fully recovered.

Plague reservoir volume increased: +100,000.

Current volume: 1,000,000.

Unlocked ability: Plague Fury!

Plague Fury

Level 1 active ability.

You can explode in fury, burning up all your accumulated plague energy and releasing it in a thirty-foot radius around you. All enemies within the area of effect will take full damage amounting to double the plague energy burnt.

10% chance that a killed opponent will turn into an undead and become your minion.

Threat rank increased! Current class: K.

The Destroying Plague

A new ability? And so awesome that it increased my Threat status? Perfect timing, I thought and picked myself up slowly. Nobody was attacking me anymore — the boss was taking aggro from the monsters left alive. There was over an hour left until midnight, and I might even be able to make it to the place of power.

All the infected and raised undead gathered behind the next dune and moved in at my call. The minions didn't move as quickly as they had in life, but still far faster than ordinary zombies. Their stats seemed to depend on their original stats.

Soon, a giant crowd of scorpids, vultures, hooked horrors, basilisks, tumbleweeds, snakes and stone worms rolled, tunneled and flew to the plowed and sundered dune, where the ragged Sharkon was finishing off the last of the mobs remaining alive. The boss had around ten million health left, and my army of the dead had enough strength to bring him down to the condition I needed. It suddenly occurred to me that with a horde like that, I could capture the Modus castle. I smiled — didn't sound likely. At least not for now.

I picked out some of the lowest level and least useful, in my view, zombies from the snakes and stone worms, and sent them at the boss. I waded in too, leveling up my archery. This time I managed to lose a few arrows, which let my skill level up to eighty.

Soon the attacking zombies fell senseless, but the mission was complete — Sharkon's health had dropped to a million. Fury, your time to shine!

_____

Plague Fury activated: released 1,892,000 energy!

Scattered bones, torn-off limbs, spikes and innards, the bodies of lying snakes and worms; all of it burst into flame and instantly burned away, and the sand thirty feet around me began to melt, creating a circle of glass with the boss and I at its center.

The air around us was annihilated under the incredible rush of energy, and fresh air rushed in to fill the vacuum. If there was any moisture around us, it all evaporated. The boss's shell blackened and fell off in ash as if eaten away by acid, baring his flesh. A heartbeat later, there was nothing left of the boss but his bones. The skeleton didn't collapse. Subject to the magic of the dead, the infected creature transformed into my undead minion, keeping all its abilities.

All hell broke loose! Virtual fireworks, sounds of triumphant fanfare constantly replacing each other depending on the subject of the notification. Windows filled my vision:

Sharkon, Underground Terror, has died.

Experience: + 661,936,813.

You leveled up!...
You leveled up!...
You leveled up!...

...

The Destroying Plague

You leveled up! Current level: 105.
325 free attribute points available!

Level 100 reached!
Rank one is now available to your skills, abilities and crafts!

Unlocked achievement First Kill: Sharkon, Underground Terror!
You are the first in the world to kill the local boss **Sharkon, Underground Terror***!*

An ancient mage suffering from an excessive sense of humor performed an experiment to cross a shark, turtle and armadillo. The animal turned out to be what he needed — deadly, armored and very stupid. His creator has long since died, and the deserted city he lived in — covered in sand. Sharkon became the terror of the Lakharian Desert and lived many thousands of years here until he met you.
Reward*: Sharkon's Mane shield.*

Sharkon's Mane
Legendary
Scalable
Unique item.
Shield.
Armor: 90.
+120 strength.
+180 endurance.
+25% block chance.

On activation: throws the shield at enemies, dealing 1000% of base damage. The shield bounces off all other opponents within a hundred feet of the current target, then returns to the owner's hand.

Gem sockets: 3.

Durability: indestructible.

Sale price: 7200 gold coins.

Chance of loss after death lowered by 100%.

All hail the hero!

Would you like to make your name public? Doing so will give +100 reputation with all the main global factions and +500 fame.

Attention! Achievement I'm on Fire! — 3 upgraded to maximum I'm on Fire! I am the Fire!

Defeat 100 enemies who are more than five times higher level than you.

This is so impossible that it speaks for itself. You're on fire, no doubt about that.

Rewards: +100% health points; **Diamond Reputation Token** (+2000 with any faction instantly).

Unlocked heroic achievement: That Doesn't Happen!

Defeat an enemy who is more than ten times higher level than you.

Hmm... You better contact tech support and make a bug report. Did the mob get stuck in the terrain? Ha-ha, just kidding. Everything is possible in

The Destroying Plague

Disgardium! What an incredible achievement!
   Reward: Legendary   Storm   Dragon *Summoning Whistle*

   Legendary   Storm   Dragon   Summoning Whistle
   Legendary
   Unique item.
   One-time use.
   *On activation, permanently gives the owner the chance to summon a flying mount — a **Legendary Storm Dragon**.*
   Requires level: 100.
   Requires riding level 10.

   I fell to the sand and smiled, looking at the stars. I urgently needed some company, so I summoned my needler.

   "Sixty-four levels gained," I said to Iggy, who was purring measuredly nearby. "I'd jump for joy, but I don't think I have the energy..."

   The pet whistled and I watched the stream of congratulatory messages come in. I waved away all the invitations to make my name public and unwillingly picked myself up to collect the loot.

   I didn't find anything special; meat, all kinds of claws, fangs and a handful of gold coins. A field day for craftspeople.

   Unfortunately, I couldn't loot the boss or the raised infected. My sense of greed complained, not to mention my prudence, which grabbed me by the throat and forced me to renounce infecting bosses. I'd made huge gains for the future; first the loot, then leveling up my *Plague Reanimation.*

My killed, or at least broken-down mechostrich had recovered by then, which allowed me to summon it and mount up to move toward the place of power. My army of the dead followed me.

I wasn't planning to retreat from any more battles. The terrifying creatures that became my servants would eat whoever they liked. Especially the former boss Sharkon, and the hermit that I'd called Toothy. Incidentally, Sharkon had started steadily growing his shell back.

I could have walked, but I couldn't wait to level up my riding skill to ten and fly my own dragon!

There were a few more skirmishes on the way, which took my level up to one hundred and eight — no more fountains of experience like what I got from Sharkon. I aggroed the mobs first to restore my plague reservoir, then set my dead minions on them.

We were in time. We reached the place of power by midnight, where the tips of stone columns eaten by wind and sand pierced through the ground. The system defined it as a separate zone, and I got an achievement for being the first to discover it.

Unlocked achievement Explorer 1.
Discover a zone that no other player has ever been to.

The Destroying Plague

Reward: +10 perception.

Scyth, you have the right to name this new zone!

You can keep the old name (Departed Temple Ruins) or come up with your own.

Unlocked level 1 Cartography skill!

Cartography is used for forming maps of areas. The skill allows you to create your own maps of previously unexplored zones, create routes for ships on the ocean, and use other people's maps to find treasure and artifacts.

In your travels around Disgardium, you can find encrypted treasure maps that point to locations where troves are buried. Using the Cartography skill, you can determine the place to go searching.

Keep upgrading the skill by exploring new lands.

Strange that I didn't get an achievement for discovering Kharinza. I thought for a moment and decided it was possible that an inhabitant of the sandbox couldn't be allowed to discover new lands outside it. I mean, it could have been that there was just no code for it.

Without thinking hard, I called the area Temple of Tiamat. If we built a new temple, the old name with the word 'ruins' wouldn't apply.

The timer should activate in a few minutes. I

ordered my mobs to patrol the area while I wasn't there, made sure that I had enough plague energy to maintain them, then did the last thing I planned to do.

I released the *Diamond Worm.*

A three-foot long sausage touched my face with its snout, sprang away from my chest and buried itself into the sand. I'd have to feed it a lot of experience in the coming days, and Iggy too; he'd fallen behind a lot in levels.

There was plenty for all the Awoken to do here.

Chapter 20

Awoken Undead

A BOMB DROPPING couldn't have had more effect than the news of the first kill of the local boss Sharkon in the Lakharian Desert. The teachers didn't let us use communicators in lessons, but in our breaks, we greedily checked all the posts and discussions, all the exaggerated versions of what happened.

New threads on Sharkon were created every second on the official game forums. Nobody doubted that the boss must have fallen to an A-class Threat, it seemed. The logic was that none of the top players would have hidden their name if it was them. There'd be no point; global feats and achievements like that got you a lot of popularity, which meant a lot of money. Some had doubts, of course, accusing the preventers of hiding a new potion from the wider public, one that let them withstand the desert debuffs. Some even shared 'insider intel'; there really was such a potion, but its recipe was deliberately kept off the market.

There's an A-class Threat in action! They exist! Ian Mitchell wrote, a journalist from Disgardium Daily. *Yesterday we received irrefutable proof. Remember how we laughed a week ago at the hapless so-called Alliance of Preventers, who let a D-class Threat slip through their fingers? The mutual distrust and sluggishness of their top players nearly led to the collapse of Modus. Last year's champions of the Arena have apparently turned into fat cats resting on their laurels. How else do we explain their embarrassing mistakes in their military operations and internal politics...*

Ian wrote derisively, dripping scorn for the preventers. This meant he only spared a couple of lines for Sharkon himself, devoting more attention to taunting and mocking the Alliance. Apparently due to a lack of information about the boss; nobody had ever seen it except me, after all.

The article ended thusly: *A-class Threat! Whoever you are, know this: I and millions of my readers are behind you! Kick those arrogant bastards' asses!*

The text had over a hundred million likes and four million comments and change. The top comment read: *Anyone know what the Threat's superpower is? Although who cares, anyone who can take out bosses past the Frontier is #1! Finally Dis has someone who can shake things up! P.S. You missed it all, Mogwai!*

The fastest growing topic was called "Hey, A-class, I want to volunteer!" and had amassed over ten

The Destroying Plague

million applications, people leaving their in-game information and expressing their willingness to join my plague-ridden crusade against the civilized world. For some reason they were all sure that's what I'd be doing, and they wanted to take part. In other threads, like "A-class Threat — who is it?" they argued about what faction I might be in, my gender, my age...

There were all kinds of speculation, but most popular of all was the idea that the Threat was a poor inwinova that had randomly found a certain artifact in a mine, allowing him to not only get his status, but also to get rich. I could only guess at who had come up with that and why. Either the preventers knew something and were sending their competitors on a false trail, or it was the mining companies pushing a 'success story' to motivate their workers.

One of the comments my eye randomly hit upon was from Zoran. *Murphy, buddy, if you're reading this... it's like I've seen Jesus! Or Satan, depends how you look at it. Yeah, I gave Ehehe his stuff back. I just wanna say thanks and good luck!*

The preventers themselves maintained an amiable silence, refusing to give any comments to journalists. Some eyewitnesses saw them mobilizing at global boss spawn points, and that made us think; the top players had stopped sitting on their laurels, as Ian wrote, and were leveling up, and all the while still building plans to capture and eliminate the Threat.

For me, Distival should become a decisive factor. I didn't allow myself the delusion that I'd be

---

without suspicion — I'd left too many traces — but I wanted to make sure. If I managed it, I'd speak to Yary and look him in the eyes. I doubted clarity would change anything, but... it would shift the priorities in my plans slightly. But there were still three more days left until Distival, and we had a lot to do by then.

That evening, first I dragged the others to the desert, then they delivered Manny and Gyula's workers to the site of the future temple. After careful consideration, I decided that the former treasury guardians would stay behind. I couldn't leave the fort entirely defenseless.

Looking around in awe, my clanmates felt themselves to make sure the heat of the desert wasn't hurting them. Infect picked up some handfuls of golden sand and watched in excitement as it ran through his fingers. The others cautiously watched my undead army as it milled senselessly around the ruins.

I didn't feel alone anymore. I was surrounded by friends and like-minded people. My feelings welled forth and I couldn't hold them back anymore. I shouted at the top of my lungs.

"Welcome to the Lakharian Desert, my Awoken!"

* * *

A day later, I sat on crest of the tallest and observed events on both sides of it.

426

The Destroying Plague

On the right, far below, two brigades were at work. I could see Manny managing the miners, gesticulating with his usual enthusiasm. They were digging the ruins of the temple of the Departed out of the sand. Gyula and his builders had begun to erect the foundation of the future temple of the Sleeping Gods in a cleared area. Now that they were undead, they all had a permanent subject for mutual jokes and mockery.

We didn't have to go far for resources — the workers mined stone and sand in situ. The other guys brought more from the fort. Just now, Crag, Crawler and Infect had gone to Kharinza for some missing materials.

Our builders were hard at work on the left, in the valley, but on the other side of the dune, a battle raged. My specially selected personal guard — five of my most powerful minions who had preserved their abilities from life, including Sharkon and Toothy — were tearing apart two basilisks. I divided my other brainless zombies equally around the construction site, creating something like a security perimeter. Throwing them all at once at a couple of respawned mobs would be foolish; they'd only have gotten in each other's way.

I quickly replaced any that fell in final death with new ones, raising dead mobs and killing three birds with one stone; keeping my overall number of minions at fifty, leveling up *Plague Reanimation* and increasing the quality of my soldiers. The last one

427

seemed to me to be something like evolution: weak zombies steadily got replaced with strong ones that preserved their abilities. Those received names and stood out not only for their greater effectiveness in battle, but also their fairly civilized behavior.

Cr-r-rash! — the gleaming flexible body of Crash flew out of the ground, throwing up a fountain of sand. The *Diamond Worm*, my new pet, had grown to sixteen feet long and had fattened up a lot, but was still a child.

"Hellish pet!" Bomber commented, climbing up to me for a rest. "Shame it's bound to this zone. I'd have taken it farming with me..."

"This zone could expand to cover half the desert, Bomb," I told him. "The habitable zone border expands half a mile every ten levels."

At that moment, Crash bit into the tail of a basilisk and hung on like a bulldog. Now that he had a grip, he turned and stabbed his drill-like tail into the creature's skin. The tail's special structure turned the pet into a mini drilling machine. The diamond drill span up to full speed in a second and began digging into the mob's body. Scraps of reptile skin flew in all directions, but the level difference was so great that it caused little damage.

To become an adult specimen, the legendary worm needed a lot more experience than epic needlers. That would happen only when it reached level one hundred. But immediately after that, it would be able to independently hunt and level up on its own, and against high-level enemies too.

"Look, your minions are doing a great job," Bomber said as he watched the fight below.

My 'guards' really were working well together. Toothy the hermit was stuck a basilisk's face and had begun a battle dance while Sharkon tanked aggro from both enemies. Apart from Crash, they were helped by the skeletal vulture Birdie, the morten zombie Kermit and the nightmarish and deadly tumbleweed known as It. The first two tore and rended a basilisk's sides with their claws, while the tumbleweed pulled a reptile's claws into itself and began to digest it rapidly.

Iggy and Whatchamacallit ran in circles nearby, firing at the enemies.

It occurred to me that a video of how the Awoken clan was progressing would have caused quite a furor, inviting envy, upset and complaints to the developers; while my army of minions tore up mobs at level four hundred, the clan members sunned themselves and occasionally smiled at another level up. In reality, this was the exception — experience was nice, but leveling up skills required personal involvement.

In the meantime, my five servants and the two pets finished off both basilisks, which respawned more often than the other mobs. There was a break in the sequence of battles. Bomber descended from the dune to collect the loot and I decided to finally get to grips with my new skill ranks.

The fun in Disgardium only really began from level one hundred; even the skill ranks below one hundred were at zero, i.e. null rank.

The previous day, after I'd dealt with the organizational questions of constructing the temple and figured out a mathematically optimal route for leveling up the clan, I'd started to get down to myself. I started by studying the ranking system thoroughly but didn't settle on a choice. The choice was final, so it demanded some serious thought.

I couldn't fall asleep for a long time that night, tossing and turning in bed, calculating builds and trying to predict how events would develop. This was mostly what determined which branch of unarmed combat would be most useful. In the end I forgot about sleep and let the calculations take over.

Everyone knew that Disgardium was a very competitive game. Success within it meant success in life, and so nobody was in a rush to share any important information.

But some information could still be obtained. For money. I didn't have a spare thousand phoenixes, so I had to climb into my capsule and pay for a pack of ranking guides with gold. I didn't have time to study them all, of course, but discarding the sections of builds that had no relevance to me (which I shared with my clanmates, of course), I read the important parts.

After rank one, you had to put in a lot more effort to upgrade your skills. Almost by a factor of one hundred. Meaning, to gain one level in a rank one skill, you had to put as much effort in as it took to level it up one hundred times at rank zero!

It was good news that all the moves and abilities related to the skill grew in level alongside it, regardless of how often they were used. That allowed me to level up *Crushing Hammerfist, Stunning Kick* and *Combo* all at once. As for *Archery* though, which was still at rank zero, *Quickshot* was now twice as high as *Explosive Shot.*

My current base damage was three hundred and eighty-two hit points. This meant that at level one hundred unarmed combat, my standard attack dealt three thousand damage and change, and my *Crushing Hammerfist* — almost two hundred thousand! But that was against a defenseless target at my level. In battles against top players and high-ranking mobs, the numbers fell catastrophically, and they were the only kind I fought...

At every rank starting from the first, skills gained new capabilities that increased their moves.

I opened the panel and focused on unarmed combat. A selection window popped up:

Unarmed Combat rank 1 reached!

Select a progression path. Keep in mind that your decision is final — you will not be able to change it. You can set an additional development path after you reach your next skill rank.

Path of Elements

Depending on your chosen element, your unarmed combat moves will hit at range, freeze enemies, deal bonus damage or ignore armor. In addition, you will be able to instantly move across short distances, slow time in battle and summon a Star Ally.

Path of Trickery

Your unarmed combat moves have a chance of maiming, immobilizing, blinding or even instantly killing the enemy.

Path of Justice

If you choose the Path of Justice, the effectiveness of all your skill's combat moves returns to its base value, but then ignores all penalties in battle against enemies at a higher level.

Path of Solitude

One who travels the Path of Solitude may resist hordes of enemies, hitting all around him with every strike.

Path of Defense

You can block and reflect enemy attacks, returning damage in part or even in full depending on your skill level and luck.

Unarmed combat wasn't the most popular skill,

but still had its hardcore fans, some of which successfully reached rank one. Almost every path had been tried and rated. Adepts of fist-fighting had come to a single conclusion: the Path of Elements was the most balanced and easily adapted to any situation, since you could switch between elements at any time you weren't in combat.

The Path of Trickery only gave a pathetic percentage that the perk would proc at low levels; only every millionth hit would kill instantly (although it worked on any target and at any level of health), and every thousandth would maim. A plus was that the blinding or broken bone debuff wouldn't heal in battle, but there were far more minuses in this path.

The adepts came to the same conclusion against the Path of Defense — too much depended on the situation and on *luck*, which few had leveled up seriously.

The Path of Solitude, on the other hand, was worth attention. Particularly in a strong clan, in contrast to the name; one hundred percent of the damage against an individual target spread out in waves against nearby enemies, which worked very effectively against packs of mobs. A player who chose the Path of Solitude multiplied their DPS[7] severalfold, which increased their value in a raid group.

Nobody ever chose the Path of Justice. Not a single player had decided to level up the skill for years

---

[7] DPS (Damage Per Second) — the average damage dealt per second.

for the sake of a remote chance to win against high-level opponents. But this branch happened to suit me more than all the others. I wasn't frightened of the prospect of the skill returning to its base values, because leveling it back up here in the Lakharian Desert was a realistic goal — it'd take a day or two in the heat of battle. And the ability to fight against any level I wanted without losing accuracy or damage was just what the doctor ordered! Especially considering one pleasant fact; as I leveled it up, the moves would ignore more and more of the enemy's armor.

I weighed up all the conclusions and made my decision.

Unarmed Combat level 1
Rank: 1 (Path of Justice).
Damage dealt without a weapon increased by 10%. Attack accuracy increased by 10%.
Continue to improve this skill by fighting enemies of your level or higher for additional bonuses and new special attacks.
6 training points available. Pay a visit to a master of unarmed combat to study new special attacks!

Crushing Hammerfist of Justice level 1
Deals 160% of standard damage.
Ignores armor: 0.2%.

A simple calculation showed that the damage

from my main attack no longer shone with fantastic numbers: just eight hundred and forty. Well, that was something I could fix. I needed to visit a trainer, upgrade *Stunning Kick* and *Combo*, and maybe check out a few other skills since I didn't need to level them up separately anymore.

Two more skills demanded my attention: *Resilience* and *Persuasion*.

Resilience rank 1 reached!
Select a skill progression path:

Path of Equanimity
You completely ignore all damage for the first 3 seconds of the battle.

Path of Life
You absorb 1% of damage taken, using it to automatically recover health, mana or your class resource.

Path of Reflection
1% of damage taken is reflected and ricochets back to the enemy.

Path of Stubbornness
A magical shield with a durability equal to 300% of your mana surrounds you at the start of the battle.

Path of Justice

The effectiveness of the skill returns to initial values, but from now on you completely ignore penalties in battles against enemies at a higher level than you.

I liked consistency. I chose the Path of Justice again. Whatever happened with the Destroying Plague and the Sleeping Gods, this choice would let me stand up against even global bosses. If, of course, I leveled up the skill again, which wouldn't be easy because of my racial ability to withstand aggressive environments and breathe underwater.

Resilience level 1
Rank: 1 (Path of Justice).

Resistance to all types of damage increased by 1%. Pain sensation reduced by 1%. If your health drops below 10%, the Diamond Skin of Justice ability activates.

Continue to improve this skill by fighting enemies of your level or higher for additional bonuses and new special attacks.

Stoneskin skill transformed!
Diamond Skin of Justice level 1
For 1 second, you are covered in a diamond skin that fully absorbs all damage. Removes all crowd control effects and debuffs.

The Persuasion skill was the fastest to deal

with. There were no progression branches there, the new rank just added something interesting:

Persuasion level 1
Rank: 1.

When talking to intelligent beings, you influence their consciousness and reduce their critical thinking. During the discussion, your reputation with your interlocutor is effectively one level higher than it is in reality.

Your eloquence is reinforced with the ability to see how your words influence the mood of those you speak to.

Once done with that, I brought up my profile to see the big picture.

Scyth, level 150 undead (hidden)
Rank: Junior Gladiator (hidden).
Clan: Awoken (hidden).
Real name: Alex Sheppard (hidden).
Real age: 16 years (hidden).
Class: Herald (hidden).

Primary characteristics
Strength: 154.
Perception: 164.
Endurance: 330.
Charisma: 179.
Intellect: 100.

Agility: 150.
Luck: 775.

Secondary characteristics

Health points: 126,600.
Mana points: 17,260.
Vindication points: 169,000 (inactive).
Plague Energy points: 1,100,000.
Restoration rate: 2475 health per minute.
Base damage: 382.
Bonus to ranged damage: +108%.
Bonus to critical damage: 418%.
Bonus to magic power: 130%.
Bonus to movement speed: 155%.
Bonus to damage resistance against insectoids: +50%.

Bonus to damage resistance from poisons: +100%.

Bonus to damage in battles against players: +5%.

Bonus to chance to stun enemy: +5%.

Bonus to chance to get upgraded loot: +30% (maximum value reached).

Bonus to chance to get a unique quest: +30% (maximum value reached).

Bonus to dodge chance: +280%.
Carrying capacity: 2890 lbs.
Accuracy: 840%.

Merchant discounts: 50% (maximum value reached).

The Destroying Plague

Chance to avoid critical damage: +5%.
Chance of critical damage: +100%.
Chance to detect invisibility: +5%.
Fame: 455.

Skills

Unarmed Combat rank 1: 1.
Riding (no rank): 7.
Crushing weaponry skill (no rank): 1.
One-handed sword skill (no rank): 1.
Cartography (no rank): 1.
Night Vision (no rank): 77.
Swimming (no rank): 66.
Stealth (no rank): 82.
Archery (no rank): 80.
Persuasion rank 1: 1.
Resilience rank 1: 1.

Crafting and professions

Cooking: Expert (195/500).

Special skills and abilities

Destroying Plague Immortality: 11.
Depths Teleportation: 11.
Ghastly Howl: 25.
Plague Reanimation: 5.
Plague Fury: 1.
Plague Pestilence: 3.

Class skills

Divine Revelation (spontaneous).
Imitation: 9.
Lethargy: 5.
Liberation: 27.
Cloak Essence: 9.

Divine abilities (inactive)
Unity.
Touch of the Sleeping Gods.
Sleeping Invulnerability: 1.
Sleeping Vindication: 1.

Achievements
Morituri te salutant! — 1
Explorer — 1
The Lich is Dead! Long Live the New Lich…
First Completion: Treasury of the First Mage
First Kill: Sharkon, Underground Terror
First Kill: Crusher
First Kill: Mok'Rhyssa, Rock Queen
First Kill: Murkiss
First Kill: Chuff, Queen of the Swamp Needlers
First Kill: Shog'rassar, God of the Sarantapods
I Came, I Saw, I Conquered — 1
I Came, I Saw, I Conquered — 2
That Doesn't Happen!
I'm on Fire! I am the Fire!

Divine emblems
Shog'rassar's protection.

The Destroying Plague

Pets
Iggy, level 91 swamp needler.
Crash, level 33 diamond worm.

Hidden status: *K-class Threat with potential* **A**.
Hidden status: *Initial of the Sleeping Gods.*
Hidden status: *Legate of the Destroying Plague.*

Money: *745,890 gold, 11 silver, 64 copper.*
Marks of the Valorous: *10.*

I liked what I'd seen and was even gladder that my numbers would be changing soon with such a rate of growth.

* * *

I cleared out my inventory before the guys came back from the fort. I'd saved up heaps of cooking ingredients by then. Some of them were well known in big Dis, but the dishes were very expensive due to a lack of resources. Which made sense; I doubted those *Tumbleweeds* got farmed often. I'd seen only two of them even after spending almost three full days in the desert.

Royalties from the cooking guild motivated me to level up the craft. My recipes (*Well-Done Carp in Sour Cream, Miner's Fish Soup, Marinated Filet of Swamp Bighead with Onion and Herbs and Fried*

Spicy Stone Grabber, Stuffed with Herbs), which I'd invented back in the sandbox, enjoyed some popularity and were bringing in around ten thousand gold every four months.

Pulling out my portable stove, I started a fire and began to equip the crafting gear that I'd so fortunately bought in Darant. *Chef's Hat, Chef's Apron, Kaizen Chef Knife.* I pulled out the *Universal Portable Stove*, spices and other ingredients, and started experimenting.

My stocks included twenty-five *Basilisk Fillets...*

"Oh, finally getting back to cooking? Nice!" Bomber interrupted my calculations, returning with some loot. "By the way, let me give you this too..."

He dumped a pile of various kinds of meat and guts at my feet and also gave me some strange ingredients, such as *Eye of the Desert Arachnid* and *Vulture Eggs.*

I started cooking, carefully experimenting and getting a negative result in the form of a ruined dish over and over again. It seemed my crafting level was far too low for the rare ingredients.

"Hey, bro!" Bomber, bustling around and actively working his nose, put a shoulder on my hand and 'helped' me ruin the next dish. "We're getting an ocean of free experience, and that's awesome, but tell me, are we planning to keep hanging around here like this?"

"Yep, Bomb, this is it until Distival," I answered, a little annoyed having failed to pull my pot off the fire quick enough. "We discussed this, the temple and leveling up are our main priorities. I need to get Iggy up to my level, and Crash needs to mature as fast as possible too. Enjoy the moment. Any player would envy you right now."

"I know, I know, bro. I'm just... bored, I guess."

Bomber took a bottle of beer out of his inventory, opened it and finally calmed down, stopped pacing and interrupting me. He lay down, took a swig and squeezed his eyes shut in revery.

Our powerleveling was actually going slower than I expected. Firstly, almost none of the guys were doing any damage, and that was a huge minus to experience. It was a good thing they were getting anything at all — in no small part because I was far lower level than the mobs, even if I was higher level than the other guys.

Secondly, most of the experience went to me. And thirdly, I then redirected it to the pets. So in two days, the guys had only reached level one hundred, and I'd gotten to level one hundred and fifty. Millions of players in Dis who thought it was good progress to make level twenty or thirty in a year would have cried to see it.

I had to admit, we had it good. I'd gotten a unique opportunity — I'd gotten a Threat status of the highest potential, and then everything went so lucky with Behemoth and the Destroying Plague. After all, if it weren't for the Sleeping God, I would have lost my freedom of choice and I'd have been eliminated very soon.

Seemed to me Bomber had had the same thought. Enjoying another swig of cold beer — thanks to the inventory, which kept consumables in the same condition they entered it in — the warrior asked:

"All the same, Scyth... Why do we need a temple? Why do we even need the Sleeping Gods? By all Ed's calculations, the Destroying Plague is way more imba than the swamp god. You think the head honcho of the dead is going to turn a blind eye to the new temple? Apart from anything else, it's gonna ruin your relationship with the Nucleus..."

"Say, do you have any cheese in your bag? Oh, great! Give it here..." I took a quarter of a wheel of *Goat's Cheese* from the warrior and cut it into small pieces, answering him as I went. "I have a feeling, and don't ask where from, that the Nucleus won't learn about the temple. Or rather, it'll learn about it, but not right away. And anyway... You know, if we let go all the sappy stuff about not wanting to see familiar NPCs as brainless zombies, the answer is simple: if the Destroying Plague reaches full strength, then the world will end. And my character too, because the Nucleus will take away my will, my control of myself."

"Are you serious? But how?

"The same way the capsule makes you believe that you got stunned. Thank the Sleeping Gods, Behemoth managed to protect me from the Nucleus' control. Apart from that, the source of the Destroying Plague's power is the Nether. It will swallow up all

Disgardium. And the Nucleus will gain strength very quick from the top players. The high-level players will be the first barrier before the legions of the undead, and they'll be the first infected — if not by me, then by Shazz. What do you think happens after that?"

"The same as in Tristad? The top players will lose their characters?"

"That's one possibility. It's fully possible that some of them will maintain control of their characters and... The Nucleus will take those in and turn them into Legates. It sleeps and sees hundreds, thousands of followers from its lair! My ceiling, even if I max out *Plague Reanimation* is a thousand dead under my command. One *Armageddon* will destroy them all, you know that spell has maximum damage. So, the more Legates the Nucleus gets, the bigger the army it can assemble.

"Oh, damn, I think now I get what that means for you..."

"Woah!" I shouted in joy, because I'd finally managed to successfully make a new dish!

All I had to do was use some logic and add what was usually put into things like this!

Attempt to create new cooking dish!
Successful! You created a new cooking recipe: Incredibly Tasty Cheesy Vulture Egg Omelet!

You created Incredibly Tasty Cheesy Vulture Egg Omelet.

_____

Incredibly Tasty Cheesy Vulture Egg Omelet.

Epic dish

Ingredients: vulture egg, vegetable oil, salt, black pepper, goat's cheese.

This omelet is a very rare delicacy; it can only be created from the eggs of the most dangerous desert vultures. The inventor of this dish, Scyth, wasted many rare ingredients before he figured out he needed to add a little goat's cheese.

Special effects when eaten: *+100 to main craft, +100% to work speed.*

Effects last: 24 hours.

Cost: 600 gold coins.

Cooking trade: +10. Current grade: Expert (272/500).

I continued cooking — unfortunately I only had one egg left — and returned to our interrupted conversation.

"Anyway, about the Nucleus. When it picks up more Legates, I'll be just one of many, and my key ability, *Immortality* will be almost unusable, since I have to be the only Legate in an area for it to activate. Then my choice will disappear once and for all, because I'll lose all my advantages and won't be able to build or protect temples for the Sleeping Gods. All the continents closed to players right now, where we might be able to build a temple in an undead body, will be available to all the top players that take the side of the Destroying Plague..."

We heard the clap of portals from below, near the workers; the guys returning from Kharinza. Crag waved to us.

"Come down!" we heard his voice through the communication amulet.

We'd bought them after all. True, ordinary ones with a range restricted to the current zone — they'd cost about ten thousand each. The absolute best communication amulets available on the market were epic ones that could hold an intercontinental connection and cost as much as a legendary flying mount. And the less said about the long-sight mirrors, the better.

I gathered up all my cooking gear and Bomber and I walked down to join the guys. The workers had already surrounded them, waiting for them to unload the resources and give each worker dinner made by Aunt Stephanie.

I pulled Gyula off to the side and gave him a couple of portions of my new dish.

"Just in time," the chief builder said. "Maybe with this speed boost, we'll be able to finish tomorrow...

"Just in time? Has something happened?"

Gyula faltered, but finally admitted:

"Um... I didn't want to bother you... Basically, there are problems in the work gang. Can't see it here, but in real life all our boys are sick. Temperatures of over a hundred. We're on our last legs. Even I'm wiped out, to tell the truth."

"What does the doctor say?"

"What doctor, Alex? We treat ourselves with grandma's remedies, everyone with something different. There's some kind of epidemic! Probably from the cold. We've had a few days of frosts; it's been a lot of colder than usual."

"Say, are all your guys sick? I mean, everyone that works with us?"

"Um... Well, my daughter in the tavern, ain't a thing wrong with her. Trixie's well too. But as for my guys, and Manny's..."

A vague worry stirred in my mind. I remembered how the Dementors suddenly fell ill when they got debuffs from the swamp needlers. The doctors couldn't diagnose them, and the guys got better when the debuff came off. The memory of my own fever after I became an undead was still fresh...

"I'll fly to you tomorrow after school and bring my Home Doctor," I said. "We need to figure out what the sickness is, and the diagnosis will make it easier to treat. By the way... you mentioned that the Sharks have been patrolling the district. Are they still there?"

"Hard to say exactly, we haven't been going outside recently, but I think things are quieter," Gyula scratched the back of his head. "At least, the men haven't mentioned anything."

"Alright, I'll risk it."

Thanking me, the foreman switched to

questions of construction. We also discussed the restoration of the first temple in Kharinza, which shouldn't have taken much time — a day and a half, no more.

After the conversation, Gyula joined the work gang and sat down to eat. I did the same, sitting down next to him.

Eating quickly, the clan and I prepared to continue our farming marathon. First our boys summoned their needler pets to join Whatchamacallit and Iggy.

Crag pulled out his cat — once small, fluffy and harmless, but now far bigger. We'd given it to Crag as a belated birthday gift. Seeing him staring at our needlers with a faraway look in his eye, I'd visited the auction house and bought him an epic battle pet. We all agreed to take the money from the gift from the clan treasury. In its adult state, the 'kitten' would become a deadly and very dangerous *Ursai Liger*, taller than a man at the withers.

The group buffed up with practiced ease as soon as we'd all summoned our pets. First Crawler put his still weak shields on us: fire, air and earth. The mage decided to level up not only the fire element and had studied the tomes I'd gotten from the treasury. That was logical; he needed to make progress in various branches.

Then Infect let loose a few of his short inspiring songs. It sounded terrible.

"Da-a-a-arrk ni-i-ight, only arro-o-o-ws zip

---

through the des-e-e-rt!" the bard howled. "Only the wind raises the sa-a-and, the stars glimme-e-er dimly..."

Our ears tried to close up, but we put on a brave face and withstood the torture. After all, we were the ones that insisted that he change his class.

After listening to our homegrown guitarist, Crag and Bomber added to our attack power with *Battle Cry*. And as a finishing touch, we polished off a portion of imba chow from *Rat Zombie Innards*.

Crash was describing circles nearby, digging in and out of the sand, and my elite undead meandered around too: Sharkon, Toothy, Kermit, Birdie and It. In the distance, staggering and emitting groaning noises, my team of forty-one other nightmarish monsters waited. Counting the guardians on Kharinza, there were exactly fifty minions.

"Everyone ready?" I asked, looking over the guys.

My clanmates answered with smiles, anticipating oceans of experience.

"Then let's go!"

The crowd of zombies advanced first. Behind, astride their newly purchased mounts, came Crawler, Crag, Bomber and Infect. Nobody had bothered to be original — they all chose the tried-and-tested mechostrich.

After making sure that things were quiet and nothing threatened our workers, I began to go down after them.

The Destroying Plague

When a weak rustle came from somewhere off to the side, my ears pricked up and I concentrated on listening. Good thing I did; a scaly, triangular head on a long neck emerged from the sand in the treacherous silence. Yellow eyes gleamed in the dusk, and the huge creature's wending body's gleamed.

Apophis, level ???
Ancient Snake
Global boss

This was the first time I'd seen a snake like this here. The reptile reached a hundred feet in length, but at the same time it moved silently. Its snow-white scales gleamed in the glow of Geala.

The snake quickly span itself into several huge rings and brought its head to my face. Its forked tongue slithered from its mouth and almost touched my lips. A sharp and foul scent made me want to throw up, although I smelled terrible myself. The huge yellow eyes burned right through me, and I watched them as if bewitched, not understanding why I wasn't saying anything or attacking. My mind screamed that something strange was happening, but my muscles had turned to stone. I didn't understand why I was losing control.

Some of the guys realized that I'd fallen back and sounded the alarm. I heard the anxious voices of builders. I couldn't even call my minions to help me — my gaze slipped past the command icons without focusing.

"Can you hear me, Scyth? What the hell is happening over there?" I heard Crawler's distorted voice through my comm amulet.

I wanted to answer, but I couldn't open my mouth. Raising its monstrous head above me, the snake froze. A droplet separated from a fang and fell onto my forehead — it felt as if a hot iron had been placed on my skin, and that was with my maximum protection against poisons. The reptile swayed back and forth as if deciding what to do, and then its maw opened and blotted out the sky.

The world shimmered, I saw the glimmering ring of a portal and I collapsed.

Interlude 3

Yemi

THE LEADER OF THE AFRICAN clan Yoruba, a ju-ju class shaman and orc by the name of Yemi, had managed to do the impossible. He had taken control of the beast-god Apophis, the White Snake. Well, taken control is a little too strong, but he *had* gained the right to make a wish (within the bounds of the snake's abilities, of course).

You wouldn't want to know what this cost Yemi. It all began when the shaman found an ancient tome that taught him all about how to talk to snakes. Simply put, he learned that skill. Since then, every time he's seen a creeping creature, Yemi has listened to its hissing instead of rushing to kill it.

At first, he understood almost nothing, just one or two words or half-formed thoughts, but as the skill grew, so did his understanding. After level ten, things really got interesting.

Talking to snakes revealed the snake god to the Yoruba clan leader. The white snake showed some interest in him, and drop by drop, his reputation with the divinity began to grow. When Yemi reached the stage of thinking about building a temple dedicated to the god in the clan's domain, their relationship moved to a new level.

The white snake named the spellcaster his first priest and gave him the first quest in the divine quest chain. It was relatively easy: destroy a hundred *White-winged Eagles* and bring the same number of their eggs to the altar. The beast-god accepted the sacrifice, swallowing the offering with pleasure, and gave the next quest in return.

Soon the shaman's reputation with the beast-god grew to *trust*. Apophis taught the caster a couple of fun tricks that increased the clan's capabilities, but the most important thing was something else. Yemi became a Threat with a potential of R.

He hid his status as long as he could, but soon started getting uncomfortable questions from his officers. And when someone voiced the correct assumption, what happened happened — the clan members became subthreats. That brought the clan closer together, and now Apophis's quests could be completed as a group.

Where was it best to hide a leaf? In the forest. Yoruba began to position itself as a preventer clan, and even became quite a successful one. In just the last year, it had eliminated two impressive threats, which allowed it to be numbered among the top thousand clans of the world.

After a couple of drinks, Yemi worked up the

courage to contact Horvac from the Travelers, offering his services to the alliance of preventers in searching for a D-class Threat, but the arrogant bastards didn't even want to talk to him!

Grr, they're going to regret that! Yemi consoled himself, deciding that the day would come when he would rise and sweep their castles from the face of Disgardium.

That meant getting a high Threat potential, and to get that, the shaman would stop for nothing. When he went to Apophis for help and the snake demanded that he bring him nine thousand nine hundred and ninety-nine intelligent creatures in sacrifice, Yemi merely asked: "Any? Do kobolds and murlocks count too?" And Apophis said any would do.

For several weeks, the clan captured intelligent mobs and NPCs all over Shad'Erung and sacrificed them, cutting off their heads where they stood by a portable altar. Blood flowed in rivers, but it was never enough for the White Snake. The situation became complicated; the first priest not only had to be present at each sacrifice, but he even had to perform the ritual.

The same fate awaited noob players, only the clan disguised themselves from those. After all, Yoruba still had a reputation to maintain.

Yemi was in a hurry. It was very important to be in time before the Alliance of Preventers or any of the lesser sharks caught the two highest threats in his memory: A and D. Nobody knew anything of the first. For a long time, there had been nothing but rumors of the second until the Alliance managed to capture one... and foolishly let him go. Yemi's chance to find a man whose name resounded throughout Dis had increased substantially.

Yesterday they made their final sacrifice of intelligent life. The beast-god had gained so much trust in the first priest by then that, albeit unwillingly, he shared some crumbs of power with him, entrusting him with unique talents. That helped Yemi to assemble a set of legendary class equipment, but he dreamed of far more than that.

Yemi handed in his quest and froze, kneeling. He lowered his head and dared not move. The beast-god's bloodthirstiness and temper sometimes led to a sharp drop in reputation due to an ill-timed word. But right now, the sated Apophis hissed in approval.

"You have earned your reward, my first priest. I will not only find the one you seek, but I will deliver him here," the snake hissed. "State his name!"

Yemi hesitated. To find him, the beast-god would need the name, race and class.

The bomb that exploded in the game community after the news of the First Kill of that boss in the Lakharian Desert had awoken Yemi's anticipation and excitement. Of course, that could be the D Threat just making progress, but what if...?

What if I risk it and order the A-class Threat? he thought. *But I don't know anything about that one...* All the same, he made his decision.

The Destroying Plague

"Great One, allow me to ask a favor of you. The one that I need most of all was in the Lakharian Desert yesterday, on Latteria. He defeated a certain Sharkon, and that is all I know of him. Although... There are rumors that he can take on the guises of others. He is very strong. He may be the strongest mortal in all Disgardium. But if this knowledge is not enough to seek him out, then I would ask you to find the warrior Crag. He is a dwarf."

"You will receive what you wish," Apophis agreed, crawling away into the gloom of the wide den he always emerged from.

It wasn't clear whom of the named threats the snake would bring, but Yemi immediately started anxiously ordering his clanmates to get ready. He climbed onto the fortress walls — to look around, gather himself and convince himself that nobody would stop the most important event in his life from happening.

With its tall, angular towers, the Yoruba castle looked like an intruder on a flat landscape without a single tree in sight. The sun fell to the horizon, breaking through the orange-pink clouds.

Barat'Uruk was considered a native land of the orcs. This harsh area of central Shad'Erung stretched out in endless steppes from the Sea of Bones in the east to the Ursai Jungle in the west. A guard post bristling with spears could be seen in the distance. It belonged to orcs from the Broken Axe clan — a local faction exalted with Yemi.

After ensuring that all was well, the spellcaster returned to Apophis' temple. Based on a careful plan, a tight circle surrounded the altar, then another and another — to make sure the Threat had no way at all to escape. The soldiers buffed themselves and hurriedly swallowed strengthening elixirs. The mages, warlocks and shamans prepared their most powerful crowd control spells.

Yemi had something else saved for a rainy day; a legendary one-time use artifact capable of stopping even a global boss.

The wait didn't last long. The huge snake didn't crawl out of its hole, but appeared in the air, and Yemi saw that the beast-god was wrapped around someone whose name he couldn't make out.

Losing his deadly rings, the White Snake freed the prisoner and he fell down in a shapeless heap. The silhouette of a man in a cloak became visible through the clouds of grey smoke, though nobody could make out any details except his eyes gleaming green from the gloom of his hood.

The Yorubas breathed noisily, glancing at their commander impatiently.

"Who is it?" Yemi asked.

"Your wish has come true, priest," the snake answered. "Know that this creature is under the protection of those who are far mightier than I. He himself is not too dangerous for now, but I feel the strength in him. He is the one that conquered Sharkon. It took a great deal of energy to bring him to you. Now I must rest. For your next such wish, I will demand thrice as much..."

Having said his piece, Apophis disappeared — it seemed to Yemi that he was exhausted. The figure by the altar stirred.

In that same instant, at their leader's signal, the entire might of the Yoruba clan descended on the Threat. The earth trembled under the smoke-shrouded body, and a destructive column of *Hellflame* shot up around him. The white lightning of *Skythunder* struck from the sky with maniacal speed, over and over in the same spot. Those two spells were usually enough to take away half the health of a high-level dungeon boss, but nobody stopped there, of course. A murderous flood swept over the outsider, a flood of darts and crossbow bolts and spears, and that wasn't counting the avalanche of other magics alongside the careful attacks of meleers, trying to strike without blocking the view for the ranged attackers.

The first two seconds of the battle convinced Yemi that everything was going according to plan. He didn't bother holding back; he immediately fired off his ultimate ability, *Scarab Swarm*. A small black cloud appeared above the Threat and began to pour tar-black bugs down on him. He didn't see what happened next with them in the developing hell, but he already knew; the scarabs would be digging into the Threat's body, ignoring all defenses, rushing toward his heart and brain. Every second with those little guests inside doubled the tick of the *DOT*.

Next the caster summoned the ghostly spirit of Apophis and...

In the center of the misty outlines of the enemy, a blinding white point appeared, instantly expanded and covered Yemi's whole field of view. Breaking through and sweeping away all defensive spells, shields, armor and resists, the evil (*dead*, the thought suddenly came to the shaman) energy killed all his clanmates with a piercing flow of energy. The raid panel showed a hundred grey portraits with skulls overlaid, and when the light went out, Yemi saw a gloomy, vague silhouette rise from its knees at the foot of the melting granite altar.

The ghostly *Cocoon of Reflection* that activated when its master was in grave danger exploded into shards. The artifact had not only saved Yemi's life. It had also saved his chance to fulfil his dream.

Right before his eyes, the unknown player had just neutralized the beast-god's paralyzing poison, which had never been known to fail, and then destroyed an entire raid of players over level three hundred in one fell swoop.

Yemi knew no spells as powerful as that. This overturned the entire balance of the game, a system of mechanics refined over decades. What was this magic against which even maxed out resists did nothing? Sure, *Armageddon* existed and was similar in its effect, but it took more time to cast than had passed since the White Snake's return!

The Destroying Plague

The shaman's intuition told him that the Threat couldn't strike so hard again a second time, otherwise Disgardium might as well shut down. The cooldown for such a strong cast had to be days if not weeks!

Confusion was replaced by fear of losing the Threat. Yemi began to approach the immobile figure and launched a destructive stunning combo at it, but unsurprisingly it didn't work.

No wonder, he thought. *If Apophis' venom didn't work...*

At that moment he saw that the entire raid had revived, and he sighed in relief. Soon they'd be here; it wasn't far to run from the graveyard to the temple. As long as the Threat didn't get away...

Although it seemed like he had no plans to do so. He burned Yemi with his gaze, and the caster could have sworn on all his wives and children that he saw a smile form in the smoky gloom beneath the hood.

"Why the hell have you brought me here?" the stranger suddenly asked, his voice vibrating and constantly changing in tone, striking horror into those that heard it. "Was that your pet, or what?"

Glancing at him guardedly, Yemi thought furiously. Was the enemy trying to distract him with smalltalk to wait for some nightmarish talent to cool down? Entirely possible.

"Great Apophis, the White Snake..." the words bubbled forth from his tongue on their own, as if the shaman wanted to confess to this stranger. "He

461

demanded we sacrifice almost ten thousand intelligent creatures to him. Many lost their heads, and rivers of blood flowed into the beast-god's altar! All so that we could find and bring you here!"

He shouted the last words, preparing to attack. Yemi could already hear the trample of his approaching clanmates and a cruel smile spread across his face. It was time for *Astral Mantrap*!

The space around the Threat began to tear with a crack. Imperceptibly fine threads began to fire at the Threat from narrow black cuts in the air, piercing his body, growing within and fixing the target fast in place with mojo. The stranger could sense something was wrong, tried to move from his spot, twitched... Yemi's mocking smile widened further, but then the trap's threads broke, flew apart into black droplets, and the cuts in the air closed up.

"Take him!" the shaman shouted as he saw his clanmates. Since crowd-control spells didn't seem to be working on the Threat, then maybe it was time to use brute force. "Tanks, grab him and hold him!"

As soon as he gave the order, it occurred to him that the Threat might be a girl; even the voice didn't give away any clues in that regard.

The strongest warriors of the clan began to hesitantly approach the enemy. For some reason, the Threat interlocked his fingers and stretched his arms above his head as if before a workout. Then he walked toward Yemi!

"So, the Yoruba clan has sentenced thousands

of sentient creatures to death so that some insane little god could bring me to this hole?" the stranger's voice rang out. "You've been killing innocent NPCs, and I'm the 'Threat'? Something's gone wrong in this world..."

The tanks finally got a grip on themselves. Some of them even managed to quickly pick up and equip the armor they dropped when they died. Six of the strongest grabbed the stranger and pulled his arms behind his back. Someone decided to snap a hunting *Choke Collar of Dominion* on the neck of the Threat hidden in smoke. It was a spiky metal collar for training particularly wild pets.

But through some miracle, the Threat managed to free both his arms and dealt a series of strikes, then, turning in the air, kicked his escort in his helmeted head. The collar cracked and smashed into shards.

"You can't hold me," the Threat said happily. "Fight!"

Yemi was covered in a cold sweat. He looked at the raid combat logs and laughed in relief. The damage dealt to his clanmates was pathetically low. A second later, everyone was laughing.

"We didn't just sacrifice NPCs to Apophis," Yemi admitted, now calmer. "But that shouldn't worry you, dead man..."

At the clan leader's signal, a hail of fire rained down on the stranger. After the first strikes, the stranger's health indicator, which was already low, dropped down to the minimum, but for some reason it froze there and fell no further.

For the next few minutes, exhausting its reserves of vigor, mana, fury and other class resources, Yoruba tried with all its might to kill the Threat. How else could it be eliminated?

The smoky silhouette shrank into itself, covering its face with its hands and patiently taking all the hits. Now it was Yemi's turn to worry: how could he deal with this bastard son of evil spirits? Apophis was ignoring his summons, as ill luck would have it.

Trying to imagine what his late Triad father would have done, Yemi snarled and extended a silver blade crafted long ago, with which he'd already put down two threats.

"Hold him!" he ordered.

The crowd pressed around the immortal creature. He didn't resist, just stood as if wondering what the caster would do next. Approaching, Yemi struck viciously and shouted:

"I banish you from Disgardium forever!"

The blade pierced up to the hilt into the stranger's chest.

But... nothing happened.

In the grave silence to follow, everyone heard the vibrating voice of the Threat quite clearly.

"Has something gone wrong?" he asked in sympathy. "Seems like none of your plans are working out. What a shame..."

The Destroying Plague

"If we can't kill you, we'll eat every part of you!" Yemi spat in fury, and immediately began to fulfil his promise.

Tearing out a black heart that filled the air with the stench of rot, he raised it above his head.

"We will take his power! Yoruba!"

"Yoruba!" the others echoed.

"Idiots," the smoky silhouette shook its head, though nobody heard him.

The clan members that had just been crowding around the Threat suddenly came alive and moved to the shaman. With the help of Francesca, his deputy and in-game lover in one, he cut up the still-beating heart and handed it out.

When everyone had a small piece, they waited for Yemi's permission and bit into the flesh of the greatest Threat of Disgardium, dripping coal-black blood.

"Well, this is interesting!" the Threat shouted, whose heart was currently being greedily devoured by orcs, sauroks, drows, minotaurs, trolls, ogres, vampires and werewolves.

Yemi realized this was a bad idea when the clanmates began to grab their throats and wheeze. The shaman saw the anthracite lines of darkening veins spreading fast across their faces; their eyes blackened, and their health dropped at a monstrous rate. Then his turn came.

You are infected with Corpse Poison!

Corpse Poison
You drank of the blood of the dead.
-10% health per second.
Duration: 1 minute.

Spasmodically pulling out a flask, Yemi uncorked it and gulped down a lifesaving healing elixir and antidote. His clanmates did the same until the healers got a grip on themselves and began to cast mass healing spells all over the zone.

"What are you?" the shaman hissed.

"Someone who's going to be back. Someone who will make sure that not a single brick of your castle stays standing, you freak..."

Yemi didn't hear the last words. A bright white spot appeared in the midst of the smoky figure again. It expanded into a blinding flame and...

You are dead.

Reviving in 10... 9...

I hope he doesn't figure out that I'm the same as him... the spellcaster thought, counting down the seconds until his revival.

Chapter 21

Nergal's Summons

I REFLECTIVELY CLOSED my eyes at the *Plague Fury* explosion, but even then, the afterglow of the flash still burned in my vision for a long time to come. In the absolute silence to follow, fanfares stacked up on top of each other and the notification window covered my field of view.

Your reputation with the Commonwealth faction has increased: +150.
Current reputation: hatred.

Your reputation with the neutral races has increased: +150.
Current reputation: hatred.

Your reputation with the Empire faction has reduced: -600.
Current reputation: hatred.

Unlocked achievement Avenger!

You interrupted an outstanding unavenged kill streak by player **Francesca** (227 kills against other players without a single death!)

Reward: title **Avenger**, passive aura **Avenger** (-1% to damage and defense of all nearby enemies).

Attention! Achievement upgraded to Mighty Avenger!

You interrupted a phenomenal unavenged kill streak by player **Babangida** (362 kills against other players without a single death!)

Reward: title **Mighty Avenger**, passive aura **Mighty Avenger** (-2% to damage and defense of all nearby enemies).

The achievement upgraded a bunch more times, getting flashier and flashier. I got the final upgrade for Yemi:

Attention! Achievement upgraded to Most Magnificent Avenger!

You interrupted the global record unavenged kill streak by player **Yemi** (6731 kills against other players without a single death!)

Reward: title **Most Magnificent Avenger**, passive aura **Most Magnificent Avenger** (-25% to damage and defense of all nearby enemies).

Unlocked achievement First Ever: Most Magnificent Avenger!

The Destroying Plague

Most Magnificent Avenger achievement received for the first time in the history of Disgardium!

*Reward: the **Magnetism** passive skill (loot from enemies you defeat is automatically sent to your inventory, with filtration options available).*

Every achievement increased my reputation with the Commonwealth and the neutrals and plunged it into the Nether with the Empire, although the result was the same with all three factions: pure, unadulterated hatred.

Unlocked achievement Punisher!
*You eliminated **10** players of an enemy faction at a much higher level than yours.*
Reward: +1% to damage against other players.

Attention! Achievement upgraded...
Attention! Achievement upgraded...
...

Attention! Achievement upgraded to Mighty Punisher!
*You eliminated **200** players of an enemy faction at a much higher level than yours.*
Reward: +10% to damage against other players.

Somewhere in the stream of notifications, including those that offered to publicize my name as a 'great hero,' I saw lines about getting a ton of exp and new levels; you got twice as much experience for PvP than for mobs. Snowstorm decided that to motivate players to fight each other.

> **You leveled up!...**
> **You leveled up!...**
> **You leveled up!...**
> **...**
> **You leveled up! Current level: 191.**
> *205 free attribute points available!*

> **Unlocked achievement It is a Good Day to Die![8]**
> *You have leveled up to 150 without dying once, and your name will go down in the history of Disgardium!*
> **Reward**: *passive skill* **Second Life** *(some chance after death to revive in the same spot with full health).*

I heard footsteps approaching. Someone wanted seconds? Apparently so. It was Yemi in the flesh. The shaman didn't rush to come too close. He stopped at a safe distance and shouted.

"Whoever you are, I, Yemi Iwobi, and all the Yoruba clan is at your service, great one! Merely summon us..."

---

[8] A war cry attributed to an Indian chieftain known as Crazy Horse, which he shouted at the Battle of Little Bighorn. 'itisagooddaytodie' is also a cheat code that gives invulnerability in the game Warcraft II. In addition, "It is a good today to die" is spoken by the protoss corsair when it appears on the map in StarCraft.

The Destroying Plague

I had a little less than no plague energy whatsoever left, so I had to use a good old bluff. I pulled out my bow, drew it... and an instant later, my fan fled my sight, quitting the game. He ran away!

Well, since my hospitable hosts had left me alone, that meant I could take their loot. I opened my inventory and swore in happiness; my bag was already full to bursting! Legendaries and epics mixed with garbage like a smoking pipe and empty potion flasks. I threw out the garbage, sighed and started picking up loot the old-fashioned way — by hand. I switched on the *Magnetism* filter at the same time, so the skill didn't pull in everything at once.

In the end there was so much valuable loot that I not only filled up my whole inventory after throwing out my cooking ingredients, but I carried a few things myself. As much as my carrying capacity allowed, of course. I even had someone's dagger between my teeth. I wouldn't have gone far that way, but I didn't have to either.

Depths Teleportation took me to the temple of Tiamat, the stunned faces of my friends and Bomber's excited voice.

"You training to be Santa Claus, Scyth? Christmas is a long way off!"

I really did look like a Christmas tree covered in dangerous toys. I dropped my hands and a pile of swords, staffs, bows, crossbows and other weapons fell to the ground. Armor fell from under my elbows. Then I threw the rest out of my inventory, and my friends' jaws dropped further with every next piece of gear until they couldn't drop any lower; every item was either *purple* or *orange*.

"What does all this mean, bro?" Crawler asked, his gaze serious.

"Did you all see the snake?" I asked, and the guys nodded. "Well, he carried me off somewhere. I was knocked out, and when I woke up, I was on Shad'Erung. I figured Horvac and his Travelers had taken me. Fortunately, it wasn't then, it was some dark clan called Yoruba. And they knew who I was! Obviously, they tried to kill me..."

They listened to me with interest and I only complained that I couldn't record any of it — Yoruba blocked video recording in their castle.

"By the way, since they have their own beast-god at their disposal... I think their leader is a Threat. Shame I didn't have time to check!"

When I finished my short story, Crawler promised to dig up everything he could on the Yoruba. My intention to take their castle to pieces for resources hadn't gone anywhere. Infect voiced the idea of putting a temple to the Sleeping Gods there, but it wasn't realistic; nobody would let us build it or keep it. The place was too easily accessible.

My friends started going through all the loot and I decided to level up my *Archery*. I took my best five minions and went to walk the perimeter of the construction site. I wanted to get the skill up to rank one before Distival, because afterwards...

The Destroying Plague

Afterwards, the landscape might change, and I wanted to be as ready for it as I could be.

* * *

The clan didn't manage to level up as far as we wanted in the previous day. At midnight, our timers activated and kicked us out of the game. An instant before I logged out, I saw that the workers were staying at the construction site at their own risk. Because of the special aura of the place of power, mobs didn't approach them, and the builders had enough sense not to leave the aura's area of effect — each of them had tried it at least once and ended up lunch for the Montosaurus. Incidentally, the lost dinosaur still hadn't shown up. Maybe it got sick from eating the undead?

In the last lesson, modern history, Greg Kovac told us about one of the most serious problems of human history — overpopulation.

"At the beginning of the nineteenth century, the planet's population was only one billion people. People died in wars, from hunger, from illness. Few lived to old age. That meant the average age was lower than in our time. Since then, the largest gain in life expectancy occurred between 1880 and 1920 due to public health improvements such as control of infectious diseases, more abundant and safer foods, cleaner water, and other nonmedical social improvements. The planet has a limited capacity to

---

generate raw materials and each year the natural resources deficit — the consumption of resources at a faster rate than the planet is able to generate them — is reached earlier. Consequently, in developing countries, overpopulation causes fierce rivalries to control resources. Some countries introduced policies to limit birth rates, but that didn't help. This meant that in the middle of the twenty first century, there were over ten billion of us, and as of now, counting non-citizens, there are twenty..."

According to the history teacher, it was precisely because of overpopulation and a lack of resources that the children of non-citizens were initially deprived of all state support. No free kindergartens, schools, hospitals — it was all on the parents' shoulders. If they decided to have children, they could bear the consequences. Mr. Kovac made it clear that he fully supported those politics.

"What can we say about non-citizens," the teacher shook his head, "if the government was forced to cut back even on your program! In my days, we studied twelve years. For you, unfortunately, your mandatory education lasts only ten years. Although up there," Greg pointed upwards, "they say that thanks to new technologies, you can absorb the study material more quickly. Think of it...!"

After our lessons, we flew by my place to grab the Home Doctor. All the Awoken accompanied me apart from Tobias. Our family gadget was far older than the premium version that could perform operations, fix broken bones and alter the state of internal organs. Nonetheless, it could at least make diagnoses by connecting to the global database, and it could perform basic treatment. I was putting my hope in that very ability; if my non-citizen friends were seriously ill, then the entire clan treasury might not be enough to help them.

The others sat in silence. Tissa was already mentally in tomorrow — we were supposed to be flying straight to Dubai for Distival right after school. Ed was probably thinking about how to deal with the loot I'd collected from the Yoruba clan corpses. The problem of transferring our game gold to real life stood out like a sore thumb.

Big Hung sat jabbing at his comm. We knew that our friend had met a cute girl from T-Modus in Dis, and he was hoping to meet her at the festival in real life.

Malik... Malik probably wasn't thinking about anything serious. He was just looking through the flyer window and smiling. Maybe he was remembering that he'd gotten his hands on some cool legendaries yesterday, a couple of which didn't have any level requirements.

We flew over the gardens of Florida, crossed the Gulf of Mexico and the Caribbean, but then, over the continent on the approach to Cali Bottom, we ran into problems. First a police bot forced us to stop. Its matt-black streamlined shape impressed us and... scared us, especially with its plasma machine guns aimed at our flyer.

"Please keep your hands visible and look in this direction..." we heard from the speakers in the flyer's cabin.

We bared our wrists with the invisible identification codes on them. The scanner's invisible ray read our data, then passed over our faces. We passed the identity check, but still weren't allowed to fly away.

"Underage dependent citizens Hung, Schafer, Rodriguez, Abdualim and Sheppard, state the purpose of your visit to the uncategorized zone Cali!"

We didn't see who the voice behind the dark glass of the police bot belonged to; it could be a robot or a person. In any case, it sounded genderless. For some time now, the police had been recommended not to introduce themselves.

Ed lightly shook his head. It wasn't forbidden to talk to non-citizens, but it did raise questions. What business could respectable citizens have, even underage ones, with the despised inwinova? Remembering how we flew through such districts with Mr. Kovac, I answered:

"We're collecting material for a school writing assignment on the subject of citizenship categories and the importance of the concept of citizenship in conditions of overpopulation."

"Wait a moment," the police voice ordered. He stayed quiet for around a minute, then spoke again. "The indicated subject is part of your school's curriculum. Thank you for cooperating and..." the voice faltered, and it became clear that it was a human speaking. "Be careful, kids. It can be dangerous here."

The police bot switched off its holding beam and we started moving again. We flew less than three hundred feet before the dot of a military flyer took off from the roof of a building and rushed toward us. One of the 'Sharks' that Gyula warned us of.

Unlike the police bot, it didn't look respectable in the least. A huge hull with enough space to store a squad of peacekeepers and an EMP cannon, alongside turrets with deadly-looking plasma machine gun barrels. This model had been actively used during the Third World War, and recently became available to private individuals.

The identification procedure was repeated. We were politely asked to show our wrists, to explain the purpose of our visit to Cali Bottom, only this time my cover story invited a different reaction.

"Well, well, well... All the Awoken clan members in one flyer. The victors of the Junior Arena, levels... hidden. Heh. How's it going, guys?"

"Who are you?" Ed asked impassively.

The Shark door opened, revealing a heavyset man in a camouflage uniform. He lifted his helmet visor and we saw that he was over forty, with grey hair.

"Speaking to you, boy, is Hairo Morales, officer of the Excommunicado clan security service. And you must be Crawler, the fire mage. What's your level, mage? And what about you, Scyth? Infect? Bomber? You guys are in the one percent of players that don't want to advertise their progress. I won't ask Tissa, she has nothing to hide... at least, yet. What is it, girl, did you hit the ceiling in the sandbox?"

"Since when has it been forbidden to hide your profile, Mr. Morales?" Hung asked, smiling widely.

"Since the preventers realized that the only people that hide it are people with something to hide. And you guys are under suspicion. Land your flyer and we'll talk. I won't ask a second time. The cops here are well fed, and there isn't anyone else to seriously investigate the tragic crash of a public transport flyer with a few students on board..."

"What a mess, ...!" Ed swore.

While I deliberately slowly flew the flyer to the roof of a skyscraper, we thought over our course of action: we'd stick to our story. We were writing a school assignment. Why in Cali Bottom? We knew some workers here from Tristad, and they'd agreed to show us their homes and tell us about their lives. Why so many of us? It was a group project!

None of that was any good. The Excommunicado security officer was far more intelligent than his clanmate Banger, the elephant man. Taking a careful look at each of us — and, I'm sure, noticing Malik biting his lip, Hung putting on a deliberately neutral face, Ed frowning and me hiding my hands in my pockets — Morales spoke. Without asking questions, just making statements.

"One of you is a top Threat. I know that for sure, because according to our intel, certain inwinovas from Cali Bottom are related to the Threat. In the future, kids, bear in mind that humans are the most unreliable of creatures. There's always at least one tongue without a spine that will give up all your plots and secrets. Just because that's human nature. Look at me, for example! I know something important! I'm involved in this! And that means I'm a big deal too! Heh-heh-heh..."

Chuckling, Morales's piercing gaze settled on me and didn't move off again.

"We knew you'd turn up here sooner or later. We weren't expecting you specifically, of course, but any citizens that dared to fly in here. There's a reason you're cooking something up with the inwinovas after all, right? There were others too, of course, but their characters were clear. Whereas yours are cloudy..."

"Mister..."

Morales, very pleased with himself, gestured for me to be quiet. He took out a cigar, bit off the end, spat it out and lit it. Exhaling a cloud of smoke, he spoke again softly.

"Alright, here's the deal, kids. Keep your fake excuses to yourselves and listen to me. We don't need any answers from you right now anyway. Got it?"

Waiting for us all to nod, he continued.

"My partner Willy and I have felt for a while that the Colonel is getting a little greedy. The main staff is living it up, while guys like me and my partner just get crumbs. Like now... We aren't going to hold you. In literally a minute you'll be flying off to get back to whatever you're plotting. And Willy and I will make a report to the chief, and then the boys upstairs will decide how to pick you up and how to strong-arm you. Of course, I value my position and I'm simply obliged to report your arrival here, but... But I could sell you some time. Maybe I could even keep the report to myself for a week. If I don't hear anything from you, it'll go upstairs. If you want to extend the deadline, then let's say — a million phoenixes a month. Gold works for us too."

"Just out of interest, how do you imagine this working?" Tissa said, having wanted to say something for a while and unable to hold back. "You realize that financial transfers so large are tracked, right? Snowstorm will have questions!"

"That's what I like to hear!" Morales said in glee. "No stunned silences, no shocked giggles, no attempts to haggle, heh-heh-heh! That means I'm right, and the amount doesn't bother you. All you need to know is the how, right? Not a problem! Ladies and gentlemen... the Goblin Auction! You know that the League respects the anonymity of its clients, right? Sure, the fees there are way higher, but do you think the corporation will miss the chance to earn a little extra from people who don't want their business made public? Especially since all the factions have access to the auction house. What, is this news to you?"

I glanced at Ed, moved my gaze to Tissa, but they just shook their heads. In the meantime, Morales got more serious and dropped the jokes.

"An unusual bar of copper ore will show up there today. One. And it will be unusual because the lot price will be precisely one million. The lot will last a week. If certain mystery customers don't buy the lot... well, then I'll have to let matters develop."

He carefully put out his cigar against the lug sole of his army boots, put the remainder back into the pack and walked back to his Shark, whistling as he went.

* * *

I returned home lost in dark thoughts. On the way back, the guys chewed out Tissa for her big mouth, argued about whether to pay the blackmailers, then started estimating the value of the trophies from Shad'Erung. I didn't bother taking part in their debates. I already knew we'd have to pay. At least until we fell off the radar. Until recently I'd believed that I didn't have to fear openly criminal acts from the preventers, but when it wasn't money at stake, but power in Dis, which had long since replaced real life for so many...

They'd kidnap me, fill me with drugs, put me in a hacked capsule and force me to personally go to their castle and ask to be eliminated. How could I prove it later, and to whom? I doubt they'd even find me. *Missing: senior student Alex Sheppard, 16 years old. Distinguishing characteristics include...* — notifications like this went around the comms daily, and that was just in our district. The sad conclusion was that we had to find shelter. And certainly not in Cali Bottom, where we'd already been made. In any case, we couldn't risk our workers' lives either.

We found them in a poor state. At least they were all on their feet, nobody was lying down and dying of fever, and the Home Doctor detected only slightly raised temperatures.

"It was worse yesterday," Manny said. "And only the ones that turned undead got sick! The others were just fine! To tell the truth, we're about ready to blame Dis, but you guys are fine, right?"

We were fine, but I recalled how bad I felt after I first transformed and pointed out that Manny's words had sense. Ed, Malik and Hung also remembered that they felt a little ill a day after they turned undead. It was a strange effect.

"Alright, we'll come around," the foreman waved his hand, exchanging glances with Gyula.

He coughed and reported on the construction progress. They'd finished building the temple in the desert and were ready to get started on upgrading the fort. I suggested that they kept out of Dis until they completely recovered and promised they wouldn't lose any pay.

Chaos reigned at home. AT was in his dog form

and seemed to be glitching out, yapping constantly, but that was the least of the problems. Mom was packing suitcases, at the same time shouting all kinds of accusations at dad. He was sitting on the couch with his face in his hands. I thought it was probably something to do with mom's affairs or dad's binges, but it turned out to be far more serious.

"We're both going to lose our licenses, and it's your fault! How am I supposed to live, you bastard?!" mom shouted.

"Don't put this on me, Helene," dad answered tiredly. "You made a mistake in your calculations..."

"On your design!" mom spat. "One million and two hundred thousand in fines! A million and two hundred thousand! We don't even have a hundred thousand in our account! You can deal with the courts yourself..."

Once she saw me, mom shut up, turned red, rushed over to me and hugged me.

"Forgive us, son!" Forgive us!" mom cried, pouring tears all over my neck.

"What happened, mom? Dad?"

"Our last order..." Dad grimaced, then decided to take the blame after all. "I made a mistake in a design for a small resort world. It's a kind of virtual planet full of champagne fountains, lemonade rivers and candy growing on trees. Not to mention more, ahem... adult pleasures. The world fell apart when it took its first batch of tourists. Long story short, we're bankrupt. If we don't pay the fine, the customer will complain and mom and I will lose our licenses and all our property, they'll knock down our citizenship status and... We'll be resettled, Alex."

"We need a million and two hundred thousand phoenixes?" I asked, thinking feverishly about the anonymous League of Goblins auction. "I'll find the money. But you're going to have to go back to Disgardium, dad. Because I don't think I can transfer the money out myself..."

Avoiding direct answers about the origins of such a fantastic amount, I told them that I had some very valuable loot and lots of it. Dad scratched his head and suddenly broke into a smile. Mom looked at us in confusion, and then dad whispered something to her. Her eyes widened, her mouth opened, but she stayed silent, just nodding.

"Everything will be fine, mom. Pack your suitcases. Dad, help mom and... No more arguments! I may not be a grown-up, but even I can see that all your problems started when you decided to divorce. Now I have things to do... including pulling your dear parental asses out of the fire!

Everyone was so stunned after that outburst that even AT, the little bastard, finally shut up and jumped onto dad's lap, wagging its tail. Like in the good old days.

The Destroying Plague

---

* * *

I rode circle after circle around the now-finished temple, but the problems never disappeared from my head. My guardian minions and other undead dragged behind me.

Upgraded riding skill: +1. Current level: 10.
You're confident in the saddle and you're ready to control a flying mount! Movement speed while riding increased by 10%.

In occasional skirmishes with respawning mobs, I focused on leveling up not only *Archery*, but also my skills with other weapons which I'd borrowed specially from Crawler to level up my skills. My level wasn't good enough for iron, but that didn't stop me from fighting, and nor did the Heavy Burden debuff that appeared when I used weapon or armor above my level (minus to stats, and gear bonuses stopped working). Thankfully, landing one hit with a sword, dagger or club on a level four hundred beast was enough to level up the skill by several grades, especially in the beginning.

In reality, I was just procrastinating on performing the temple dedication ritual. I was afraid that the Destroying Plague would learn of the treachery, and I hadn't managed to level up everything I wanted to, but I was even more worried about Behemoth... who had remained in the lair of the Nucleus of the Destroying Plague. When I activated *Balancer* and prepared to fire at the ruler of the undead, the I heard the Sleeping God's weak voice:

"Stop, Initial! While the parasite is fed by its channel from the Nether, you cannot kill it. Leave me here. I will try to disentangle its weavings and close it off from the source. Moreover, I will find something to replace the gifts it has given. But remember, Herald! Your thoughts are protected from the parasite, but if anyone else learns of me, it may figure out what is happening. No living soul must learn of this, otherwise my presence in this world will be ended."

"What should I do?"

"Leave me in that pool of scum. As for you, use your abilities from the parasite to become stronger and strengthen your allies. Reach the place of power and build a temple to Tiamat. Once she appears, she will remove the undead curse from you, and I will try to find out more about the parasite and all the rest in the meantime... Hurry! An assault from the Nether is coming, and its power is unprecedented. The Destroying Plague is merely one of its heralds. If we, the Sleeping Gods, do not gain enough strength, the Nether will swallow up Disgardium."

Had I become stronger since then? Naturally. But had I leveled up enough? Of course not.

And right now, I needed to finally decide whose side I'd play for. My imagination saw legions of the undead, and myself at their head. I could get rid of

The Destroying Plague

the lich Shazz by building a stronghold of the Destroying Plague in the Commonwealth itself. All the top players would gather for such a serious event, and if I put myself nearby in the disguise of another, then the lich would die alongside his minions. The Nucleus would have only one Legate left — Scyth. I wouldn't allow any new ones to appear. The Sleeping Gods? My promise to Behemoth? The world had somehow lived and gotten along fine without them for more than one era.

I imagined returning to Latteria after leveling up to a thousand on Holdest, Meaz and Terrastera, and going on to conquer the entire Commonwealth, and then the Empire! How I would take down the entire preventer army and crush their castles with a single *Plague Fury* for a million damage. I pictured processions of envoys waving white flags both from the clans and from the corporations, coming to bend the knee and beg for mercy. And they'd either have to make me a category-A billionaire with my own space yacht or find themselves a new game to play. I was sure they'd try to bribe me.

Once rich, I'd be able to help my non-citizen friends. Trixie would be able to travel where he wanted, with a premium capsule. The workers' kids would be able to study in private school.

Only thanks to the Destroying Plague did I have the power to solve my parents' problems and pay for university for myself and the former Dementors. Thanks to the undead curse, I'd be flying to Distival tomorrow! Only thanks to the curse had the Sleeping Gods gotten their new temple; both on Kharinza and here, in the Lakharian Desert. And I was still in doubt; who's side to take...?

Alongside the Destroying Plague, I could bring the entire system to its knees!

Nether, I *was* the Destroying Plague! Because life is death, but there is no death in service to the Destroying Plague! The entire world will bow before its might...!

"Are you alright, Scyth?" Crag's calm voice brought me back to reality.

"We're all worried, bro, but why eat sand?" Bomber asked.

Raising my head, I realized that my mouth was full of sand and my body was buried up to the waist in a pit which I must have dug out myself. The sun had already gone down, and only the light of Geala lit my friends' concerned faces. How much time had passed?

I raised my hand and saw the broken bones of my fingers. Not realizing what had happened and why they were in such a state, I shook my head and nearly fell, losing my balance when my head span three hundred and sixty degrees. The thought of the Destroying Plague's power burned bright in my mind...

What? Those weren't my thoughts! That bastard had pulled me into its ranks by force, and only through Behemoth's intervention had I kept my control of myself. But the Sleeping God was weakening, the Nucleus's influence growing. If something happened to Behemoth, I'd lose my character. And then not only would I never see riches or fame; everything would be lost!

I let that thought grow stronger, crowding out ideas from outside my mind. And I made my decision, doubting no longer.

I descended into the valley, leaving my clanmates and my zombie minions. I walked into the temple and approached the altar.

Level 1 Unconsecrated Temple

Consecration requires an adept with a status of at least 'priest'.

Identified: Initial.

Requirements met.

As soon as I put my hand on the altar, my sensations all disappeared. I found myself in an infinite space surrounded by huge misty figures. A barrage of foreign emotions washed over me, each one somehow with a sense of belonging to someone specific. Leviathan uplifted me, Kingu calmed me, Abzu made me want to laugh, Tiamat couldn't hide her joy at her upcoming reincarnation in the world, and Behemoth... Behemoth felt terrible, but for some reason beamed with happiness.

The illusion subsided. I saw the dark room of the temple again, with my hand on the altar.

Scyth, do you wish to consecrate this temple to the Sleeping Gods?

I confirmed it and chose Tiamat from the list of the Sleeping Gods.

Second Temple of the Sleeping Gods, dedicated to Tiamat
Level: 1.
Initial (1/1): Scyth.
Priests (3/3): Patrick O'Grady, Manny, Tissa.
Adepts: 169/169.
Faith points until next temple level: 1/28561.
Restore the First Temple of the Sleeping Gods or build a new one to increase your adept cap.

The icons of the divine abilities I'd gained from Behemoth all lit up at once. *Unity* came back, increasing my stats based on number of adepts.

A dragon's face appeared on the altar, and then I felt *her* presence. A gentle hand descended on my shoulder.

"Greetings, Initial," a soft female voice said in the silence. "We have much to discuss, but not now. I am weak. I must gain strength to remove the curse from you and your allies. My brother asked me to tell you that he is very proud of you, but he asks that you hurry. If he is found, he will be disincarnated, and the Sleeping Gods will never reach full strength without him. You must complete the parasite's quest to return to it and get Behemoth out of there. He has done what needed to be done."

"Will *vindication* help? I have a supply."

"No," the goddess shook her head sadly.

Your reputation with Tiamat the Sleeping God has increased: +500.

Current reputation: trust.

Behemoth's quest wasn't over, apparently considering the special circumstances — it asked me to restore the first Temple, and, first, to get the quest giver out of the lair of the Destroying Plague. But how could I do that if Kharinza was riddled with the undead...?

I didn't have time to figure out the details; I barely had time to appreciate Tiamat's beauty and majesty before she disappeared. A few moments later, a column of cold light struck the temple, bright and blinding. I stood frowning and heard a piercing buzz growing, making my bones vibrate. The walls of the temple shook, dust fell from the ceiling, and just as I'd begun to think the building would fall down, the noise abated, and the light faded.

I heard Crawler shouting through the comm amulet.

"Scyth, get over here now! We have an emergency!"

My vision hadn't recovered yet, and I felt my

way out of the temple.

It was lighter in the desert than in the daytime, but the falling light wasn't warm. It spoke of the presence of another god; Nergal the Radiant. Crag crawled on all fours on the dune's slope, clutching his head. Bomber, Infect and Crawler stood nearby, weapons bared. The warrior's sword, bard's guitar and mage's staff were aimed at Crag!

I ran over to them. When I reached them, Nergal's light had gone out and finally disappeared, letting the night seep back in. Crag was already getting up, raising a calming hand.

"Guys, guys, everything's fine. You can put your weapons away."

"What happened?"

"Bullshit happened," Crag wheezed, shaking sand off himself. "Sorry, Scyth, I messed up…"

"What the hell happened; can you tell me?"

"Listen, I don't know how this became possible, but it seems Behemoth hid his presence on Kharinza from Nergal, so the Radiant didn't know anything. But now that you've summoned Tiamat…"

"Now that was a sight!" Bomber butted in, unable to restrain his excitement. "A huge red dragon all across the sky!"

"Dragoness," I corrected him automatically.

"We're busted, in other words," Crag resumed. "Nergal saw the temple of the Sleeping Gods through my eyes and it sent him into a fury! He demanded that I destroy the temple! And it's… It's a quest. With insane, awesome rewards!"

"And?"

"What do you mean 'and'? What am I going to do to you? You're immortal, damn it! Plus, you know my secret and you won't attack first."

"What happens if you don't take the quest?" I asked.

"The Radiant threatens to take away my imba *Nergal's Fury* ability and then curse me to hell and back too. The curse is awful, it's a huge penalty to stats. Forever."

"All we needed..." Infect sighed.

"Listen, Craggy, what if we take you out?" Bomber suggested in a sly voice. "We'll share the rewards after, of course..."

"I doubt I could stop you, Bomb. But we're friends, right? Maybe let's calm down and give me a little time to think? Especially since we don't have a lot of time — if I don't complete the quest, the talent will drop by a level each day, and when it reaches zero, it'll be gone."

"Alright, Toby," I agreed, paying no attention to the others. "You can crash here or on Kharinza if you don't have anywhere to hide your character. We'll be in touch."

Thanking me, Crag said goodbye and left the game, leaving me to tackle the question of why Nergal was so indifferent to the Destroying Plague, and even to the fact that his subject had turned undead.

"Shouldn't have let him go," Crawler grumbled.

"What stops him going to the preventers and selling not just himself, but our base too? He'd be a rich man."

"No point in trusting only halfway. Do you remember how Mr. Wetmore explained to us that every betrayal has its price? Nether with all that. I trust Tobias, and if he betrays us, then that's one less friend. But if he doesn't, then our friendship with him will be worth more than all the rewards of the treasury!"

The Radiant God must have heard us. Immediately after my words, a global notification resounded:

Nergal the Radiant declares a holy crusade!

To the heroic and the courageous! In the Lakharian Desert, traitors of all that is light have founded a temple to the nightmarish Sleeping Gods. All Disgardium is in danger!

Don't let this awoken evil gain strength; destroy it first and Nergal the Radiant's reward will be generous!

Global event begins in 7 days.

A ceasefire has been declared between the Commonwealth, Empire and neutral races!

All who wish to join the holy crusade will get temporary immunity to the deadly heat of the Lakharian Desert.

"Damn it..." Crawler swore, stunned. "That's all we needed!"

The Destroying Plague

"Just seven days!" Infect howled. "So little time!"

"Little?" Bomber laughed. "A week ago, we were all under level thirty, but now? We're going to be at the top of the leaderboard at this rate! Anyway, I'm sure Scyth has some ideas!"

"Just one," I dodged Bomber's friendly jab with a weighty fist. "I think I'll need to be a Legate of the Destroying Plague a little longer to protect the temple. If the Nucleus has no objections, of course. And I'm going to need wings too...

Digging around in my inventory, I pulled out a *Summoning Whistle*. I span it in my hands, thinking of how much it could be worth, then blew into it. A thin whistling song on the edge of ultrasound flew out into the skies.

A ball of lightning fell nearby, and the measured, unhurried crack of monstrous wings descended on us.

Looking up, the boys slowly sat down on the sand.

"Holy..." Bomber wheezed. "That's the most beautiful thing I've ever seen!"

My new mount, so enormous that all the Awoken would have easily fit on its back, landed carefully without so as not to hurt any of us. Little charges of lightning ran across its dark-blue skin covered in mithril plates.

A powerful, sonorous roar echoed through the desert. We weren't the only ones to instinctively jump back; even the dead minions did. The pets, headed up by Iggy, bolted off to the side. Crash, now grown to around the size of an aerotrain, peaked his head out of the sand and stared at my new pet with interest.

Storm Dragon
Legendary
Flying mount.
+1500% movement speed.

The Storm Dragon, the last of its kind, the true ruler of the skies. It has never had rivals in the skies or on earth, which is what caused its extinction; every intelligent creature considered it a duty to find and destroy the eggs of the Storm Dragons.

An ancient mage preserved this dragon by sealing its essence in an artifact.

Storm Dragon is a battle pet and can take part in conflicts. Apart from basic moves, attacks with a precision lightning strike.

Requires level: 100.
Requires riding skill.

Sinking into the sand, the dragon approached me and lightly nuzzled me with its powerful triangular snout. Touching it, I felt the reptile's measured breath, looked deep into its giant snake eyes and saw the wish to fly and fight. And at the same time, I somehow knew; it was a she!

"You'll be Storm," I declared, and turned to my friends. "Well, guys? Let's fly? We can take a look at the desert from above, and I'll level up Cartography..."

I didn't have to ask twice.

I'd thought the last week had been hot. But the real fire was only just beginning.

End of Book Three

An Afterword From the Author

I'M WRITING THIS many months after I finished working on the book, specially for the English edition of *The Destroying Plague.*

When I'd just started working on it, the book's provisional title was *The Colonization of Kharinza* because I planned to focus on the development of the Awoken clan. But then, suddenly, the Destroying Plague came, followed by the fall of Behemoth's temple. At least that's what the dice decided (I do use them occasionally, just to avoid predictability story-wise).

When things went from bad to worse and Scyth did die, the story moved in a totally new direction. I wouldn't say it came as a surprise, but I had to completely rework the outlines for this and the following books.

What's going to happen next? You've just read Book Three out of the seven that I planned. The next book, titled *The Holy War,* should come out in spring 2020. It will up the ante further: the characters will visit Distival where all kinds of encounters await them; Scyth will visit the Goblin League and the Temple of Fortune while an enormous allied army summoned by Nergal the Radiant will invade the Lakharian Desert... There'll be battles, there'll be wars, but first Scyth needs to find himself some trusty allies...

I'd like to thank the book's translator Alix Merlin Williamson for his wonderful work and the deep understanding of my characters; my publisher Alex Bobl who graciously accommodated my failure to meet deadlines; his colleague Simon Vale who kept helping me with promotion; Taylor Sloan and Ian Mitchell for their support and proofreading; Michael Atamanov, Vasily Mahanenko and Alexey Osadchuk for their amazing worlds and inspiring stories... and Ramon Mejia, of course! Ramon, you know why, don't you? You're a man of great heart.

But my biggest gratitude and appreciation goes to you, my Reader. Thank you for sticking with me! For buying and reading my books, rating them and leaving reviews! See you later this spring on the pages of *The Holy War*!

Faithfully yours,

Author
Dan Sugralinov

Want to be the first to know about our latest LitRPG, sci fi and fantasy titles from your favorite authors?

Subscribe to our **New Releases** newsletter:
http://eepurl.com/b7niIL

Thank you for reading *The Destroying Plague!*
If you like what you've read, check out other LitRPG novels
published by Magic Dome Books:

Level Up LitRPG series by Dan Sugralinov:
Re-Start
Hero
The Final Trial
Level Up: The Knockout (with Max Lagno)
Level Up. The Knockout: Update (with Max Lagno)

Disgardium LitRPG series by Dan Sugralinov:
Class-A Threat
Apostle of the Sleeping Gods
The Destroying Plague

World 99 LitRPG Series by Dan Sugralinov:
Blood of Fate

Adam Online LitRPG Leries by Max Lagno:
Absolute Zero
City of Freedom

Reality Benders LitRPG series by Michael Atamanov:
Countdown
External Threat
Game Changer
Web of Worlds
A Jump into the Unknown

**The Dark Herbalist LitRPG series
by Michael Atamanov:**
Video Game Plotline Tester
Stay on the Wing
A Trap for the Potentate
Finding a Body

**Perimeter Defense LitRPG series
by Michael Atamanov:**
Sector Eight
Beyond Death
New Contract
A Game with No Rules

**The Way of the Shaman LitRPG series
by Vasily Mahanenko:**
Survival Quest
The Kartoss Gambit
The Secret of the Dark Forest
The Phantom Castle
The Karmadont Chess Set
Shaman's Revenge
Clans War

Dark Paladin LitRPG series by Vasily Mahanenko:
The Beginning
The Quest
Restart

Galactogon LitRPG series by Vasily Mahanenko:
Start the Game!
In Search of the Uldans
A Check for a Billion

Invasion LitRPG Series by Vasily Mahanenko:
A Second Chance
An Equation with One Unknown

**World of the Changed LitRPG Series
by Vasily Mahanenko:**
No Mistakes
Pearl of the South

**The Bard from Barliona LitRPG series
by Eugenia Dmitrieva and Vasily Mahanenko:**
The Renegades
A Song of Shadow

The Neuro LitRPG series by Andrei Livadny:
The Crystal Sphere
The Curse of Rion Castle
The Reapers

Phantom Server LitRPG series by Andrei Livadny:
Edge of Reality
The Outlaw
Black Sun

Respawn Trials LitRPG Series
by Andrei Livadny:
Edge of the Abyss

The Expansion (The History of the Galaxy) series
by A. Livadny:
Blind Punch
The Shadow of Earth
Servobattalion

Interworld Network LitRPG Series by Dmitry Bilik:
The Time Master
Avatar of Light

Mirror World LitRPG series by Alexey Osadchuk:
Project Daily Grind
The Citadel
The Way of the Outcast
The Twilight Obelisk

Underdog LitRPG series by Alexey Osadchuk:
Dungeons of the Crooked Mountains
The Wastes

AlterGame LitRPG series by Andrew Novak:
The First Player
On the Lost Continent
God Mode

An NPC's Path LitRPG series by Pavel Kornev:
The Dead Rogue
Kingdom of the Dead
Deadman's Retinue

The Sublime Electricity series by Pavel Kornev
The Illustrious
The Heartless
The Fallen
The Dormant

Citadel World series by Kir Lukovkin:
The URANUS Code
The Secret of Atlantis

Point Apocalypse *(a near-future action thriller)*
by Alex Bobl

Captive of the Shadows *(The Fairy Code Book #1)*
by Kaitlyn Weiss

The Game Master series by A. Bobl and A. Levitsky:
The Lag

You're in Game!
(LitRPG Stories from Bestselling Authors)

You're in Game-2!
(More LitRPG stories set in your favorite worlds)

Moskau by G. Zotov
(a dystopian thriller)

El Diablo by G.Zotov
(a supernatural thriller)

More books and series are coming out soon!

In order to have new books of the series translated faster, we need your help and support! Please consider leaving a review or spread the word by recommending *The Destroying Plague* to your friends and posting the link on social media. The more people buy the book, the sooner we'll be able to make new translations available.

Thank you!

Till next time!